Vinyl Highway

A Memoir

DEE DEE PHELPS

ALTERGATE
Publishing
LOS ANGELES

ISBN 978-1-934321-75-1 (13 Digit)/ ISBN 1-934321-75-3 (10 Digit)
Previously ISBN 1-4120-7383-9

Library of Congress Control Number: 2006910743

ALTERGATE
Publishing

Offices in the United State of America
Los Angeles, California

Information address:
Altergate Publishing
15332 Antioch Street, Suite 716
Pacific Palisades, CA 90272
USA

Phone 310 281-1183
Fax 310 573-9771
e-mail: www.support@altergate.com

Publisher's Cataloging-in-Publication
(Provided by Quality Books, Inc.)

Phelps, Dee Dee.
Vinyl Highway / Dee Dee Phelps—1st ed.
p. cm.
LCCN 2006910743
ISBN-13: 978-1-934321-75-1 (Altergate)
ISBN-10: 1-934321-75-3 (Altergate)
ISBN 1-4120-7383-9 (Trafford)

1. Phelps, Dee Dee. 2. Singers—United States—
Biography. 3. Dick and Dee Dee. 4. Popular music—
1961-1970. I. Title.

ML420.S787 2007   782.42164'092
QBI06-600712

I dedicate this book in loving memory of George and Betty Sperling, Dick St. John and Bill Lee, all of whom shared the experience; Kane Phelps for thirty years of love; Chris and Christine Lee, Jesse and Vanessa Phelps and Caroline Phelps (my beautiful children and their spouses); and Ashton and Ronan, my grandchildren. You brighten each and every day.

ACKNOWLEDGEMENTS

Special thanks to: Leah Komaiko, David Fryxell, Aram Saroyan, The Maui Writer's Retreat Support Team, Samantha Dunn and especially Reeva Hunter Mandelbaum for guiding and shaping the process; author Helen Winternitz for her help with "more texture, more detail, more snappiness;" and Chris Lee, for the countless hours of computer monitoring, web site work and for believing in the dream.

In 2001 the thought came to me, "You need to write a book about your singing experience." I immediately rejected it. "After all," I reasoned. "I'm too busy living life. Who wants to take time to revisit the past?" But the thought haunted me…. "You need to write a book about your singing experience." I finally realized the project offered an assignment and an opportunity. The assignment was to complete the book. The opportunity challenged me to grow and change in the process.

"But I can't do this alone!" was my next thought. And then I realized I am never alone. My love and gratitude go forth to God, Christ, Paramahansa Yogananda, and guidance from the Angels. When I turned it over to them, the book wrote itself.

TABLE OF CONTENTS

SECTION ONE

"The Mountain's High"

CHAPTER ONE

Little Mary's on the Radio

The shimmering asphalt stretched before us as Dad steered our massive, pea-green '58 Pontiac north on Highway 5 past Fresno, toward the faraway oasis of our holiday spot near Seattle. Although our vacation destination promised a cooler temperature, at eighteen I knew it definitely wasn't cool to be traveling with my parents on a family vacation. I frowned at the thought of my friends sprawled out on the sand in Santa Monica basking in the ocean breeze, while I sat trapped in a sweltering car.

Dad drove on. There was no point in asking him to stop to use the rest room because Dad never hit the brakes until he'd logged at least two hundred miles. Dad's hands clasped the steering wheel calmly.

It was quiet, too quiet. The car tires droned. I slouched in the front seat against the passenger door, miserable but careful not to ruin my hairstyle, a teased, sprayed, helmet like a tower, called a "beehive." Pressing against the window, I tried to put as much distance as I could between myself and the rest of the family.

Mom sat in back braced as a formidable barricade between my two younger sisters so they wouldn't hit and kick each other, which they would have done for miles without ceasing.

The California farmland wilted in the noonday sun as we blurred past, leaving Santa Monica farther and farther behind. Too limp to even fan myself, I silently raged, "This is the last family vacation I'm ever going on! Why did I ever agree to one last vacation with my irritating family?"

My sister Doris snapped her bubble gum, snap, snap, snap. She was capable of driving anyone crazy. At age fourteen, Doris thought she knew everything, but I'll bet she didn't even know how many more hours we'd be riding in this damn car! I inwardly groaned. How much more of this familial togetherness could I take?

I might have leaned my head against the window and tried to try to sleep if it wouldn't have damaged my "beehive" hairdo and created a giant headache when my head banged, with each jolting bump, against the window. To drown out my sister's infuriating bubble gum snapping, I stretched out my arm into the dead zone near Dad and flipped on the radio. A top-forty rock and roll song, filled with pulsing drums and electric guitars exploded forth. I heard a boy and girl sing about a high mountain and a deep valley. As I realized what I was listening to I let out a scream, "Aouahhhhhhhh," the kind that shrieks out when you least expect it.

Dad, always in perfect control, suddenly jerked the steering wheel to the right and careening out of control, drove into a ditch. We bounced against a few small boulders, accompanied by the terrible scraping sound of rocks carving numerous patterns into the metal hub caps, and finally, miraculously, shot back onto the highway. Dad kept going, but his hands trembled on the steering wheel.

"What the hell is wrong with you?" he shouted.

My voice shook. "That's my record, but they're playing the wrong side!" I felt conflicted between the joy of hearing my voice streaming over the air waves across much of northern California and simultaneously feeling a knot in my stomach because the mountain song was junk filler for the back side of the most beautiful ballad I'd ever sung.

The disc jockey announced, "You just heard a revolutionary new sound by a new recording duo, Dick and Dee Dee." (Dee Dee was me—that is, the name the record producers had given me.) "That was 'The Mountain's High,'" he continued, "a smasheroo record on the Bay Area's coolest station, the boss of the Bay, KYA."

I said, "Oh my gosh! Our record wasn't even scheduled for release." My mind could not absorb this. I was a nobody, but my voice was being heard by thousands, maybe hundreds of thousands, maybe millions of people. To make it more unbelievable, the disc jockey played the wrong side of the record!

With that realization I fell back against the sweaty leather seat, totally destroying the back of my hairstyle. I didn't care. As the radio played a Doublemint Gum commercial, Dad reached forward and lowered the volume. For the first time since the trip started, the five of us sat in silence, stunned and frozen. At that moment, I realized something huge had taken place. The equivalent of a 9.2 earthquake reverberated inside me. Somehow I knew that my life would never be the same.

* * * * *

The next moment, Dad's attitude changed. With a new-found respect in his voice, he addressed Mom. "Well, what do you know, Betty," Dad said, twisting to see her in back. "Little Mary's on the radio."

Mom's voice floated over my sister's strangely silent breathing. "But what happened to the song you wrote, Mary? You know, 'I Want Someone?'"

Adrenaline shot through me. I barely heard her. My mind raced as I remembered all my hopes and dreams for "I Want Someone," the other side of the record, the song that had earned Dick and me the recording contract we'd signed three months ago. "But why are they playing that mountain song?" Mom persisted.

As if I were explaining it to a two-year-old, I sarcastically retorted, "They've obviously turned the record over."

I wildly fanned my face with a copy of Dig Magazine I'd grabbed from the car floor and turned the volume level higher on the car radio.

"Tossing and Turning," a national hit by Bobby Lewis, exploded through the car. I started singing along, super loud.

* * * * *

Not that I was counting, but we heard "The Mountain's High" eighteen more times before we traveled out of range of the San Francisco broadcasting area and into Oregon. Each time it played, I acted like I could care less, but inwardly grew more and more excited. The song must be destined for greatness; otherwise, why would they play it so much? Was it possible that Dick and I might have a hit record? How cool would that be?

When we finally reached the farm, I immediately telephoned Dick in Santa Monica. When he said "hello," his image flashed through my mind: six feet tall, short brown hair (practically shaved off on the sides), small pinpoint eyes, leaning against a wall, the phone to his ear, his face red with annoyance.

"'Where have you been?" he shouted. "You told me you'd be in arriving in Seattle two days ago."

"In my dad's ancient car, it took much longer to get here then we expected."

"Do you know what you've been missing?" He didn't wait for an answer. 'The Mountain's High' is climbing the charts on two top-forty radio stations in San Francisco."

"Dick," I said. "I already know that. I heard it eighteen times on the radio while trapped in my parents' sauna of a car on the way up here. But why did the Wilders decide to promote 'The Mountain's High' as the A side of the record?" The Wilder Brothers- George, Walt and Warner- had signed us to a recording contract and produced our first record.

"The Wilders told me that Bob Mitchell, a San Francisco disc jockey, mistakenly put the wrong side on his turn table. The station's phone lines lit up for half an hour with requests for 'The Mountain's High.' Bob Mitchell told the Wilders, 'You've been promoting the wrong side of the record.' The Mountain's High' is the side that's going to be the hit.'"

I wondered how anyone could prefer "The Mountain's High," with that tin can drum and strange "whee oohs" sung in Dick's falsetto voice to the lush orchestra and string section on "I Want Someone." This was totally embarrassing.

* * * * *

"So why were you desperately trying to reach me?"

"We're booked on 'The Dick Stewart' television show in San Francisco in three days. He's like a West Coast Dick Clark. You've got to fly down here."

"The show's in three days?"

"The Wilders reserved hotel rooms for us. I'm flying up tomorrow morning with my mom. Whadda ya think?"

That stopped me cold. I took a deep breath. "Dick, I just arrived at the farm with my family. You know Dad's never going to let me leave."

"Do you realize what's at stake?" Dick sounded agitated. "We're already booked on the show. We can't cancel. I can't sing 'The Mountain's High' on television alone. Do you want me to talk to your parents?"

That was a terrible idea. "No, I'll take care of it. I'll call you back."

I slowly placed the receiver back in the cradle.

* * * * *

I found Dad sitting in the living room. A tall man with thinning dark hair and a pleasant face, he puffed on his pipe as he read the evening newspaper. My dad, "Mr. George E. Sperling, Jr." as it said on his business cards, was corporate counsel for Carnation Company in Los Angeles, and he sat on the Board of Directors.

To achieve his goals he applied single-minded focus and steel determination to hard work. One of the perks of his new board position was a week's vacation every few years at Carnation Farms, a company-owned getaway near Seattle.

Mom sat nearby, knitting a sweater. Mom worked as an executive secretary before retiring in her early thirties to raise three children. She stood about five-four, with short, dark hair. Her pretty face and beautiful blue eyes masked her true age and most people thought she was much younger than forty seven.

Sometimes I felt sorry I didn't show more appreciation towards her. I truly loved Mom. I never remember her uttering an unkind word to anyone. Although she'd developed a deep faith in God, she kept her views to herself and worshiped the Almighty by service to others.

Mom used to tell us kids constantly, "If you can't say anything nice, don't say anything at all." Unfortunately, as far as her daughters went, most of her advice fell on deaf ears.

"Guess what?" I said, trying to bluff my parents and act super casual. "You know how we kept hearing 'The Mountain's High' on the car radio driving up here? Well, I just talked to Dick. Can you believe it? Our record is a big hit in San Francisco. Isn't that fantastic? He says I have to fly down there right away. We're booked on a television show this Friday."

Dad slowly closed the newspaper and shook his head. In a stern voice he said, "That's not the way we do things, Mary. Didn't Dick know about this before today? It's not reasonable to expect you to give up your vacation to fly down there on such short notice." He casually sucked on his pipe.

"Dad," I pleaded, starting to feel anxious. "I don't think Dick was given much notice either. That's just how things go sometime. I agree it's rotten timing, but my leaving here doesn't ruin the vacation for you and Mom. You can still stay."

Mom calmly continued to click her knitting needles. "Who is going along as chaperone?" she asked.

"I don't believe this," I said. Inwardly I chanted, "Stay calm. Stay calm."

"Dick's Mom, Mrs. Carroll. She'll be there."

Dad tapped his pipe against the side of the ash tray, sending burnt tobacco ashes into a small volcanic pile. He set the pipe down and looked directly into my eyes. In his most authoritative voice, the voice I'd hated during most of my teens, he said, "Well, I don't think it's right. Maybe they can change the date of the show to next week and we can all drive down to San Francisco as a family."

A family? That was it. I felt desperate and ready to scream.

"Dad," I said, trying to keep my shaky voice under control. "This is an amazing opportunity. Just think… they want us to sing on television." I paused, and then pleaded, "Trust me just this once. I'll be fine."

Dad and Mom exchanged glances. Dad finally leaned forward and picked up his newspaper. "All right, but under one condition: I want to know the name of the hotel you're staying in and exactly when you're returning to Los Angeles."

Barely controlling my excitement, I ran to the telephone and called the airlines. The next available flight left Seattle the following afternoon. I booked a reservation, then immediately called Dick.

"I'm arriving in the San Francisco airport at 4:00 p.m. tomorrow on PSA. Dad needs to know the name of the hotel we're staying at."

"The St. Francis. Mom and I will meet you up at the airport baggage area."

I hung up the phone and leaned back in the wooden desk chair, watching the sun stripe the wall through the Venetian blinds. It's so weird how things turn out, I thought, not quite believing this wasn't a dream. It had all happened so quickly: Dick and I had recorded our first record just three months ago, and only three months before that, Dick magically re-entered my life.

"Little Mary"—Age 5

The Sperling Girls (from left to right):
Patty, Doris and me (with my 'Beehive' hairdo) and Mom in front.

Dad, attorney George E. Sperling, Jr.

CHAPTER TWO

The Roller-Coaster Ride Begins
December, 1960

Of all the people in my life, the last one I'd expected to end up singing with was Dick. Here I am, about to be famous with a guy who messed me up the first time I met him. This was the guy who cut off most of my hair, and it wasn't normal hair either, but a shiny, auburn mane, hanging half way down my back. I brushed my hair one hundred strokes a night, dangling my head upside down to encourage the blood flow to my brain and enhance the hair roots.

When I was fourteen, I'd sat across from Dick Gosting in a math class at Paul Revere Junior High School in West Los Angeles. He wore a letterman's jacket, although he never played sports (I never asked him if he stole it from the boy's locker room). Dick styled his brown hair with what appeared to be shiny grease and combed it back into a trendy "ducktail."

But anyone could see Dick wasn't really trendy. He was tall, slightly overweight, with puffy skin. He bit his nails and wasn't as cool as the guys who slunk around in jeans and tee shirts tattooing their girlfriend's names on their arms with blue Bic pens.

Nevertheless, we struck up a conversation in math class and he invited himself to my house after school. The day he followed me home, he insisted I bring him a pair of shears from my Mom's sewing cabinet.

"We've got to do something about your hair," he said. "Long hair is just so not happening. Why don't you let me cut it short, like Audrey Hepburn's?"

I felt weird. "I don't know," I said. "I've worn my hair long for some time now and I'm used to it."

"Oh, come on," he insisted. "You're not that attached to your hair, are you? Do you always want to look slightly dorky?"

I knew nothing about guys. I'd been raised with two sisters and wasn't sure how to behave around male energy. Did guys always insult you?

Dick waved the shears in the air. "Come on. Just let me trim off a little. It will look so much better. Here, face this way."

Dick turned me toward him, away from the mirror. I stared at his chest as I heard snipping. Several dark brown locks floated to the floor. At one point I tried to pull away, but Dick yelled, "Stand still!" After about two minutes, long hair strands covered the tile. When I finally turned back to the mirror and saw my hacked-off, choppy head, I gasped. I looked like the neighbors cactus plant. I knew I could never go outside again for at least a year.

Dick smiled. "You look great," he said. "Trust me. You'll get used to the haircut and you'll thank me for not even charging you for it."

Too distraught to even comment, I ran for my bedroom and slammed the door. Dick let himself out of the house and we didn't speak again until my hair grew long enough to curl with rollers, about six months later. And even then, our conversations consisted of only "Hello," and "How are you doing?" as we passed in the school hall.

I moved to Santa Monica in the eleventh grade and switched schools. Dick and I drifted apart, not knowing we shared a common bond of songwriting and the common belief that music was our generation's salvation.

* * * * *

Four and a half years later, in late 1960, during my Christmas break from college, I got a job at a See's candy store. Hundreds of See's stores dotted Los Angeles. They all looked alike. The store walls were painted white, with black trim.

We salesgirls wore white uniforms resembling nurses outfits, with large, frumpy, black bows pinned to our chests. Mandatory spider-web-like hair nets clutched our tresses, pulling all loose strands to the back, where they hung in a limp bun. In those outfits, I am surprised we didn't scare the customers away.

When I first started working for See's, I'd noticed a large black and white photo of a kind-looking, elderly woman on the wall opposite the candy counter. Smiling sweetly, Mary See watched me continuously. Although she'd passed away, her benevolent smile encouraged me to sell more of her product.

* * * * *

One day, on a lunch break from my job, I rounded a corner and bumped into Dick Gosting, who looked like a taller version of the pale-faced boy I knew as the scissor wielder in junior high. Our eyes met, and I glanced away, wanting to protect myself from intimidation. He was eager to speak.

"Wow, is it really Mary Sperling in that ridiculous outfit? Why are you wearing that? It's two months past Halloween."

"It's nice to see you, too," I said. "Seriously, I work for See's Candies. This is the uniform of choice." I glanced at my watch.

"How's the pay?" Dick asked.

Did he really have to know? "Terrible. It's minimum wage and they don't ever let you sit down." I heard Mom's voice in my head. "If you can't say something nice, don't say anything at all." I tried to think of something positive to say. "The cool thing is you can eat all the candy you want."

Dick's eyes widened with the joyful news. He practically drooled. "Are they hiring?"

"Dick, the problem is you're not a woman. Out front it has to be ladies wearing these lovely outfits, but guys do sometimes work in the back room as box boys during the Christmas rush. Anyway, I've got to get back." I looked at my watch as I turned away. "Well, see you."

As I took off down the street, I glanced back. Dick stood where I'd left him, staring in my direction. I had a feeling I hadn't seen the last of him.

* * * * *

About a week later, the store manager called me into the back room. "We hired a new box boy for the holidays. Dick, come here."

Flabbergasted, I saw Richard Gosting walk toward me. Out of hundreds of See's candy shops in the Los Angeles area, he had finagled a job in my store.

He grinned. "Pleased to meet you," he said.

There wasn't time to talk because the store manager stood guard, pursing her lips, annoyed that an extra second of work time had been wasted. Soon I was back behind the counter stuffing chocolates into boxes at a rate that could have qualified me for the Olympics if box stuffing was an Olympic sport.

Milling around the counter were two-dozen customers who had lost their Christmas spirit. In the middle of all this pre-Christmas cheer, Dick appeared, lugging three tall cartons of weighty candies from the See's delivery truck. As he passed through the main part of the store, carrying them from a truck to the storage room, I heard him muttering, "This candy is damn heavy."

When he reached the end of the candy counter he dropped the boxes with a thump. They landed on the floor near the feet of the startled customers. He then reached around the counter and grabbed a handful of caramels. He popped one in his mouth and stuffed the rest in his pants pocket. Grinning at the customers, he hoisted the cartons back up and headed towards the storage room, making loud, slurpy noises as he sucked the candy. When I saw the customers' shocked expressions, I had to dig my fingernails into the palm of my hand to keep from laughing.

The wave of humanity crushed back against the counter, but I had a funny feeling something was wrong. When I had a moment to look up, I saw the picture of dear Mary See transfigured. Someone had pressed one of our most popular candies, a chocolate-covered marshmallow with a jelly-like green top, over each eye. Her eyes were now green squares. I couldn't contain myself. I burst out in raucous laughter.

The manager noticed the decorated photo and yanked the candy away from Mary's eyes, leaving a sticky, gooey, snail-like trail on the glass. She squinted her eyes and glared at us sales girls as if to say, "Before this day ends, someone will be terminated."

After the store closed there was hell to pay. The store manager made us stand in a row like a police line-up and demanded a confession from the guilty party. Everyone denied their part in the vandalism, but I noticed a big smirk on Dick's face.

"It wasn't me," he told the store manager. "But I think it improved Mary See's appearance, don't you?" I wondered if Dick would make it through the rest of the week, but since no one saw the culprit in action, Dick did not get fired.

* * * * *

As the Christmas holidays progressed, Dick and I spent time together on our lunch breaks. We never mentioned our early adolescence and the disastrous haircutting episode. I felt more relaxed around him now. His hilarious and irreverent sense of humor eased any remaining tension between us. I realized that since our junior-high days, Dick had morphed into one funny person.

One day we sat in the nearby Apple Pan Restaurant, polishing off large slices of apple pie.

"So what do you do when you're not selling candy?" Dick asked.

"I'm currently enrolled at Santa Monica City College, but as you know, it's Christmas break. If I didn't have to work at the candy store every damn minute, I'd be writing songs."

I launched into a conversation about how I'd formed a girl's singing quartette in the tenth grade, writing all the material we sang.

Dick's eyes widened. "So do you still sing in the group?"

"No. Let me tell you what happened. After classes one day, one of the girls who had a driver's license drove us to Beverly Hills so we could audition for a record executive."

I told Dick how the record executive expected us to deliver a demonstration tape of our songs but since we didn't have one, we launched into our first song live, a ballad with soaring four-part harmonies. The man furrowed his brow and started drumming his fingers on the desk. He told us he'd heard enough of that song and asked us if we had anything else.

Undaunted, we sang the introduction to our second song. We'd barely started when the phone rang. The man answered and got into a heated argument with someone on the other end of the line. He talked through most of our performance, paying absolutely no attention to us. Finally he slammed down the receiver and shouted, "Stop!"

Dick dropped his fork on the floor. He bent down, picked it up, stuck it in his water glass, dried it on his napkin, and used it to spear another piece of pie. I inwardly blanched, and then continued my story.

I told Dick how the record producer requested we sing the final note of the song again, holding it out in one long "Ahhhhhh." The man leapt to his feet, waved his arms in the air and shouted, "Go write a new song around that one note and you've got a hit record."

"What a jerk," Dick interjected.

"Yeah, well, get this. When we stood to leave, he asked us to deliver a package to an address in Beverly Hills. Now he wanted us to be his messenger service! But, of course, we did what he asked."

I told Dick that when we reached the house I dashed out of the car. But before I had a chance to ring the bell, the front door swung open and I found myself staring at my favorite actress, Doris Day.

You have to realize that Doris Day was my idol. As one of America's top box office draws, she starred in all my favorite movies. She also sang—cheerful, positive songs. Doris Day, with her short blond hair, blazing blue eyes and cheerful demeanor, haunted my dreams. She was everything I wanted to be.

When I saw her standing in front of me, my brain short circuited. I found myself unable to even smile. Like a robot, I silently handed her the package.

"Are you an employee of the record company?" she asked.

I staggered back and managed to stammer, "No. Actually I was there for an audition."

Her eyes flashed. "That's wonderful," she gushed. "Good luck to you."

I managed to stumble back to the car and convinced the driver to start the engine, even though the other girls wanted to storm the fortress to see Doris Day for themselves.

Dick broke into my reverie. He could care less about Doris Day. "So I take it you never got a record deal."

I sighed, crestfallen. "No, by the time tenth grade ended, all the girls had quit. But I've continued writing songs on my own ever since."

How could anyone ever understand why I loved song writing? Sitting at the piano, facing a blank sheet of paper, my fingers automatically pressing different keys at random, that magical moment arrived when a melody floated up from somewhere deep in my subconscious mind.

Then I'd start with a sentence and try to rhyme the last word until lyrics spilled

out, one word following the other. But the joy occurred when I sang the completed
song for the first time.

With eyes closed, I expressed my feelings and emotions, transporting myself
to another place and time, creating a flow that, by the end of the song, completely
transformed me. I can only describe it as being in a shower of total creativity that
cleanses every cell of your body. But who would understand this?

Dick broke into my thoughts. "That's just what I'm doing, writing songs that is.
Do you want to get together sometime to share material?"

What were the odds of finding someone who shared my songwriting passion?
I said "Okay."

* * * * *

Christmas of 1960 and then New Year's Day 1961 came and went. The crowds
thinned at See's. The manager laid Dick off, but before Dick left work, he handed me
a slip of paper with his phone number scrawled across it.

One Saturday I drove to Dick's home in Santa Monica Canyon. The older home
sat modestly on a narrow, tree-lined street. I parked in the driveway under a large
sycamore, grabbed my folder of song lyrics and knocked on the front door.

Dick opened it. "Come on in," he said, his eyes shining. He escorted me into a
dimly lit corner of the living room where an old upright piano sat against the wall.

"You can sit here," he said, patting the piano bench. Dick appeared eager, excited.
I felt nervous, but happy to be there sharing my songs.

Dick placed his beat-up reel to reel Wollensac tape recorder on the floor, turned
it on and gave it a kick to get the spools turning. Accompanied by his pounding piano
playing, an original song, written and sung by Dick, blasted from the speakers.

"I'm showing this material to some big-time record producers," Dick boasted.
I was impressed. "Wanna know how I met them? I went to a party at a friend's house.
This kid's dad was a hot-shot movie producer. When no one was looking, I snuck
into the dad's office and went through his address book. Under the category Music
Arrangers I found the name and phone number of Don Ralke. I wrote it down on a
cocktail napkin."

Dick waved the paper napkin in front of my face to prove what he was saying.
I wondered if he felt guilty sneaking into someone's office and copying down a phone

number from someone's personal address book. A shamefaced feeling rushed over me, followed by grudging admiration for Dick's boldness.

"So now I have an appointment to show my songs to The Wilder Brothers. You know who they are, don't you?"

Feeling naïve, I said, "No."

"They're a hot new production company. They actually are brothers, three of them, George, Walt and Warner, and they're searching for acts to record."

"Groovy," I said, genuinely happy for Dick.

"Yeah," Dick said. "I know I'm going to make it big as a solo artist. That's my destiny." He stared off into the distance, and then condescendingly turned to me. "Oh, by the way, did you bring your songs?" I waved my folder in his direction, the folder I'd been clutching the entire time.

I opened it and handed him lyrics to a ballad I'd composed, entitled, "I Want Someone." Dick stared at the words, and then flopped onto the piano bench, his large fingers playing the stained ivory keys.

"Listen to this," he said. Soon he was singing my words to his music. It was a miracle. The words and tune fit together exquisitely as if they'd been created by a single mind.

Sitting beside Dick with eyes closed, I let the melody envelope me. Within ten minutes I was adding a harmony part. Dick grabbed a small plastic microphone from the floor and attached it to the top of the piano. He turned on the tape recorder and we sang the song into the microphone, heads pressed together, and mouths inches from the recording device. Each time we sang it, the song sounded better and better.

As we listened to the played back song, I started spontaneously singing another harmony, higher than the first one, adding a third part to the song. Not to be outdone, Dick began singing the melody an octave higher and in falsetto. We instantly sounded like a quartette.

"Listen to that," Dick muttered. "We sound like a huge group. I wish there was a way to tape all the voices."

"It's awesome," I said. We just looked at each other. That moment heralded the birth of the Dick and Dee Dee sound. Ta-daah!

It sounded so good Dick decided to include the ballad of "I Want Someone" on the tape of songs he intended to play for the record producers. There was only one problem. How would they hear our higher harmonies?

Dick said, "There's a little recording studio in Hollywood that charges by the hour. But if you record at six in the morning, they only charge half-price. Let's record our higher voices there."

"Great," I said. "I'll split the fee with you."

* * * * *

A week later, before my college classes began, we drove to the studio. It resembled a laboratory, white everywhere. We entered a small room with a tiny sound booth on one side. The sound engineer, yawning into his coffee, waved us into the main studio and turned on the equipment. With Dick accompanying us on piano, we quickly recorded our lower voices to "I Want Someone." Then we sang our higher voices on another track, and the sound engineer mixed them together.

"That's far out," the man commented. His eyes sparkled for the first time "That song's a gas, very commercial sounding."

We paid him and thanked him for his time. As we left, Dick clutched the tape to his chest.

* * * * *

The next day, Dick drove to Westwood to meet the arranger and producers. He telephoned me that evening. "The Wilder Brothers heard my demo tape and loved it," he said. "They decided to record me as a solo artist. Oh, and incidentally, I'm changing my last name, from Gosting to St. John. I think it sounds better."

"Congratulations," I replied. I waited a few moments, but he didn't mention our song. Finally, I had to ask, "What did they think of the song we sang?"

Dick paused for what seemed like a long time. I made a face. Did he even show them our song?

"Oh, they want us to record 'I Want Someone' at the same session as my solo songs. They told me, 'Whoever that girl is, bring her along too.' They want to duplicate the sound we got in the small studio. So, we have to go to Gold Star Recording Studios in Hollywood in a few weeks. It's going to take them a little time to hire musicians."

I felt my heart lunge and my face flush. Was I ready for this?

"Wow," I said. "That's incredible!"

* * * * *

I was so jittery I immediately telephoned my boyfriend, Mike. I imagined him standing in the hall at his parents' house, lifting up the black phone receiver.

"You won't believe this," I babbled into the phone. "You know that song I wrote, 'I Want Someone'? Well, I have a songwriting partner and he put my words to music. I just found out some record producers want to record us."

Mike and I had been a couple for over a year. We never discussed marriage but there was the possibility that might happen some day. I felt comfortable with him. He stood about five feet nine inches tall and wore his dark hair cropped short. He tanned easily and, when he smiled, it made my day.

He was Jewish and I was Presbyterian. Although he didn't join me and my family on Dad's mandatory Sunday visits to the local Presbyterian Church, his family always invited me to dinner at their home for Passover and other holidays. They tried to make me feel welcome. I felt comfortable most of the time, except when I had to drink borscht.

"That's cool, Little Boo," Mike said, using his nickname for me. He usually called me either "Little Boo" or "Kitten."

"You write great lyrics. While you're at it, you should try to write a follow-up to 'Poison Ivy.'" Then he launched into the song, one of his old favorites by the Coasters.

I laughed and hung up. I didn't want Mike to know how much the upcoming studio event occupied my mind or how excited and nervous I was. I walked into my turquoise and yellow tiled bathroom and stared into the mirror. My face looked flushed, my eyes wide. I wondered if Mike thought I was pretty. I slammed the medicine cabinet door and walked to my wall calendar. What date would the Wilders choose for our recording session? I stared at the calendar for a long time.

* * * * *

More than thirty musicians gathered in Studio A at Gold Star Recording Studios in Hollywood that warm afternoon in spring, 1961. By the time I arrived, I found them perched in folding chairs, their instruments beside them, studying sheet music propped on music stands. Dick walked out of the control booth and grabbed my arm.

"You're finally here," he said, although I'd arrived ahead of time. "This is Don Ralke, our arranger." I nodded at the short, bald man. "Don, this is Mary." Don's kind face broke into a broad grin and his eyes gleamed as he smiled at me.

"You've written a nice song," he told me. "I think you'll like what I've done with the string parts."

I blushed. Before I could think of anything to say, a tall man with reddish hair and a big smile came out of the control booth.

"I'm Warner Wilder," he said. "Dick tells us you've written lots of songs. We really like the sound you two got on 'I Want Someone.'"

Don looked at his watch and turned to us. "Now, if you'll both go into that little booth over there, we'll get started." The booth stood in one corner of the studio. We entered it, peering through a small glass window.

Don rehearsed the orchestra several times, and then clicked his baton on the music stand to quiet them.

"Time is money," he announced. "Let's get going."

Then Don pointed his baton in our direction. We adjusted our headsets and started to sing. It was thrilling to weave our voices around the violins, rhythm instruments, and guitars. I stared at the small army of musicians playing the song I'd written the lyrics to. It sounded like the Los Angeles Philharmonic Orchestra. Joy flooded over me.

Listening to "I Want Someone" played back through huge studio speakers, I smiled. It sounded beautiful, absolutely gorgeous. It wasn't Shakespeare, but it was dramatic enough to convey the teenage angst I had felt when I wrote the song several years ago, before I met Mike.

I smiled and swayed, slightly dazed. I couldn't believe I'd written lyrics that had actually been recorded. The musicians took a break and we recorded our higher voices on the open track. Then suddenly it was over.

Dick gently pushed me toward the door.

"You don't need to stick around," he said. "I'm going to record my songs now. We'll be in touch." When I acted confused and hesitated, he shoved me harder. He was obviously trying to get rid of me.

"Thanks for coming," Don Ralke said, as he waved his baton in my direction. Reluctantly, I left. The studio door slammed.

* * * * *

Several weeks passed. Then one day Dick telephoned to announce that the Wilder Brothers were convinced "I Want Someone" was destined to be a hit single. They wanted us to go back to the studio to record another song for the flip side of the disc.

"Just throw anything on the back," George Wilder suggested. "No one ever listens to the B side of a record."

"Come over to my house and help me go through some lyrics I've written," Dick said to me. "I'm sure we can figure out something to put on the record's back side." There was no mention of me bringing my folder of songs.

When I arrived, Dick rustled through a stack of papers sitting in his piano bench. "Here's something," he finally said, pulling out some scribbling on lined paper. In a loud voice, Dick started singing his words and melody to the first verse. It was about someone who couldn't get to the other side of a mountain. It didn't make any sense to me. Then I thought, "No one is going to hear this song anyway. It really doesn't matter."

I helped Dick rewrite several lines and suggested an order for the verses. We repeated the first verse at the end. The song finally stretched to the proper length for vinyl singles, just under three minutes. We rehearsed the song for about ten minutes.

"This should work," Dick said, smiling at me. "Now we know two songs together." "Yes," I thought. "If you call those strange mountain lyrics a song."

* * * * *

The following week we drove to an address on Formosa, a residential street in Hollywood. We entered a small home studio, located over a three-car garage. The studio belonged to sound engineer Armin Steiner, who sat hunched in a tiny control booth. Instead of an orchestra, I counted only five musicians. The Wilder Brothers played some of the instruments themselves, accompanied by a young man on drums.

We ran through the song several times. The Wilder Brothers joked and laughed.

I suddenly relaxed. This seemed a lot easier than the Gold Star recording session. When it was time to actually record the song, Dick and I stood in the studio and sang "The Mountain's High" into an ancient microphone. When Armin played the song back, the tape machine shuddered and changed speeds. It sounded scary.

"Don't sweat it," Armin said. "It takes awhile for the machine to warm up."

Dick grimaced. He leaned over and whispered in my ear, "We sound like Alvin and the Chipmunks," referring to a then popular record with voices sped up to resemble chipmunks singing.

Finally the tape machine kicked in and played our song at a normal speed. Then there was much discussion about the sound on the drums.

"Man, it sounds like I'm playing a tin can," the drummer said.

Armin tried placing the microphone in several different positions, sometimes closer and sometimes farther from the drum heads, but nothing changed the fact that the drums sounded tinny.

"This is really a drag," Dick whispered to me. "We've gone from first class to last class."

I smiled at him. I was just happy to be singing. I felt confident the Wilder brothers and Don Ralke knew what they were doing. Watching them through the window in the control booth, I noticed they didn't appear upset with the drum sound or anything else. They finally requested we add our high voices, which we did in one take. When they played the song back through booming speakers, they actually laughed!

In less than two hours after we'd arrived, George Wilder came out and shook our hands.

"Congratulations!" he said. "We've got a flip side."

* * * * *

Driving home from the recording session, Dick cruised down San Vicente Boulevard, nearing my house.

Rousing himself from his deep thoughts, he said, "The Wilders are drawing up song writing contracts. So the record label will read, 'I Want Someone' by Mary Sperling and Dick St. John and 'The Mountain's High' by Dick St. John." I sat in disbelieving silence.

"Wait a minute. What do you mean 'The Mountain's High', by Dick St. John?"

I asked, puzzled. "We both contributed to the song. It was just fragments scribbled on paper when you showed it to me."

Dick clenched his teeth. His voice rose in anger. "I wrote the entire song before I ever met you." My insides started to flutter. Taking a deep breath, I tried to stay calm. Try to reason with him, I thought. That usually works with Dad.

"Dick, we worked on that song together, remember? We changed it a lot."

Dick tried to control his body. His knuckles whitened as he gripped the steering wheel. He suddenly pounded on the dash board, sending his knit argyle dice attached to the rear view mirror swinging like a pendulum.

He shouted, "'The…Mountain's…High'…is…MY…song!"

His anger frightened me. I felt like I'd been punched in the stomach. I'd never seen this side of him before. It's going to be alright, I told myself. I folded my arms, disappointed and genuinely hurt. "Why don't we let the Wilders decide?" I finally said quietly. "We can tell them what we both contributed."

Dick's foot shot out and slammed down on the brake pedal. The car stopped abruptly, throwing me forward. My right arm crashed heavily against the dashboard. I felt something snap. Severe pain shot up my entire arm.

"Ahhhh, my wrist," I cried, carefully cradling it in my left hand.

"I wrote that song alone!" Dick shouted.

With my good hand, I opened the car door. Sliding out, I slammed the door as hard as I could and ran down the block and into my house without looking back.

* * * * *

I'd sprained my wrist. A doctor verified this by x-ray. He also told me a sprain can be more painful than a fracture. When Dick telephoned, I refused to talk to him, preferring to sulk in my room. What a jerk, I thought. I don't want anything to do with him.

Several days later, the doorbell rang. Without thinking, I swung the door open. Dick stood on the porch, a big smile on his face.

"Here are the contracts." He handed over a small pile of papers. "Because we're under twenty-one years of age, our parents have to sign, too."

I just stared at him, a cold expression on my face. Had he forgotten about our last encounter?

"My wrist still hurts," I said.

"Sorry." Dick replied, and then quickly changed the subject. "Look, I'll be back tomorrow to pick up the contracts. Aren't you excited? Our record will be released soon!" Before I could answer he raced down the steps, jumped into his car and drove away.

Clutching the documents, I retreated into the house. Sure enough, just as he'd predicted, the songwriting contracts showed Dick as the sole writer of "The Mountain's High."

I started shaking. My stomach felt like kittens were chasing each other around inside it. I paced back and forth in my living room, wondering what to do. Raised in a society where women acted as the supporters/nurturers, I'd observed that men remained in control and it was best to keep my mouth shut. But this was totally unfair. What could I do about it?

Should I tell him I didn't want to sing with him anymore? That would really screw things up for the record producers. They'd invested time and money in this project. Besides, I'd be hurting my own chance for success.

Then I remembered something Dick once mentioned about songwriting. He said that if you didn't copyright a song officially, you could put a copy of your artistic work in an envelope, take it to the post office and send it registered mail to yourself. If you kept the sealed package unopened, the postmark showed you made claim to title on a specific date. Apparently, this type of claim stood up in court.

I played "The Mountain's High" on my piano, singing the melody in a shaky voice. After I recorded it, I placed the tape in an envelope, went to the post office and mailed it to myself.

For years the package remained in my dresser drawer. I forgot about it until I found it six or seven years later. By then, the statute of limitations supporting any legal claim had expired, and I threw the tape in the trash.

* * * * *

But in 1961, the day Dick handed me the contracts, I still felt upset. The only other person I told my sad situation to was my boyfriend Mike. I left out the part about my sprained wrist.

"I don't know what you're so concerned about," Mike said. "Fifty percent of some thing is better than 100 percent of nothing. In other words, you potentially have a career ahead, singing as a duo with Dick. If the act breaks up over who wrote "The Mountain's High," what would that solve? Then you'd have nothing."

"But it's the principle of the thing," I argued. "I worked hard on that song. I feel like Dick cheated me."

Mike sighed.

"Little Boo, it's only the back side of the record. Who's even going to hear it? There will be other songs and other opportunities. Why don't you wait to see what happens?"

I reluctantly agreed with him and decided to continue on with the act, although the breach of trust created a protective shield around me that remained throughout my entire career with Dick. I never again let Dick get too close.

* * * * *

That night my Dad studied the singing and songwriting contracts intently. "You know, the Wilders are giving you a tiny percentage of the royalties. If they lease your songs to a major label, as they have the right to do, their royalties will be more than yours and Dick's combined." I didn't care.

"Dad, right now we have nothing. If we cause trouble, they're just going to drop the entire project. Please sign the contracts." With a sigh of resignation, he finally signed.

When Dick showed up the next day to pick them up, Mom opened the door and handed them to him. I watched from the upstairs window.

"Where's Mary?" I heard him say.

Mom vaguely replied, "Oh, she's occupied. She said to give these to you."

Dick looked thoughtful as he retreated to his car.

* * * * *

About a month later, Dick dropped by again. By now my wrist had healed. I thought of the tape stating I wrote half of "The Mountain's High," sitting in my dresser drawer. Somehow the thought of my secret maneuver made me smile.

Dick stood on the front porch, his eyes worried and hands trembling.

"Here it is," he said in the sweetest voice imaginable. "This is your copy of our record."

He handed the vinyl record to me like it was made out of spun glass. I stared at the 45-rpm disc. My heart pounded with excitement. The black vinyl wore a beautiful dark blue label that read "Lama Records." I liked the color of the label, but my stomach sank when I read the label's wording. It read, "'I Want Someone,' by Dick and Dee Dee!"

"That is so lame." I stammered in disbelief. "They got my name wrong! They know my name is Mary. Why did they call me Dee Dee?"

Dick stood there biting his fingernails. "I knew you would be upset," he replied. "But I didn't have anything to do with it."

I didn't know whether to believe him or not. It was then that I realized it wasn't a mistake.

"It was intentional, wasn't it? I can't believe they changed my name without even asking me!" I stared again at the record label. "I notice they didn't change your name. It should have been 'Mick and Mary.' That sounds cool."

Dick said, "The Wilders told me that Tom Donahue, a disc jockey in San Francisco, named you Dee Dee after his daughter, Deirdre. It's a compliment."

"His daughter didn't sing on the record!"

"Well, I wouldn't sweat it. The Wilder Brothers are area testing 'I Want Someone' in the Bay Area on their small record label, Lama Records. If it does well, they hope to lease it to a major label. Maybe they'll change your name back to Mary on the next release."

I sighed and looked at the writing again.

"You'll get used to the new name," Dick said confidently. After he left, I put the disc on the turntable and turned up the volume. "I Want Someone" soared through the house. I thought well, it does sound absolutely beautiful. None of the rest of the petty stuff matters.

Turning the record over, I started to listen to "The Mountain's High," but turned it off halfway through. It sounded even worse than when we recorded it.

CHAPTER THREE

Maybe, Someday, I'll be a Star

My flight from Seattle took several hours. When I walked to the baggage area at the San Francisco airport, Dick and his mother stood waiting. Mrs. Carroll, a large woman with grey hair and a take charge attitude, grabbed me in a bear hug.

"Oh, it's so wonderful you kids are going to be on television," Mrs. Carroll thundered. "I always knew Rich was going to be a star." Dick rolled his eyes.

"Are you worried about singing on tv?" he asked.

Before I had a chance to reply he said, "There's nothing to get nervous about. We don't even have to sing live. When they play the record, we just mouth the words. It's called 'lip-synching.'"

Mrs. Carroll smiled at me. "I know you'll look beautiful on television," she said, "as long as you remember to smile." She and Dick acted so excited, I started to laugh. Their enthusiasm flooded over me. I have to admit it, as cool as I tried to be, the thought of performing on television thrilled me too.

We took a cab to the television station, a modern building on a narrow street. Dragging our heavy luggage, we stumbled through the tall glass doors. A receptionist raised her head.

"We're here to perform on the Dick Steward show," Dick said. "We're Dick and Dee Dee," I looked around, expecting a third person. Then I remembered that I was Dee Dee.

"Yes, Mr. Stewart's been expecting you. Please go through that door at the end of the hall."

She buzzed the hall door open, unlocking it so we were able to enter. A crew member dressed in casual clothes waved us over. Dick and I dropped our suitcases and Dick turned to his mother. "Can you watch our things for us?" She nodded. The man escorted us to a vast, cavernous room. I noticed a stage set, with a podium and dance floor, cameras and floor cables.

"Sit there," he commanded, pointing at two stools.

Another man approached. He was five-feet-seven, with a handsome face and flashy white teeth, dressed in a sport coat and narrow tie.

"Hi," he said. "I'm Dick Stewart. I'm glad you could make it." He waved his arm towards the left. "The dressing rooms are over there." I felt awestruck by the celebrity glow surrounding the man. I knew kids considered him a huge star in the San Francisco Bay area.

"This is your first television show, right?" Dick Stewart beamed with professionalism. I nodded. "Well, there's nothing to be nervous about. We're going to have a run-through and then you can go change." He yelled to someone in the sound booth, "Hit it!"

"The Mountain's High" blasted from a nearby speaker.

"Always look at the camera with the red light on," Dick Stewart said. "That's the one taping you." We moved our eyes from camera to camera as the red light alternated between them. It blinked on and off. We stared into the lens and sang along quietly while the song played. This was fun- no pressure here.

"Excellent," the disc jockey said. "See how easy that was? Now, when we actually tape the show, we'll have a short interview after the song ends. Why don't you go change your threads? The audience arrives in about fifteen minutes.

"Oh, incidentally," he added. "Several local performers go on before you. But when it's time for your number, a stage hand will bring you here from the dressing rooms."

Dick and I hauled our heavy luggage down a hallway. I opened the door to one of the dressing rooms, shoved my suitcase inside and entered. With a thud, the door slammed behind me. Startled, I looked around and realized I was alone.

I unfastened the two clasps on the front of my Samsonite suitcase, lifted the lid and surveyed the wrinkled terrain of mangled garments inside. I decided to wear a skirt and top, the only outfit that had survived the trip without creases, and changed clothes quickly.

Suddenly I heard a loud knock.

"You're on," a stage hand announced.

I couldn't believe how quickly the time flew. Back in the hallway, I joined Dick. He wore a sport coat and must have been hot, because his face looked red and moist. He pulled my arm nervously, prodding me down the hall at a fast pace.

We followed the crew member through a polite crowd of teens to the wooden stools, now bathed in a brilliant spotlight. Heat flooded over my body. It felt warm and welcoming. All the tensions of the past week dissolved as the spotlight transformed us from awkward, inexperienced teens to competent recording artists. I took a deep breath and smiled.

Dick Stewart stood behind a podium. The red lights on the television cameras flashed on.

"Today," he said, "we have two special guests, visiting us all the way from Los Angeles. Their record is number-one on the charts in the Bay Area. Let's give a warm San Francisco welcome for the singers of 'The Mountain's High,' Dick and Dee Dee." Dick and I gaped at each other. Did he say our record was number one?

Over loud applause, "The Mountain's High" started playing. We smiled, watched the camera and sang to the record.

When the music ended, microphone in hand, Dick Stewart approached us. "Dick and Dee Dee, welcome," he said. "So you're from the Los Angeles area. I know you're both teenagers. Are you boyfriend and girlfriend?"

"No, we're just friends," Dick said.

"How long have you been singing together?"

After a brief instant of calculation, Dick told him, "Only three months."

"And, Dee Dee, what's it like having a hit record?" I cleared my throat. It was difficult breathing. "It's great so far."

"Well, you kids have a far-out disc and a righteous career ahead of you. Thanks for joining us. Let's hear it for Dick and Dee Dee!"

We left the stage accompanied by polite applause. Mrs. Carroll stood in the wings. "You kids were good, real good." she bellowed. "You were the best ones on the show."

I appreciated the vote of confidence, even though I found out later that the only other performers were a ventriloquist and a trained dog act.

As we headed toward the dressing rooms, from behind the cameras and lights, a short, nervous-looking man with dark hair approached Dick and me.

"Bob Mitchell," he said, sticking out his hand. "Boss of the Bay on KYA."

I realized that he was one of the disc jockeys responsible for helping make "The Mountain's High" a hit in the Bay Area.

"I really dig the disc," he went on. "Why don't you join me at my record hop tonight in Redwood City? You can get up on stage and sing along to the record. It's great promotion." He smiled at us invitingly, and then added, "I'm heading there right now."

Dick and I looked at each other and at Mrs. Carroll, uncertain what to do.

"Hey, it's no biggie," he reassured us. "I'll drive you there myself."

Dick shrugged. "Well, let's go," he finally said. Puppy like, we trailed after the disc jockey from the building to the parking lot.

After depositing our suitcases in the trunk of his car, Mrs. Carroll, Dick and I squeezed into the compact vehicle. Bob drove about an hour before we finally pulled into an American Legion Hall parking lot.

I noticed a line of teenagers standing in front of the building, waiting to purchase tickets. I realized that Bob Mitchell must be receiving money for the show, yet he expected Dick and me to perform for free. But, as he said, "It's great promotion."

Passing several police cars parked in front, Bob circled the building and finally swung the car into a parking space at the rear. He then led our small group through a side door into a deserted dressing room.

"Just hang your coats there," Bob said, pointing to a battered metal clothes rack. Several folding chairs sat under a dim, naked light bulb. The clothes rack and chairs appeared to be the only furnishings.

Bob went on, "When I announce your names, just climb up on stage and start singing along to your disc, you dig? On the turntable I'm gonna play 'I Want Someone' first and then 'The Mountain's High.' You cool with that?" We both nodded.

I felt nervous. The audience suddenly cheered. My stomach lurched.

As I stood backstage, I peered out from behind the curtains, studying the faces of the teens on the dance floor. I realized they would soon be staring at Dick and me. The room started to spin. Was I going to faint?

"Hey, kids," Bob shouted into a microphone. "Cool it. Time to pay attention. Whamma, Whamma, Whamma! I've got a duo with me from the Los Angeles area. They're going to sing their hit record, 'The Mountain's High.' Let's give a big Boss of the Bay welcome to Dick and Dee Dee!"

The kids shouted and applauded. We ran out on the stage. Perspiration covered my forehead. I took a deep breath and tried to steady my shaky body. As "I Want Someone" started to play, the kids began slow dancing. We sang along with the recorded music and were generally ignored.

But when Bob Mitchell flipped over the record and the musical introduction to "The Mountain's High" started, the hall came alive with cheers and shouts. With great enthusiasm, we threw ourselves into the performance.

Near the end of the song, the needle got stuck on the record and one line started repeating itself over and over. Dick and I frantically gestured to Bob Mitchell, who poked the needle with one finger, causing it to slide across the disc, creating a terrible screeching sound. The needle finally landed at the end of the song.

At first the kids appeared confused, but when the song ended they cheered anyway. We gave an awkward bow and exited the stage.

"That was horrible," I said to Dick as adrenaline rushed through my body. Still, the shaking was gone. I felt like I could run for miles, sing for hours and dance all night.

"Don't sweat it," Dick answered. "The kids loved it."

* * * * *

When we got back to the dressing room, Mrs. Carroll was nowhere in sight.

"Where did my mother go?" Dick asked several people milling around the hall.

They shrugged. Finally someone mentioned that while we were singing, they saw the police lead an older woman outside to a squad car.

Dick took off in a dead run out the backstage door and around the building, with me in pursuit. We finally found Dick's mother sitting in the rear of a police car, puffing with indignation.

"RICH !" she bellowed. "Get them to take these handcuffs off me. Tell them who I am!"

"What do you think you're doing?" Dick shouted at the officer.

"This woman was in the dressing room going through coat pockets," the policeman explained, grim-faced. "We've arrested her for attempted robbery."

"That's my son!" Mrs. Carroll yelled, pointing at Dick. "He's a singer. I was going through his coat pockets trying to find a damn Kleenex."

"How could you do this to my mother?" Dick shouted. "Does she look like a common thief?" The policeman scratched his head. I noticed he did not answer the question.

"We've had a rash of burglaries here lately," he said. "I thought I finally caught the culprit." In seconds, he freed Mrs. Carroll from the handcuffs. She sat glaring at the officer.

"I demand to go back to the hotel immediately," she ordered.

"The show's almost over," Dick said, reaching out an arm to help her out of the car. "Come on. Let's go back inside."

Mrs. Carroll winced, blinked a few times and struggled to her feet. She glared at the policeman. "Next time why don't you ask a few questions and make sure you have a real criminal!"

* * * * *

Later, when we finally did arrive back at the hotel, Bob Mitchell reached over the front seat and patted Mrs. Carroll's arm.

"I'm sorry the arrest happened," he said. "But, hey, the police were just doing their job. Look, I'm going for a drink. Can I buy you one?" He aimed his words in the general direction of Mrs. Carroll, but looked at Dick and me to let us know that the invitation was really meant for us.

"I just want to go back to my room," Mrs. Carroll said. "This has been a total nightmare."

"Would you guys like to join me? We won't be out long."

"Mom, are you all right going back to the room by yourself?" Dick asked.

"Do I look incapacitated? I'm fine. Before I go to sleep, I'm going to write a letter of complaint to the mayor of Redwood City." As she got out of the car, Mrs. Carroll warned, "Don't you kids stay out too late."

* * * * *

Bob Mitchell drove us to a nearby bar. The décor resembled early Hawaiian. Black lava rock Tiki gods leered down from the walls, their beady red electric-light eyes flashing on and off. The waiter apparently knew Bob.

"Good to see you again, Mr. Mitchell. What'll it be?"

"Bourbon on the rocks for me. Bring the kids a Mai Tai."

What a joke, I thought. Anyone can tell we're not twenty-one. What is he thinking?

To my surprise, even though we were under the legal drinking age, the waiter did not ask us for identification. When the drink arrived I took one sip and almost gagged. It tasted disgusting. I poured it into a potted plant when Bob wasn't looking.

"'The Mountain's High' is number one in San Francisco," Bob said after several sips of bourbon. "But that doesn't mean it's going to be number-one nationally." He shook his head. "No, No. Lots of records have a great start but die along the way."

There was a brief pause out of reverence for the dead records. He patted us consolingly on the shoulders. "But I'll tell you what I am willing to do. I'll give you each ten thousand dollars if you sign your future royalties for 'The Mountain's High' over to me. If not, you're taking a big gamble. This record might go right into the proverbial toilet."

With great dramatic flair, Bob Mitchell produced a document and pen from his jacket and propped them up on the bar before us. He patted his puffy coat pocket.

"Ten thousand dollars each," he whispered. "Cash! I've got it right here. Think what you could do with all that money."

Our eyes bulged at the thought. Then reason set in. Dick spoke first. "Naw, I think 'The Mountain's High' has a good chance of becoming a national hit. I'll take my chances."

"You're making a big mistake," Bob growled. He turned to me, his voice taking on a softer tone. "What about you, Dee Dee? I'll give you ten thousand dollars cash right now if you sign over your half of the singing royalties to 'The Mountain's High.'"

In a moment of instant clarity I realized that I had climbed onto an enormous roller coaster. The ride would take Dick and me to great heights, but would also fling us sideways and finally down. No matter how high we climbed, one thing was certain: what goes up comes down. The ride would stop someday and we would have to get off. Did I want to give up anything at this point in our career, with the roller coaster ride just beginning?

"No, I'll take my chances too."

Bob took a big swig from his glass and glared at me. He exhaled a boozy breath as he warned, "Your record will probably bomb out and you'll wind up working as a waitress in a sleazy bar somewhere, married to a guitar player."

"What's wrong with guitar players?" I thought, but kept my mouth shut.

Bob downed the remainder of his drink. He drove us back to our hotel in silence.

* * * * *

We left San Francisco and returned to Los Angeles. With the memory of Bob Mitchell's ten thousand dollars apiece hanging over us, both Dick and I realized our poor financial status. We'd spent all our savings on food and lodging in San Francisco. Although we owned a signed contract with the Wilder Brothers, the document did not provide for any advance money. We would not get royalties until records sold and accountants calculated our percentage.

Desperate for money, Dick got a job handing out free samples of cigarettes in Santa Monica. Back I went to my former Christmas job, working behind the counter at See's Candies. The candy company transferred me from the Westwood See's to their Santa Monica store, and I watched Dick passing out cigarettes from the store window.

Meanwhile, the Wilder Brothers shopped our record around Los Angeles, trying to get the best lease deal they could. Based on record sales in the Bay Area and the fact that "The Mountain's High" reached the number-one slot there on the top two radio stations, Liberty Records snatched it up. We glowed when George Wilder predicted that we might have one of the hottest records in the country.

* * * * *

Liberty Records released "The Mountain's High" in Los Angeles in June 1961. KRLA, the top radio station in town, chose it as a "Discovery of the Week," resulting in airplay every hour for a week.

Right at this time, AFTRA, the recording artists' union, decided to strike and record promoters were not allowed to cross the picket lines with new product. All over Los Angeles the top-forty charts remained frozen for three weeks. During the strike, "The Mountain's High" continued to play every hour on the hour, twenty-four hours a day. When the strike ended, our record jumped from "Discovery" to number-one.

Dick and me calling our friends, celebrating our first hit record
in Los Angeles, 'The Mountain's High."

CHAPTER FOUR

Heat, Cactus, and Segregation

Several weeks later, mid-summer of 1961, Dick called me at See's Candies.

"We just received an offer to go to Texas on tour," he said. "The Wilders feel this is an excellent chance to promote our record outside California. The tour is booked for the month of August." I looked over my shoulder at the store manager and pressed the phone tighter against my left ear.

"They're offering us $150 each per week," Dick went on. "Of course, we have to pay for our air fare and hotels. But the promoter provides transportation from show to show."

"Look, I'm not supposed to take personal calls at work," I whispered. "Let me call you back at home tonight."

I realized that $150 a week outperformed my salary at See's, but I also realized that traveling to Texas meant quitting my job. The store manager would never let me take a month's leave. What would I do for income when I returned?

I finally decided to let the future take care of itself. I'd find another job in the fall, a part-time job while I attended college for my sophomore year.

That evening I spoke to my parents about the tour. They agreed I could go, but Mom remained adamant about my finding a chaperone. I had a feeling Dick's mother would not travel on an extended trip. Was there anyone else available to satisfy Mom's demands? I finally promised her I'd find someone, although

I didn't have a clue who that someone might be.

* * * * *

Dick and I met the Hollywood Argyles band at a shabby rehearsal hall in Hollywood for a pre-tour rehearsal. As we walked in, we noticed instruments set up in the corner of the room. Some of the band members appeared slightly hung over.

"I can't wait to get to El Paso," the lead guitar player was saying. "I just want to go across the border to party in Mexico."

The other musicians snickered. I imagined partying was a large part of their lives. These guys were older and more experienced than any of the young men I'd been around. I felt slightly apprehensive.

"So, what songs do you want to rehearse?" the leader asked us.

We pulled out simple chord charts to "I Want Someone" and "The Mountain's High" that arranger Don Ralke had written up for us and handed them over.

"This is a no-brainier," the band leader said.

The band read music and played the songs perfectly, including the part in "I Want Someone" where the key changes and everything is raised up half a tone.

"We're also doing a Mickey and Sylvia song, 'Love Is Strange,'" Dick said. "That's cool. What key?"

Within half an hour, we'd finished and walked out the door. A teenage girl and her mother stood on the sidewalk, studying the address on the building. The girl's pretty face and brown hair spoke of youthful eagerness.

"Are you Dick and Dee Dee?" the girl asked. We nodded.

"I'm Kathy Young and this is my mother. I'm booked on tour with you."

Mrs. Young smiled at us. We shook hands. I certainly knew who Kathy Young was. Her record, "A Thousand Stars," currently topped the record charts nationally.

"Since I'm only sixteen, my mom is going on the tour as my chaperone," Kathy added.

Her mother smiled. Suddenly it hit me. I'd found the perfect solution to my chaperone problem. I grabbed her arm. "Mrs. Young, would you be willing to call my mother and tell her you would act as my chaperone as well?"

Mrs. Young smiled. "I'd be happy to," she replied. I quickly wrote my home phone number on a slip of paper and handed it to her.

Kathy said, "Did you know that Ray Peterson is headlining our show? He's going to sing for about forty-five minutes."

I knew that on group tours most of the acts sang only two or three songs, but the headliner sang longer, twenty minutes to half an hour. Ray Peterson's hits included "Corinna, Corinna," and "Tell Laura I Love Her."

"He can't come to L.A. to rehearse," she went on. "He's going to practice with the band in Texas before the first show. He's only staying with the tour one week. The second week Gary U.S. Bonds is the headliner."

Gary's record currently held the number-one slot in the nation.

"I love 'Quarter To Three,'" I said, referring to Gary's hit record.

"You'd better rehearse now." Mrs. Young interrupted our conversation.

Kathy sighed. "See you later," she said.

"Yeah, we'll see y'all in Texas," Dick drawled.

* * * * *

I felt excited to be traveling with famous singers, but worried that we might appear inexperienced in comparison. With all the focus on the quality of the shows, I never once considered the fact that Gary U.S. Bonds and his musicians were black. We would be traveling as an integrated tour in a segregated state.

At that time in the South, racial segregation remained deeply woven into the social fabric. In 1960, after four black freshmen from North Carolina Agricultural & Technical College refused to leave a "whites only" lunch counter at Woolworth's, civil rights demonstrators from Harvard, M.I.T., Boston University and other colleges descended on the Southern states, often riding in buses as an integrated group. The press named them "Freedom Riders."

The Freedom Riders were met with great resistance, sometimes putting their lives on the line for their cause. Such was the climate as we flew to Texas in August 1961 for our own integrated bus tour.

* * * * *

Our plane landed in Dallas on a hot, sticky morning. The tour promoter stood by the luggage carousel.

"Bob Plastad," he said, sticking out his hand.

I gripped his hand in a firm handshake.

"It's going to be a scorcher," he continued. "Here, let me help with the bags. The van's outside."

Parked by the curb sat a white van with "GARY U.S. BON DS TO UR" painted in huge red letters on either side.

"What does the 'U.S.' stand for?" Dick asked.

"Ulysses Samuel, apparently Gary's middle names."

I presumed they'd designed the giant printing on the side of the van to promote the tour. Eventually I discovered it also served to identify us as singers, rather than Freedom Riders.

Bob swung open the door to the van. "This is Ray Peterson," Bob said, introducing Dick and me to a tall, lanky man sitting in the front seat. He wore his dark hair brushed back, and his face was pale. He didn't look too healthy.

Ray shook our hands firmly.

"And you know Kathy Young and her mother."

We waved at them through the van window. They sat in the middle row, looking hot and uncomfortable. After we loaded our luggage into the back and climbed into the rear seat, Bob slid shut the heavy van door and started the engine. Cool air went on automatically. Mrs. Young gave a sigh. The temperature on a bank building read 102 degrees and it was still mid morning.

"Everybody ready?" Bob asked. "I'm not only promoting this tour, but I'm also doubling as the driver. If you have any complaints, I'm the one to talk to."

We laughed politely. We were in what was known as the "honeymoon" phase of the tour. Who knew that later we'd barely speak to each other?

Bob put the van in gear and we rolled out of the parking area.

* * * * *

The van became our home away from home, our refuge from the heat and crowds, our place to sleep and dream as we drove along miles of highway, with nothing more to view from the windows than an occasional cactus or dead armadillo. I'd brought along a suitcase full of books to escape the tedium with wild adventures of other places and times.

We drove most of the morning and afternoon, stopping only once for a quick lunch. I felt excitement at the prospect of singing live onstage for the first time.

No lip-synching on this tour. Audiences expected us to be professional. I felt more than a little nervous. What if the band played our music wrong? What if I forgot the words to the songs?

By late afternoon we finally pulled into the parking lot of a huge auditorium in Austin. We stared at the building.

"My God, that's gigantic," Dick said to me. "That auditorium holds hundreds of people." We exchanged nervous glances.

The show promoter gave me my own dressing room. From my suitcase I selected a dress with a full pink skirt, shook out the wrinkles and put it on.

Moments later, I stood in the wings mesmerized as the band walked out on stage and started playing, the dazzling spotlight transforming them from grungy men who had driven all day in the desert heat to glittering rock stars.

It was as though someone had scattered fairy dust over everyone, making them instantly beautiful. Magic ruled the moment. I forgot I'd soon be on stage myself.

After the band's introduction, Kathy Young walked on stage wearing a pastel dress with a full skirt. She launched into her opening song, "A Thousand Stars." Since I'd heard it hundreds of times on the radio, I stood behind the curtains and watched, transfixed.

I glanced out at the audience.

"We need to say a prayer," a voice said. Startled, I looked up and saw Dick standing beside me.

"We need to pray that we'll do well."

Although I'd never known Dick to be religious, I thought petitioning the Lord was an excellent idea at this point in time and bowed my head.

"Dear Lord, help us to do well."

Suddenly, we heard a loud voice over the sound system, "And, now, all the way from Los Angeles, California, with their first hit record, 'The Mountain's High,' Dick and Dee Dee!"

This was it. My heart leapt and I started shaking. Dick shoved me from behind and I stumbled out onto the stage, into the blinding lights. All I could think about was making it to the single microphone set up on the front of the stage.

Little twinges of pain shot through my stomach. My knees wobbled and my hands felt clammy. I remembered the Wilder Brothers encouraging us to smile onstage, but I could only manage a maniacal grimace.

Standing side by side, Dick and I began singing "I Want Someone," the song once destined for greatness. It was the worst possible opener, because of the slow tempo. Better to have an exciting, fast song first, but, alas, the Wilders wanted us to save "The Mountain's High" for last.

I could not figure out what to do with my hands. They apparently had a life of their own, flopping around like chickens on speed. I clutched the sides of my dress in a death grip, forcing my hands to stay put.

The spotlight blurred my vision. The crowd felt like a living ocean of energy, hidden in the dark… anonymous, scary. Sheer furnace-like heat radiated from the footlights. I started to sweat profusely and feared it would stain my dress.

The audience politely applauded after the first song. Then we started to build momentum with the rhythm-and-blues song, "Love Is Strange," originally recorded by Mickey and Sylvia. The song was supposed to have some spoken dialogue in the middle. At that moment, however, I felt a lump growing in my throat and doubted I could utter a sound. We managed to sing the start of the song and then we reached the spoken part:

Dick: "Oh, Dee Dee."

Dee Dee (hoarsely with a croak): "Yes?"

Dick glancing at me, slightly concerned: "How do you call your lover boy?"

Dee Dee: "Ah, Ah, AUGGGHH." I cleared my throat and forced out the words in a harsh whisper: "Oh, Lover Boy."

Dick: "What? I can't hear you."

Dee Dee (a louder hoarse growl): "Oh, lover boy."

Dick slapped me on the back a few times to help me clear my throat.

Dick, agitated: "Speak up!!!"

Dee Dee (straining and shouting): "OH LOVER BOY!!"

Dick stared at me, so startled he forgot to sing. The band played our final line by themselves and abruptly ended the song. I heard polite applause. The audience appeared confused, but not as confused as I felt.

Suddenly the band launched into "The Mountain's High" and the audience came out of their stupor and roared with approval. Totally startled by this reaction, I struggled to remember the lyrics. Oh, yeah: "The mountain's high and the valley's so deep…" My voice returned at last and I made it through the song, ending on a positive note.

After an awkward bow, I ran off the stage and found solace behind a coat rack in the dressing room. After several deep breaths and a silent prayer of thanks, I slipped out the side door. The heat of the night felt oppressive.

I stood in the dark. One of the doors to the auditorium remained open and, through it, I watched Ray Peterson perform. He sang for a long time, his beautiful voice soaring. Enthralled by the music, I forgot my onstage ordeal, and focused on the enchantment of the moment. This is how it's supposed to be, I thought. Will we ever look and sound so inspirational?

* * * * *

The first week passed rapidly, a blur of van travel, desert panoramas, junk food and always, evening shows. I eventually got used to performing onstage. At the end of the first seven days, Ray Peterson left the tour.

The morning Ray departed, the day started hot. I woke in yet another hotel room, threw on a pair of Capri pants, tank top and sandals, and dragged my luggage down the hall and into the elevator. This was the day Gary U. S. Bonds joined the tour as the "headliner." I looked forward to meeting Gary. Bob left the hotel early to pick him up at the airport.

Dick and I hauled our suitcases from the hotel lobby to the van now parked at the curb and started hoisting them into the rear baggage area. Bob climbed down to help.

"Man, this bag is heavy," Bob said, lifting my suitcase of books up over the fender. "What's in this thing?"

I felt defensive. "Gold bricks!"

Dick smiled. He knew hardcover books lined the suitcase.

I heard the sound of the heavy sliding van door and Gary and his two musicians staggered out. Bob turned and noticed the musicians.

"Oh, this is Gary Bonds," he said. "Gary, Dick and Dee Dee."

Gary's smile brightened the morning. His perfect white teeth blended with the equal perfection of his narrow nose and sparkling brown eyes. Short, curly dark hair topped his light tan complexion.

He's incredibly good looking, I thought. Embarrassed, I lowered my gaze, realizing I was staring at him.

"And this is Mel and Earl, Gary's sidemen," Bob added. "Earl's a jazz sax man and Mel plays bass."

Grateful for the diversion, I turned my attention to Gary's musicians. Mel appeared young, maybe in his early twenties. He was dark-skinned, also good-looking. But Earl looked old enough to be my father. The whites of his eyes contained red streaks like he'd either been crying or drinking. I suspected the latter. He appeared slightly shaky on his feet.

"Hey, man, what about breakfast?" Dick asked Bob.

"You haven't eaten? Man, that's a drag." Bob sighed and looked at his watch. "Look, I've got to fill the gas tank, and make a few phone calls. If you can eat quickly while I'm doing that, go for it, but you haven't got more than half an hour."

"Kathy and I have already eaten," Mrs. Young said. "You told us to be ready to go by eight thirty, so we had room service."

Bob turned to us. "Find the nearest restaurant and meet us back here. I don't want to have to come looking for you."

Mrs. Young and Kathy climbed into the van. Bob gently put the vehicle in gear and drove off.

Dick and I, Gary and his two musicians stood on the hot sidewalk. For a moment, no one said anything. "So do you want to join us for breakfast?" Dick asked. "I think we should eat in the hotel dining room. It's the closest place."

After a moment's hesitation, Gary nodded.

Dick and I, Gary and his entourage entered the formal hotel dining room. When no one greeted us, we seated ourselves at a round table. Under a crystal chandelier, sparkling light reflected off the water glasses and polished silverware. China plates sat on starched linen table clothes.

I tried not to stare at Gary. Since menus were already there, we studied them hurriedly, knowing that Bob wanted to launch into the long drive ahead and did not expect delays.

We sat without service for what seemed an excessively long time. Dick tapped his fingers nervously on the table. Finally, a waiter dressed in black pants and a white shirt approached.

"Finally!" Dick said. "We're in sort of a hurry today. I'll have scrambled eggs, toast and juice."

The waiter abruptly walked away without writing down Dick's order. We saw him in whispered consultation with several other waiters at the back of the restaurant. Then he returned to our table.

"I can't serve 'em," he said to Dick, nodding in the direction of Gary, Mel and Earl. We stared at him in disbelief.

"What? Why not?" I asked, totally confused.

In a low voice he whispered to me, "Miss, we have a whites-only policy here. Y'all can eat, but I can't serve them."

With that, he turned and headed to the kitchen.

My face burned with shame and discomfort at what Gary and his musicians were going through. I felt shocked, outraged.

"It's all right," Gary said with resignation. "I'm from Florida. I'm used to this kind of thing. Why don't y'all order breakfast and we'll wait outside." He rose to leave.

Earl muttered, "Damn honkies," and stood up.

Dick raised his voice to a near shout: "Waiter, could you come over here, please?"

The man scurried over, his eyes avoiding the side of the table where Gary and his musicians now stood.

"Look," Dick said. "We're performers and we just need a little food before leaving town for the next show. That's not unreasonable, is it? Can't you just make us something quick so we can get out of here?"

"I'm sorry," the man replied, choosing his words cautiously. "Ordinarily, I would be happy to serve you, but we have to honor the restaurant policy."

I watched Dick's hands start to tremble. I saw him take a portion of the linen table cloth that was resting by his knees and tuck it into his waistline, behind his belt. Then he stood up.

"We're all leaving," he announced.

I rose to leave with the group. As Dick moved away from the table with the tablecloth still firmly tucked into his jeans, all the china plates, glasses of water, and utensils came crashing down behind him.

"Oh my goodness, look what happened," Dick said in mock dismay, studying the catastrophe on the floor. All shocked eyes of the restaurant patrons remained riveted on us. Dick pulled the cloth loose from his pants.

"Sorry," he said in a whiny voice, imitating comedian Jerry Lewis.

As we quickly exited, we found Bob and the van parked by the curb. We climbed aboard immediately. Bob started the ignition and we drove off. I peered out of the rear of the van through the luggage to see if anyone chased us, but the sidewalk remained deserted.

None of us spoke for the longest time, each absorbed in private thoughts. Despite the van's air conditioning, my face felt flushed and perspiration broke out on my brow. I couldn't even look at the others.

"Did you have a good breakfast?" Bob asked cheerfully, finally breaking the silence. "I hope you ate a lot because we have a long drive ahead. We're crossing the desert and there won't be any food until nighttime!"

Earl muttered something unintelligible under his breath.

No one else bothered replying.

* * * * *

Trapped in the van that day with nothing to do but stare out the window, sleep or read, I observed my fellow travelers.

Bob was easy to figure out. Slouched in the driver's seat, his right arm on the steering wheel and left arm resting against the side window, he really didn't want to get involved with any of us on a personal level. He spoke as little as possible. His job was to get us to the shows on time.

Our job was to relax and go along for the ride. I noticed that the usually exuberant Kathy Young and her mother said very little. They'd drawn an invisible wall of self-enforced solitude around themselves.

Stuck in the rear of the van, I watched Gary, Mel and Earl, who sat in the seat directly in front of Dick and me. Gary kept silent much of the time, leaving the conversation up to his friends. I wondered if he was shy.

Mel, apparently a good friend of Gary's as well as his bass player, often muttered comments to Gary in low tones that only Gary could hear. Gary usually laughed, so I presumed the remarks were amusing.

Earl acted bored with the tour and disgusted with finding himself in Texas. Maybe he'd hadn't been exposed to "in-your-face" segregation for awhile or, if he had, he'd found ways to numb the pain long ago.

* * * * *

When Bob finally pulled into a gas station at midday, everyone piled out of the van to stretch, grab something to eat from the vending machines and use the restrooms. Several other cars pulled in near the gas pumps. The occupants of the vehicles gaped at us like we were circus performers.

I noticed a crude sign, made of cardboard, taped over each restroom door. One read "Women," the second "Men," and the third "Colored." Smaller signs labeled the two drinking fountains, "White" and "Colored."

Angrily I yanked on the vending-machine handle, trying to retrieve a candy bar stuck in the down chute. A few good tugs and it finally fell out.

We all climbed back in the van and Bob started it up. No one mentioned the signs or the staring people. I felt unsettled, rattled. There was so much hatred aimed our direction because we were an integrated group. This was as strange to me as being onstage for the first time had been, but I didn't ever want to get used to this.

* * * * *

We arrived in Corpus Christi in time to check into a hotel before the show, but to my surprise, Bob first steered the van to a seedy part of the city and pulled into the parking lot of an antiquated motel. Everywhere I looked, I saw only black faces.

"Where are we?" Dick asked, startled awake as the van jerked to a stop.

"We're dropping Gary and his musicians off at their motel," Bob said matter-of-factly.

Oh my God, I thought. We can't even stay in the same hotel together.

Mrs. Young stared at the surroundings, an appalled look on her face.

With resignation, Gary reached over and pulled open the van door. It made a whooshing sound. He staggered out, followed by Mel and Earl, blinking like owls in the bright sunlight.

Bob jumped down and opened the rear of the van, helping the musicians pull out their luggage.

"You've got a reservation here," Bob told them. "I'll be back to pick you up at seven."

We left them standing in front of the office, as they watched a little boy circle them on his tricycle.

* * * * *

Bob drove us to another motel, this one on the white side of town. We checked into our rooms, ate a quick meal in the coffee shop next door, and changed into our stage clothes. I wore a sheath and heels and Dick put on a sport coat and tie.

As we climbed in the van, I noticed Mrs. Young's face appeared relaxed after the brief break. I guess she'd taken a shower and cooled off.

On the way to the auditorium, Bob drove to the other side of town and honked the horn outside the motel where the others were staying. Gary, Mel and Earl walked out. Their appearance had changed radically. Mel and Earl wore ties and black suits. Gary was dressed in a custom-made gold lame outfit, with tight pants and a toreador jacket. The contrast with the seediness of their surroundings couldn't have been greater if they'd just stepped off a spaceship.

Wordlessly, they climbed into the van and we left the tumbledown motel behind.

* * * * *

When we arrived backstage at the auditorium, Gary and his musicians disappeared into their dressing room. Out front, the all-white audience filled every seat. I realized that segregation applied to live performances as well as restaurants, hotels and gas stations.

I also realized that fame superceded prejudice. The audience was there primarily to see the headlining act, "Gary U.S. Bonds," yet folks of his same race were barred from admittance. I wondered what I could possibly do to make a difference.

We sang in the same order as when Ray headlined the tour. First Kathy Young went on stage, then Dick and I. After our performance we stood near the back of the auditorium in the dark, eager to watch Gary's act.

All eyes focused on the stage. A local disc jockey walked to the microphone.

"And now, the man who brought you the current number-one record in America, 'Quarter To Three,' Gary U.S. Bonds!"

The auditorium erupted into screams, shouts and wild applause. Mel and Earl ran out on stage and, picking up their instruments, joined the Hollywood Argyles Band. Gary followed. The gold lame outfit shimmered in the lights like the morning sun off the ocean.

As Gary sang, he flashed a huge smile. The audience appeared instantly mesmerized.

"Gary, Gary, Gary," the girls shouted.

The intensity built, song by song, until the audience stood shouting. They finally collapsed in their seats after Gary left the stage. The band played its final number.

Dick and I slipped out the side door before the lights went on and made our way back to the dressing rooms.

"He's incredible, isn't he?" I said to Dick.

"Yeah," Dick said. "After this tour we should do that song in our set."

* * * * *

After the show, while the band packed their instruments, I walked by the open door of Earl's dressing room. He sat by himself, saxophone to his lips. An empty bottle of scotch lay sideways on the table next to him, its final drops spilled on the dirty wood.

In his own world, with eyes closed, Earl played the sax for over half an hour. His haunting melodies drifted down the corridors of the armory, drowning out the sound of the band packing up their instruments on stage. Stage hands walking the halls quieted their steps and listened. Back in my dressing room, I listened to the blues through the wall. The notes went straight to my soul, bringing melancholy to my heart and tears to my eyes. I finally shut off the lights and joined the cast in the van.

* * * * *

That evening we were invited to a party at a disc jockey's house. Mel and Earl declined and took off for parts unknown. Bob agreed to drive the rest of us and to stay there until it was time to go.

We pulled up in front of a tract home in suburbia. The disc jockey, a tall man wearing a reddish toupee that made his face appear ashen, waved us into his garage and shut the garage door after the van entered. We entered the house through a door leading from the garage to the kitchen.

Gary became the center of attention. Everyone crowded around him, staring at him, wanting to get close. Several people asked for his autograph. I couldn't understand how "stardom" appeared to be the only thing eliminating prejudice. I looked at all the Caucasian faces at the party and wondered how they would feel if the door flew open and half the black community entered. Gary appeared to be the exception to the segregation rule, at least at this party, because he'd achieved fame.

I became infatuated with Gary along with the rest of the crowd. I stood nearby watching him interact with the young people. He must have felt my eyes on him, because he turned and glanced at me. We stared at each other across the room. Then a young girl grabbed his arm and took his attention away.

When it was time to leave the party, Bob walked through all the rooms of the house, trying to round us up. He instructed Gary and me to get in the van while he routed out the others.

I walked with Gary through the house, out the kitchen door, and into the garage. Gary pulled the sliding door of the van open and waved me into the second row of seats, climbing in front himself. As I passed, my arm brushed his hand and I felt a tingling all over my body.

Gary must have noticed my reaction because he glanced at me shyly and then looked away. Then he reached out and slowly stroked my arm. Just then the kitchen door burst open and Dick St. John, Kathy Young and her mother entered the garage, chatting loudly. Gary quickly withdrew and turned back around on the front seat, facing forward.

Everyone climbed in and we drove off, heading to one side of town to drop Gary off in the black section, then back across town to where we were staying. I lay awake in bed a long time, thinking about Gary. After hours of restlessness, I finally fell asleep.

* * * * *

As the tour progressed we played San Antonio and Fort Worth. Our routine was always the same: drive for hours each day until we reached the town or city where we were performing, find the "colored" section of town and drop off Gary, Mel and Earl at their motel, then travel to the "white" section to check into our rooms. We kept hoping things would get better and the segregation issues would lessen, but they only got worse.

In addition to the horrible feeling of injustice the segregation policies brought up for me, I felt tired and depressed by it all. Driving all over town consumed a huge amount of time. Often we barely made it to the auditoriums in time for the show.

Gary and I were never alone together after that one night at the party, but we gave each other furtive glances in the van and were definitely attracted to each other.

* * * * *

One night we arrived in town so late we drove straight to the concert hall without checking into our motels first. Bob reserved a number of rooms by phone at a motel near our performance venue, thinking that, even though the motel had a "Whites Only" policy, we'd sneak into our rooms in the middle of the night and leave at the crack of dawn before anyone saw us.

After the performance, under the cover of darkness, Gary, Mel and Earl dashed from the van to their rooms. All went well until a group of fans cruised through the parking lot, honking and yelling Gary's name.

A frantic call from Bob jolted me awake. "Get your bags ready. We're leaving now!"

Stumbling out of bed, I hit my knee on the nightstand. Holding my knee with one hand to numb the pain, I tried to throw my clothes in the suitcase as quickly as possible.

Outside the window I heard the muffled sound of voices, someone running down the corridor and the sound of the van warming up. I jumped when Dick pounded on my door.

"Are you ready?" he called. "Come on. We've got to get out of here."

I threw open the door and dragged my suitcase over the doorsill. Dick carried it to the van for me, hoisting it up and tossing it on top of the other baggage stored in the rear.

With my numb body and groggy mind, this felt like a dream turned nightmare.

Somehow I managed to climb into the van, shivering although it was warm and humid. The door slammed shut. I looked around at everyone else. Mrs. Young did not look happy. Her mouth appeared anesthetized. Kathy's lip trembled like she was going to cry. Only Gary and Mel seemed to think the nighttime jaunt smacked of adventure. Mel poked Gary and they both started laughing.

As we drove through the silent streets, we suddenly heard a police siren. The squad car followed us to the outskirts of the city, and then pulled over to watch us pass the city limits sign.

The next day, Kathy Young and her mother abruptly quit the tour. Bob drove them to the nearest airport and we all waved goodbye. Farewell to my chaperone. I'd now become the only woman left in the "Gary U.S. Bonds Road Show." But I felt safer with the group of men inside the van than with those outside it

* * * * *

We drove through Waco, headed toward the town armory, our performance venue. After Waco's top disc jockey publicized the event on a popular rhythm and blues radio station, a large crowd of black folks gathered outside the building, hoping to see the show. The Waco promoters wrung their hands, trying to decide what to do.

Finally, they allowed some blacks to sit in the balcony while hundreds of other teens, white and black, gathered outside demanding entrance to the sold-out show.

We made it through the evening performance to the finale. As Dick and I joined Gary on stage to sing "What'd I Say," our new group finale, the crowd outside broke down a side door and flooded in. They shoved their way to the front, blocking the view of the audience seated in folding chairs.

"Down in front," someone yelled.

The promoters pulled the power switch, shutting off the microphones and lights. The building plunged into darkness.

"The show's over," the promoter's voice shouted. "Please leave the armory."

The kids in front started yelling, and then someone threw a chair. Before we knew it, numerous folding chairs flew in the dark. One landed with a crash on stage. I froze, terrified.

"Get under the piano," Dick shouted, and we huddled under a baby grand.

A riot erupted. Someone called the National Guardsmen stationed nearby. When they finally arrived, they turned fire hoses on the crowd. Two men escorted us off the stage, out the back door and into the van. I folded my arms over my chest to stop the shaking.

That night, as I lay on the bed of my crummy hotel room and stared at the ceiling fan slowly rotating above me, I wondered how Gary went out there and gave such dynamic performances, knowing that the very promoters who hired him and made their livelihood off his name prevented people from attending his shows based on the color of their skin. At times, I'd wanted to throw a few chairs myself, but now I felt numb.

* * * * *

From far away it looked like a Western ghost town and when we got closer we saw not a whole lot had changed from its frontier days. We'd driven through other faded, dilapidated dots on the map, but this one reeked of centuries-old dust and decay. Driving down the tiny, one-street town somewhere in rural Texas, I felt exhausted. We were in a time warp. Not a good place to be.

"God, look at that," Bob said.

We stared out the window at two tiny diners, their window sills covered in a thick film of dirt. Torn, faded awnings hung forlornly on rusted poles. A pale sign proclaimed "Good Eats." As we rolled by we saw "For Whites Only" signs in the windows. Further down the block we passed a Greyhound Bus station café with filthy windows and a few rusty, dented cars parked nearby.

Bob pushed his foot down gently on the brakes. Our van rolled to a stop.

"Look, I'm going for gas," Bob said. "Your best bet is the Greyhound Station. I think you'll all be able to get something to eat there. I'll be back in half an hour. Don't be late."

We piled out into the scorching sunlight, wilting in the furnace blast. Bob drove off leaving Dick, Gary, Mel, Earl and me standing on the sidewalk. In our exhausted state, we started in the front door of the Greyhound Station restaurant, but were met by a burly man who blocked our path. He stood about six-foot-three, with beefy arms and a beer belly handing over his too tight Levis overalls. His face looked like someone had sandblasted it. He wore a cap advertising some kind of tractor company.

His tiny, black, pencil-point eyes bore into us. He glared at the boys.

"The colored entrance is around back."

I stood perfectly still. As Gary, Mel and Earl turned around abruptly and marched in resignation around the building toward the back of the restaurant, something inside me snapped. After a month in Texas, I'd had enough of segregation policies.

"Let's go eat in the colored section," I said to Dick.

Dick stared at me, and then grinned.

"Sure, why not?" he said. "We shouldn't leave the Lone Star state without at least touring the 'colored' section of a restaurant."

The burly man glared at us.

Dick and I turned our backs on him and tagged along behind Gary.

"Do ya'll know what you're doing?" Gary asked, stopping at the broken screen door entrance out back. "These folks take this business pretty seriously."

"We're tired of this shit," Dick replied. "Let's just order our food, eat and get out of here. If it gets bad, we'll ask for food to go."

I studied the rickety back door, a torn screen puckered on one side and the "Colored Only" sign nailed above it. It looked like a child had written the sign with green crayons. Gary pushed the creaky door open and we followed him inside.

A little girl wearing tiny braids on her head tugged on her mother's arm. "Mama, look." She pointed at us.

"Hush." The mother pulled the child around in her seat, facing her toward the wall.

I noticed mixed expressions of fear and discomfort registered on the faces of the black customers. We marched to a table and sat down.

"Y'all better leave or there's gonna be a heap of trouble," the waitress whispered, glancing around nervously.

Dick gave her a big smile.

"I'll have a bacon, lettuce and tomato sandwich," Dick replied loudly. "No pickles."

After Dick gave his order, the diners around us began to relax. Their voices rose in quiet chatter. I started to feel less self conscious.

We all gave our orders and I had a chance to glance around the room. I realized that it had probably once been a storage shed/bathroom and now, as a memento, it still housed an old, unused toilet in the corner of the room. The floor was worn. Gray linoleum squares peeled away from the walls. Faded, broken blinds covered the back windows and several dead flies graced the floor. I found the room disgusting.

A plastic partition, covered in mesh screening, separated us from the white dining room. You could sort of make out the forms of the white diners. Their blank, confused stares in our direction told us they were aware that two Caucasians had entered the "colored only" dining area.

It was quiet in that section, too quiet. I wondered what everyone was thinking. They probably imagined we were Freedom Riders trying to integrate their small town.

My sweaty hands stuck to the cheap paper placemat and I could feel my pulse like a drum beating. Dick began to hum quietly. Suddenly the room became perfectly still. It felt like the calm before a Los Angeles earthquake. The only competition to Dick's humming was a droning fan on our side of the partition. Dick's hum turned to singing and increased in volume until both words and melody, familiar to everyone, floated through the partition.

"God bless America, land that I love,

Stand beside her and guide her…"

I looked at him in shock. Was he insane?

Through the partition I saw the shadows of three men, as they leapt to their feet and ran out the front door. I knew trouble was coming.

"We've got to get out of here," Gary shouted. His voice ricocheted off the walls, echoing in my head. I felt a surge of fire rush through me. A voice in my head shouted, "Danger, Danger!!"

We dashed out the back door. Frantically running down an alley into the street, I saw our van cruising toward us. I wildly waved at Bob. He slowed to pick us up, as if he had all the time in the world. Just then the three men, now carrying baseball bats, emerged from behind the Greyhound depot and ran at us, like a bull heading for a red flag.

The man who'd blocked our entrance to the "white" section led the charge, his face screwed into a tight, perspiring image of hatred. The other two men wore dirty white tee shirts, stuck to their bodies with sweat. One tall, lanky man with short cropped hair was missing two teeth in front.

"Get 'em," he yelled.

Bob saw the men and turned pale. He froze like an armadillo in front of a semi doing ninety. We ran toward the van, trotting alongside it as it slowly rolled by. Gary reached up and unlatched the sliding door. It swung open with a "whoosh." The boys in our group pushed me up into the van and started to climb in after me. But Bob saw the ugly, twisted faces of the bat-wielding men growing closer in his side mirror and panicked. He gunned the accelerator. The van lurched forward before Dick could climb aboard. He ran down the street alongside the van, desperately trying to keep up.

"Don't leave Dick!" I cried.

Bob slowed the van briefly. That gave Gary just enough time to reach out and grab Dick's arm, pulling him up and inside. Then Bob floored it, but not before one of the bats smashed down on the rear fender, -CRASH -, putting a huge dent in the metal.

"Are you crazy?" Bob screamed at all of us. "What did you do to those men? We've tried to keep a low profile this entire trip. Do you want to get us all killed?"

I retreated into a depressed silence, too exhausted to even speak. I was totally burned out. I realized we had been on tour a long time, way too long, because when I tried to visualize my bedroom in Santa Monica, nothing was there.

*　*　*　*　*

That night, after the final show, Bob called us into the box office. Dick and I stood before him, while he studied our contract. Then he reached into a canvas bag and started pulling out hundreds of dollars in fives, tens and twenties. Counting out two hundred and fifty dollars each for the two weeks' work, he handed Dick and me a stack of money. Dick folded his share in half and put it in his coat pocket. I stuffed mine in my purse.

"Well, I guess this is it," Bob said. "Thank you for joining the tour. It's certainly been interesting."

We shook his hand awkwardly. By the time we walked outside with him, we noticed the band had packed their instruments and left. Gary and his musicians were nowhere to be seen.

Bob drove us back to our motel, gave us a final wave and took off. I felt tremendous disappointment that I didn't get a chance to say farewell to Gary.

When I awoke the next morning and telephoned Dick's room, he informed me that the band had already started their drive back to Los Angeles. Gary, Mel and Earl remained somewhere on the other side of town in a segregated motel. We were on our own. His news only added to my feeling of emptiness.

"I can't believe no one said goodbye," I told Dick.

"So what did you expect? A farewell party? A brass band?"

We packed our bags, checked out and sat by the side of the highway atop our luggage, waiting for a bus to take us to the airport. It was hot and desolate, with a mild wind rustling the tumbleweeds.

Dick sighed and stared up the highway. "Well, the tour's over," he finally said to no one in particular. "It's time to move on."

A dark cloud, invisible yet tangible to me, settled over my head and shoulders. I felt very alone. The wind blew around the cactus, stirring up the sand.

The breeze suddenly stopped. It became so still the desert appeared to fade into a brownish blue hue. I finally realized what was so strange about this tour: It's that everything could change from joy and inspiration to dullness and depression in a Texas minute.

CHAPTER FIVE

The Monk

What a difference a month away from home made. In L.A. the season changed from summer to fall. The sky presented a vivid blue cover and the sun remained warm, but the air held a crispy snap. All the heat and smog of summer receded as nature turned inward. Fall has always been one of my favorite times of the year.

It took at least a week to recover from the Texas tour. I spent that time sleeping, getting caught up on the family's activities and trying to reconnect with my boyfriend, Mike. He'd started a new job and was quite busy.

I felt like I needed time before I saw Mike. I'd changed so much on the Texas tour. Gary remained a strong force in my mind. How would I feel about my relationship with Mike when I saw him again?

* * * * *

After four days, Dick called.

"I just talked to George Wilder," he said. "He told me that while we were in |Texas, a promoter telephoned Liberty Records. This man wants to book us on a tour with Jan and Dean in the Midwest. Liberty thinks the tour will help promote 'The Mountain's High' there."

The news startled me. I couldn't imagine touring again for a long time.

"When would we go?"

"Sometime in late October or November."

I realized that if we continued on the road, I would not be returning to college for my sophomore year. I no longer knew what I wanted to do with my life. Did I want to go on singing as Dick and Dee Dee or return to school? Events were moving too quickly.

"We've got to do this tour," Dick insisted. "It's the only way to make our record a national hit."

"I need some time to think."

"What do you need to think about? You're either committed or you're not. What's your problem?"

How could I explain something I didn't understand myself? "I'll call you tomorrow," I said, and quickly hung up.

Grabbing my car keys, I climbed into my Corvette convertible. Driving aimlessly, I headed west on Sunset Boulevard toward the ocean. Maybe a walk on the beach would clear my head.

When I drove through Pacific Palisades, I stopped at a stoplight in the village and watched a crossing guard escort three small children across the street. How simple their little lives are, I thought. When you're a child all decisions are made for you. You just have to show up. Maybe that's all I have to do, too. Just show up.

As I headed around the last curve of Sunset I noticed a beautiful park on my left. An occasional break in the trees revealed a small lake, with several swans floating serenely. Without thinking, I made a left turn, drove through the gates to the parking lot and turned off the ignition.

A small dirt path passed a charming wooden cottage and led from the lot around the lake. I followed it, intrigued. I remembered I'd been here before. When I was going to high school, I used to drive over here and feed the ducks. I'd forgotten all about this place.

The path curved in a large circle, surrounding the lake. I passed a man-made waterfall with a huge statue of Christ above it. This was obviously some kind of religious place. I'd never noticed the statue before.

A visitor's directory and other free literature sat in attractive wooden shelves situated on the path. I lifted up the directory. The first page told how sacred places are valuable to visit because they are permeated with the vibrations of the great souls that walked the grounds. The vibrations remain long after the souls depart. Because these souls have communed with God, it's easier for others to do the same in sacred locations. One's life can be changed for the better by a single pilgrimage to a sacred place.

The sound of the koi fish splashing in the water and the honking swans interrupted my reading. I realized I felt better than I had in a long time.

A man dressed in an ocher-colored robe approached me on the path. He was bald, with a shiny smiling face and kind eyes. "Hello," he said. "Is this your first time at the lake?"

"Actually, I used to come here and feed the ducks when I was in high school."

"Ah, but today you come for another purpose," he said gently.

I looked away, unable to continue eye contact. How much should I tell him about the dark cloud I'd carried back from Texas and my confusion over the choices I had to make? When I glanced back he was watching me with a gaze that seemed to look deep into my soul.

"No one comes here by accident," he said. "Everyone who enters these gates is drawn by a deep need to experience peace. And no sincere seeker goes away empty handed."

"Do you have a minute?" I blurted out.

"Let's sit on that bench over there."

We walked to a cement bench near a second waterfall and sat down. The sound of the rushing water filled my ears. I felt emotions welling up in my throat.

"I just don't know what to do," I said as tears sprang to my eyes. "I should be happy. I sing as part of a duo and it looks like we might have a national hit record. But I have to decide if this is really what I want. I started out writing songs. But this hit record thing is changing my entire life. I don't know if I should just let it happen, or drop out of the record business and continue on with college."

"Can you do both?"

"No, not really, because becoming a singer means constant travel on the road. You have to tour to promote yourself. I don't even know if this is what I'm supposed to do with my life. I'm so confused!"

"Something else is going on here," the monk replied. "It's fear. Fear of the unknown. Staying at home and going to college is familiar. It's secure and safe. Traveling brings many changes, people and circumstances into your life. You learn, grow, and expand. Traveling is the more difficult path because most of the time you are forced to let go and surrender."

He paused and looked at the lake, then back at me. He went on, "So now you're reluctant to commit to something you think you might later regret?"

I nodded. "I just don't know what I'm supposed to do with my life."

The monk studied me in silence for a moment. I listened to the sound of the waterfall and watched the sunshine send sparkling reflections off the lake.

"I predict this singing career is the start of a grand adventure for you," he said at last. "I see your destiny as traveling all over the United States and other parts of the world, singing to thousands of people, bringing joy to their lives with your songs. It will be incredibly rewarding but also incredibly difficult because you're a deeply sensitive person."

He thought for another moment, and then reached into his pocket. "Here," he said. "Take this." He handed me a rose quartz crystal that almost filled the palm of my hand. I marveled at the color and the coolness of the stone against my skin.

The monk explained, "When things get tough, retreat to a quiet place and hold this crystal in your right hand. Close your eyes and let the peace of the crystal fill your being. Know that you are following the path you created for yourself and that everything will indeed work out for the highest good."

He stood and smiled.

"And now I must go," he said. "He who has cows takes care of cows." His eyes twinkled and his laughter shook his stomach.

For the first time in a long time, I laughed, too.

* * * * *

Several days later Mike called. "Hey, Little Boo, you rested from the trip now?"

"Hi, Mike." Suddenly it felt very good to hear his voice.

"Want to go for dinner tonight? We can get a pizza at Mario's Restaurant in Westwood and see a movie afterward."

"Sure, that would be great."

I dressed attentively for my date with Mike, carefully applying makeup and rolling my hair in curlers. Although I was ready half an hour before he arrived, when he knocked at the front door, Mom opened it before I could get there.

"Hello, Mike," she said. "Mary will be down in a moment."

"I'm right here," I said, rounding a corner to the entry hall. Mike and I looked at each other, then back at Mom. "I won't be late," I said, as we escaped out the door.

I climbed in Mike's convertible. The top lay flat against the back of the seat, exposing the cool night air and star-filled sky. The new moon loomed close. I thought, "Fall has definitely arrived."

Mike headed down Wilshire Boulevard toward Westwood. We finally pulled into the restaurant parking lot and entered Mario's. The smell of garlic and tomato sauce reminded me how hungry I was. Fortunately, within minutes a casually dressed waiter escorted us to a booth.

"So, I can guess what you want to order," Mike said. "Tuna pizza."

I smiled. On the Texas tour many things had changed for me, but my eating habits remained the same. I'd ordered tuna pizza at Mario's since junior high.

"You're right about that."

After the waiter took our order, Mike leaned his head back against the fabric of the booth and studied me intently. "You look good," he said. "Looks like you lost a little weight."

"Yeah, well, usually there was no time to eat before the shows and afterwards we always had to drive half the group to the other side of town. By the time we got back to our hotel, we found the restaurants closed."

"Sounds bizarre. Well, you're home now."

Mike pulled the paper cover off his straw and then tossed it back down on the table. "So, have you registered for the fall semester yet?"

I paused. "I don't know if I'm going back to SMCC . Liberty Records wants Dick and me to travel to the Midwest for a few weeks on a singing tour with Jan and Dean. Since it takes place in October or November, I can't do both."

Mike picked up the straw and started drawing random lines in some water on the table. "I think you really need to examine your priorities," he finally said. "How long do you think this singing thing is going to last? You don't want to be a college sophomore when you're thirty years old!"

I pouted. I didn't like the parental tone in Mike's voice. Defiantly I muttered, "Maybe I won't go back to college at all."

"Now you're really thinking crazy," he said, pointing the straw at me. "Do you really imagine there is any longevity to what you're doing? It's one thing to have a little fun but a whole other thing to throw away your entire education."

I thought of what the monk at the lake had told me. Mike would never understand that this might be my destiny.

"I think touring is something I'm supposed to do," I responded. "I'm getting a major education traveling. In fact, in Texas, I learned more about human nature in one month than all the eighteen years of my life, although much of it was not pleasant."

Mike frowned. "But that's a different kind of learning. You're going through basic experiences, but it's not the same as getting a rounded education. You know, you need to study history, psychology and so forth."

I took a deep breath and tried to return to the peace I'd felt at the lake. "Mike, I'm just burned out now. The experience of segregation in Texas wore me down. It shattered my positive belief in the goodness of mankind. Nothing makes me happy now."

"Not even seeing me again?" Mike looked at me with that special look that usually melted my heart. Then his face furrowed with concern. "What do you think is going to happen to us if you start to travel all the time? How can we possibly stay connected?"

My eyes filled with tears. "That's so unfair. Why do you have to say those things, just when I'm trying to figure out my life?"

"For once I agree with your parents," Mike continued as he lifted a spoon and violently stirred his Coke. "You know how important education is to them. They will not want you to drop out of school."

"Oh, great," I cried. "Now you're turning into Dad."

Mike's face softened. "Hey, let's not ruin our night together. Let's only talk about fun things and put this on hold for awhile."

We did manage to change the subject and attended a movie after dinner, across the street at the Bruin Theatre. But I found it difficult to concentrate on the film.

My mind kept returning to the choices I needed to make.

* * * * *

The next morning, the phone rang.

"Mary, Dick's on the phone!" my sister Doris yelled. "Don't talk too long. I'm expecting an important call."

"Yeah, right," I said and then changed my tone to super nice as I lifted the receiver. "Hello?"

"I thought you were going to call me. The Wilders assume we're going to the Midwest. They want to send the contracts back so the promoter can book the shows. You are going, aren't you?"

"Relax, Dick. Yes, I am going on the Midwest tour."

"All right," Dick breathed. "That's all I wanted to know. This tour is going to push 'The Mountain's High' to number-one in the nation. Do you realize that?"

I wondered if I was secretly afraid of that happening. Things already appeared out of control.

"That would be unbelievable," I said in a low voice.

CHAPTER SIX

Mentor Sharon

Prior to the Midwest tour, the Wilders decided we needed publicists, someone to put our name in print in Los Angeles. They signed us up with a flamboyant guy who flooded the teen magazines and trade papers with news of our so-called activities.

The publicist telephoned me one morning.

"Darling," he intoned. "I have marvelous news. You're going to a super party, thrown by none other than Miss Sharon Sheeley herself. Before you say, 'Who's that?' I want you to know she's the top song writer in Hollywood. Over 352 songs of hers have been recorded and that's no small potatoes.

"Anyway, lovey, Sharon is throwing a party for her song-writing partner, Jackie de Shannon, and Teen Magazine's photographing the event. It's a photo op you and Dick do not want to miss. So you call your partner and insist he accompany you to the party of the year. Now get a pen and take down the address." I dutifully jotted it down. Later that evening, Dick and I drove to the party.

A woman I presumed to be Sharon stood on the front steps of a large Spanish home in Hollywood. In her late teens or early twenties, she appeared tall and thin, with long straight dark hair and slender hands. She wore tight black Capri pants and a tan sweater, practical, not glamorous.

"Welcome, welcome," she called. "When the valet gets back, he'll park your car." Ignoring the valet, Dick and I parked on a side street and walked back to

Sharon's. As soon as we entered the living room Sharon grandly waved her friend over.

"This is Jackeee," she announced, pulling her writing partner into the circle of photographers. She looked at us. "And you're?"

"Dick St. John," Dick said, sticking out his hand. "And this is Dee Dee."

A small man with a gray goatee and a vivid green sport coat shoved his way into our small circle. He addressed Dick and me.

"Jackie and Sharon are signed exclusively to Liberty Records' song-writing publishing company. And Jackie is signed as a recording artist with Liberty. Great going, I must say." He waved a glass of champagne in Sharon's direction. "And you've helped Jackie. Congrats!" he shouted.

We hung around the party for several hours, but soon tired of the frantic activity and the popping flash bulbs from the press cameras.

"Do you want to go?" I asked Dick.

"Yeah, but we should thank Sharon for inviting us."

We found Sharon in a circle of reporters.

"Going so soon?" Sharon asked. "Well, if you must. But please do come back and visit. It usually isn't so wild."

* * * * *

Several nights later, Dick and I found ourselves within blocks of Sharon's house. Since we didn't have her phone number, we decided to just drop in.

"Dick and Dee Dee," she smiled, as she swung open the door. "What great timing. A few of my friends are here writing songs. Come in. Come in."

She escorted us through the ornate living room, now quiet and serene, into a small den.

Seated on the sofa was Phil Everly of the Everly Brothers and Jackie de Shannon. Both singers held guitars. They glanced up at Dick and me inquisitively.

I felt a surge of energy rush through my body from the shock of seeing my favorite singer, Phil Everly. In high school, my best friend Elaine and I sang Everly Brothers songs constantly in the car on our way to school. I knew the lyrics and harmonies to practically every song they ever recorded.

Trying to act nonchalant, I sat on a sofa facing him, a pleasant smile on my face.

Phil nodded at Dick and me and went back to tuning his guitar.

"What if we change that song to the key of G," Jackie said. "And add another verse before the bridge."

Sharon left the room, returning with a large pot of tea.

Dick and I sipped our tea in silence, at a loss for words. It became apparent that Jackie and Phil were writing songs together and we'd somehow interrupted them.

I tried to act cool, but my body tingled. Sharon suddenly stood up.

"They're busy working," she said, pointing to the duo. "Let's leave them alone for awhile."

When we exited the den, the performers didn't even glance up. I felt like we'd somehow breached protocol, but wasn't sure exactly how it had happened.

"Well," Dick said, "we didn't mean to barge in. We were nearby and just wanted to stop by and say hello. Actually, we have to go now."

We made a swift exit out the front door. As we walked down the path past several large rose bushes, Sharon called, "Be sure to come back again sometime."

* * * * *

During the next few days, I thought about Sharon. She lived the life I'd dreamed of, writing songs, buying a large home on her own, and surrounding herself with a circle of wonderful friends. She had a life and she didn't have to go on tour. I wanted to know how she did it. I decided to visit her on my own, in the daytime, without Dick.

The next morning, I drove to Sharon's. I found her puttering around her rose garden. She acted delighted to see me, not the least bit surprised at my impromptu appearance.

"Come in, luv," she said. "I was about to make a pot of tea."

Rather than sit in the massive living room, we sat on sofas in a small den where Jackie and Phil wrote songs the night before. The room looked different in the daytime, muted colors, shawls draped over the sofa backs.

"I got in the habit of tea when I was in England," Sharon said.

"When were you there?"

Sharon paused. Her eyes took on a dreamlike quality.

"Oh, it's been several years now."

The mood suddenly shifted, like a large cloud covering the sun.

"Do you remember Eddie Cochran?" Sharon asked casually. An image of the deceased rock and roll artist flashed through my mind.

"Eddie Cochran? Oh, wow! When I was in high school I played volleyball at State Beach during the summer. His hit record, 'Summertime Blue' blasted over everyone's transistor radios. Everyone thought that record was so cool. I remembered seeing him on American Bandstand, too. What an extraordinarily good looking guy!"

"We were engaged," Sharon continued. "Eddy took me to England when he toured there with Gene Vincent. Everywhere we went, girls screamed and fainted over Eddy, but he told me they were only in love with his image. He said our love was real. We were going to get married after the tour."

Sharon paused and glanced out the window. A bird warbled in the late afternoon sun. Suddenly tears filled her eyes.

"The last day in England, on our way to the airport in a taxi, we had a horrible auto accident. Another vehicle demolished our cab. They took me unconscious to the hospital where I stayed for several months."

"I didn't mean to bring up any unpleasant memories," I said, afraid of her reliving the trauma.

"No, it's alright. It helps to talk about it."

She took a deep breath and then continued. "My back and neck were broken in several places. I kept asking where Eddy was, but no one would tell me. As time went by I became more and more depressed. I knew something was terribly wrong."

Sharon's voice dropped so low I had to lean forward to hear the rest.

"They finally told me the truth. This nun came in and after beating around the bush she finally said, 'Sharon, Eddie's dead.' When I actually heard her say 'Eddy's dead', I wanted to die too."

Our tea had cooled to room temperature and shadows filled the den.

Sharon suddenly looked around and shivered.

"Oh, the tea's cold. I'll heat some more."

Before I could protest she swept into the kitchen, returning quickly with a fresh pot.

"So, one of the Catholic nuns at the hospital kept talking to me. She told me

I had my whole life ahead. She believed I had an important destiny. 'Like what?' I thought. 'What do I have to live for?' Anyway, after many months, my body healed and I was able to return to California. But my soul never healed."

Sharon stared at the floor. She looked like a young girl, devastated and alone. "I'll never get over Eddy's death, never. He died at the prime of his life. You know, he was so talented. He would have become the next Elvis…." A long pause followed, as Sharon's thoughts drifted into private memories.

"How did you start writing songs?" I finally asked, changing the subject.

Sharon smiled at the memory.

"I was in high school and like everyone else in America; I used to watch the Ozzie and Harriet Show on television. I loved Ricky Nelson. I knew he'd become a huge recording star if they ever gave him a chance to sing on the show, so I wrote a song just for him…. 'Poor Little Fool.'"

I stared at her in amazement. That record, by Ricky Nelson, catapulted to the top of the charts and indeed, Ricky sang it many times on the family TV show.

"The only trouble was I didn't know how to get the song to him. Finally I bought one of those maps to movie stars' homes from someone on Sunset Boulevard and discovered that The Nelsons lived in Beverly Hills. I staked out their place. I knew if I could just get to Ricky alone, I might talk him into recording my song.

"One day the Nelson gardener told me the family was away on vacation, but they were due back in a day or two. I pitched a small tent on their side lawn under the trees and waited for their return. Unfortunately, they arrived late at night, when I was sound asleep." Sharon laughed.

"I was rudely awakened by Ozzie Nelson, Ricky's dad, shining a flashlight in my eyes, demanding to know who I was. I told him I'd written a hit song for Ricky that would make him the number one singer in America." Sharon smiled impishly.

"To this day, I don't know why he didn't throw me off the property but instead, Ozzie listened to me. There in the tent, under the stream of light from the flashlight, I half read, half sang the words to "Pool Little Fool." I don't know if you know this, but I can barely sing on pitch. It sounded like hell. But Ozzie saw something in it. You know the rest. It became a number one record for Ricky."

With a burst of energy, Sharon leapt off the sofa and raced to her record cabinet.

"Speaking of hits, you've got to hear this. Jackie just brought the album back from New York." She placed a vinyl album on the turntable. "It's called 'Freewheeling' by a new folk singer, Bob Dylan."

After we listened to her favorite cut she asked, "Did you ever hear anything so incredible?

" Words failed me. Did Sharon think this guy might actually make it as a vocal artist? Did she think this song was possibly going to be a hit record?

"He sort of talks the song." I stammered.

"He's a genius," Sharon proclaimed. "It's not about his voice. Listen. Listen to what he is saying. I predict he will become the hottest singer/songwriter of our time." I wasn't sure. Bob Dylan didn't sound like any of the popular singers of our day. He didn't sound like Elvis or the Everly Brothers, Bobby Vee or even Eddy Cochran. Could Sharon be right? But I did listen. And the record player droned over and over, "The Times They Are a Changing."

CHAPTER SEVEN

Life in a Sedan

One night, after dinner, while Mom served her famous lemon meringue pie, I said, "Our producers, the Wilder Brothers, think we should go on a tour to the Midwest to help promote 'The Mountain's High.' Our song is number one on the West Coast, but isn't getting much air play in the rest of the country. They think a personal tour might turn the situation around."

Mom placed a generous slice of pie in front of me and said, "I don't know why my meringue always develops little drops on it when I put it in the refrigerator. They look like tears."

Dad stared at me. "When do they want you to go?"

I took a deep breath. "In two weeks."

"Two weeks! What about school?"

"I've decided to take some time off. I'll go back to college in the spring."

Dad slowly lifted his fork, speared a bite of pie and put it in his mouth. I watched anxiously as he chewed and swallowed it.

"Sounds like you've figured it all out," he said. "I hope you're darn sure this is what you really want to do, because you're giving up a lot."

"I am sure," I assured him. "I've given it a lot of thought." They must have trusted my judgment. This time they didn't mention a chaperone.

* * * * *

The weeks passed quickly. Dick and I left Los Angeles for Chicago on a clear fall morning. As we exited the plane at our destination, a smiling gentleman with dark hair rushed forward to greet us. The man appeared to be in his forties, with a stocky, solid build.

"I'm T.B. Skarning," he announced. "You must be Dick and Dee Dee." I assured him we were.

Dick planted a big grin on his face. He actually seemed happy for the tour to start. I felt an excited energy rush through me. This was where I belonged. I suddenly felt sure I'd made the right decision in deciding to go back on the road.

We made our way down the escalator to the baggage area and I identified my suitcase. Mr. Skarning hoisted the large bag up with a strong arm. Dick grabbed his luggage.

"This way," T.B. commanded, heading for the exit door. He acted like a man in a hurry.

Outside I noticed a large, nondescript, four-door sedan sitting by the curb. What really caught my eye were the two young men leaning on the car, Jan and Dean.

Jan appeared to be the taller of the two. He had thick blond-brown hair and bushy eyebrows. Dean looked thinner, with blond-brown hair and a narrow nose.

"Do you know Dick and Dee Dee?" T.B. asked them.

Dean nodded. We'd all gone to the same high school—University High in West Los Angeles. That seemed like centuries ago now.

I climbed in the car. Wedged between Dick and Jan in the backseat, I tried to find a comfortable position. My feet rested on a carpeted hump, forcing my knees up against my chin.

How long can I sit like this? I wondered.

T.B. started the engine. He turned his head and looked at us crammed in back.

"Everyone comfy?" he asked. No one bothered answering. He forged on, "We're going to drive all day and most of tomorrow to get to our first gig in Fargo, North Dakota. You might as well relax and enjoy the scenery." I gave him a weak smile.

We drove the entire morning, stopping at a Howard Johnson's for a quick lunch. Then we headed back on the road again. Time dragged. I tried to remain alert, but occasionally drifted into sleep, waking each time my head fell forward.

By late afternoon, Jan started to groan. He was stuck in the backseat directly behind T.B, his long legs folded in a torturous position. Clearly restless, Jan grabbed a large bag of M&M's from the floor of the car and tore it open. He popped M&M's into his mouth, one by one, until all that remained were a handful of red ones. He suddenly flicked an M&M into the front seat, toward the back of Dean's head. The candy hit Dean in the neck, and then fell down the passenger seat behind him. Dean turned and grinned.

Then Jan let an M&M fly toward T.B Skarning. It spun toward the back of his head, bouncing off his hair. T.B absentmindedly touched his head, as if brushing away a fly, and continued driving. Dick gave a snort and covered his mouth with his hand.

Several minutes later, Jan flicked another M&M at T.B. This time the candy landed on top of his head. It resembled a small red Frisbee in a sea of black waves. Dean put a magazine over his face. His body shook with uncontrollable laughter as he turned his head away from T.B. and looked out the passenger window.

"I can't stand being cramped!" Jan suddenly shouted, shooting his long legs forward. He pushed against the back of the driver's seat. The entire seat lunged forward, forcing T.B. into the steering wheel.

The brakes screeched and the car spun on the icy road, rolling to a sideways halt. I stared out the window at the deserted stretch of highway, shocked and startled by our near accident.

"Don't ever do that again!" T.B. yelled, turning toward the back and glaring at Jan. "We could have been killed."

"I can't stand being cramped," Jan muttered.

T.B. looked at his watch. After firing a final angry look in Jan's direction, he started the ignition and sped off down the highway. It was close to midnight before we pulled into the parking lot of a Travel Lodge.

"We've got reservations here," he said. "I'm requesting a 5:00 a.m. wake up call for all of you. Don't be late."

Dick dragged my suitcase to the hotel room assigned me and left for his room next door. I fell on the bed, my legs aching. Suddenly I felt a strong urge to call Mike. Picking up the motel telephone, I automatically connected with the office. The office phone rang and rang. No one answered. Then I noticed a small sign on the desk. It read: "Switchboard closes at 11PM." Exhausted, I fell back on the bed and slept with my clothes on.

The next morning our blurry-eyed group assembled in the dark. We shivered and blew steam from our mouths with each breath. Dean hopped up and down and muttered, "Man, it's really cold."

"Get in the car," T.B. said. "I'll put the heater on."

We resumed our contorted positions and T. B. took off.

Several hours later, when he stopped for gas, T.B. said, "I have to run up the street to a stationery store to buy a map. Don't leave the car. I'll be right back."

The second he vanished from sight, Jan started looking around.

"Are you hungry?" he asked Dick and me. "Hey, there's a drug store across the street. Come on. Let's get something to eat."

We crossed the road and entered the building. Dean and I wandered the aisles looking for the food section. I glanced up. Through the store window, I saw across the street as T.B. approached our empty car. He looked inside, then around in every direction. Finally his eyes landed on the drugstore.

"Here comes T.B.," I said. Jan and Dick ducked down behind a counter.

As T.B. entered the store he walked up to Dean and me and loudly reprimanded, "I thought I told you to stay in the car. Where's Jan?"

Dean gave him an innocent look. "I don't know. He was here a minute ago."

"Damn!!!" T.B. shot out the door and raced up the street, running into clothing stores and dry cleaners.

"Come on," Jan said, popping up from behind the counter. "It's time to get back in the car." We all ran back across the street, giggling like third graders.

When T.B. finally returned to the car, huffing and red faced, he found us waiting for him.

"Where have you been?" Jan asked, innocence permeating his being. "We've been looking all over for you. I thought you were in a hurry!"

T.B. slammed the car into drive and peeled out of the gas station. From then on, he only spoke to us when it was absolutely necessary. I guess traveling around the Midwest with a car load of teenagers wasn't his idea of fun.

"Want to see the inside of a human body?" Jan asked.

Startled, I shifted my gaze from my book and looked over at his. The book showed photographs of abdominal surgery taking place.

"How am I supposed to remember this stuff?" Jan complained, throwing the book to the floor of the car. "I can't concentrate when we keep hitting bumps in the road."

"Here, read this," Dean said, tossing him the latest copy of Mad Magazine.

Dean turned his attention to his pen-and-ink drawings.

"So, are you going to be a doctor or something?" Dick asked Jan.

"Yeah, man, you can't make a living singing 'ooh-wee-ooh' your whole life."

Dean muttered, "I'm going to be a commercial artist. Maybe I'll design album covers."

"Before I started singing with Dee Dee, I decided to enroll in the Art Institute in Los Angeles," Dick said. "That was before our record took off. Now I can't imagine being anything but a singer."

"Jan's right, this isn't going to last forever," Dean smiled. "You might as well enjoy it while you can."

"No, I'm always going to be singing and writing songs," Dick replied adamantly.

"I'd like to write a book someday," I said.

Startled, the three young men stared at me. They'd apparently forgotten I existed.

"Hey, you don't need to worry about a career," Jan interjected. "You're a girl. You'll get married and raise kids."

That was the last thing I'd considered. I had no idea what I wanted to do with my life, but I knew one thing for sure. I didn't want to get married until I figured things out.

"Maybe," I said. "But for now, singing is great."

"Yeah, it's bitchin'," Jan replied.

* * * * *

The day dragged on. I thought about Mike a lot. I bought him a post card at a gas station. It showed a picture of corn fields and said, in red writing, "Welcome to Illinois." After I wrote, "Hi, what's going on in L.A.? I miss you," I tore it up. Mike didn't want a casual post card. He wanted a phone call.

"I'll call him," I thought. "I really want to hear his voice. I'll call at the next available place."

* * * * *

That night we drove miles out on a deserted highway into a forest, suddenly coming upon an ancient wooden building in the woods. Left over from an era of swing and ballroom dancing, the old ballroom echoed forgotten memories with its wooden floors and big band size stage.

I studied the photos lining the walls of the foyer. There were photos of square dancers, of country singers decked out in suede, fringe and cowboy hats, pictures of people holding accordions and several rock stars of our era, including Bobby Vee.

"You like the photo collection?" someone asked. I spun around and faced a heavyset man wearing overalls and a railroad cap.

"I've been cleaning this place for thirty years," he said. "There ain't a singer come through here I didn't meet." His eyes narrowed. "Except a few. Those rock and rollers who died in a small airplane, I didn't meet them."

"Do you mean Ritchie Valens and the Big Bopper?" I asked.

"Yep, that's them. They were on their way here to perform that night. 'Course, because their plane crashed, they never made it. It was terrible. All those town kids crying and what not. We finally got a local kid to fill in so the show could go on. Ol' Bobby went on to become pretty famous himself. There he is."

The man pointed to a picture of Bobby Vee.

"Dick and I record on the same record label as Bobby, Liberty Records."

"Ever meet him?"

"No, not yet."

"Nicest guy you ever want to meet. When you do see him, tell him Charlie Richards says hello. Say, what's your name?"

"Oh, I'm Dee Dee Sperling of Dick and Dee Dee. We're performing here tonight."

"You certainly are," the man commented. He pointed to a new poster attached to another wall. "You're starring on the bill."

I noticed our names were in larger print than Jan and Dean's. Somehow that shocked me.

I heard a loud voice over the P.A. system, "Testing…one, two…testing."

"I have to go rehearse," I told Mr. Richards. "Nice meeting you."

Since T.B. requested that Dick and I sing for twenty minutes twice a night, we'd learned several new songs to fill out our act. We chose a gospel song, "Swing Low," and also "What'd I Say," last performed as a group finale in Texas. We kept our standards: "Love Is Strange," "I Want Someone" and, of course, "The Mountain's High."

That evening something unusual happened. Halfway through our first song, Dick reached around behind me with his left arm. He grabbed the back of my dress and started to slowly pull me back from the microphone. Balancing precariously on high heels, I tried not to topple over backwards. I glanced at him questioningly, but he just glared at me.

He kept this up periodically throughout the rest of the set. Unable to concentrate on the words to the songs, I tried to focus and kept smiling.

"What on earth was that all about?" I asked when we walked off stage.

"You were way too loud. I was adjusting the volume by pulling you back from the microphone."

His comment didn't make any sense to me. "So you're an expert on sound balance?"

"I can always tell when you get too loud. The audience gives us strange looks."

I sighed and looked at the stage. "Dick, there's only one microphone up there. If we stand an equal distance from it, we'll both be heard."

"I should sound louder. I'm singing melody. You're just background."

"We need to be balanced," I said quietly. I felt hurt, compromised. This brought back memories of Dick slamming on the brakes and hurting my wrist. I felt myself shrinking from him.

Dick glared and walked away. He pushed his way out the side door of the ballroom and walked to T.B.'s car. It was unlocked. He climbed in, slammed and locked the door, leaned back against the seat and closed his eyes.

With one eye on my watch, I nervously watched as Jan and Dean started their second set. I knew we followed directly after them. As the duo completed their final number and took a bow, Dick suddenly appeared at my side.

"That's it. Let's go."

After the announcer introduced us, we ran onto the stage. During this set, Dick only pulled me away from the microphone once or twice. As we exited the stage he said, "This time, you sang quieter."

I felt relief at his approval but realized, when under his control, I felt less than whole.

* * * * *

With several days and more performances behind us, we headed for Des Moines, Iowa. T. B. took pity on me in my cramped position in the middle of the back seat and rotated us one by one to the passenger seat in front. I liked the front seat. I rolled up a sweater, placed it next to my head, leaned against the window and went to sleep.

No matter how many books I read, after awhile my eyes just wouldn't focus anymore. I stared out the window as mile after mile of snow-covered countryside rolled by, broken by an occasional silo or farmhouse. Outside, the landscape was white, quiet, still and solemn.

I usually slept during the morning ride, lulled to sleep by the droning motor, exhausted from the previous evening's show. Performing gave me a huge energy boost. It took hours to get to sleep after each show. But by lunch time, everyone started rallying. Then, boredom and restlessness really set in.

With everyone awake in the car, we struggled to shift our positions in a futile attempt to get comfortable. We read magazines, wrote and occasionally talked. I felt detached from the group, withdrawn. And, as usual, I was the only woman.

* * * * *

After the first week on the road, I felt incredibly lonely. I finally picked up the receiver of a pay phone at a gas station and telephoned Mike.

"Hey, it's me." I announced.

"So you finally decided to call," Mike responded, listlessly. "How's it going?"

I felt defensive and slightly guilty for not calling sooner. "Oh, it's okay. The shows are going well."

There was a long pause of silence. I continued, "I miss you."

"Really? I would never have thought that with the exciting life you're now leading."

I felt defeated, deflated. "It's not what you think. There's very little glamour. We're mostly sitting around in a car."

"Well, at least you have plenty of guys to keep you company."

Mike was on a roll. He continued, "What about Jan? I'll bet he's pretty cool."

"Why are you acting like this?" I asked. "You know I'm just friends with these guys."

"Right, well hurry home," Mike commanded. "I can't wait forever." He hung up the phone.

* * * * *

Life on the road resembled a time warp. Sometimes I forgot what day of the week it was. Since we occasionally drove over state borders at night, I rarely knew which one of the United States we were in. I only knew that T.B. drove and that we rolled down a highway somewhere in America.

Sometimes I felt great contentment as I gazed out the car window, watching frozen landscapes pass by. In those moments, I felt performing and traveling were my sole purpose in life.

Other times, great waves of loneliness passed over me. I felt isolated from everyone. I felt my life had little meaning and thought no one would notice if I just vanished from the Earth altogether.

At those times, I questioned what I was doing traveling aimlessly around the country, when I could be involved with friends and family in more meaningful pursuits. Often, I grabbed a notebook and pen and tried to turn my feelings into song lyrics.

The tour continued. We sang six or seven days a week, two shows a night. After the ballroom show, apparently satisfied with the sound systems, Dick refrained from pulling me away from the microphone. The shows turned out to be the highlight of our existence, the only purpose to our days.

I found I missed my family and Mike, especially in the middle of the night. I'd lie in bed surrounded by darkness, my thoughts miles away. I felt insecure about my relationship with Mike. He just couldn't grasp what touring was like for me, how difficult it was to keep up the pace, traveling from city to city, usually sleep deprived. I knew things probably wouldn't change for the better until I returned home and saw him in person.

I preferred the days to the nights. The distraction of my companions, the scenery out the car window and good books helped the time pass.

* * * * *

T.B. booked the final show of the tour in St. Paul, Minnesota. We pulled into the city and T.B. checked us into a downtown hotel. For once the band, who traveled in a separate van, stayed in the same place we did. Since our final show wasn't for two more days, T.B. gave us some time off. He vanished after checking us in, telling us that he would see us before the show.

It snowed the entire time we were there, which pretty much confined us to the hotel. I again gave thanks for the suitcase of books I had brought. The others weren't so lucky. They entertained themselves by dropping water balloons out the windows of their rooms on unlucky pedestrians walking on the icy sidewalk below.

Luckily, the hotel had a twenty-four hour switchboard. I phoned Mike.

"The tour's almost over," I said. "Can you believe it? I'll be home in two more days. I can't wait to spend some time with you."

"I'm going to free up the weekend," Mike responded. "I'm looking forward to seeing you, too. I love you, Little Boo." My heart soared as I counted down the remaining days.

Few people attended the final show of the tour. The radio station failed to properly promote the event and hardly anyone showed up. Even the band acted depressed.

T. B. paid us our money in the ballroom office, handing over stacks of bills. I shoved my huge wad in my coat pocket. He drove us back to the hotel.

"Well," he said. "It's been nice working with you."

He shook our hands. I noticed with shock that his jet black hair had turned steel gray. After the tour, we never saw him again.

Dick and I stood at the desk in the hotel lobby checking out, when I decided to return to my room to see if I'd left anything behind. I found the room filled with toilet paper streamers. The decorations were compliments of the band. Apparently they had found my room empty and decided to improve the decor. Dick appeared in the doorway.

"We have to go. Our cab is here."

"What about all this damage? I can't just walk out without trying to fix it."

"If we don't get in the cab NOW , we're going to miss our plane."

I reached up and started pulling streamers off the curtains and lamps. Dick caught my arm.

"Don't worry. This happens to hotel rooms all the time. Someone will clean it up. We have to go."

I sighed. Dick shut the door behind me and we headed down the hallway toward the elevators.

It felt strange leaving the tour and Jan and Dean. Would I ever again stand in the wings and hear Jan and Dean sing "Baby Talk?" We'd formed a comfortable alliance. But since it was over, all I wanted to do was go home.

SECTION TWO

"Tell Me"

CHAPTER EIGHT

Growth Brings Change

Mike picked me up in his convertible and we headed up the coast to Malibu. The sun danced joyously off the foamy ocean. Several surfers sat on their boards in the far distance, waiting for the perfect wave. Mike pulled over to the side of the road and we watched the surfers for awhile.

"So, where are you now?" Mike asked.

"What do you mean?"

"What's going on with you after that Midwest touring experience? I guess I really want to know why you never called."

"Mike, it's really hard to explain what life on the road is like," I said. "You just try to survive. In the Midwest, our only phone access was in gas stations or hotel rooms. But the problem with talking in gas stations was we were there for such a short time and everyone wanted to use the one pay phone."

"So what was wrong with the hotel phones?"

"Usually the hotel switchboards shut down at midnight and we generally returned to our rooms after one or 2:00 a.m. Let's face it. Most of the time we were trapped incommunicado in the car."

"I don't know," Mike responded. "It was like you vanished into a black hole. There's always a way to call if you really want to."

Anger and frustration rushed through my body. Didn't he believe me? With a hurt expression, I turned and looked at the ocean. We both sat staring at two children building castles in the sand.

"So is this going to continue?" Mike finally asked. "This touring thing? I mean, you only had a year of college. Don't you want to finish school?"

I took a deep breath, trying to remain patient. "Don't you realize what an education it is to travel around the country, meeting people from different parts of the United States? Can't you tell how much I've changed and grown? Give me a break, Mike. Do you want me to give all this up before I find out where it's all going?"

"Yeah, I guess I do," he finally admitted. "If it means we're never going to see each other."

"You were the one who advised me not to quit that time I was mad at Dick. Now you've completely changed your mind."

We watched as the children on the beach kicked down their sand castle and poured buckets of ocean water all over it. Within minutes, nothing was left but flat, wet sand. How quickly things come and go in life, often without leaving a trace.

"It's not good for us to have long separations," Mike finally said. "I don't think this is going to work."

I felt a deep sorrow, but at the same time I realized how much I'd changed. Was that what traveling on the road did? Was I changing radically and rapidly while everyone back home remained the same? I mourned the loss of who I had been and felt genuinely sorry I couldn't be that same person for Mike.

"So what do you want to do?" I finally asked with resignation.

There was a long pause. Eventually Mike answered. "Let's start seeing other people."

I felt a lack of feeling rise in my body. "Whatever you want." I barely choked out the words.

Then sadness rolled over me. It was so intense, so deep that it welled up from the core of my body, threatening to overwhelm me. Tears rolled from my eyes.

Mike started up the car and drove me home.

* * * * *

I mourned the loss of my relationship with Mike for a long time. He had been my first serious boyfriend, and he represented who I'd been during high school and college. But I was not the same person anymore.

After Mike dropped me off, I suddenly remembered the rose quartz crystal and raced up the stairs to my bedroom, tugging open my dresser drawer. There it sat, pink and shiny. I picked it up with my right hand, feeling its icy coldness against my palm.

Placing it back in the drawer, I climbed in my car and drove ten minutes to the Lake Shrine grounds. After parking, I quickly walked around the lake on the dirt path, looking for the bald-headed monk. When I didn't see him, I approached a gray haired man in an orange collarless shirt, pruning the roses.

"Do you know if any monks are around?" I asked.

The man turned and stared at me with fathomless eyes. "Who are you looking for?"

"This monk was medium height, bald."

The man smiled in recognition. "I'm sorry, he's not here."

"Oh," I said. My voice registered deep disappointment.

"Can I help you with something?"

"No, that's alright. I had a question for him, but it can wait. Thank you anyway." I walked around the lake, experiencing peace as it descended over me. Even without talking to the monk, I felt better.

* * * * *

Shortly after I returned home, I received a special phone call.

"Dee Dee? Al Bennett."

Oh, my gosh! It was the president of Liberty Records. We'd never met, but I certainly knew his name. I put on my sweetest voice.

"Hello, Mr. Bennett."

"Did you enjoy your tour of the Midwest?"

"Oh, yes. It was great."

"There's a little matter I have to discuss with you. We just got a bill from a hotel in Minneapolis for $400.00 damage to your room. How did that happen?"

Shock and embarrassment flooded my body. I felt my face turning red.

"It's a big mistake," I stammered. "I mean, the damage was done, but not by me. The band trashed the room."

"Well, don't worry about it," Al assured me. "We'll just deduct it from your royalties for 'The Mountain's High.'"

I eventually discovered many things were deducted from the royalties, including all recording costs, costs of pressing the records, and the percentage that went to the Wilder Brothers, although it took awhile to find these things out.

CHAPTER NINE

Trains, Snow, and Six Meals a Day

The Wilders informed us it was time to produce a second record. They hoped to release it as soon as "Mountain's High" hit the top of the charts nationally. "We need to have something in the can, ready to go," Warner Wilder said.

Dick and I arrived at the studio with memorized melodies and harmonies to a "Mountains High" clone which Dick wrote, entitled "Goodbye to Love." I didn't think much of the song, but then again, I didn't think much of "The Mountain's High" the first time I heard it.

Since that day in the car last spring, when Dick slammed on the brakes and my wrist hit the dashboard, Dick never again mentioned writing songs with me. We managed to stay clear of that particular subject. I remembered our origins, how happy we were to get our first record deal. I felt like an equal partner then. Now I spoke cautiously, avoiding the "elephant under the rug." I skated around Dick on thin ice.

Swept along with Dick's confidence that "Goodbye to Love" would be our next big hit, I dutifully sang my part. For the flip side we'd prepared our rendition of an old gospel song, "Swing Low, Sweet Chariot," which we'd performed onstage in the Midwest.

At the recording session, the Wilders were in a congratulatory, happy mood.

"'The Mountain's High' is number one in cities all over the West Coast,"

Warner Wilder shouted. "We know it's going be a hit nationally. Let's make record history and do it again."

During the recording session, Warner pulled out a long, narrow, wooden percussion instrument. When he took a mallet and scraped the deep grooves edged into the sides, it sounded like a sick duck in heat. While we sang, Warner enthusiastically played percussion: "Scrape, quack, quack, Scrape, quack, quack."

"I don't know about that duck sound," I muttered. Dick laughed nervously.

"Hey, it's great," Warner replied with enthusiasm. "Every song needs a gimmick." George Wilder gave us the thumbs-up sign from his control booth. The scraping quack sound stayed.

Mike called once, just to see how I was doing. When I told Mike the title of our new song was "Goodbye to Love," he replied, "That's appropriate."

* * * * *

Al Bennett, President of Liberty Records, telephoned the Wilders and told them "The Mountain's High" had climbed record charts in the Midwest and the South, but wasn't getting much air play on the East Coast. He wanted Dick and me to go there for a promotion tour, all expenses paid by Liberty Records. This involved traveling around the major Eastern cities meeting disc jockeys. A Liberty Records promotion man planned to set it up and accompany us.

It didn't take much to convince us to go. I always wanted to see New York City and thought this sounded like fun. No live shows were involved.

The East Coast tour prevented me from signing up for the spring semester at college, so once again, I deferred my education to a later date. My parents never commented on it. I finally felt able to make my own decisions.

When I told Mike I intended to leave for New York, he just said, "Don't do anything I wouldn't do."

We arrived in New York City on a cold evening in April, 1962. Ed Silvers, the Liberty Records promotion man for the East Coast, met our plane. A good looking, dark haired man in his thirties, he wore a top coat with a wool scarf wrapped tightly around his neck.

"It's freezing here," I said, breathing out steam with my breath. "It's spring in Los Angeles."

"You'll get used to it." Ed's eyes met mine. "This time of year it usually gets much colder than this."

Ed escorted us to his car and Dick helped me load my luggage into the back. Miraculously, all the bags fit in Ed's small trunk.

"I don't usually travel with the Liberty acts," he told us. "The guy who does this job is ill. So I hope you'll cooperate with me in every way to make this promotion tour as pleasant as possible.

"Here's the deal. My job is to take you to major cities to meet the top disc jockeys. We'll be primarily traveling by train, sometimes planes. I just don't want any screwups. You need to be willing to follow a specific schedule."

"Just tell us where you want us. We're good about punctuality," I promised.

Ed gazed at us as if he questioned my comment. To test our reliability, after helping us check into a mid-town Manhattan hotel, Ed announced he would pick us up at 7:00 a.m. the following morning and left.

* * * * *

Although Dick and I waited in the lobby for half an hour the next morning and, when Ed did arrive, greeted him with cheery smiles, Ed didn't look happy. His nose and eyes appeared red and a scowl covered his face. He stared at his watch and studied a train schedule he held in one hand.

"Come on. We haven't much time."

Ed grunted as he tried to lift the first of my two suitcases into the trunk of the car.

"What do you have in this thing, cement?"

"Books," I replied. "I didn't want to run out of reading material."

Ed stared at me as if he couldn't believe what I just said. "Pick out two or three," he ordered. "You're leaving the rest of them at the hotel. They'll store them for you until we return."

I flipped open the suitcase lid, exposing my books to people passing by on the street, searching for the book I was currently reading.

"They probably think you're selling those things," Dick muttered.

Grabbing two books, I quickly slammed the suitcase shut. Together, we dragged the suitcase back into the hotel and up to the front desk. The desk clerk agreed to keep the suitcase until we returned in several weeks.

* * * * *

After boarding a train in Grand Central Station, we finally arrived in Albany, New York. A distributor for Liberty Records met our train and drove us to a radio station. After a brief wait outside the control booth, the local disc jockey came out. "Hey, hey, it's Dick and Dee Dee," he said, putting out his hand.

We shook hands and followed Ed, the distributor and the disc jockey back to the car. The distributor drove us to a nearby restaurant, where he ordered us a fabulous lunch. I was starting to think that meeting disc jockeys and dining in great restaurants might be better than we'd anticipated.

"So, 'The Mountain's High' is a hit on the West Coast," the disc jockey said. "I don't know if it's the kind of record kids would like here."

I saw Dick bristle. "Oh, I don't know," he commented. "Kids are pretty much the same all over."

"Well, to tell the truth, I like the flip side, "I Want Someone" better. Why don't you promote that side?" Dick's face turned red.

Ed smiled at the disc jockey and commented, "It's interesting you would think that. Some people have been saying that Dick and Dee Dee might have a doublesided hit, so play both sides.

""Tell you what," the disc jockey added. "I'm going to have a contest on the air and ask the kids to vote on which side they like the most."

"That's a great idea," Ed said. "Let us know the results."

After the lunch ended and Ed paid the bill, we dropped the disc jockey off at his radio station, Ed turned to Dick.

"Always be grateful for any air play they agree to give you."

He smiled at the distributor and then turned back to us. "We're now going to the competing radio station." Whatever you do, don't let them know we just had lunch with their rivals. They're in a ratings war. Just pretend we came all this way to visit with them only."

We drove to another radio station and Ed introduced us to the top disc jockey there.

"Let's go eat," the man said. "I'm starving. Besides, that will give us a chance to get to know each other."

I glanced at Ed, incredulous; I was so full I didn't think I could even waddle to the car.

"Great idea," Ed said. "Where do you want to go?"

Fortunately, the disc jockey picked a different restaurant than the one we'd just eaten at! He ordered a major meal. Trying to pretend we hadn't had lunch, we ordered salads. The disc jockey kept passing me the bread, commenting, "You've got to try this garlic bread. They're famous for it."

When we finally left Albany and boarded a train headed for the next town, I felt like a stuffed duck.

Dick whispered to me, "We're going to gain fifty pounds if we keep this up."

Ed heard him. "The idea is that if we can sit down and share a meal together with the various disc jockeys, they will get to know you and Dee Dee personally. Eating several extra meals is a small price to pay for that kind of publicity. The disc jockeys really are impressed you came all this way to meet them. They always play your records big time after you leave town."

I realized I should be grateful for all the promotion Liberty Records was giving us. If only I wasn't so tired and cold all the time. I felt stuffed and bloated, but decided to try to be as cheerful as possible.

* * * * *

We arrived at WJZ TV studios in Baltimore. Dick and I were scheduled to appear on "The Buddy Dean Bandstand," a popular rock 'n' roll television dance show with a huge following. I decided to wear heels and a fitted turquoise dress.

Buddy waved us over during the run through.

"No sense practicing to the record," he said. "If you don't know how to lip-synch by now, you ain't ever gonna learn."

He smoothed his sport coat. "When the cameras roll, just stand on this white marker, look at the camera and sing. We'll have the interview afterward."

The room filled with teenagers, wildly excited and ready to dance. Buddy stood cool and calm under blazing lights, facing the kids and camera.

When the cameras finally rolled he shouted, "Today we have a duo with us all the way from California. Let's give a big hand for Dick and Dee Dee!"

As the applause started, so did the musical introduction to "The Mountain's High." Dick and I mouthed the words and smiled at the camera. When the song finally stopped, Buddy approached us. Wedging himself between Dick and me, with his right hand he stuck a microphone in Dick's face.

"So, Dick, you wrote the song?" he asked.

Dick nodded.

"What gave you the inspiration for that?"

As Dick started to reply, I felt the oddest sensation on my back. I realized Buddy was using his free left hand to unzip my dress from behind. Already he had zipped it down below my shoulder blades!

I glanced up at him, but his face wore an angelic expression. He acted as if everything Dick said sounded utterly fascinating. His right hand held the microphone steady near Dick's mouth and his left, hidden from the audience, continued to unzip my dress. Oh my God! I knew if I didn't do something quickly, my dress would fall off.

I lifted my right foot and moved it back, instinctively guided the small, pointed high heel toward Buddy's left shoe. When I felt his toes under my heel, I managed to shift my weight backward so the pointed heel pressed sharply into his toes. He gasped, abruptly letting go of the zipper, and tried to squirm away.

"So," he said, acting as though nothing had happened. "How do you like Baltimore?" He moved the microphone in my direction, almost banging me in the mouth.

I felt like saying, "We just arrived here by train two hours ago. It's freezing cold and I'm so congested I can hardly breathe. The only things I've seen in Baltimore are the insides of a taxi cab and the television station. And now I've got to put up with you unzipping my dress. So I have no idea how I like Baltimore. In fact, I didn't even know I was in Baltimore."

But instead I replied through a fake smile, "It's a wonderful city and it's so special to appear on your show." At that moment I realized I was becoming the ultimate phony. I wasn't proud of it.

* * * * *

With the rumbling train as a sound effect, we traveled on. I felt as if I might be coming down with a sore throat, but Ed prodded us forward. We continued to Philadelphia, Boston, Cleveland and other cities. Between the freezing weather, six to eight meals a day, and lack of exercise, both Dick and I came down with the flu. Our extra weight didn't help strengthen our immune systems.

After several weeks of continuous travel, we staggered back to New York each ten pounds heavier. But it was worth it. "The Mountain's High" took off like a soaring rocket and climbed the charts rapidly all over the East Coast.

We were so sick we overslept and missed our flight from New York to Los Angeles. Feverish, Dick and I barely spoke in the cab on our way to the airport. The ticket agent assured us there were empty seats on the next flight.

When we finally boarded and our plane cleared the runway, I glanced out the window. My eyes widened in shock. There below us, sticking out of the icy Atlantic Ocean stood the tail section of an Eastern Airlines airplane that had apparently just crashed. I grabbed Dick's sleeve and pointed at it.

When I asked a flight attendant if she knew anything about the plane crash, she glanced out our window and turned pale. Without saying a word, she headed up the aisle toward the cockpit. Several minutes later she returned.

"Please don't mention it to the other passengers," she whispered. "We don't want to make them anxious."

Anxious? What about us? We'd already seen it.

I started dwelling on thoughts of death. What if we'd been on that plane? Did the fact we were still alive mean we'd received some type of divine protection? And if so, why didn't the people who passed away escape their fate as we did? I felt overwhelmed with gratitude to be alive, but deep sorrow for those who had died.

* * * * *

Mom picked me up at the airport. She arrived late and didn't find out about the plane crash until I mentioned it in the car. Mom fell silent for several minutes, and then she said, "What a tragedy for the victims and their families."

I flopped back in an exhausted heap against the back seat. My body ached and I found it difficult to breathe. "Yes, it's horrible," I finally commented, closing my eyes.

CHAPTER TEN

Struggling for a Hit Record

I lay on my bed; the wrinkled sheets tossed in every direction like a war had taken place. My nightstand held a giant glass of water. The thermometer, which for the past three days rarely dropped below 102 degrees, lay on the floor.

After four days of nightmarish fever, I finally forced myself into an upright position, swung my legs over the side of the bed and weakly made my way to the dresser. Pulling open the bottom drawer, I tenderly lifted up the rose crystal given to me by the monk at the lake.

It felt as cold as ice in my hand. I studied it intently. One side was practically flat and fit perfectly in my palm. The top side rose upward at a slant, creating a jagged point in the middle. The rock glistened as if someone had painted pale pink nail polish all over it.

What was it the monk said to do? Put the rock in my hand and think of something, but what? Oh yeah, think of peace. I'd better think of healing as well.

So I climbed back in bed, clutching the rock in my right hand, and imagined walking around the lake again. I visualized the swans peacefully paddling and the snapping turtles climbing onto the rocks to sun themselves. I placed the cool crystal on my forehead. That felt good.

When I awoke several hours later, the fever had broken. I felt sure the crystal had something to do with it.

* * * * *

The phone rang long and incessantly before I finally lifted the receiver.

"Hello?"

"A ghost of the past reappears. How are you?"

"Oh, hi Mike," I said. I felt confused and disoriented.

"I just found out about the Eastern Airline crash. My God, you could have been on that plane."

"We could have been." Both Mike and I remained silent. I could hear the pounding of my heart.

I leaned over and turned on the dial to my radio. A record by the Shirelles began to play, titled "Will You Still Love Me Tomorrow?"

"So is touring everything you expected?"

I tried hard not to cough. "I'm a little under the weather right now, Mike. Dick and I caught the flu. It was rough. We weren't prepared for the cold weather and it snowed heavily from Baltimore on."

"So have you had enough of touring or are you going back out again?"

"Right now we're getting ready to go back into the studio. But I presume we'll go on another tour soon."

Mike abruptly changed the subject. "Well, I have to go. I'm really busy with school and my new job. Call me sometime if you want to get together."

I heard a click, and I listened as the dial tone harmonized with the Shirelles. Feeling sad, I pulled the covers over my head and went back to sleep.

* * * * *

Two weeks later, after a complete recovery from the flu, Dick and I dropped by Sharon's house. On her coffee table sat the latest copies of Billboard and Cashbox, musical trade magazines containing national and international data on the latest hit records.

"Look," Sharon said, stabbing her slender finger at a list of information. "'The Mountain's High' is number 37 on the British charts."

How remarkable, I thought. Our voices are reaching parts of the world we've never even traveled to.

We looked at the United States record chart for that week. "The Mountain's

High" held the number two slot nationally. Another Liberty Recording artist, Bobby Vee, sat in the number one slot with "Take Good Care of My Baby."

"Hey, we're almost there," Dick said. "Maybe next week we'll hit number one."

"Hmm, you'd better check this out," Sharon commented, frowning and waving her hand in the air. "If I were you I would march into Liberty Records and demand to see their accounting figures."

"Their accounting figures? Why?" I asked.

"The thing is, Bobby Vee is signed directly to Liberty and you and Dick are only leased to them through the Wilder Brothers.

"Liberty's in-house producer records Bobby, and they're not about to release his number one position if they can help it. Bobby Vee's record has sat at the top of the charts for a long time. That's a tremendous feather in the in-house producer's cap. But something isn't right. At this point in time, you are probably selling more records."

"But how do you know that?" Dick asked.

"Well, it's predictable. When a record sits at the top of the charts it eventually loses momentum. Your record is the hot newcomer. It's got to be selling more. You need to get your hands on some official sales sheets from Liberty and compare your record with Bobby Vee's. You should be in the number one slot already."

We realized we'd never even stepped through the doors at Liberty. We had never met anyone there personally. Dick called the Wilders and demanded that they set up an appointment. At first George resisted, but he finally arranged for us to meet the president of the company, Al Bennett, the same man who had called me about my trashed hotel room in Minneapolis.

* * * * *

When Dick and I walked into in the lobby of Liberty Records on Sunset Boulevard in Hollywood, the receptionist ignored us. But when we told her we had an appointment with the president, her attitude changed dramatically.

After a brief wait, she escorted us into Mr. Bennett's office. A large man with a round face and pale skin sat behind a massive desk. He smiled, left his spot behind the desk and walked around it to slap Dick heartily on the back and shake my hand.

"Congratulations, you've got a massive hit record, a monster." Al walked back behind the oak desk and pushed a button on the intercom.

"Send in Snuff and the staff. I want them to meet Dick and Dee Dee."

I was thankful he hadn't brought up the trashed hotel room.

Still smiling, he asked, "Do you kids want any coffee or a Coke?"

"Oh, no thank you," I said. "We just had lunch."

Several staff members entered, their radiant smiles revealing dazzling white teeth. They shook our hands and then left. Mr. Bennett glanced back at his desk and then at his watch.

"Well," he said slowly. "If there's nothing else…"

Dick coughed. "Actually there is. We were wondering if we could see some of the accounting sheets for 'The Mountain's High.'"

Mr. Bennett's smile abruptly left his face. "I've given all that information to the Wilders." He nervously tapped his desk with his manicured nails. Click, click, click. Click, click, click.

He added, "Look, you're talented kids, good singers. Just stick to singing and leave the accounting to the pros."

Dick and I exchanged looks. Then we waved a halfhearted good-bye and trudged out.

"I'm going to talk to George," Dick said. "He'd better take a closer look at our accounting sheets."

George did study the figures and reported to Dick that, as far as he could tell, everything appeared normal.

* * * * *

By mid-year, Liberty released our second single, "Goodbye to Love," the song with the duck call. Expecting "Goodbye to Love" to sell a million copies, following a hit single like "The Mountain's High," they pressed up thousands of copies of the record and shipped it to their distributors.

"Goodbye to Love" turned out to be what was termed in the industry a "bomb," as in bombing out. "Goodbye to Love" didn't sell well after the first big promotional explosion. In fact, when the record stores returned their unsold copies to distributors and the distributors returned their unsold copies to Liberty, the record company discovered they had more copies returned than they had even pressed!

It appeared that bootleggers, confident that the follow-up record of "The Mountains High" would be a given best seller, printed up black market copies on their own. Somehow the bogus copies also got mixed in with the legitimate ones and were returned to Liberty.

I'd had a premonition about the commercial success of "Goodbye to Love." The duck call, the attempt to create another "Mountain's High," none of it felt right to me. Although disappointed, I still intuitively knew we'd have another hit record.

* * * * *

Dick's first single by himself, "Gonna Stick by You" was finally released by the Wilder Brothers. From the beginning of our singing career, Dick made it clear that he saw himself as a solo artist. When "The Mountains High" became a hit, I presumed his thoughts of a solo career had diminished, since he seemed happy with our success. But an occasional comment told me he still desired personal acclaim.

"I'm going to have a hit record myself," Dick said one day. "Don't be surprised when that happens. The first time we started working together, I told you that was my goal."

"Gonna Stick by You," (an ironic title, considering his desire to branch off on his own) was released around the same time as the second Dick and Dee Dee single. His song marched hand in hand with "Goodbye to Love" to the rock and roll graveyard.

* * * * *

It was time to go into the studio again. Dick blamed the failure of "Goodbye to Love" on the record's duck call. Humbled and chagrined by the failure of "Goodbye to Love," the Wilders planned another session. This time they booked the date at Gold Star Recording Studio in Hollywood.

"You kids need to try something different," George told us. "Let's use your beautiful harmonies and record a ballad, something like 'I Want Someone.'"

Again, Dick went into his songwriting mode. It was a solo effort. We wanted to stay far away from another songwriting controversy, like the one that erupted over who wrote "The Mountain's High."

My thoughts often went back to the advice Mike had given me when we first started singing. "Fifty percent of something is better than one hundred percent of nothing." I believed that arguing with Dick would only result in a fight and lead to the eventual break-up of the duo. So I kept silent and never complained about his selecting all the material for us to sing. A voice inside me said, "It's alright; you have talent and will survive no matter what direction Dick takes." I'd learned my lesson about arguing with him. I simply withdrew and waited to see where it all landed.

* * * * *

Dick wrote a new ballad entitled "Tell Me."

"What do you think?" Dick asked after singing and playing it over the telephone. I thought it was beautiful. It had great potential, especially the way it soared in certain parts. Another Dick St. John song, "Will You Always Love Me?" graced the back side of the record.

In a virtual replay of the session at Gold Star just nine short months before, we sang in the same dark booth, surrounded by an entire orchestra. Again, the strings sounded beautiful, inspiring. Everyone there loved it.

However, the Liberty Records staff wasn't too thrilled with our new single.

"We thought you were going to give us another 'Mountains High' type song," Al Bennett told George.

"The kids wanted a change of pace," George Wilder replied. "I trust their judgment. And you know what? I've got a good feeling about this record."

* * * * *

By late 1962, Liberty did release "Tell Me," although in limited quantity. The song took off immediately and climbed the national charts. Orders poured in from around the country and Liberty did another major pressing and shipping. When Dick and I saw "Tell Me" climb the charts in Los Angeles, we congratulated each other.

"I knew you kids would have another hit," George Wilder told us, a big grin on his face. "You're not one-hit artists."

I felt great happiness because I believed in this song and loved the arrangement and sound the Wilder Brothers got on the record. This validated my belief that I somehow knew how to recognize hit material.

"Tell Me" reached the number 22 position on the Billboard charts and, although it didn't sell as many copies as "The Mountains High," it did establish us as legitimate recording artists. We immediately started gathering material for our first album, to be titled "Tell Me the Mountain's High."

* * * * *

Dick and I often went to the Wilder's studio with rehearsed material written by Dick. After selecting a few songs, the Wilders turned us over to arranger Don Ralke to create beautiful string arrangements. We spent considerable time with Don at his home office in Studio City working out chords on the piano.

* * * * *

The Wilder Brothers decided I should record a single as a solo artist, just as Dick had. I believe now that it was simply an attempt at fairness—and the fact that they were always experimenting, recording various lounge acts they came across in Las Vegas. They tried many times to get a hit single with one of their Vegas discoveries, Wayne Newton, but to no avail. The irony is, years later Wayne became known as Mr. Las Vegas, one of the most popular entertainers to ever play there.

For my solo venture, The Wilders chose a song titled, "The Torch Is Out." It sounded like a former hit record "Angel Baby" by Rosie and the Originals, but slightly more up-tempo. I recorded the song in the Wilders' studio one afternoon, with George, Walt and Warner on instruments, accompanied by a hired drummer. Don Ralke played piano.

As I stood in the center of the musicians, facing a single microphone, out of the corner of my eye I saw Dick huddled in the corner of the room. I tried to ignore him, but that proved impossible. First he snickered, just loud enough for my ears. Then he started making horrible faces, as if he'd bitten into a sour pickle. Just as I was getting ready to sing the middle of the song, he pretended to throw up. I froze. The music continued to play but nothing came out of my mouth.

"Cut," George Wilder shouted. The music stopped. "You're doing fine," George said. "Just take deep breaths."

"Yeah," Warner added. "Stand on the balls of your feet and try to breathe from your diaphragm."

"Think high," George added. "Try to sing higher than the pitch."

With great effort I focused on my breathing. I tried to sing high. Finally, after what seemed an eternity to me, they appeared satisfied with the take. I still felt shaky and insecure.

In Dick's car on the way home, he told me, "Well, it finally sounded alright, but you have a problem. You sing flat at times. Luckily, you don't have to worry about it. It's wonderful what they can do by adding echo to your voice."

I felt limp and defeated. After that conversation, I didn't care what happened to the song.

Just as they had with "The Mountain's High," the Wilders released "The Torch Is Out" on their own label. Once again, they changed my name. Instead of calling me Mary or Dee Dee, this time they named me "Lindy Lou!"

The record project proved to be short-lived. "The Torch Is Out" didn't take off and the torch of their enthusiasm waned. The Wilders soon went searching for their next "discovery."

By this point, I felt convinced Dick possessed the only talent in our duo. In all matters relating to our music career, I silently deferred to him. After all, he possessed a three-octave range, took charge of everything and let me know it would not be a wise decision to cross him in any way. Inside, I sank deeper into withdrawal.

* * * * *

Without warning, Dick's favorite aunt died. Deeply affected by her passing, he wrote what I considered to be one of his best songs, entitled "Life's Just a Play." We recorded it and released the song as our follow-up to "Tell Me," with "All I Want" on the flip side. Few people bought the record.

We started our career with a massive hit record, "The Mountain's High", then had a failed attempt with "Goodbye to Love", then a hit with "Tell Me", now another failed attempt. Dick retreated to his living room piano and started writing songs again.

* * * * *

At that point, I decided to find my own place to live. After the freedom of touring, I no longer wanted to live at home with my parents and two younger sisters. I needed to control some aspect of my life.

After searching the West Los Angeles area, I finally secured an apartment on Bundy Drive in Brentwood. It was only a five-minute drive from my parents' house in Santa Monica.

The apartment, a small, nondescript one-bedroom unit, faced a busy street.

I decorated it with odd discards from my family's home. For my bookcase, I used bricks and boards. Mom gave me leftover, mismatched plates and cups. While most young adults my age were decorating dorm rooms in college, I struggled to create a feeling of home in my little one-bedroom apartment. But, no matter what I did to it, the apartment felt temporary.

CHAPTER ELEVEN

Confronting Liberty Records

One morning Sharon Sheeley called. She said she had something important to show us and insisted we come over immediately.

Lots of changes had taken place while we were touring. Sharon and Jackie's relationship deteriorated and they were not speaking to each other. They'd even dissolved their song writing partnership.

"You wouldn't believe some of the things Jackie tried to pull," Sharon finally said. "Bottom line is, you have to choose. You can be my friend or Jackie's, but not both."

I glanced at Dick.

"Don't worry, Sharon, we're on your side," Dick assured her. "We don't even know Jackie that well."

I nodded. "Sharon, we've been good friends for awhile. There's no way I'm going to abandon our friendship." Sharon smiled at us, reassured. From that day forth, I never heard Sharon mention Jackie's name again, unless it came up for professional reasons.

Liberty Records had just released our first album, Tell Me the Mountain's High. At Sharon's house, Dick and I eagerly scanned Billboard and Cashbox magazines in anticipation of a rapid climb up the Top 100 album charts. Although our album received wonderful reviews, its climb appeared nonexistent.

"Do you want to know the real reason your album isn't on the charts?" Sharon asked Dick and me.

I said, "Of course."

"It's due to bad promotion on the part of Liberty Records. Look, this is why I invited you guys over. I want to show you something."

Sharon brought out her most recent statement from BMI, a company that pays publishers and songwriters for the air play their music receives. Another statement showed records sold.

It startled us to discover that a song Sharon wrote sold more copies than what we'd been told "The Mountain's High" sold. Our record, though, ranked higher on the national charts. Was Liberty not reporting all our record sales to us? Something did not make sense.

"I'd sure ask to see the accounting records if I were you," Sharon said.

"We already tried that," Dick muttered. "It didn't work."

"You'd better talk to your record producers. Someone has to do something!" We left Sharon's house deeply concerned.

Dick approached the Wilder Brothers and again complained about the accounting at Liberty. By requesting an audit, the Wilders got Liberty to admit they'd made an error. Liberty suddenly credited one hundred thousand more record sales to our account for the hit single, "Tell Me."

"Can we get out of our contract with Liberty?" Dick asked the Wilders. "I don't trust them."

George responded, "No, they won't release you. We already asked them. In the beginning we leased you to Liberty Records under a five-year contract. You still have four years left."

"If we did get a release, would it be possible to sign with another record company?"

"Are you kidding? You've had two hit records! We could sign you to any label you wanted."

We went back to Sharon's to discuss our situation. When we told Sharon our dilemma she leapt off the sofa. "You've got to talk to Al Bennett personally," she said, referring to the president of Liberty Records. "I know him well. Al is extremely emotional and does not like confrontations. Show him you're upset. Convince him that you have to be released from Liberty."

As we drove home from Sharon's Dick said to me, "Our entire career is at state here. Liberty's roster is too large. We're getting lost in the shuffle. They aren't promoting us or giving us accurate accounting information. We have to do something."

"Since the Wilders struck out, how are we going to convince the president of Liberty to release us?"

"I don't know yet. But I do know one thing. It's time for action." He added, "I feel like throwing a rock through the window of Liberty."

We sat in depressed silence for a few moments.

"Let's go there tomorrow." Dick continued. "We won't let Al know we're coming. That way there's an element of surprise. He won't be prepared. I'll call first thing in the morning to make sure he's going to be there."

"But what are we going to say to him?"

"I don't know yet. I'll think of something. Just be ready to go by ten o'clock tomorrow morning. I'll pick you up."

* * * * *

The next day dawned beautiful and sunny, but when I climbed into the car and saw the scowl on Dick's face, I felt internal storm clouds gathering.

"I've decided what to do," Dick informed me. "Sharon said Al is emotional. The only way to get our release is to appeal to him through his emotions.

"I'm going to tell him the accounting situation upset me so much I'm about to have a nervous breakdown. I'm going to say that my mother is in the hospital and I can't take all this pressure."

I watched a billboard on Sunset Boulevard whiz past.

"You're going to have to get upset, too," Dick continued. "Do you think you can start to cry?"

"I-I don't know," I stammered.

"Ok. We have to start thinking of really sad things. We have to walk in there upset. What if everyone you knew died? What if you were all alone in the world, with every cent you ever earned stolen by Liberty? What if you wound up on the street with no home?"

Dick worked his way into an emotional frenzy. I found it difficult to pretend

I was sad, alone, broke and homeless, but I managed to plant an unhappy expression on my face.

By the time we pulled into the parking lot behind Liberty Records, Dick's hands trembled. Determined, with faces frozen in frowns, we marched through the front doors of the record company. The receptionist looked at us blandly.

"Can I help you?" she asked.

"We're here to see Al Bennett." Dick responded.

"Do you have an appointment?"

"No, but we have to see him now. It's an emergency. Just tell him Dick and Dee Dee are here."

Glancing down at her intercom, she pressed a button. Al's voice boomed into the reception area.

"What is it? I told you I didn't want to be disturbed."

"Dick and Dee Dee are here. They say it's an emergency and they have to see you now."

"Tell them to wait," Al shouted, unaware his voice carried loudly throughout the reception room. "I'm doing something important."

The receptionist clicked off and glared at Dick and me.

"He's busy." She commented, as if we hadn't heard his voice through the intercom.

"I have to see him now!" Dick shouted. "I'm too upset to wait!"

He bolted past her desk and headed down the hall toward Al's closed office door. I meekly trailed behind.

"You can't go in there," the receptionist yelled, as she leapt from her seat and tried to block Dick's path.

Dick ignored her. He reached Al's door before she did and flung it open. Al sat alone at his desk, working on some paperwork. He looked up startled, and then planted a big smile on his face.

"Dick," he said, rising and sticking out his hand. "And Dee Dee. It's so nice to see you. What can I do for you today?"

He nodded to the receptionist that it was alright for her to go back to the reception area. She quietly shut the door behind her.

"I can't take this anymore," Dick said intensely. "I think I'm having a nervous breakdown."

Al pointed to a sofa. "Please, sit down."

Dick ignored the sofa and sat on the edge of a chair, directly facing Al. Al remained standing behind his desk. I collapsed onto the sofa, sinking into its soft comfort, trying to become as invisible as possible.

"Now, how can I help you?" Al said, looking genuinely concerned.

"Liberty hasn't done all they can do for us as artists," Dick said. "When the Wilders questioned our royalty statement, you suddenly came up with one hundred thousand more record sales. How do we even know that figure is correct?"

Al tried to answer, but Dick barreled forward. "My mother is in the hospital and I'm under a lot of pressure right now. I don't need this aggravation. I'm getting more and more upset each day. In fact, I might be having a nervous breakdown. Sometimes I don't think I even want to live anymore." Dick started to sob. I stared at him in alarm.

"What can I do?" Al finally choked out.

"You can release us from Liberty so we can go elsewhere, somewhere where we will be appreciated. Isn't that right, Dee Dee?"

I nodded.

"I appreciate you," Al said convincingly. "We all love you at Liberty."

"I'm going crazy," Dick shouted, leaping to his feet. "I don't know what to do." Dick approached Al's desk in a menacing manner. Al looked startled. He reached under the desk and apparently pushed a call button because within seconds, two men burst through the door.

"You all know Dick St. John," Al sighed in relief. "He's a little upset now."

He turned to Dick and lowered his voice, talking in a calm, quiet tone.

"Now, why don't you sit down so we can discuss this further?"

Shaking uncontrollably, Dick backed up, never taking his eyes off Al, and bent his knees to sit back down on the chair. Unfortunately, Dick misjudged the chair's location and instead of sitting on the chair, fell backwards onto the floor.

Before anyone dared laugh, Dick picked himself up off the floor and put his hands over his face. He started to wail.

"My mother is in the hospital. I can't take this pressure. I'm just going to quit singing."

Al exchanged glances with the two men. I'm sure Dick and Dee Dee's record sale history flashed through their minds. Yes, "The Mountain's High" and "Tell Me" rose high on the national charts. But our current single, "Life's Just a Play" and our first album remained in limbo. How important was it to keep us on the label?

"All right," Al sighed. "I'll tell you what I am going to do. I'm going to release you from your recording contract so you can get your life back together."

"Thank you," Dick sobbed.

"But I'm warning you," Al continued, "If you try to sign with another record label I will make sure you never have another hit record again. Is that clear?"

Dick looked at him through tear-filled eyes.

"You're always welcome to come back to Liberty at any time. In fact, I predict you'll come crawling back on your hands and knees."

Dick sniffled and slowly shuffled forward to shake Al's hand.

"Thank you," he choked out. "We really appreciate it, don't we Dee Dee?"

"Thank you," I echoed in a tiny voice and followed Dick from the room. My face felt hot and my heart fluttered. How embarrassing. I just wanted to get out of there.

I glanced back and saw the three men staring at us with the strangest expressions on their faces.

When we got in the car Dick placed both hands on the steering wheel for several seconds until the shaking stopped. He turned and looked at me.

"Well, we got our release," he said. His voice sounded flat, drained of all emotion. "I told you we would. But you could have done something more dramatic. You just sat there."

"Well, anyway, it worked, Dick. We're free from Liberty!"

"Yeah, but Al Bennett said he'd make sure no record label would ever sign us." Dick acted defeated, subdued. "I sure hope the Wilders knew what they were talking about when they said every label in town wants Dick and Dee Dee on their artist's roster."

I, too, wondered if we'd done the right thing. Only time would tell.

When I got back to my apartment, I discovered that someone had tried to break down the front door. Apparently the deadbolt held, but the door looked like someone had attacked it with an axe. I shuddered to think what it might have been like had I been inside. My sense of adventure of living on my own and my feeling of safety vanished. Was someone trying to get to me personally or was it a random attack? I didn't know, but I felt so shaken I immediately moved back home.

SECTION THREE

"Young and in Love"

CHAPTER TWELVE

Two Excellent Career Moves

Hardly any time passed before the Wilder Brothers signed us to Warner Brothers Records. Great relief and joy shot through me when I heard the news. The career of Dick and Dee Dee appeared far from over.

Joe Smith became our contact person at the new record label. Warner Brothers hoped to transition from representing middle-of-the-road singers to pop acts, so the timing appeared perfect.

The Wilders decided that, unlike our relationship with Liberty Records, it was important for us to be personally involved with the record company from the beginning. After they signed the contracts, Dick and I met Joe Smith in his office.

Joe, a short man with dark hair, stood and walked to the door to greet us. He shook our hands. "Welcome to Warner Brothers," he said. "I know we're going to have a wonderful relationship. Come on. Let me introduce you to some of the staff."

Joe led us through the art department and introduced us to some of the record cover designers. He turned us over to a secretary, who acted as tour guide to the various departments at Warner Brothers Records. When she returned us to Joe's office, we knew a lot more about record production and promotion than we did walking in.

"Just let me know if you need anything," Joe said, as he escorted us to the door. "We try to keep in close contact with our artists." We left with positive feelings about how Warner Brothers Records intended to promote us and account for our record sales.

Dick wrote another song in the "Tell Me" style; a similar melody but different message. "Tell Me" talked about lost love. His new song, "Young and in Love," described love in full bloom.

* * * * *

By now, we'd joined the big leagues. Don Ralke, the Wilder Brothers' partner and our arranger, hired the hottest studio musicians in the business: Hal Blaine or Earl Palmer on drums, and Ray Pohlman or Carol Kaye on bass. Don excelled with his string arrangements, which we recorded with a small orchestra.

Warner Brothers Records released our first single on their label in early 1963. "Young and in Love" immediately climbed the national charts. The threats from Al Bennett became a moot point.

Dick decided that I would have much better luck talking to Joe Smith than he would, simply because "it's harder to say 'no' to a girl!" He often told me to telephone Joe for a favor.

The first time I called Joe Smith, it took all my courage, but once I got him on the line, I felt better immediately. When I asked Joe if Warner Brothers would arrange a photo session for us, we got it right away. When I suggested that Dick and I release an album as soon as possible to capitalize on the success of our first Warner Brothers hit, he agreed. Joe acted supportive and positive no matter what I asked for. What a nice change from the way Liberty Records had treated us. At Joe's suggestion, Dick and I started gathering material for an album to be titled "Young and in Love".

* * * * *

Dick decided the small, one-man booking agency in Hollywood wasn't doing the proper job for us. As "Young and in Love" climbed the national charts, Dick wanted us to sign with a larger, more prestigious agency.

He prodded the Wilders until they finally set up an appointment for us to meet Bill Lee, an agent with the William Morris Agency in Beverly Hills.

I didn't know as Dick and I entered the ornate lobby of the William Morris Agency that spring day in 1963, that I was about to meet a man who would change my life forever.

In the elevator, Dick coached me.

"Don't be nervous," he commanded. "If they decide to sign us, it will be a huge boost to our career. So you need to try to make a good impression.

" The other people in the elevator stared at the ceiling, pretending they weren't listening.

"Let me do the talking," Dick said. "You just smile and act friendly." One man gave an amused glance to a fellow passenger.

The elevator doors swung open. Dick and I got off. We found ourselves standing in a large reception area. After giving our names to the receptionist and listening to her announce us over the intercom, we sat for a long wait.

We read the latest copies of Billboard and Cashbox magazines. Dick pointed silently to "Young and in Love," number twenty three on the record charts nationally. Finally the receptionist escorted us into Bill Lee's office.

The agent wore a dark business suit and trendy narrow tie. He appeared to be about twenty-five years old. His dark tan face contrasted with his expertly groomed brown hair. I thought instantly that he was using Man Tan, a bottled tanning agent. The lotion had a tendency to turn your face slightly orange.

Bill's feet remained propped up on his desk and he held two telephones, one pressed against each ear. With a nod, he indicated we were to sit on the sofa facing him, and then continued to carry on two telephone conversations at the same time.

When he was speaking to one individual, he cupped his hand over the mouthpiece of the other phone.

"Look, Tony," Bill said. "I've got him on the other phone and he doesn't like the bottom line. I can't help it if he doesn't see things our way. Wait a minute. I'll ask him."

He cupped his hand over the mouthpiece of the first phone, so the individual he'd been speaking with couldn't hear, and then spoke into the second phone. He shouted, "Joel, I'm doing all I can, but Tony doesn't listen to reason. I know. I know. I'm on your side, buddy. But I can't force the guy!"

Back on the first phone, he commented, "Tony, he's going to have to think this one over. Can we call you back?"

He finally ended both conversations and stared at us, as if suddenly wondering how we had appeared on his sofa. Then he pulled his feet off the top of the desk, leapt up and stuck out his hand.

"Bill Lee," he said. "Lee—L…double E."

We stood.

"I'm Dick St. John." Dick shook his hand. "And this is Dee Dee Sperling." I shook his hand also.

"Please, sit down," Mr. Lee said.

We sat awkwardly on the edge of a plush leather sofa. Bill sank down into his massive leather desk chair. He placed his elbows on the arms of the chair and pressed his fingers together.

"Let me tell you what is going on with William Morris," he said. "The agency has decided to branch out. We're adding rock and roll artists to our client roster."

"Cool," Dick replied. "There's a growing demand for rock and roll, Mr. Lee."

"Call me Bill. None of the older agents know anything thing about this new branch of, uh, show business, so they hired a woman in New York named Roz Ross to create a rock and roll 'department' there. I'm her counterpart in Los Angeles."

Bill suddenly leapt off the chair and raced to a turn table in the corner. He put the needle on a record and "Papa Ooh Mau Mau" by the Rivingtons blasted forth.

"Listen to that!" Bill shouted. "Isn't that great?"

I quietly said, "Great?" To me, those song lyrics made no sense at all.

Bill snorted and glanced over, as if seeing me for the first time.

Dick jabbed me in the side with his elbow.

"Yeah, great record," Dick enthused.

"Anyway, we're signing every act we can that is currently on the national charts. And that includes Dick and Dee Dee."

"We'd love to sign with William Morris," Dick said.

"Because you're under twenty-one, we'll need your parents' signatures on the documents, as well as yours. The standard contract for William Morris locks you up in all areas of show business. Why don't you step out into the outer office and my secretary will give you contracts to take with you. Oh, incidentally, I need them back in twenty-four hours. That's essential."

The telephone started ringing and Bill eagerly grabbed it, waving us out the door with the other hand. We waved a feeble goodbye and collected our contracts from the secretary before leaving.

Wow, what a strange experience, I thought as the elevator doors closed behind us. Who is that guy, anyway? How could he have such a powerful position at such a young age? And does he really think that bottled tan looks natural?

As we rode down to the lobby, my stomach lurched from more than the speed of the elevator.

"Isn't this fantastic?" Dick practically leapt off the sidewalk. "We've finally hit the big time. Just think what an agency that powerful might do for us."

"It's cool they want to sign us," I said.

"Not only that. Think what he said about locking us into all areas of show business. That means television and motion pictures. There's no limit to what we can achieve. I've always wanted to be an actor, you know."

* * * * *

That night, I told Dad that, because we were minors, he had to sign our agency contracts. I imagined it would be a simple procedure for him to read them, give his consent, and sign them as my legal guardian. Mom and Dad and Aunt Doris sat at the dining room table where so many of our discussions took place throughout the years, enjoying their dessert. After Dad read through the contracts, he squinted and stared at me.

"The William Morris Agency is trying to control you and Dick in all areas of show business. They want to sign you in television and motion pictures as well."

"I know. Isn't that great?"

"All you wanted the agency to do was have them represent you for touring. You're giving away too much. It's not necessary."

I sighed. "Dad, what difference does it make? We're lucky they even want us."

"Nevertheless, we shouldn't sign the contract until I make several changes."

He noticed my unhappy expression for the first time.

"Don't look so sad. I'm just trying to protect you. Only your family and good friends truly care about what's best for you, not strangers."

I nodded, but I didn't feel convinced.

"At the end of your life, if you can count your true friends on the fingers of one hand, you're really doing well. Do you know who your best friends are? They're the people sitting around this table right now."

Mom smiled kindly and Aunt Doris nodded in agreement.

"We're the only ones who truly have your best interests at heart. So let's make the changes to the contract for your benefit."

My stomach felt tight. I knew how important it was to get the contacts back to Bill immediately and sure enough, Dick called after dinner.

"Are the contracts signed? I need to come by and pick up them up."

I paused and then said quietly, "Dad's making a few changes. He doesn't think we should be tied up in all areas of show business. You and I might want to sign with another agency for television and motion pictures."

"He's doing what?" Dick's voice rose. "Your Dad has no right to change anything."

"Dick, he's giving it some thought. I can't grab the contracts away from him before he thoroughly reviews them. He's a lawyer, for God's sake. He needs to study them before he signs."

Dick slammed down the phone.

The next morning Dick phoned again. His voice shook.

"Well, now you've done it," he said. "I called Bill and told him we'd have the contracts back shortly, but a few changes were being made by an attorney. He got extremely agitated and said the contracts were standard and unchangeable. He said we could forget the whole thing if we didn't sign them as they were. He said he was giving us until five o'clock today to get them back. If you screw up this deal for us…" "My dad doesn't even get home from work until after five," I wailed.

"You're going to have to explain this to Bill, not me."

I approached my father that evening, the moment he walked into the house.

"Dad, our agent at William Morris said we have to get the contracts back immediately, with no changes, or they aren't going to represent us."

Dad acted totally unimpressed. He waved his hand at me, impatiently.

"Anything worth doing is worth doing right," he commented. "The William Morris Agency is just trying to scare you."

"They're doing a good job of it."

"You have the right to have an attorney look over your documents and make changes, if need be. Don't let that guy at William Morris push you around."

"Dad, you don't understand," I pleaded. "We're just one of twenty or thirty acts they're trying to sign. I'm sure if any of their acts give them trouble, they just drop them."

Dad walked past me, heading for the kitchen. "Well, no sense standing here any longer. Since I haven't read the contract, I'm not going to sign it yet."

I wailed, "Well, when are you going to read it?"

"I can't read it tonight because I have to prepare a brief for an important case in Seattle tomorrow. And I'm catching a plane out first thing in the morning." He observed my confused, distressed face. "I'll tell you what I'll do. I will review the contract thoroughly on the airplane and make the recommended changes so you'll have them next week when I return."

"William Morris is going to drop us," I said with a sob. "And Dick will never speak to me again. That's it. The act's over." I started crying and ran upstairs. Why did Dad act so stubborn? I felt like my whole future, everything I'd struggled for, was swirling down the drain and there was nothing I could do about it.

Despite my final pleas, Dad left for the airport the next morning with the contracts in his briefcase, unsigned. I finally got the nerve to telephone Dick with the news.

"I should never have left you to handle things," he shouted. "Your dad is out of control. He's ruining everything."

Before I knew it, his car screeched into the driveway. I heard pounding at the front door. Dick grabbed my arm and pulled me toward his vehicle.

"Come on. We're going to the airport. We have to get those contracts back before he leaves."

I remembered Dad telling Mom he intended to fly on Pacific Southwest Airlines. When we reached the airport, the information board listed his departing gate. We ran down the corridors, finally arriving at the boarding area, huffing and out of breath. We found my father in the boarding area, reading a newspaper.

"Mr. Sperling," Dick said, his voice shaking. "My mother has already signed the contracts and I would like you to sign them too. We had until last night to return them and now we're late."

Dad glanced up, surprised.

"There are items that should be changed," Dad firmly replied.

Dick's hands trembled. "They're just standard contracts. The agency won't change them for anyone. We have already put this tremendous opportunity at risk. But if we make any changes they are definitely going to drop us." I stood by Dick's side, wringing my hands.

Dick continued, "Our career will pretty much be over if we don't sign with William Morris."

"Alright," Dad finally said. "I could get a much better deal for you if we had more time, but since you refuse to wait a few more days, I'll sign the contracts."

Moments before the passengers boarded, we got his signature on the line. As Dad walked away, he glanced back once. I gave a smile and a feeble wave. He just stared. As he rounded the corner to board the plane and I looked down at his signature on the dotted line, a great wave of relief flooded over me. Dick and Dee Dee still had a future.

* * * * *

In the car, on the way back to Santa Monica, Dick started a tirade against my father.

"He's created a huge problem," Dick commented. "We've violated the deadline."

"But we're just one day late."

"I don't care. I want Bill to know the late contracts are your dad's fault, so he still has a good impression of me. I might sign as a solo artist someday and I want him to know that at least I'm reliable. You can return the contracts to Bill's office yourself. And if he gets upset, you'll have to explain why the contracts are late."

This was a startling new development, because I rarely went anywhere professionally without Dick. But I agreed to drop them off.

When I got back to the house I telephoned the William Morris Agency in Beverly Hills and requested an appointment.

"It's urgent," I told the receptionist. "I need to meet with Bill Lee immediately." She made an appointment for three p.m.

* * * * *

When I arrived in Bill's reception area, he kept me waiting for over half an hour. The longer I sat there, the more concerned I became. What if Bill freaked out about the delay in returning the contracts? What if he no longer wanted to represent us? How would I ever justify that to Dick?

Finally the secretary told me I could go in. I cautiously opened the door and saw five lanky black men standing around an imaginary microphone in the center of Bill's office. The tallest member, who sang bass, boomed out the lyrics. The rest of the group danced around in a circle. Bill stood behind his desk, clapping with delight, shouting "I love it! I love it!"

They all stopped and stared at me as I entered.

"I'm returning the contracts," I stammered. "I'm sorry we're late with them but..."

"Wait! You've got to hear this," Bill shouted. Pointing at the lead singer he commanded, "Sing it again! Sing 'Papa Ooh Mau Mau!"

The group danced in a circle again with Bill gleefully urging them on. The phone rang. Bill waved them to continue, as he launched into a conversation.

"Right, Abe is trying to sign Streisand. What? That noise? That "noise" is a new rock and roll group I'm signing. I know. I know. You don't have to understand what we're doing here." He winked at the group.

"The Rivingtons are a hot act." There was a pause. Bill finally sighed and commented, "Okay, let me know when the Streisand meeting is." He slammed down the phone and stared in my direction.

"Hey," he said to me. "Thanks for dropping off the contracts. We'll be in touch.

" * * * * *

I nodded and, waving a polite goodbye to the Rivingtons, backed out of the room. As I shut the door they broke into another raucous chorus of "Papa Ooh Mau Mau." Feeling relieved I'd gotten off easy, I raced toward the elevator.

CHAPTER THIRTEEN

Destiny Brings a Key Player

As I lay on the single bed in the little room off my parents' garage, (which I converted to meet my needs when I moved back home), I opened my eyes to the sound of the garbage trucks dropping trash cans on the street. My clock read 5:00 a.m. I groaned and pulled the pillow over my head.

An hour later the phone rang.

"Hi, sorry to call so early," Bill Lee said. "I didn't wake you, did I? I usually get to the office by six to reach Roz on the East Coast."

Feeling groggy, I cleared my throat and tried to think.

"Listen, I was wondering. Would you like to have dinner with me tonight?"

He was asking me out? Oh my gosh! Instantly, I felt alert. What was tonight?

"Uh, sure." I stammered.

"We'll go to the Broken Drum on Wilshire in Santa Monica. Your address is on the William Morris contract. I'll pick you up at eight."

After I hung up I wondered if I'd dreamt the phone call. Why did he want to go out with me? He didn't even know me. I'm sure he realized I was six years younger. I felt nervous, but excited. "Take a deep breath," I told myself. "You need to act mature and sophisticated."

I pulled on a pair of faded jeans and a tee shirt and staggered into the house. As I passed through the kitchen on the way to the bathroom, I smelled eggs and toast.

At this early hour, it didn't smell particularly good.

From somewhere upstairs, through the bathroom ceiling, I heard music coming from my sister's room. It sounded like Kyu Sakamoto singing "Sukiyaki." I stopped and listened intently. The washcloth I held dripped water all over my tee shirt. I raced out of the bathroom and called Dick.

"Rich is sleeping," Mrs. Carroll announced. "Why, you're up early this morning. Is it important?"

"No," I said. "But please have him call me when he gets up."

I headed to the kitchen. Mom stood by the stove, wearing a yellow and white apron and holding a large serving spoon in her hand.

"I made extra scrambled eggs. Do you want some?"

I didn't, but since she'd saved some for me I thought I'd eat them.

After I ate, I walked out the back door, through the yard past the orange and lemon trees, and into my little room off the garage. I looked around, as if seeing it for the first time.

The phone rang.

"My mom said you called." Dick sounded bored.

There was a pause. Finally Dick asked, "Well, what did you want?"

"Oh, I wanted to tell you that Bill Lee called and asked me out to dinner."

"What? Fantastic! If you start going out with him, think what that could do for our career."

"Dick, I'm going out with him because I think he's interesting."

"Well, just make sure you don't do or say anything to ruin things for Dick and Dee Dee."

Why did I bother calling him? I realized I'd been seeking brotherly advice in the wrong place.

"I'll be sure to tell him you send your regards," I said and hung up the receiver.

* * * * *

Bill picked me up in his white Corvair and we drove a short distance to the restaurant. The Broken Drum sat on Wilshire Boulevard in Santa Monica near 6th street. The sign outside the restaurant read, "The Broken Drum, You Can't Beat It."

We entered a small room. A fire burned cheerfully in the fireplace. Starched linen, silverware and a beautiful vase of fresh flowers sat on every table. Piano music played softly in the background.

After we were seated Bill studied his menu.

"Do you like escargot?" he asked.

I blanched at the thought of eating snails. "I've never eaten them," I answered, trying not to shudder.

"I'm going to order some. You can try some of mine. You never know if you're going to like something until you try it."

I coughed and quickly gulped some water.

The waiter took our orders. I ordered a Caesar salad and lightly grilled salmon. Bill passed the basket of sour dough rolls, helping himself to one.

"So how's Dick doing?" Bill asked.

"He's fine. He's working on some new material."

The waiter appeared carrying a dish of escargots. He placed it in front of Bill, placing a special pronged tool next to them. Bill gave a big smile.

"Ah, escargot," he said. "What a delicacy."

He took the pronged tool firmly in one hand and pulled the snail out of its shell with a small fork. It stretched, ominously. Bill looked at it fondly before dipping it in butter and placing it into his mouth. A look of rapture came over his face as he chewed.

"You've got to try this," he said.

I tried not to recoil in horror as Bill extracted another snail from its shell, dipped it in butter and moved the fork toward me. I took the snail into my mouth and valiantly chewed it, feeling like I was going to throw up.

"Do you like it?" Bill asked.

"Uh, tastes like chicken," I managed to gasp.

Bill appeared happy with that answer and finished the rest of the escargot by himself. Then he turned to me.

"I want you to know something," he said. "I'm married."

I stared at him. Why was he telling me this?

"I'm separating from my wife this weekend. I've rented an apartment on Granville in West Los Angeles and I'm moving in on Saturday."

"How long have you been married?" I stammered.

Bill stared at the table. "Just a few years. Actually, this is my second marriage. I got married in my teens to my high school girlfriend, who dumped me a short time later."

Bill picked up a sour dough roll, tore off a piece and popped it in his mouth. "I was so hurt by the breakup I vowed to find a woman who prized loyalty above all other qualities. So when I met Marsha, I knew she was the one. There was only one problem. I wasn't sure I loved her."

"You didn't love her and you married her?"

"Oh, I loved her, but I thought something more would eventually develop. She's really a wonderful girl, but it just didn't work out."

"Why are you telling me this?"

"I want to be upfront with you, because I didn't want you to find out I was married before I could tell you myself."

Bill stared at me with large blue eyes. I felt emotion and sincerity behind his words.

Suddenly I choked up with tears. Where were these feelings coming from? My face started to flush.

I stammered, "I really don't know what to say."

"Don't say anything. Just hang in until I get settled and start the divorce proceedings. What I'm saying is, I'd like to see more of you, but I want things to be right. This is very difficult for Marsha. She can't understand what went wrong in the marriage, as we rarely fought. She thought everything was perfect."

I glanced at Bill. It was difficult to comprehend what he was talking about.

"Marsha had no idea how unhappy I was. That's why I spend every waking moment at the William Morris Agency. My job is the most important thing in my life." "Well," I finally said. "Let me know how the move goes."

Bill reached across the table and took my hand. "I'll invite you over for dinner as soon as I get settled."

He released my hand, grabbed the salt shaker and pretended it was a microphone.

"Ladies and gentlemen," he said loudly. "We'd like to present the winner of the

Irving Salzburg award to Dee Dee Sperling, for tasting escargot and living through the experience."

I burst out laughing. A couple at a nearby table gave us an amused look. We ended the evening with coffee and Bill drove me home.

I lay in bed that night, wide awake and reliving the evening. I thought the dinner went well. Bill's take-charge personality intrigued me. But he was married. Well, at least he told me about it and, after all, he'd soon be living apart from his wife and divorcing her.

* * * * *

Bill's talk about moving started me thinking about my own housing situation. Things again felt restrictive at home with Mom and Dad. My former apartment in West Los Angeles represented my first fledgling efforts at self sufficiency, ending sadly when someone tried to break the door down. Now, maybe it was time to find a new place to live, somewhere safe and attractive. Somewhere I could retire to between tours.

The next day, I grabbed the Los Angeles Times and started reading the classified ads. One ad in particular caught my eye. It advertised apartments for rent in a high-rise, one of the first to be built on Wilshire Boulevard in West Los Angeles near Barrington.

Bill had mentioned he intended to move to Granville Avenue, which was located several blocks away. What would it be like living within walking distance of each other?

* * * * *

A sophisticated, immaculately dressed rental manager met me in her office at the Barrington Plaza. She told me the apartment prices and various choices. The only apartment I felt I could afford was a single on the eleventh floor.

"Let's take a look at it," I said.

I loved it the minute she opened the door. It was a corner unit, and windows covered two of the four walls. I felt like I was in an airplane. One view looked toward hills separating the Valley from the West Side and the other view faced Santa Monica and the Pacific Ocean. Below, a massive pool sparkled in the sunlight.

I signed the rental agreement that day, anticipating I would move in two weeks later.

After a week Bill called, sounding tired but happy.

"I'm in West Los Angeles," he announced. "The movers just left. What a long day. But the worst is over. Now I just have to put things away."

"Where is your wife living?"

Bill paused. "She's moving back with her parents temporarily. She is very unhappy. Fortunately, she wasn't there when the movers arrived."

He suddenly changed the conversation. "I'd like to have you over for dinner next week. By then I'll know where my pots and pans are."

I smiled. "I'd love to see your apartment. And I've got some news for you. I just signed a year's lease on an apartment nearby. It's in the Barrington Plaza, those tall towers on Wilshire. I'm moving in at the end of this month."

There was silence on the other end of the line. Then Bill said slowly, "You're moving two blocks from where I live?"

"Yeah," I continued. "Wait until you see my apartment. It's on the eleventh floor. I've got a view of the ocean and mountains. Maybe I can even see your building from the window."

After a long pause Bill said, "Well, I've got to go. I haven't a clue where the sheets and towels are packed."

He hung up abruptly. I wondered if Bill felt concerned about my plans to move so close.

Several days later, Bill called again. He shouted, "Get out your calendar! You and Dick are going to play the hottest club in town, Pandora's Box. You don't need to thank me. Just send chocolates."

I laughed, but sobered when I realized he didn't mention seeing me alone again. I telephoned Dick.

"Bill is starting to book us," I told him. "We're playing Pandora's Box in Hollywood."

"That's so cool," Dick replied. "You must have said the right things when you went out with Bill. You can be in charge of the bookings from now on. Just let me know when they are, so I can put them on my calendar." I sighed. I realized a new responsibility had just landed on my lap.

* * * * *

Pandora's Box sat on a small traffic island on the corner of Sunset, near Highland. The quaint house contained remnants of the fifties Beat Generation, sporting black walls and a continual smell of stale cigarette smoke. In previous years, the club bore the name, "The Renaissance."

When I was in high school, I drove there with Mike to see shock comedian Lenny Bruce. I spent most of the evening trying to duck out of sight behind a pillar so he wouldn't single me out to attack for the sake of a laugh.

Another time, I saw Bessie Griffin and the Gospel Pearls. Those ladies rocked the place with their full-volume, joyous gospel music. And now I'd return to Pandora's Box, this time as a performer.

* * * * *

The afternoon of our performance, we met with the small group hired to accompany us. The band leader introduced himself. "I'm Leon Russell." When we handed him our music for "The Mountain's High," "Tell Me" and "Young and in Love," he barely glanced at the sheet music before playing the songs on an old upright piano. His style felt relaxed and soulful.

The club's tiny stage stood against one wall of what must have once been a living room. There was barely room for a four-piece band and their instruments, let alone Dick and me.

That evening we walked on stage and smiled at the audience. The intimate setting helped me relax. With Leon's awesome musical backing, the place rocked out. Exhilarated and joyful, Dick and I finally left the stage after being called back for two encores.

"What a great band," Dick said. "Too bad we can't play with them every night."

"I wish," I said.

"We sounded great too," Dick added. "For once you weren't too loud."

I turned and headed for the dressing room, Dick trailing after me. Our tiny closet- like dressing room held two chairs. As I collapsed into one of them, grateful to be off my feet for awhile, we heard a knock at the door.

"Dick? Dee Dee?" Bill Lee's voice said. "Can I come in?"

Dick almost tripped over his chair racing to open the door. "Bill, oh wow, we haven't seen you for awhile. How are you?"

"I'm great. You guys really brought down the house tonight. This is the first live show I've ever seen you do. You're incredible!"

Dick motioned for Bill to sit in his chair.

"No, that's okay. I've been sitting all evening. Can I get you something to drink? You must be thirsty after that workout."

"No thanks." Dick quickly responded. "We'll get something later. But I'm glad you're here. I wanted to discuss something with you."

Bill nervously blinked several times. "Oh, sure, what's on your mind?"

"We need more national exposure, especially on the East Coast. People hear our records, but have no idea what we look like. Is there any way you could book us on a tour of that area?"

Dick paused and looked at Bill expectantly.

"Strange you should ask. I'm right in the middle of packaging a Dick Clark Caravan of Stars Tour for the East Coast. Roz is booking the acts that live back East and I'm signing artists out here. I submitted your names last week."

"Oh, man, that would be so great. When do we find out if we're going?"

Bill smiled with pride. "Right now. That's what I came here to tell you. The offer came in this morning. You're booked."

Dick clapped his hands together. "Fantastic, that's just what we need. We've never even done Bandstand. And now we get to travel with Dick Clark. What other acts are on the tour?"

Bill smiled and pulled a list from his coat pocket. "Are you ready for this? Gene Pitney, The Dovells, Paul and Paula, The Crystals, The Thymes, Barbara Lewis, Rockin' Robin, Lou Christie, Johnny Tillotson, The Orlons, Bobby Sox and the Blue Jeans, Ruby and the Romantics, The Chiffons, Gladys Knight and the Pips…I don't know, there are others. Incidentally, you leave in two weeks. You'll be gone for two months, practically all summer."

Dick and I glanced at each other, stunned.

Bill stood and opened the door. "I'll be right back."

After he left the room, Dick jumped up. "Wow, things are moving fast. I've got to get some fresh air. I'll be back before the second show."

Left alone, I leaned back in the chair. Thoughts rushed through my mind. I had a lot of planning to do before I left for the summer. For one thing, I needed to move into my new apartment! I felt nervous, excited. A knock on the door jolted me out of my reverie.

"Open the door," Bills commanded. "My hands are full."

I crossed the room and swung the door open. Bill stood there, a cup of coffee in one hand and an iced drink in the other.

"Your choice," he said, nodding at the drinks. "Coffee or seven up? This place doesn't have a license for alcohol." I took the coffee and thanked him. He entered the room, shutting the door behind him.

"Is seven o'clock on Friday a good time?" Bill asked.

"For what?"

"For dinner at my place." He looked at me with a soft, caring gaze. "Incidentally, I'm glad we're going to be neighbors. I want to cook a special meal for you."

I felt a rush of joy. He wasn't angry I decided to move so close.

"Seven is perfect," I replied. "Can I bring something?"

"Just bring yourself." He paused and stared at me for a moment. "Come outside. I want to show you something."

We walked out to the street and approached Bill's Corvair. He put the key in the trunk lock, opened it and took out his briefcase. I noticed several items stored in a huge cardboard carton; glass mayonnaise jars filled with water, numerous cans of tuna, a can opener and a machete.

"What on earth are those things for?" I asked.

Bill looked pleased with himself. "Those are my safety rations in case Castro decides to bomb us. I don't have a bomb shelter but I could escape L.A. in my car. You can live quite awhile on water and tuna."

I couldn't believe what I was hearing. "But the machete?" I asked. "Are you going to cut a path through a jungle?"

Bill laughed. "No, the machete is to protect my food."

I thought it was a bit over the top and looked at him to see if he was joking. His eyes showed a hint of fear.

He put the briefcase back, slammed the trunk and stared at his watch.

"I was going to show you the schedule of the towns and cities where the Dick Clark Caravan of Stars Tour plays, but I don't have it with me. I'll give it to you later. Come on. You've got a second show to do."

All throughout the second performance I thought of Bill. He stood in a doorway in the back, leaning against the door frame, watching us perform. Joy filled my heart. He wouldn't be staying so long if he didn't have some interest in me.

After the performance, we grabbed our coats and walked outside to our parked cars. I hesitated, wondering how Dick would feel if I rode home with Bill. But Bill suddenly glanced at his watch.

"Gotta run," he said. "Believe it or not, I've got to review another act this evening. I'll call tomorrow."

He climbed in his car and took off, leaving me to ride home with Dick.

* * * * *

Several days later, the doorbell rang. Dick stood on the front porch of my parents' house, beaming.

"Look," he said, pointing to a shiny new maroon Cadillac sitting in the driveway. It gleamed in the morning sunshine. "It's my new car. I paid cash for it, too. Wanna go for a ride?"

My mouth fell open. I knew Dick received song writing royalties, but I didn't think he'd saved enough to purchase a Cadillac. Speechless, I climbed into the passenger's side.

We cruised around several blocks. Dick drove cautiously and timidly, in total contrast to the way he usually drove.

"Check this out," Dick said, raising and lowering the electric windows. He pushed several buttons and the radio's speakers blasted from the back seat, as well as the front.

My dad happened to be home watering the lawn that Saturday and watched in surprise as Dick and I drove back up the driveway. Dick proudly showed him some of the car's features.

Dad muttered, "Nice car." Within a month, Dad purchased a Cadillac for himself, albeit a used one.

To date, Dick and I had received very little money in record royalties. Although the Wilders signed us to Warner Brothers Records for approximately seven percent of the gross sales, Dick and I only got one-and-a-half percent each, with a slight graduating scale built in over remaining years of the contract. The Wilders received the rest.

Our only immediate cash came from touring. However, before we received money from the tour promoters, the William Morris Agency took ten percent from the initial deposit. Dick and I split the rest, but we also had to pay all our travel expenses, hotel and food costs, plus any clothes and essentials. After expenses, there wasn't a lot left over, certainly nothing to save.

But saving didn't seem to be a priority. In fact, we didn't give it a thought. As long as we continued singing, we believed the money would roll in, enough money to buy clothes and whatever else we wanted. We'd get three hundred dollars a week for the Dick Clark Caravan of Stars Tour.

* * * * *

Friday night finally arrived and I spent hours getting ready for the dinner at Bill's apartment. My stomach quivered with excitement and my hands shook as I applied my makeup. I wore a brand new designer pants outfit. A hairdresser in Beverly Hills had styled my hair, piling curls on top of my head. With a final look in the mirror, I shouted "goodbye" to my Mom and drove to Bill's new apartment.

Bill lived in a two-story, stucco building on a nondescript street. Sure enough, the Barrington Plaza loomed in the distance two blocks away. In fact, my future window faced the direction of Bill's apartment.

Bill swung the door open the moment I rang the bell.

"Hello," he said. "Enter." He was wearing khaki pants and a stylish shirt. His face looked tanner than usual.

I walked into a typical one-bedroom apartment. Bill gestured toward a modern sofa, tastefully covered with a beige fabric. "Please sit down. Dinner is almost ready." My eyes scanned the room. Designer striped pillows spilled across the sofa. Across from it sat a comfortable arm chair and matching hassock.

The small dining area held a round Danish Modern table that normally sat four, but was now set for two. On the table were attractive placemats, Mexican handblown dishware and glasses, candles and flowers. The most wonderful aroma drifted out from the kitchen. It carried a hint of garlic.

"I'm just waiting for the tomato sauce to reach perfection," Bill said, as he entered the tiny open kitchen and uncovered a large pot. Inside, homemade tomato sauce simmered.

A large Caesar salad sat in a gigantic wooden bowl, ready to be served. Bill broke a raw egg over it and stirred in the rest of the ingredients to make the salad dressing. He pulled open the oven door and took out garlic bread, beautifully toasted and fragrant, which he piled on a platter and set on the table.

"Well, it's all ready," he announced. "Please sit down."

Bill uncorked a bottle of red wine and poured me a glass. We sat down and started eating the salad and garlic bread. It was simply the best thing I had ever tasted. I couldn't believe Bill knew how to prepare such food.

During our meal, the phone rang several times. Bill jumped up and buried his phone under pillows on the sofa, so the ring became muted. The next time it rang, he cranked up the volume on the record player to cover the noise.

Was his wife on the phone? They'd just separated. Did she miss him? Was she trying to get him back? I felt like the "other woman." To distract myself from the ringing phone I shouted, "So how did you get your job with William Morris?"

"I had a job as a cue-card boy for a television show at NBC. I held up giant cue cards so the audience knew when to laugh or applaud. One day I held up the wrong card and everyone laughed during a serious moment. I didn't last long there." Impressed that Bill kept his sense of humor after losing his job, I smiled.

"When I started working for William Morris they put me in the mailroom. That's where everyone begins. It's sort of like an initiation. It's one of the most boring jobs in the world, but you learn who the key players are."

"I guess if you're reading their names on the envelopes you figure out quickly who's who," I observed.

"Right, eventually I worked my way up the ladder. Now, of course, I'm the West Coast agent for the Rock and Roll department." Bill smiled modestly.

"That position is mostly misunderstood by the old timers. They have no idea what rock and roll music is about, except that it makes money and is extremely popular. Of course, it is just a fad and won't last."

I totally disagreed. Rock and roll reflected the values and taste of my generation. I never heard anyone close to my age call it a fad. Was there so large a gap between Bill's and my age?

"What makes you think it won't last?" I asked.

"The only people of lasting value are people like Barbara Streisand and Shirley Bassey, the truly talented singers. They'll always be able to play Vegas and do concerts. But rock and roll acts? They're a flash in the pan."

Bill looked at me intently. "Enjoy what you're doing while you can. You're in one of the most futureless professions in the world."

I felt a wave of concern flood over me. I never thought much about the future. I just assumed it would all work out. But without a college education, what might happen if the singing stopped?

Bill leapt up and put a 45 rpm single on the record player.

"I hate to interrupt dinner, but you've got to hear this. It will prove my point." Bill placed the phonograph needle on the disc. Surf music blasted forth.

"This is a new group called the Beach Boys. We're thinking of signing them to William Morris. They're capitalizing on the surfing craze. Listen to this. It will probably be a number one hit. But do they have staying power? Of course not. Where are the Beach Boys going to be five years down the line? Do you see my point?"

I nodded but added, "Well, everything comes and goes eventually. But who knows what is going to last? I think talent always shines through, no matter what form it is presented in."

"Do you call that talent?" Bill asked, gesturing toward the record player. "It's a gimmick aimed at a certain segment of teens. It will come and go, trust me."

I realized that there was a generation gap between Bill and myself. Although I'd turned twenty I thought Bill looked to be about twenty-six. He had not been raised with rock and roll. He didn't relate to it. I felt disappointed.

"So are you signing them to William Morris?"

"The Beach Boys? Not yet," Bill grinned. "They're a family. The dad is something else. His name is Murray. He comes into my office or calls almost every day telling me how talented his sons are and how far they are going to go in show business."

"He sounds persistent."

"He bent my ear for so long I finally introduced him to Nick Vinet over at Capital so he could bug Nick for awhile. Next thing I knew, Nick signed the Beach Boys and is going to record them from now on. The song you're hearing, 'Surfin,' appeared on a small label. It sounds commercial. What do you think?"

"Oh, it will be a hit in California and Hawaii for sure. I don't know what people in the Midwest will think of surfing. I mean, they don't even have oceans in those states."

Bill laughed. "You're right. It's probably a West Coast phenomenon. How could they relate to that in Kansas?" We both laughed.

The phone rang again, long and incessantly. Bill stared at the sofa. He did not appear comfortable until the sound finally stopped. The phonograph arm automatically lifted and retracted, lowering itself into position to start playing the record again.

After dinner, I helped Bill wash the dishes. When he walked me to my car, he put his arm around me and for a brief moment, held me close. Then he opened the car door and bowed.

"It was an honor having you over for dinner. I hope I see you soon.

" * * * * *

The next week I moved into my new apartment at the Barrington Plaza. I loved everything about it. A parking structure sat under the building. After parking my car I took an elevator to either the lobby, where the doorman stood, or directly to the eleventh floor. My apartment door stood just down the hall from the elevator.

Since my apartment had no bedroom, I searched for a sofa that would convert into a bed at night. Just down the street from the apartment I found a hotel supply shop with the perfect piece of furniture.

I eventually got a small round table for dining in the corner of the living room. I also sat and ate on a barstool in the kitchen, looking out over the city of Santa Monica and the ocean. I often saw a blue expanse with several sailboats in the distance, merging into the sky. I could also see a layer of brown smog on a polluted day.

My first night there I felt so tired I called down to an Italian restaurant on Wilshire and asked for a meal to be delivered. They brought it to the doorman, who delivered it to my apartment. It was like living in a hotel. I could order down for room service any time I wanted to. I felt very privileged and happy with this arrangement.

I also hired a locksmith to put a deadbolt on the door, since I would be gone for two months on the Dick Clark Caravan of Stars Tour. Finally ready to show the apartment to others, I telephoned Bill at work. The secretary put me on hold for a long time. Finally he took the call.

"Yeah?" he answered.

"I wanted to tell you that I'm completely moved in and wanted to invite you over for dinner tomorrow night. I thought it might be nice to share a meal before Dick and I leave for the Dick Clark tour."

"Listen, can I call you back?" Bill said in a stressed voice. "This isn't a good time to talk."

"Sure," I replied, my feelings slightly hurt. "If you want to call me tonight, I'll be home."

Bill hung up abruptly. What was going on with him? I waited all evening, but Bill didn't call. Several times I peered out my windows in the direction of his building. I could see the roof and front of his apartment, but not the carport behind where Bill parked his car. I finally gave up waiting and went to bed.

* * * * *

Two days passed. I tried to busy myself organizing the apartment and packing for the trip. I constantly listened for the phone to ring. Finally, around ten o'clock at night, the evening before we were scheduled to leave for New York, it did.

"Hello?" I answered expectantly.

"Sorry I took so long to call back," Bill stated. "I was in the middle of a major crisis."

He paused and I wondered if he was going to go into the details.

"I've been fired from William Morris," he flatly stated.

"What? How did that happen?"

Bill acted evasive. "Oh, it was over my servicing one of the William Morris lounge acts in San Diego. This male singer, who shall remain anonymous, wanted me to line up some girls for a party in his hotel room after the gig. I invited some chicks from the audience, but he called several other girls on his own.

"It turned out his girls were hookers and the whole group got busted. I bailed him out of jail but it hit the local papers there. The singer blamed me. He said I hired the call girls. Since this guy's a major star and brings in a considerable income, the William Morris Agency took his word over mine. Anyway, they fired me."

I struggled to find something comforting to say. "I'm really sorry that happened. You're a great agent. There's no one else there who even knows the rock and roll department."

I heard silence on the line. Finally Bill spoke. "I don't know what I'm going to do next. I need some time to regroup."

"Why don't you join the Dick Clark tour for awhile?" The idea flashed across my mind and out of my mouth before I had time to think. "You know who the acts are. You helped book them. You might make some personal contacts with both the acts and Dick Clark, and getting out of L.A. for awhile might give you a chance to analyze your situation."

"I'll give it some thought," Bill said. He didn't exactly jump for joy. "Right now I just want to go to bed." Then he hung up.

I lay in the dark for a long time, trying to sleep. I always felt unsettled the night before I left on tour and this time was no different. But this time I had Bill on my mind. Would he decide to fly east? And if he did, how would that work out with us? The clock said 2:00 a.m. before I finally drifted off.

Our Warner Brothers Records Publicity Shot, circa 1963.

Agent Bill Lee at the William Morris Agency in Beverly Hills.

Sonny and Cher and Dick and me backstage, circa 1963.

Backstage in dressing room at Pandora's Box.

CHAPTER FOURTEEN

The Dick Clark Caravan of Stars

I tried calling Bill at home the next morning, but he didn't answer his phone. I caught a cab to the airport. Our flight left Los Angeles International Airport mid morning and we arrived at La Guardia Airport on the evening of July 14th 1963.

As we drove from the airport to the city, from the cab window I stared at the slick, bustling New York streets, feeling lonely and empty. Dick and I hardly spoke in the cab.

I finally said, "I think it's going to rain."

Dick didn't bother answering. He stared out the window, absorbed in his own thoughts. I hadn't told him Bill no longer worked for the William Morris Agency.

I imagined Mom in California cooking dinner, my sisters racing through the house, filling the rooms with laughter. In my mind, Mom stood at the stove with a large spoon in her hand, stirring the gravy. The house radiated warmth and security. I felt lonely. What was Bill doing? Had he decided to join the Caravan of Stars? If so, when would he arrive? I felt insecure and jittery.

The cab driver suddenly spoke, "It already rained today. Tomorrow's going to be a scorcher." By then I'd forgotten I'd mentioned rain.

We checked into a large hotel on Fifth Avenue near Central Park. Both Dick and I decided to order room service in our separate rooms and go to bed early. I requested a 4:00 a.m. wakeup call.

* * * * *

The next morning, the phone jolted me awake. I fumbled into my clothes and groggily followed the bellboy to the lobby. Dick stood there, looking disoriented.

Morning arrived hot and muggy with the promise of more heat to come. I saw no signs of breakfast anywhere. The coffee shop sat dark and silent.

Dick and I pulled our bags out to the sidewalk. A bus sat at the curb, waiting in anticipation for passengers to climb aboard.

The early morning sun slowly appeared, sending tentative rays down between the cement buildings, warming the city streets and highlighting the walls and concrete.

Slowly, in various states of disarray, fifteen to twenty people started gathering. Everyone looked disheveled, dazed. Eventually the group grew to forty or fifty. Who were these people? I didn't recognize anyone. One thing became apparent. At least half the acts were missing. Someone said that the absent entertainers planned to fly directly to the rehearsal in Hull, Massachusetts.

An older gray-haired man and a man in a bus driver uniform appeared on the sidewalk.

"We're boarding in ten minutes," the older man shouted. "Make sure your bags are loaded under the bus before you board."

As the bus driver slid open the large aluminum side panel, revealing storage space under the vehicle, Dick hoisted our bags up and the driver helped shove them in.

Glancing down the street, I saw a food cart open for business. I dashed to the stand and bagged up cherries, grapes, a plum and a few apples. I never considered how long they had sat there, exposed to germs and grit on the grimy New York streets. It never occurred to me to wash the fruit before consumption.

I climbed inside the bus, taking a seat halfway down on the right. Talent agents roamed the bus aisles, shaking hands with singers. An attractive man noticed me and stuck out his hand.

"You must be Dee Dee," he said. "I'm Wally Amos, from the William Morris Agency. I'm handling rock and roll acts here in New York."

"It's nice to meet you," I responded, shaking his hand.

"Maybe I'll see you again sometime," he said over his shoulder as he followed the other agents off the bus.

Years later, Wally created Famous Amos Cookies. I did see him again when I found his face smiling at me from the front of a cookie package on a shelf at Ralph's Market.

* * * * *

After the bus driver secured the door and started the engine, the older man with gray hair stood in front, facing us.

"I'm Ed McAdams," he announced. "And I'm in charge of this bus. There are a few things you need to know. Each night we stay in a hotel, you will be given the departure time for the next morning. It is my job to make sure everyone is on the bus at the proper time. If you're late, we leave without you and you'll have to get to the next town on your own. We don't wait for anyone. Is that clear?"

Everyone nodded. I stared out the window, feeling excited but also jittery and jet lagged. There was no sign of Dick Clark. Was I really on the Caravan of Stars tour or had I just climbed on some strange tour bus for who knows where?

The bus started with a shudder and after half an hour of battling traffic, it pulled out of the city and onto a highway. I looked over my shoulder. The passengers either talked to their seatmates, stared out the window, or leaned against the backs of the seats and tried to sleep. Considering the early departure, I'm surprised anyone remained awake. I finally fell asleep leaning against the air-conditioned bus window.

Around noon I awoke. Everyone else slept. The bus droned along, a hypnotic, sleep-inducing sound. I reached into my brown paper bag and grabbed a handful of cherries, carefully eating around the pits. I followed that up with a plum and then an apple. Feeling slightly better, I leaned back in the seat and dozed off again, taking a long afternoon nap.

* * * * *

Later that day we pulled into a huge parking lot, exited the bus and entered an auditorium. The temperature inside felt chilly with the air conditioning cranked up full blast. A band sat on stage. I listened as Ed McAdams started calling up various acts to rehearse in some predetermined order. No one looked particularly happy. I just wanted the rehearsal to be over so we could check into a hotel and get some rest.

I sat on a folding chair, shaking with cold and stage fright.

"Man, I'm tired." Dick slouched into a chair next to mine. "I didn't sleep at all last night. I've never heard so much racket in my life. Doesn't the traffic noise in that city ever stop?"

"It's New York City. What did you expect? Anyway, the challenge now is how to sleep on a bus."

"You've got the charts, right?"

I patted the leather pouch sitting on the chair beside me. It held the musical scores to the three songs we planned to perform on the Dick Clark Caravan of Stars Tour.

"Where's Dick Clark, anyway?" Dick continued. "He obviously doesn't come to rehearsals."

"Why should he? All he needs is a list of the performers and the order they go on stage. He's just the announcer. He doesn't have to rehearse the band."

"I hate waiting," Dick said. "I'm going to walk around. If you decide to leave this area, don't go out of earshot of the stage. They might call us up at any moment."

Ed McAdams, his brow furrowed, walked on stage carrying a large black briefcase. He paced back and forth, scowling as one of the acts left the stage.

I thought back to what Bill told me about the formula Dick Clark used for his tours. He hired as many acts as he could afford, each scheduled to sing two or three songs, all backed by the same band.

Dick Clark acted as Master of Ceremonies in the shows, a role perfected from years of hosting American Bandstand. Often sixteen or seventeen acts appeared on the bill. The shows traveled the East Coast, touring sixty to ninety days non-stop. Would I be able to last months on the road, sitting in a bus for hours on end?

* * * * *

Then I heard Bill's voice in my head. Think how lucky you are to be booked on the Caravan of Stars Tour. Think how the tour will expose you to East Coast audiences and help promote future record sales.

I remembered how excited we'd been when Bill told us about the tour. Just the thought of Bill gave my heart a little ache.

I gave up watching the band rehearse and started wandering around the ballroom. The music stopped and over the microphone I heard "Dick and Dee Dee. You're next."

Dick and I bolted toward the stage from different parts of the hall. We climbed the stage together and shook hands with the band members. Dick passed out sheet music for "The Mountain's High," "Tell Me," and "Young and in Love".

The band acted serious and professional. They ran through our song charts quickly and perfectly. I noticed no one laughed or joked around.

It became intense. Standing there, pounding out the proper tempos with our feet and signaling breaks with our arms, my head throbbed. I attributed it to the fact I'd eaten no real food all day, except the bag of fruit.

The rehearsal took complete concentration. This was our only chance to get the music right before the evening performance. I felt exhausted. Dick and I sat on electric amplifiers and tried to make it through our last song. The band finally indicated that they knew the material, and we left the stage.

* * * * *

By evening I'd developed a major headache and my stomach felt queasy. I remained in a solemn mood, exhausted and jet lagged. The girls' dressing room felt unbearably hot. Cigarette smoke drifted listlessly around the light bulbs. I crossed the room and opened a window.

The Crystals and Paula (of Paul and Paula) sat on an ancient sofa, laughing and joking about a former show they'd worked on together in New York. I didn't know a soul, and no one introduced themselves. I felt awkward and out of place.

Ed McAdams hammered on the door.

"Dick and Dee Dee," he bellowed. "Let's go."

I joined Dick in the hallway, a forced smile on my face. Suddenly, we both froze. Between us and the stage were approximately six thousand kids, dancing wildly. Whoever had designed the auditorium apparently forgot to place the dressing rooms near the stage! Clearing my throat to address Ed, I yelled, "How do you suggest we get through the crowd?"

Ed grabbed my arm. "Police escorts. Here they come now. Just follow the men in uniform. Don't stop for anything, either coming or going. And whatever you do, no autographs. Just keep moving."

Then he turned to the police. "Alright, boys, move 'em out."

Surrounded by police we crept forward. Dick gently shoved me from behind.

"Keep up with the bodyguards," he shouted.

I gripped my newly purchased tambourine like a mighty shield. Mostly, the kids ignored us. Flushed and covered with perspiration, they appeared to be in a trance. They danced wildly, ignoring the police pushing us through the crowd.

At the stage steps, Dick turned to the police officers.

"Thanks for the escort. But I really think we can get back on our own."

One officer's eyes widened. "Are you sure? This crowd gets pretty wild."

Dick nodded.

"Alright," the other officer yawned. "Whatever you say. That'll give us a chance to get some coffee."

We stood at the bottom of the stage steps. After Ruby and the Romantics took their final bows, Dick Clark entered from the opposite side of the stage. He walked toward the audience and stood before the single microphone.

He looks incredible, I thought. He looks exactly like he did on American Bandstand when I was in high school. He never ages!

His voice sounded as familiar as an old friend's. I felt a chill of excitement run down my spine.

"A while ago you heard a boy/girl duo that came from Texas. You remember that Paul was extremely tall and Paula was just a short little thing. This next couple you're about to see are both tall. They hail from Santa Monica, California and record under the name Dick and Dee Dee!"

Perspiring, my hands dropped the tambourine. I bent over to recover it and the spotlight hit me. All I could do was smile foolishly and straighten up. I climbed the stairs and walked rapidly to the microphone, followed by Dick. The crowd gave polite applause. Then silence. Everyone crowded around the stage, waiting in anticipation. "'The Mountain's High is first,'" Dick hissed to the band.

The group shuffled through their sheet music, finally finding the proper chart and launched into the introduction. We started to sing the song.

In the middle of the first verse a girl in the front row reached up and grabbed Dick's ankle. He looked startled. The girl grinned and tightened her grip. Dick solved the problem by moving back fast, breaking her hold. I backed up too, landing directly on the bass player's foot with my spike heel. He moaned, but didn't miss a note.

We finished the first song and started to sing "Tell Me." A girl standing to one side screamed, and then she burst into tears. Bending down to see if she was alright, I banged my head on the microphone. The loud crash resounded throughout the ballroom. The kids in front started laughing. I bravely smiled, pretending I had done that on purpose.

Somehow we made it through "Young and in Love," managed a bow, and exited. Before our performance, the crowd hadn't recognized us, but now they knew who we were. With the police escorts nowhere to be seen, Dick grabbed my arm as we launched into the sea of excited fans.

Someone jabbed me in the arm with a pen, trying to get an autograph. Dick turned pale. I could barely breathe. I stumbled and felt my shoe fall off, but there was no way to bend down and retrieve it.

Someone accidentally hit Dick in the head with a hot dog, splattering his brown hair with mustard and relish. Some of the mustard dripped onto his shirt. I clutched his arm, afraid the crowd might separate us. After what seemed like endless hours, we finally fought our way back to the dressing rooms.

"You could have been injured!" Ed McAdams shouted. "Next time, do what I tell you."

I gathered my belongings and hobbled to the bus on my remaining shoe. I felt depressed. Why did Ed have to yell at us? We didn't deserve that! I sat in the dark, listening to the muffled music coming from the auditorium. Finally, the rest of the cast staggered to the bus and we drove to a hotel.

* * * * *

I awakened in the dark to a jangling telephone. It wouldn't let me sleep. It rang and rang. I finally groped for the receiver.

"Good morning," the hotel operator said. "It's your 6:00 a.m. wake up call." "It's a mistake," I croaked. "I didn't leave a wake up call."

Her voice lowered, taking on a confidential tone. "It was Dick Clark himself. He told me to be sure to call everyone on the tour and tell them that the buses are leaving promptly at 7:00 a.m."

I dropped the receiver on the floor. We'd checked into the hotel sometime after 1:00 a.m. What were they thinking? We'd only had four hours' sleep!

Somehow I threw on some clothes, splashed cold water on my face and dragged my bag down through the lobby to the street. Two buses sat by the curb. Ed McAdams faced the crowd of exhausted singers, a black briefcase chained and handcuffed to one wrist.

"If you're in the band, or if you perform in the first half of the show, get on bus number one. Dick Clark's in charge of that bus. If you perform after the intermission in the second half of the show, you ride bus number two. I'm in charge of that bus. Alright, let's go."

Dick and I climbed aboard Bus Two.

As soon as Dick Clark climbed aboard Bus One, the vehicle pulled out, but apparently three people remained missing from Bus Two. The Orlons finally dragged out of their rooms fifteen minutes later. Rosetta was the first to climb onto the bus.

"Shit," she said. "I barely got to bed. What's with this?"

Ed waited until the girls were seated.

"I'm only going to say this once more," he said, "so you better listen up.

" One of the singers in the rear of the bus dropped an apple and it rolled down the aisle. After it was retrieved, with a bite out of it, Ed continued.

"For those of you who were not on this bus yesterday, I'm saying this one last time. The bus rolls on schedule. Do I make myself clear? If you're not on it, you'll be left behind."

"That sucks," Rosetta muttered.

"That's 'cuz you don't know how to get your tired ass out of bed," another Orlon replied.

Everyone laughed. Ed sank into the front seat, his black briefcase still chained to his arm, and the bus roared into motion. I presumed the briefcase held box office revenues. For the rest of the tour, Ed carried that briefcase locked to his arm at all times.

* * * * *

We drove all morning and most of the afternoon. No one had any idea what our destination was. Mostly people quietly talked, tried to sleep or read books or magazines.

I sat by the window, watching trees rush by the side of the turnpike. The bus tires hissed and the air conditioning created moisture on the bottom of the glass windows. Dick sat next to me, reading a magazine.

We drove for hours, covering hundreds of miles. We eventually discovered our bus driver erroneously headed in the wrong direction. What was supposed to be a three-hour ride turned into a twelve-hour marathon. Around seven-thirty that evening, after we passed a "You Are Entering Johnson City" sign, a policeman flagged us over. Ed worried about a speeding ticket, but the officer had something else on his mind.

"Where have you been?" the policeman shouted. "The show promoter called the highway patrol to find you. Is the other bus following you?"

Ed turned pale. "You mean the other bus isn't here? They started way before we did."

We arrived at the packed auditorium in Johnson City, New York, at ten minutes to eight. The only way to reach the dressing rooms was to walk across the stage to the other side. There were no curtains.

As we staggered across the wooden platform, dragging luggage, in wrinkled traveling clothes, aching from sitting on bus seats all day, blurry eyed and half starved, the crowd rose from their seats and cheered. I felt surprised and relieved by their support.

At the last moment, while we swiftly changed clothes, Bus One pulled into the parking lot. When someone announced the show's start would be delayed so the musicians could set up, everyone yelled and applauded. The audience sat patiently for over half an hour waiting for the show to begin.

It must have been one hundred degrees in the auditorium. The heat felt insufferable. To keep the acts as comfortable as possible, Dick Clark arranged for folding chairs to be placed outside where we could get fresh air. We sat several feet from the rear entrance so we could hear the acts scheduled to perform next.

I slumped against the hard wooden slats of the folding chair, listening to the acts coming and going. In the distance I heard Ruby and the Romantics singing, "Our day will come, and we'll have everything." In spite of the heat, a chill rose in me, inexplicable in the warm night. A nearby police officer smiled at me as he waved away an autograph seeker that tried to get close.

Then intermission arrived. The back door to the auditorium burst open and the musicians staggered out. They looked like they might pass out. Their faces glowed in various shades of red and perspiration poured off their bodies.

I heard a shout and turned to see several men appear at the door, caring an unconscious girl by her arms and legs. She was placed on a blanket right at my feet.

She slowly opened her eyes and cried, "My hands are paralyzed. I can't move them."

"You'll be alright," I said to her in what I hoped was a soothing voice.

Shortly an ambulance arrived and the attendants carried the girl away on a stretcher.

"What happened to her?" I asked the girl's distraught friend.

"She was so excited to see the show that she got out of her seat and crowded forward near the stage. I was right with her. But she suddenly turned pale and said she couldn't breathe. We were trapped in the crowd. It was impossible to move in any direction.

"There was very little air. Finally, she just fell to the floor. The kids surrounding her didn't notice she was on the ground. In fact, several people stepped on her to see over the crowd. When they finally discovered her, she was in a state of shock."

More shouts interrupted her dialogue. This time the men brought out two more heat exhaustion victims and placed them on blankets on the ground.

"This is the gig from hell," one of the musicians muttered.

"Intermission is over." Dick Clark's voice boomed forth from the stage door. "Come on, guys. The Crystals are next."

I listened as the show started up again. The Crystals launched into "Da Doo Ron Ron." a song about someone named Bill.

Bill...I wanted to tell Bill about the tour he'd booked us on, that we were exhausted, hot and hungry, that this wasn't the great experience we'd expected. But there was no telephone in sight. He probably wouldn't be there anyway.

I took a deep breath, watched the stage door and waited for Dick Clark to call us on stage.

* * * * *

After an all night bus ride, we rolled into Syracuse, New York the following morning and checked into a hotel. I decided to have my hair washed and trimmed at the hotel beauty parlor before sleeping the rest of the day.

One minute I sat under the dryer. The next minute the room started to spin and I collapsed on the floor. The beauticians crowded around me, shouting, "Get back! Give her room to breathe! Someone call a doctor!"

I heard myself gasp, "Find someone from the Dick Clark tour. We're staying at the hotel." Then I blacked out.

The next thing I knew I was whizzing through the hotel lobby in a wheel chair. Confused, I turned to see who was pushing me. It was Ray Hildebrand (Paul of Paul and Paula). I felt a tremendous pain in my stomach.

"What's happening to me?" I asked Ray.

He didn't answer. I started laughing, then began to sob uncontrollably. The world spun dangerously. Ray put his hand on my shoulder.

They took me in a cab to a specialist.

The doctor examined me and said, "Young lady, you've got an acute case of stomach virus, probably combined with food poisoning. Did you eat anything unusual?"

I thought for a moment. "The day before yesterday I ate some fruit off a stand in New York City."

The doctor looked perplexed. "I'm not sure bad fruit would stay in your system this long, although God knows what poisons they sprayed on it. In any event, you need medication and rest."

He gave me a hypodermic in the arm and all went foggy. I vaguely remember the taxi ride back to the hotel. The hotel bellman helped Ray wheel me to my room. Ray picked up the telephone and tried calling Dick St. John, but there was no answer. He and the bell man helped me from the wheelchair to the bed. I climbed in, fully clothed.

I must have slept a long time, for it was dark when I opened my eyes. Dick and Bill sat in chairs by the window. I stared at them and then struggled to sit up. "Bill!" I whispered. "How did you get here?"

"Don't move," he said kindly. "You need plenty of rest." He gently pushed me back into the billowing pillow.

Bill quietly said, "In L.A., after you suggested I join the tour, I thought about it and decided you were right. I made plans to join you in Syracuse. Dick St. John knew about it. But I wanted to surprise you. Anyway, now that you're sick, I'm glad I'm here to help."

I struggled to move again. "I have to get up. It's almost time for the show."

Bill and Dick exchanged glances.

Dick smiled. "You're not singing tonight. I'm going on alone."

I tried desperately to comprehend what he said. I pulled myself off the pillow. My hair flopped in my face. Things didn't make much sense. Suddenly the whole memory of fainting in the beauty parlor and visiting the doctor rolled back over me. My eyes filled with tears.

Bill sat beside me on the bed. He glanced into my eyes with a caring, concerned look on his face. I didn't have time to sort out my emotions, but it felt good having him by my side.

"Dick volunteered to go on stage alone for as many nights as it takes for you to recover," Bill said. "You need to relax. Try not to worry. Everything's been taken care of. All you have to do is get better."

I tried to move and again felt a stabbing pain in my stomach.

I groaned, "What about tomorrow when the tour leaves for the next town? What if I'm not well enough to get on the bus?"

"Let's worry about that tomorrow," Bill replied. "Here. Take this medication and then try to sip some of this soup."

I obediently swallowed the pill, washing it down with a glass of water that Bill handed me.

"We're going to leave you here to sleep," Bill said. "I'm going with Dick to the show to make sure things work out alright there. The door will lock automatically behind us, so you don't have to worry about getting out of bed."

He paused and looked at me lovingly. "I hope you feel better," he added, bending over and kissing my forehead.

I watched them leave the room, my eyes brimming with tears. I slowly sipped the soup. It did taste good. The pain in my stomach abated slightly.

About ten minutes later I heard a knock at the door. Maybe Bill forgot his key. I swung my legs over the side of the bed and tried to stand. Lightheaded and shaky,

I slowly made my way to the door and opened it. There stood Dick Clark.

I stared at him, speechless and awestruck. All those years of watching American Bandstand turned him into a hero. And there he stood in the hallway, live and in person, a concerned look on his face.

"I just wanted to see how you were doing," Dick remarked. "I hope you feel better, Dee Dee. Don't worry about the show. Dick St. John will do a good job."

"I know," I replied. "Thank you for your concern. I think the worst is over."

We both tried to laugh. I thanked him again and crept back to bed. I had no problem sleeping that night.

* * * * *

The next morning I dressed rapidly, weak but determined. I called a bell hop to carry my bags down to the lobby and found, to my surprise, I was the first one there. As the acts started gathering one by one, Lou Christie, male singer of the hit record "Lightening Strikes," came up to me.

"We heard you were sick," he said. "Are you feeling better?"

I nodded. Dick and Bill appeared, startled to see me.

"This is not a good idea," Bill said.

Bill wore a button-down blue shirt and khaki pants. His hair appeared perfectly groomed. I suddenly became aware of how weak I felt.

"What if you have a relapse on the bus?" Bill said. "There would be no medical help available. Why don't you stay here a few more days, and we can make arrangements for you to rejoin the tour."

"I'm going to be fine," I insisted, feeling annoyed. "I just have to take it easy, which I can certainly do on the bus. The important thing is to watch what I eat and take the medication."

I suddenly felt restless and abruptly changed the subject.

"So, how did the show go last night?"

"Dick sounded great!" Bill enthused. "You would have been proud of him. When Dick Clark made an announcement that you were ill, the crowd acted tremendously supportive."

I felt sad that I hadn't been part of the action, but smiled, vowing to get better and continue on the tour.

"The buses are here," Ed McAdams shouted.

All the performers started crowding toward the hotel exit. I grabbed my cosmetic bag and purse and moved forward. Bill grabbed my arm.

"There's still time to go back to your room," he said. "I really think you're putting yourself at risk."

"I'm going on the bus," I muttered. Determined to have my way, I pulled free from Bill's grasp.

My head hurt and I started to feel lightheaded, but I looked Bill in the eye. "I really appreciate your concern, but my place is with the tour. I'll be okay."

Before he could say anything else, I dragged myself outside and climbed up the bus steps, flopping into a seat near the front. Bill and Dick followed me. They sat in the seat directly behind mine, leaving me the entire seat to myself.

"You can stretch out and sleep," Bill said. His voice boomed over the seat from behind.

I nodded and without turning around, pulled my legs up and leaned against the bus window. When the Dick Clark Caravan of Stars Tour pulled out of the city, I continued on with the performers.

* * * * *

We headed for Canada. By the end of the first day, after I appeared stable, Bill stopped worrying about me. In fact, when Dick Clark told him he could use some help organizing the first bus, Bill transferred to Bus Number One. I couldn't believe it. He'd barely arrived and now he was, for all intents and purposes, gone. But I told myself it was important for Bill to get to know Dick Clark and to find a new career direction.

Two days later, our buses reached Montreal, Canada. We sang outdoors in Fauscher Stadium to a crowd of over twelve thousand people. We broke all attendance records at the stadium to date. In fact, a package tour hadn't drawn so many people since Elvis gave a concert there in the 'fifties.

After our concert in Montreal, I climbed aboard Bus Number Two for yet another all-night bus ride. Since no one ever thought to clean the buses, soft drink cans and bottles rolled up and down the aisle every time the bus turned a corner or went up a hill. The clanking racket only added to whatever noise the singers in back were making.

Tonight, from the back of the bus came screams and shouts. Now in excellent spirits, the group in back decided to party. I looked at my watch and groaned. It was after three in the morning.

* * * * *

When the buses stopped for gas at 4 am, Bill left Bus One and climbed back up the metal steps of Bus Two, waving at Ed McAdams in passing.

He slid into the seat beside me. "How are you doing?"

I smiled and gestured toward the rear of the bus. "Oh, my stomach pains are completely gone. The problem now is lack of sleep. Looks like they're into all-night partying back there."

Jerry, one of the Dovells, turned in his seat and yelled over his left shoulder, "Hey youse guys, how about toning it down a little? Some of us are trying to sleep." There were jeers and laughter.

A voice yelled back, "If you don't like it, leave the bus." The uproarious laughter, yelling and shouting continued.

Bill leaned over and tapped me on the shoulder. "How does flying grab you?"

"What?"

He pointed to the rear of the bus. "They're going to keep this up all night. You need rest. You should fly."

"Fly? What planes are available at this hour?" I asked. "Are we even near an airport?"

"We will be shortly."

Bill walked to the front of the bus and talked to Ed McAdams and the bus driver. Several miles down the road, the bus pulled off the highway at an airport exit and we pulled up in front of Canadian Airlines.

"Who wants to fly?" Bill asked the sleepy singers in the front of the bus. Two of the Dovells (Mike and Jerry) and Dick and I immediately stood. I grabbed my purse and makeup bag from the overhead rack.

Bill told the driver, "Leave their luggage on the bus. Just deliver it to them at the hotel in the next city."

He picked up his small bag, the only one he'd brought on the trip, and climbed off the bus, followed by the four of us. Glancing back at bus Number Two the last thing I saw were singers hanging from the back windows shouting, "Defectors!" and throwing peanuts at us.

Inside the airport Bill pulled me aside.

"We haven't had much time to be alone together since the tour started, but I need to talk to you. I have to go back to L.A. and since we're at an airport, I might as well fly out of here tonight."

I felt a cold chill in my stomach. I wasn't sure I'd heard him correctly. He was leaving? He'd only been on tour four or five days, most of that time spent on Bus One.

"You're going now?" I asked. "Why?"

"Well, as you know, I've been helping Dick Clark with some matters on Bus One. I also got to know some of the acts on this tour. I've done a lot of soul searching and decided that I'm going to become a personal manager.

"I've already talked to Paul and Paula and the Dovells. They want to sign with me. I'd like to sign Dick and Dee Dee, too." Bill paused and glanced at me expectantly.

I felt hurt and confused that Bill decided to leave the tour so suddenly. In my weakened, tired condition, none of this made any sense. I suddenly felt scared. Did Bill and I even have a relationship? I couldn't understand his attempts at closeness and then his withdrawal and distancing from me. And now he was saying he wanted to manage Dick and me?

"Have you talked to Dick about this?"

"Of course. He said signing with me would be the greatest thing that could happen to your act. But what do you think?"

I experienced conflicting thoughts and emotions. From a practical standpoint, Dick and Dee Dee needed a personal manager, and with all Bill's experience and contacts, he would be perfect. On the other hand, I was sorry this took a priority over our personal relationship.

Bill waited, expectantly.

"You'd be a great manager," I said, believing it to be true.

Bill grinned. "I'm going back to LA to formally establish my management business. For the time being, I'm going to turn my apartment into an office. I want to get everything organized and ready to go. Then, I'll be back to join you on tour for the last two weeks."

That would be at least a month from now, maybe longer. Feeling neglected and abandoned, my emotions started to deaden. My body felt frozen and my mind went blank.

We heard a voice over the loudspeaker announce our flight to Toronto, and everyone gave Bill a goodbye hug. When he hugged me, he didn't look me in the eye.

Dick slapped him on the back and said, "Take care. We know we're in good hands."

As we walked down the corridor to board our plane, we left Bill standing alone in the airport. When I turned to look back he gave a slight nod of his head. He appeared sad. Maybe this was hard for him too. I knew it was terrible for me. Bill had been there when I was sick, he'd taken charge of the buses, and he was a vital part of the Dick Clark Caravan of Stars Tour. How would I survive the rest of the tour without him nearby?

* * * * *

We had no maps in front of us and even if we had, it would have done little good. On a trip such as ours, where most days and nights were spent on the bus, the highway stretched endlessly. Our only stops were to use the rest rooms and refuel the buses at gas stations, or to grab a quick meal at Howard Johnson's on the turnpike.

Our schedule ran something like this: one night we would check into a hotel and sleep there after the show. The following morning we would drive all day to the next town and perform that evening. Then after the show, we would climb back on the bus and drive all night and part of the next day to the next town, arriving sometime in the late afternoon. We'd check into a hotel, sleep a few hours, perform that night, and climb on the bus afterward for another all-night bus ride.

We headed south toward Raleigh, South Carolina. I no longer slept through the night. Often I'd wake several hours after falling asleep, and stare out the bus window as the dark silhouettes of trees and houses rolled past. Life no longer presented a sense of time or place. The bus interior remained my only contact with day-to-day reality.

My personal world became a bus. I imagined we would drive forever, going in circles, going nowhere. Dawn would come with pale streaks across the sky and then I would think of Bill and wonder if and when he might return to the tour. Every time I called him from a hotel, his answering service picked up. Where was he?

Just when I stopped thinking about him, he reappeared. One night, I looked down from the stage and there he stood, grinning. I almost forgot the lyrics to the song. My heart started beating rapidly and I had trouble breathing. I smiled as genuine joy filled my being. After the show, Bill gave me a big hug. He climbed on the bus, sliding into the vacant seat next to me.

"I came back early," he announced. "Things are going great. I've got my office set up and I'm also working on booking a tour of the Midwest. Of course, that tour includes Dick and Dee Dee." The joy surging through my being surprised me with its intensity.

"How long are you here for?" I asked, still unable to believe he had suddenly reappeared.

"I'm here for the rest of the tour. Dick Clark wants me to handle Bus Number Two. Ed McAdams is going to ride with him in Bus Number One."

This was, indeed, great news. I gave Bill a big smile.

"You'd better watch out," I told him. "Bus Two is pretty rowdy."

"People usually do what I ask them to do," Bill said. I felt confident that they did.

* * * * *

Filled with relentless heat, August in the south scorched. The air-conditioned bus offered some refuge. We traveled unattached to the outside world, as silent as statues, watching cities and towns roll by. I noticed several Confederate flags hanging in store windows and shivered. Memories of the Texas tour flooded back.

Bill commandeered Bus Two with authority. The singers listened to him. One afternoon, as we left North Carolina and entered Virginia, suddenly and inexplicably our bus broke down. The driver maneuvered it off the road and parked on a green knoll. Bill looked at the roadside tavern located at the bottom of the hill.

"I'm going down there to call for a replacement bus," Bill announced to the singers. "Everyone stay put until I return."

"Can I go with you?" I asked. "I need to use the restroom."

Bill thought for a moment, and then smiled.

"Okay. Let's go."

Our black bus driver, Martin, Bill and I marched down the hill and entered the tavern to call the bus company. Several large guys playing pool, faces flushed from the heat and alcohol, turned and stared. I froze. Were we back in a segregated state again?

As our driver entered a hallway to use the pay phone, the waitress left her position behind the counter and walked to the window, looking up at the grassy knoll and parked bus. By then everyone had climbed off the vehicle and stood on the grass. About sixty percent of the singers on Bus Two were black.

"Y'all are freedom riders," she stated with scorn, slapping her dishrag on the counter. She glared at me. "I just want to know one thing. What are ya'll doing hanging out with a bunch of colored folk?"

"They're not freedom riders, they're singers," Bill replied. "And I'm managing the bus. We're part of the Dick Clark Tour. Have you ever heard of Dick Clark?"

"Go on!" she exclaimed. "I can't believe that. If it was the Dick Clark Tour, Dick would be there." She peered out the window again. "Nope, he ain't there, that's for sure."

She paused and looked at Bill, squinting and pursing her lips. "I know what you are. You can't fool me. Even if my Ma says I'm so dumb I can't pound sand in a rat's hole, I'm still smart enough to know freedom riders when I see 'em. You know folks around here don't cater much to freedom riders."

I glanced around and noticed the guys in the back stopped playing pool and huddled in the doorway, pool cues in hand, listening to the conversation.

Bill walked down the hall to the pay phone. The bus driver hung up. "They're sending another bus," he told Bill. "They said it would take about an hour."

"We can't wait in here," Bill replied, looking over his shoulder. "Let's go back to the bus."

As we climbed the hill and got within earshot of the singers, Bill shouted to the group assembled on the grass. "They're sending another bus. But in the meantime, we need to get back on board and wait inside."

"No way," one of the guys complained. "The air conditioning is off. It's hotter than hell in there."

"Well, people are a little uptight in the tavern. We don't want any trouble."

One of the female singers from Philadelphia put her hands on her hips. "Well isn't that too bad. Hey, man, I'm hot, hungry and tired and I've gotta go pee. I'm going down there to use their bathroom."

Bill panicked. "No, don't do that. You need to wait until I go down and talk to them about that."

"Damn!," the singer said.

When Bill returned to the tavern to negotiate bathroom trips for the singers, I trudged after him. We noticed with relief that the men now ignored us, racking up pool shots with clicking intensity.

"Look, the bus bathroom is broken," Bill told the waitress. "I'd like the singers to come use this bathroom, but I'll send them down in small groups so they don't overwhelm the place."

"Did y'all here that?" the waitress shouted. "These here freedom riders wants to use our bathroom."

She turned to Bill. "Because I'm a kind, God loving citizen, I'm gonna let 'em use the bathroom. But they can't come into the restaurant or pool hall." Bill and I returned to the bus with the news.

Bill told the performers to stay in groups of two or three and take turns walking down the hill. He also reminded them to stay out of the restaurant area. Several people complained, but no one challenged him.

In groups of two or three, performers walked down to the tavern, used the restroom and returned to the bus. Two hours passed. The sun's heat remained oppressive and unrelenting.

One of the band members said, "I'd rather die in a sauna than from sun stroke." He climbed back on the sweltering bus.

"I can't imagine what's taking the replacement driver so long. I'm going down to the tavern to call again," Bill said. He glanced at me. "Come with me. I may need your help."

We walked down the hill and cautiously entered the restaurant. A large grill sat behind the counter, where several hamburgers sizzled. A counter and bar stools faced the grill. An open door led to the attached pool hall. The men stared at Bill and me as we walked in. All talking ceased.

"Listen," Bill pleaded to the waitress. "We're waiting for another bus to arrive but in the meantime, everyone is starving. Can I order some hamburgers to go?"

The waitress/cook put her hands on her hips and chomped on her gum. "Now you ain't foolish enough to think I'm gonna cook food for all them folk." She gestured out the window toward the bus. "What do you think this place is, a damn freedom rider rest stop?"

"What if I cook the food," I heard myself say. I was as surprised as everyone else when that popped out of my mouth.

The waitress looked at me like I was insane. "You want to cook the food?" She laughed. "That's rich. Be my guest. But we're going to charge you plenty. Prices have just doubled."

I glanced at Bill wondering what to do.

"Go ahead. Cook the food Dee Dee," Bill instructed in a calm, low voice.

I cautiously walked around the counter and faced the grill. I remembered what to do from my days at Neenie's Famous Weenies, where I worked when I was sixteen. I slapped hamburger after hamburger on the grill, watched while they sizzled, then flipped them over with the spatula. Bill came behind the counter. "I'll help you," he said in a low voice. "It will take less time."

We set up an assembly line. He lined up forty hamburger buns, tops and bottoms face up, and slapped mayonnaise and ketchup on them. We worked quickly and efficiently. When the burgers were cooked, we wrapped them in wax paper and stuck toothpicks through them to hold the buns in place. Bill started stuffing the burgers into large paper bags the waitress threw in our direction.

"Put some chips in too," he muttered.

I took handfuls of chips and tossed them into the bag. The waitress frantically scrawled on her pad, adding figures.

"What about drinks?" I asked Bill.

The waitress's eyes widened in disbelief. "Now, how are y'all gonna carry forty cups of Coke up that big ole hill. Any fool could see that would take you 'bout twenty trips." We heard a shout and looked behind us.

"Well, ah declare!" One of the men staggered out of the pool room and approached Bill. "Now ah seen just about eva 'thing—a white man carrying food to some niggas on a bus. Where ah come from, ain't nothing like that gonna happen."

Bill pulled two one-hundred dollar bills from his wallet and handed them to the waitress.

"Keep the change. Come on, Dee Dee, let's go."

The man stood blocking the hallway, but we pushed past him, hauling the bags of hamburgers in our arms.

I slowly climbed the hill, one foot in front of the other. I felt danger from behind, as if someone held a gun to my back. I didn't dare turn around.

"Just act normal," Bill said. "Walk slowly and don't forget to breathe."

As we staggered up the hill a cheer came from the group assembled on top. We sat on the grass in the small amount of shade the bus created and opened the bags of food.

Down below, two cars pulled up and parked next to the tavern. Six guys got out of each car and went inside. A short time later, they came back out, accompanied by the men who had been playing pool. The men still held their pool cues. About eight men stood at the bottom of the hill glowering up at us.

One of the Orlons began to sing, with attitude, "Mine Eyes Have Seen the Glory of the Coming of The Lord."

Another female singer started screaming. "I'm from Philly. I have a hit record. I don't need to take bullshit from anyone."

"Oh my God," Bill muttered.

The men started up the hill just as four highway patrol cars pulled up behind our disabled bus. The officers jumped from their patrol cars, ordered us back on the bus and had the driver close the door. When the men holding pool cues saw the police, they reluctantly retreated to their cars and drove off.

"Y'all know better than to cause this kind of trouble around here," one of the officers said to Bill. "Y'all better get going as soon as you can."

Fortunately, within another ten minutes, the replacement bus arrived.

* * * * *

Dick Clark heard about our bus experience from Bill and approached me after the show.

"I heard you made hamburgers for everyone." I nodded.

Dick just shook his head. "Sometimes we have to overlook the bad things and just get the job done. You did well."

His praise meant a lot to me. Dick Clark strived for perfection and I was honored that he appreciated my efforts. I carried his praise within me like a warm blanket next to my heart.

* * * * *

After four particularly difficult days of driving all day and night, Dick Clark took pity on us. When we finally got to a town where we could check into a hotel, he decided to throw a huge party for us after the show.

Reserving a small banquet hall in the hotel, Dick turned the party into a major production. Dick Clark had us secretly draw names of the other performers on our tour from a hat. We were to get up on a makeshift stage with the band backing us and perform at the party as if we were that person whose name we drew (some males drew females, and vice versa). To stand up there by myself and sing a song I hardly knew filled me with major anxiety.

I drew the name of Barbara Lewis. Her hit single "Hello Stranger" topped the charts at that time. I would have been better if I'd picked the name of someone in a group, because the thought of all eyes on me while I attempted to sing "Hello Stranger," as a solo act made my body go numb.

Much laughter and conspiracy buzzed around the hotel. Everyone created costumes, fashioned from hotel bath towels and whatever garb could be borrowed, like women's wigs and heels. The party plans consumed everyone. An excitement and joyful anticipation filled the singers and the exhaustion and fatigue from the all-night bus rides momentarily faded away.

As we sang at the local arena that evening, I stood in the wings watching Barbara Lewis perform, willing myself to memorize her song by heart. When Dick and I went on stage and sang "The Mountain's High," I could hardly get through the song, as the dread about my upcoming party performance mounted.

That night the acts raucously joined in with the festivities. The hotel provided a catered meal and unlimited alcohol. I felt much too nervous to eat.

Finally Dick Clark tapped his knife against a glass.

"Alright, everyone, listen. We're going to start the show now. I'd like to ask the band to come up and take their places. We'll follow the same order we do every night. I'll announce each act and whoever drew that name will come up and perform instead. LET THE SHOW BEGIN ."

The band staggered to their instruments as the singers yelled "Way to go!" and "Yeahhhhh!"

The first act called up was the Crystals. Instead of the usual girls who made up the group, four males, including one of the Dovells and Dick St. John raced up. Several of them had borrowed women's wigs and they all wore lipstick. They were dressed in skirts, fashioned from towels wrapped around them, secured by safety pins. I laughed until tears ran down my face.

The band launched into the introduction to "Da Doo Ron Ron." A member of the all male Dovells acted as the lead singer of the Crystals. He forgot most of the words, but filled out the verses singing, "La, La, La," in a loud, drunken voice. The song sounded completely out of his range, but he managed to get through it in a falsetto voice.

"Yeah, way to go, hooo, hooo!" the crowd yelled.

Dick Clark announced each act, until I heard "Barbara Lewis." I walked to the microphone, grabbed it with one hand and sang in a throaty voice, "Hello Stranger." Everyone yelled and screamed, drowning me out.

I saw Dick St. John leaning against a wall, laughing at me. I felt all confidence leave, and started to shrink inside myself, wanting to be invisible. But I managed to forge ahead, batting my eyelashes and "camping" it up. When I finished everyone roared their approval.

Dick Clark recorded our little show and, before the tour ended, gave each performer a reel-to-reel tape to play on our home recorders. When I finally listened to it I realized how small and frightened my voice sounded. But it really didn't matter, because everyone yelled and cheered me on. Somehow, I'd survived.

* * * * *

In late August, after numerous overnight bus rides, our buses finally pulled into New York City. Most of the group appeared in bad shape. All everyone wanted to do was go home, soak in a tub, climb in bed and collapse for a few weeks.

It's strange how some tours end. Sometimes people never say goodbye, they just drift away. One minute people are grabbing their bags from the luggage racks and the next minute they disappear.

Dick Clark and Ed McAdams vanished into a nearby hotel. Dick, Bill and I caught a cab for the airport and boarded a jet heading back to Los Angeles. Bill didn't say much during the return flight. He kept reading a mystery novel he'd picked up in the airport. I sat next to him, wired but tired.

When I finally got back to the Barrington Plaza, I wearily rode the elevator up to my apartment and opened the door. Things were exactly as I had left them. Still wearing my traveling clothes, I pulled out the duo bed, climbed on top of it and slept for fourteen hours. Home, sweet home.

CHAPTER FIFTEEN

Speechless Dick

Bill flung open the door to his apartment and Dick and I entered. Nothing looked familiar. Book shelves lined one wall. Copies of Billboard and Cashbox magazines littered the coffee table. A huge desk sat by the window with two telephones perched on it. Bill's sofas and chairs faced the desk. Bill's living room now resembled his office at the William Morris Agency.

"Sit down," Bill said, waiving his hand toward the sofa. He sank into his desk chair and picked up a folder. "Before I rejoined the Clark tour, this is what I worked on for you two. I'm trying to get you work locally, to fill in the time before you take off for another extended period."

I noticed how focused Bill appeared, totally concentrating, all business. Did we even have a personal relationship?

"Where would we work locally, in clubs?" Dick asked.

Bill smiled. "I've booked you with an up and coming local surf band, The Beach Boys. Their first record is climbing the charts so they have some name value as an opening act. They're also going to back you."

He addressed Dick's question. "No, not clubs, you're going to play high school assemblies."

I smiled as I remembered eating dinner at Bill's house and our conversation about the Beach Boys. How many months ago was that? And now that their record had started to sell, I guess Bill liked them after all.

"The assemblies are in the daytime. You'll perform with the Beach Boys once or twice a week, until we run out of high schools in Los Angeles. Anyway, this will keep you busy for awhile, but will also give you free time for recording."

Bill shuffled through some more papers on his desk, finally handing over a list to Dick and me. "Here's a schedule. Your first show is in a week."

"Wait a minute," Dick said, studying the sheet of paper. "There's no rehearsal time on here. We can't perform with a band that has never played our music before." Bill looked startled, as if he hadn't anticipated a rehearsal request.

"Oh, sure, no problem. The Beach Boys are extremely cooperative. I'll set up a rehearsal for the end of this week."

He paused dramatically. "And now for the exciting news." He pounded his hands against the desk, imitating a drum roll. Drum, drum, drum, drum, drum.

"You're going to England!"

Dick and I sat in stunned silence.

"What do you think I was doing in L.A. all the time you were struggling on the Dick Clark Tour? I was working my butt off for you, that's what I was doing. I talked to Joe Smith at Warner Brothers and they are willing to send you to England on a promotional tour."

"Far out," Dick said.

"Warner Brothers hopes to launch you as an international act. They think television exposure will greatly increase international sales, which at this point are virtually non existent. I'm not sure when you're going, so you have a few months to work around here before you leave."

"Hey, man, thank you, thank you," Dick leapt to his feet and shook Bill's hand. "Wow, that's so cool. I knew you'd be a great manager." Bill smiled modestly.

For the first time, Bill's eyes caught mine. He smiled, a slight grin, prideful, like a cat presenting its owner a dead bird.

"He's doing a great job, isn't he?" Dick asked me, nodding in Bills direction.

"Yeah, awesome." I said. When we left Bill's apartment, everyone was very smiley.

* * * * *

Dick drove me in his maroon Cadillac south on the 405 Freeway past the airport toward Torrance. Following directions written on a slip of paper, he steered the car onto an off ramp and maneuvered through the side streets until we came to a deserted warehouse. Through the open back door we saw the Beach Boys setting up inside. Dick and I left the hot California sun and entered a cool, dark building.

"Hi," Dick said, putting out his hand to a short, stocky young man heading in his direction. "I'm Dick St. John and this is Dee Dee Sperling. We've brought our charts with us, so the songs should be pretty easy to learn."

"I'm Carl," the young man announced. "These are my brothers, Brian and Dennis Wilson."

I thought, "They're so young. They look like they're still in high school. Will they be able to back us?"

Dennis laughed. With a strand of blond hair flopping over one eye, he slowly walked to his drums and sat down, picking up the drum sticks. The group picked up their instruments and launched into their hit record, "Surfin' Safari."

They played it with great enthusiasm and volume. It sounded slightly off key and I wondered if they had tuned their guitars. It didn't sound exactly like their record, but I had to admit it was a catchy song. When they'd finished they looked at Dick and me expectantly.

"Great song," I finally said. Dennis snorted.

"Here are chord sheets to "The Mountain's High,"" Dick told them, waving the music in the air. "It's pretty basic, just a four-chord progression in the key of F#. It modulates to G after the bridge."

Dennis Wilson laughed. He brought the drum sticks down on his cymbals with a crash. Everyone looked at him.

"They only play in the key of C," he commented nonchalantly, pointing his drum stick at his brothers. "They haven't learned any other keys yet."

"Oh, yeah," Carl said. "Can you sing "The Mountain's High" in the Key of C?"

Dick and I exchanged concerned glances. Were they joking? We usually sang the song in the Key of F#, which was six notes higher than the key of C. What would we sound like singing in low, low voices?

"Well, if that's the only key you play in, I guess we'll have to," Dick's hands shook as he passed out the music. He did not look happy.

The Beach Boys struggled through "The Mountain's High" then attempted to play "Young and in Love." Both songs sounded way too low. We stood in awkward silence as the song ended. Was there any point in continuing?

"We'll be doing some other songs, too," Dick finally said in a husky voice. "We'll have to rehearse them at the high school assembly on Friday." He lowered his voice and gave me a concerned look. "Come on, Dee Dee. Let's go."

As we drove north on the 405 Freeway, Dick pounded the steering wheel.

"I had to stop singing. I almost blew my voice out singing so low. We're going to Bill's apartment. He has to do something about this."

* * * * *

When Bill opened the door he acted surprised to see us, but waved us in anyway. "What's going on?" he asked.

"We've got a problem," Dick said, his voice shaking. "They only play in one key."

"Who are you talking about?"

"The Beach Boys, the surf band you booked us with. They only play in one key."

"That's impossible."

"They're cool guys," I said. "But all our songs sound exactly alike and the music is so low, we can barely hit the notes."

Dick took a deep breath, trying to control his anxiety. "They sound fine on their own music, but they shouldn't be backing other acts because they're so inexperienced."

Bill put his hand in the air to slow Dick down. "Explain to me exactly what happened."

Dick took a deep breath. "We managed to rehearse "The Mountain's High" and "Young and in Love" in the key of C, the only key they play in, but the songs were pitched so low I started to strain my voice, not to mention how strange it sounded. This just isn't going to work."

Bill took a deep breath, and stared down at his hands. He finally said, "Look, you're not making much money off the high school gigs. Plus I'm taking fifteen percent off the top as your manager. It costs way too much to hire an entire band for just your part of the show. Since the Beach Boys play instruments and are willing to back you, why not try to make it work?"

"That's easy for you to say," Dick replied angrily. "You don't have to stand up there in front of hundreds of kids blowing out your throat and making a fool out of yourself."

"Look, we've got contracts signed with high schools all over L.A. It's too late to cancel. Can you think of anything you could do to make it better?"

"Yeah, we can get another band."

I thought for a moment. "Maybe if we add two or three simple songs that have a straight four-chord progression and aren't too rangy, like the Gary U.S. Bonds song, "Quarter to Three," songs that would sound alright in the key of C."

Bill looked at Dick. "Are you willing to try that?"

Dick shrugged. "I don't know. What other choice do we have?"

* * * * *

In the next few days, Dick and I scrambled to find four more songs to fill out our portion of the twenty minute set. We finally chose "Quarter to Three," "What'd I Say," "Love Is Strange" and "Tell Me."

On Friday, we drove to the gymnasium of a local high school. With less than half an hour to rehearse before the bell rang to summon students to the concert, we nervously climbed onto a makeshift wooden platform and tried to smile at the Beach Boys.

An ancient microphone faced us, propped on a tall mike stand. I didn't think it worked and moved my face closer and closer until I practically touched it with my lips. Suddenly it boomed forth with loud feedback. In pain, I clamped the palms of my hands over my ears.

"Hey, do you guys know "Quarter to Three?" Dick asked. "It's a simple four-chord progression."

The Beach Boys started playing it and we sang along. It actually sounded good. We rehearsed the rest our songs in the Key of C. Some of them were a little low for our voices, but we were able to pull it off. The public address system sounded horrible anyway, with occasional feedback and muffled static.

Suddenly a loud bell rang and kids started filing into the gymnasium. With great excitement and anticipation, they climbed into the bleachers, shoving and pushing to get a good seat.

There were no curtains. The Beach Boys, dressed in matching striped shirts, stood awkwardly on stage tuning and retuning their instruments. Dick and I waited on the floor behind them, leaning against a wall.

The high school principal walked to the microphone. He gave it several taps, and then read several school announcements. He finally announced, "And now, what you have been waiting weeks for, I'd like to bring onto the stage—DICK AND DEE DEE."

We ran on stage and started singing "The Mountain's High." Thrilled to be out of class and excited about the concert, the teens yelled and screamed. They didn't appear to notice how low we sang or that both the music and vocals sounded quite different than our records. Nothing mattered to them but hearing the rock and roll guitars and having fun.

Our portion of the act ended with an encore, "What'd I Say." We left the stage with smiles on our faces and returned to our spot against the gymnasium wall, behind the Beach Boys.

When the Beach Boys started playing their current record release, "Surfin' Safari," the crowd went wild. The kids knew all the words from radio air play and started singing along. I instinctively realized the Beach Boys' first single for Capital Records was destined for greatness.

After the show ended and everyone filed out, Dick and I shook hands with the band members.

"Hey, thanks for the great job," Dick told them. "The kids loved it."

"Yeah," Brian said. "It was pretty cool."

We left with good feelings toward the Beach Boys. For the next several months, we traveled to high schools in the Los Angeles area several times a week, singing together on rickety, makeshift gym stages in front of ancient microphones. But after every performance an inexplicable joy filled my being.

* * * * *

One morning, Dick called me. "My throat is really bothering me," he said. "Every time I sing for ten minutes, I get a sore throat. I'm going to a doctor to have it checked."

Several days later, he called back. "What a bummer! I've got nodules on my vocal cords. They're like calluses on your fingers when you first learn to play guitar. Unless I have surgery to remove them, my voice is always going to sound rough and husky."

"That's terrible," I said. "Are you sure they won't go away on their own?"

"Do you think I want to have surgery? Don't you think I explored every option? No, they won't go away." Dick sounded angry. "The only thing to do is go ahead and cut them out. The surgery is scheduled for a week from today." Dick paused and coughed. "It's going to take a month to recover afterwards so I won't be able to talk, let alone sing. This is such a huge drag!!!" He slammed down the phone.

After he hung up, I tried to think how this was going to impact our career. Dick usually took charge of everything. How would he continue in that role if he couldn't speak?

* * * * *

The day before the surgery, Dick called again, sounding depressed. "Listen, I can't talk for long. After the surgery, when you telephone my house and I answer, I'm going to ring a little bell. That will let you know I'm on the line. I won't be able to talk to you, but I'll be listening so you can say whatever you need to say."

"Good luck with the surgery, Dick."

There was a moment of silence. "Thanks, I'll need it."

* * * * *

Several days later, the phone rang. When I picked it up, I heard a strange sound on the line.

"Ding, ding, ding."

"Dick, is that you?"

"Ding, ding."

"Did the surgery go alright?"

"Ding, ding."

"Oh, I guess you can't talk. Anyway, I'm sure it went well and that you are starting to heal. Listen, you know Bill tried to cancel all our gigs for the next month, but we have to do one show in Las Cruces, New Mexico. Bill tried to get the promoter to let us out of our contract, but he refused to do it. He said he's already promoted the show and hundreds of kids have already bought tickets."

"Ding, ding, ding, ding, ding, ding, ding, ding."

"I know you're upset about this, but Bill assured me it would work out. The promoter says we can lip-synch to our records. I know we're going to look ridiculous, but the man says he'll sue if we don't appear."

"Ding, ding, ding, ding, ding, ding, ding, ding."

"Why don't you write Bill a letter? That's the best way for you to communicate your feelings. Anyway, Bill's still working on it. I'll keep you posted."

"Ding, ding, ding." Then a long moment of silence.

"Well, I hope you're doing alright. Goodbye."

I hung up the phone.

* * * * *

The show promoter in New Mexico demanded we honor our contract. Dick, for once mute and silent, and I flew into New Mexico. A local disc jockey met us at the airport. He was tall, with fiery red hair and a goatee. A cowboy hat topped his head like a star on a Christmas tree. I thought people in New Mexico might be mellow, but this guy acted like his body ran on diesel fuel.

"Hey, man, I heard about your surgery," he said to Dick, talking at a rapid clip. "Sorry about your throat, man. But, hey, you get some time off. If it was me, I'd go to Hawaii and mellow out."

Dick glared at the man.

"Anyway, there's obviously no need for a band rehearsal, hah, hah, hah, since you're not singing live. At least you don't have to deal with that."

Dick looked at me and rolled his eyes.

The disc jockey turned toward me. "So, Dee Dee, you're going to have to run the show tonight." I froze.

"What do you mean 'run the show'?"

"Well, the kids are expecting you and Dick to sing live with the band. You're performing in a large dance hall and the kids want to boogie. You're going to have get up there and explain why you and Dick are lip-synching to records. You need to tell jokes and entertain them since you and Dick aren't singing live. Otherwise, the kids might get hostile."

I felt my face flush. I'd never spoken on stage, never, ever. Dick did all the talking between songs. He welcomed the audience and introduced certain songs. I felt my words freeze up in my throat.

Dick set his lips in a firm line. He looked like he wanted to punch the disc jockey. He fired a hostile glance at me. I felt shivering in my stomach.

"I can't do that," I finally stammered. "I mean, you know, act as master of ceremonies and tell jokes. I don't even know any jokes. Why can't we just sing along to the records, one after the other?"

"Now think what that would look like. The one thing you want to avoid is dead air time. It's going to take awhile for me to find the right song on the album and to put the needle in place. You can't just stand there. They're a pretty tough crowd here in Las Cruces. No, they want a show. And you're going to have to provide one."

Dick leaned against the car window and shut his eyes. This was his worst nightmare come true, on stage with me and unable to talk.

The build-up for this show was far worse than any nervousness I'd ever experienced, far worse than the first show we did in Texas. My entire body shook. It felt like a rock pressed against my stomach. I felt clammy and jittery. The only sound I could force from my frozen throat was a hoarse, barely audible, shaky whisper.

We stood backstage in a large hall. The audience danced wildly to the live band. I could tell from the general volume of the voices and the yelling that much of the audience had been drinking. Native Americans hung out together, warily eying the Caucasian population. I wondered if a fight might break out.

After a loud band finale, the musicians left the stage. The disc jockey, now dressed in a red-sequined sport coat that clashed with his hair, raced toward the single microphone. He faced the crowd, a sloppy grin on his face.

"Alright, is everyone having a good time?"

Cheers and shouts.

"The band is going to take a break now, as we bring out our featured act, all the way from Los Angeles, California, the act that brought you 'The Mountain's High,' and 'Young and in Love,' DICK AND DEE DEE!"

Applause. Dick and I trotted out onto the stage. The disc jockey left, giving us the thumbs-up sign. We stood in silence in front of the microphone, looking at the audience. Everyone stared back. I felt my knees start to buckle and gripped the microphone stand with my clammy hands. You can do this, I told myself.

Taking a deep breath I managed to whisper, "Hello. We're Dick and Dee Dee."

Everyone just stared, expressionless.

Louder, I told myself. Force it out. I cleared my throat. "Ah hum. Normally we sing live? But Dick just had surgery on his throat to remove some nodules and he can't talk or sing for a month. But we didn't want to disappoint you by canceling the show. I mean, some of you bought your tickets in advance and were already planning to come, so we decided to fly here and 'lip-synch.' 'Lip-synching' means moving your mouth to a record, but not really singing."

I was on a roll. The babble fell out of my lips and over the audience like silent rain. You couldn't shut me up. Dick, an alarmed look on his face, reached behind me and tried to pull me back from the microphone. I yanked free. This was my moment. This was the break I'd dreamed of. Nothing was going to stop me from finishing what I had to say. I moved in closer to the mike.

"It's not really hard to lip-synch. I mean, you don't have to worry about matching up the words on the record exactly because, if you sort of sing along quietly, it looks like you're singing. Of course, Dick can't sing along because of his throat surgery, but he can mentally sing, and that will match up his lips to the records, I'm sure."

The audience appeared confused.

"Anyway, we're now going to sing, I mean lip-synch, our first hit for you. We recorded it on a tiny label, but finally leased it to Liberty Records after it became a hit in San Francisco. I think you remember this one. It's titled, "The Mountain's High."

Several people in the front row cheered.

The disc jockey dropped the needle onto the vinyl and the musical introduction started to play. Dick and I moved our mouths to the song, pretending we were singing. I had a flashback of lip-synching at the armory with Bob Mitchell and remembered how the needle screeched across the record. That felt like eons ago.

We finished "The Mountain's High" without incident. Everyone applauded and looked at me again. They expected me to say something, but what?

"So, are you having a good time tonight?" I heard a few cheers and cat calls. "That's great because we are too. It's really interesting being here in New Mexico. We've never played this state before, but I hope we can come back and visit. We love

Mexican food, especially with the Southwestern seasoning."

I glanced at Dick. He was perspiring and his face looked pale. He wiped away the sweat off his forehead with a handkerchief.

Glancing behind me, I saw the disc jockey squinting at the record as he held it up to the light, trying to read the titles written in tiny print on the label. What song is he looking for? Oh yeah. We are going in chronological order of our hits. Let's see. That makes the next song, "Tell Me."

"Anyway, sometimes things don't always go well in our lives. Sometimes the person we love the most just walks away without a word. Sometimes we're left desolate and inconsolable—you know, really, really sad. We'd like to do a song about lost love. It's called, "Tell Me." The record started to play.

I listened to Don Ralke's plunking string parts and the soaring vocals. This song wasn't half bad. We certainly sounded better on the record than when we sang it live with the average band. When we finished, the audience applauded.

"Thank you. And I'm sure Dick thanks you, too."

Dick shot me a nasty look, and then turned toward the audience, forced a minismile on his face and halfheartedly waved.

"There's always light at the end of the tunnel. After you lose your true love, and you think you will never find love again, the perfect person comes along and everything changes. Suddenly the world becomes brighter, more alive. It's like you're looking through pink-tinted sun glasses. Everything is rosy."

I felt Dick tugging at the back of my dress again. I squirmed free.

"So, when that happens you know you are "Young and in Love." The song started to play. It felt like the perfect segue. Hey, this wasn't so bad. Maybe I should talk more on stage.

As the song faded away, I realized it was time to pick up the tempo, but with what song? When we sang live, we did "Love Is Strange" and "What'd I Say," both recorded by other artists. What song was the disc jockey going to play next? I didn't have a clue.

I started to babble. "Dick has this huge vocal range. I mean, it's about four octaves. It's too bad he can't demonstrate it tonight. Anyway, when we can sing, Dick sometimes does that song, "Summertime." It was in the play, Porgy and Bess?

Anyway, he does each verse in a different octave. People can't believe it when he hits the final verse, he's singing so high."

"Ahhhhh."

Dick suddenly elbowed me in the back. I fell forward into the microphone, hitting it sharply with my forehead. The mike wobbled back and forth on the stand before settling back with a thump.

I glared at Dick and rubbed my sore back with one hand.

"So, anyway, on that happy note we're going to sing another song. No, not sing. We're going to lip-synch another song. And I'm not even sure which song we're doing, but we'll find out when we hear it."

I laughed nervously. Dick glared daggers at me. The disc jockey struggled to place the album on the turntable and just when he placed the needle on the vinyl, the record player broke. As the machine lost power, the song slowed to a warped pace and faded to nothing.

For one long, horrible moment, no one knew what to do. The disc jockey kicked the table the record player sat on. Dick took one look at the disc jockey, glanced at me and turned and walked off stage. I stood alone in the spotlight.

"Well, we seem to be having technical problems. I want to thank all of you for coming here tonight. The band will be back on stage shortly, so don't go away. It was great performing for you. Have a great evening."

I left the stage to scattered applause.

"Where did Dick go?" the disc jockey yelled. "As soon as I fix this damn turntable, I want you to go out there and finish the show."

"It is finished," I said, as I watched the band members climb back up on stage.

I found Dick pacing in the parking lot. He had tears in his eyes and his face was red. He'd never looked so miserable before. He pointed at his watch and at his throat. Then he imitated popping something in his mouth and taking an imaginary drink of water. I realized he needed to go back to the motel to take another pain pill.

I saw a pay phone on the curb by the street. Lifting the receiver, I called a taxi, which arrived in less than five minutes. Dick and I rode back to the motel in silence.

The next morning, we returned to Los Angeles. We never heard from the disc jockey again, but he did send our money to Bill and honored our contract. I didn't see or hear from Dick for several weeks. Bill kept busy lining up more shows for us to play with the Beach Boys at local high schools while awaiting news of our tour to London.

When Dick's voice returned, so did his good disposition. He never mentioned the gig in New Mexico. He didn't even mention the fact that we still sang all our songs with the Beach Boys in the key of C. I guess he was just happy to have his voice back again.

* * * * *

"Young and in Love," is starting to fall off the record charts," George Wilder told Dick and me. "We need to record a follow up single before you leave for England."

Dick and I drove to Don Ralke's home in the San Fernando Valley. In Don's music room, Dick played and sang several songs he'd written while recovering from the surgery. Then Don played a song he'd written with his wife, titled, "Love Is a Once in a Lifetime Thing." The lyrics spoke of a deep love Dick and I allegedly felt for each other. Near the end of the song Dick would sing solo, "Oh, Dee Dee, I love you," and I was to sing, "Oh, Dick, I love you." Oh, gross, I thought, so totally inappropriate, so "Paul and Paula."

I felt uncomfortable pretending Dick and I were involved in a romantic relationship, but Don said, "People enjoy a good love song. Look at Paul and Paula. They don't even speak to each other, but they had a huge national hit with 'Hey Paula.' It really doesn't matter."

"I think we should do this song," Dick told me. "It has a great chance to be a hit record."

We chose two other songs to record; a song written by Dick St. John entitled, "Guess Our Love Must Show" and a song I'd written the lyrics to on the Dick Clark Caravan of Stars tour, "Where Did All the Good Times Go?"

I accidentally left the lyrics to the song in Dick's car one night. When he found them, he put music to my lyrics. Without ever sitting down and working with him in person, I suddenly had become his writing partner again. I took this as an overture towards an improved relationship and sincerely hoped we might again collaborate on songs together.

Several weeks later, we recorded the songs at the Wilders Recording Studio.

When the session ended, everyone gave us the thumbs-up sign.

Warner muttered, "I think 'Where Did All the Good Times Go?' is a hit. It's a gas."

Of course, he'd said the same thing after he put the duck call on "Goodbye to Love."

* * * * *

For our next single, Warner Brothers released "Guess Our Love Must Show." It barely broke onto the record charts, and then quickly dropped off. Warner Brothers put the London tour on hold until we could travel there with a proven hit record in America.

Somehow, without my noticing it, Bill changed from boyfriend to manager. He wore his "manager" hat more regularly, more jauntily. His professional attitude flowed into our personal lives, interfering with intimacy and leaving me wondering what our relationship was all about.

Bill's work consumed him. I saw less of him and started to despair at the new state of affairs.

"Turn Around" and "Thou Shalt Not Steal"

CHAPTER SIXTEEN

"Turn Around"

"The Wilders want us back in the studio," Dick said. "We've got to get some new material together. We need another hit record. We've got to try something different, maybe another ballad, like "Young and in Love."

One day I went to Dick's house to listen to material. He played me some songs on his tape recorder. N one of them struck us as "hit-record" material. Then Dick remembered a song he had heard on a recent Kodak commercial. It told a beautiful story about children growing up. He contacted the publishers of the song and learned its title, "Turn Around," co-written by Harry Belafonte.

When I heard the song for the first time, something inside resonated deeply. I knew it would be a hit.

The Wilders scheduled a session at their garage studio to record "Turn Around." The day of the session we were startled to see a stranger enter. He wasn't carrying an instrument.

"Who's that?" Dick questioned.

The Wilders laughed. "It's a professional whistler," George replied. "Jeff, meet Dick and Dee Dee."

"I'll bet I can whistle just as well as he can," Dick whispered to me. As the musical introduction to the song started, Jeff intently studied the music chart. At the perfect moment he launched into a remarkable whistle, following the melody perfectly.

Dick's eyes widened and he smiled.

I felt joy deep within myself. This was my favorite song of anything we'd recorded so far. As we sang the song of children growing up and leaving home, I felt tears well up in my eyes. Dick stood before the microphone, pouring his soul and feelings into the lyrics. He held the last note a long time. The profound moment stretched into silence. Then, a voice sounded in our ears from the control booth," That's it. We got just what we need."

When the session ended, George Wilder cornered us in the sound booth.

"You know we really have a good thing going here," George said. "I'm talking about our collaboration. It's a great combination with Don, who's an excellent arranger, and Walt, Warner and myself, who also happen to be professional singers and musicians, giving input and direction to what the two of you are doing.

"I just hope you don't become dissatisfied at any point and decide to find other record producers. I don't think you would have good results because when you change one of the members of a group, the whole dynamic changes."

I studied him intently, startled at George's serious demeanor.

George continued. "We're a team here. A team effort has produced three hit singles. I just want to caution you about making changes."

Dick looked surprised. "We don't want to make any changes," he commented. "We're perfectly happy with you producing our records."

"Well, that's good," George remarked, smiling at his brothers. "I just wanted to remind you that 'united we stand, divided we fall.'" Dick and I exchanged glances.

I wondered why George worried about us leaving his production company. We now had three hits to our credit and a potential fourth with "Turn Around." Would we soon be receiving offers from other producers?

* * * * *

Warner Brothers released "Turn Around" as a single in late 1963 and it started a slow and steady climb up the charts. In conjunction with its release, Dick decided to purchase two poodles from agent Roz Ross, who had just moved to Los Angeles from New York. He telephoned me the day he brought them home.

"You've got to come see my new dogs," he said. "I named them Rocky and Roland, but their nicknames are Rock and Roll. There's one dog left in the litter.

It's a male. You've got to get it."

"Dick, I already have a German shepherd. My parents take care of it because we travel so much. I really don't know if I should get another dog."

"This is different. These dogs are small. You can easily handle a dog this size in your apartment. And, you can take them practically anywhere. Just come over and see them."

I drove to Dick's house to see Rocky and Roland. The wiggling, squirming bundles of brown fluff rolled with each other on the floor and frantically licked my hand. They were the size of large cats, chocolate brown, with deep, trusting eyes. I had to admit they were adorable.

Bill heard about my ambivalence to adopt a puppy and volunteered to bring the last available dog to my apartment for a visit. One afternoon I heard a knock at the door and Bill entered, carrying the puppy cautiously, like a newborn baby.

"You've got to be careful with him," Bill said. "These dogs are extremely intelligent and sensitive. He'd be a great companion for you. Incidentally, he's paper trained."

The little brown puppy squirmed in my arms and licked my face. "He's so happy," I said. "I'll name him Peppy." Bill gazed into my eyes.

"It's good for you to have a puppy to love," Bill commented. I wondered if it was also good to have a man to love.

But I did adopt the dog and changed the spelling of his name to "Pepe," a French aristocrat, when I discovered the dog's high-strung and finicky nature.

Faced with the task of taking the dog outside to do his business, I made a deal with the doorman. I would call down and tell him Pepe was on his way. When the elevator door opened on my floor, I pushed the lobby button and placed the dog inside and waited for the doors to close, leaving Pepe to ride down alone.

When he reached the lobby level, the doors to the elevator opened and the doorman escorted Pepe to the outside bushes, where he stood until Pepe finished his business. Then he placed Pepe back in the elevator and called to announce Pepe's return.

Again, the elevator brought Pepe back up to my floor. Without my having to get dressed first, I'd found a solution for walking the dog. But mostly it amused me to think of Pepe riding down in the elevator alone.

When we went out of town, Dick and I left the dogs at a boarding kennel in Beverly Hills. That way all three brother dogs roomed together. Pepe, Rocky and Roland always looked great when we picked them up and acted happy to see us. As time went by, I was very glad that I had decided to adopt Pepe.

Warner Brothers Publicity Shot, circa 1964.

CHAPTER SEVENTEEN

The Day the World Changed Forever

By November of 1963, we were back to performing at high schools with the Beach Boys. To our surprise and great joy, their musical skills improved considerably. Brian Wilson changed the entire feel of the show when he stood by himself at the microphone and sang The Beach Boys' new release, "In My Room."

The song was a haunting reminder of how we all need a sacred space for introspection and an indication of the new direction the Beach Boys had decided to take. This song rapidly climbed the charts to the number one position.

On November 21st I went home for a family dinner. Mom and I and my two sisters sat around the table in the family room. I brought Pepe and convinced Mom to dog sit him the next morning while I traveled to Santa Ana for a high-school assembly with the Beach Boys.

The evening passed rapidly. I decided to spend the night there.

The morning of November 22, 1963, I woke early. My watch read 8:00 a.m. Dick planned to pick me up at ten to drive to the designated high school south of Los Angeles.

I walked downstairs and into the kitchen to get some breakfast. Mom stood in front of the ironing board with the television turned on. As she turned and gazed at me, I saw tears rolling down her cheeks.

"Mom, what's wrong?" I felt shocked seeing my mother cry. I'd only witnessed my mother in tears one other time, the day she heard the news that her father had passed away. I don't know if I was more startled by the news that was being broadcast at that moment or the fact that my mother was crying.

I walked close to her to give her a hug.

"The President's been shot," Mom said, glancing back at the television. We both stared at the television screen. In an emotion filled voice, the announcer said that the President had been taken to Parkland Memorial Hospital in Dallas where he was struggling to survive. Descriptions of the shooting assaulted our senses like bullets tearing through our own bodies.

Disbelief and anguish rose within me. This just wasn't possible. How could such a horrible thing happen? How did this guy get his hands on a gun? No one carried guns unless they were police officers, military personnel or hunters. It was totally inconceivable.

I picked up the phone and called Dick.

"Do you have the TV on?"

"Oh my God, it's so horrible. Kennedy's fighting for his life." Dick paused. "I'm sure they're going to cancel our show at the high school today. We can't possibly stand up there and sing."

"Let me try to call the school," I said, relieved to find some type of meaningful activity. "I'll find out what's happening and I'll call you back."

I spent ten minutes trying to track down the principal of the high school, but no one knew where he was. Nor did they know whether or not the assembly had been cancelled.

"We're going to have to drive down there," Dick told me when I called him back. "If we don't show up, we could be sued for violating the contract."

"This is just ridiculous," I said.

"I know, but I think it's important to go there in person so the principal sees we did honor our agreement."

I slowly dressed, still stunned and shocked. Dick pulled into my parents' driveway. I silently climbed into the passenger seat of his Cadillac. We'd barely entered the 405 Freeway heading south when the news came over the radio, "President Kennedy, the 34th President of the United States, is dead."

"My God, what's the world coming to?" I cried.

I stared out the window, tears running down my face. All the cars gradually slowed to about twenty miles per hour and, one by one, turned on their headlights. We found ourselves in an unplanned freeway funeral procession, as hundreds of grieving drivers struggled to understand the inconceivable.

Dick and I drove twenty miles an hour in silence until we reached the freeway off ramp and the high school parking lot. I felt deadness, like an invisible blanket covering my body, blocking out all sensation from the world.

Judging from the bustling activity and the joyous normality of the students, they apparently did not yet know what had happened. We slowly made our way to the principal's office. He greeted us with a smile. "Are you ready for an exciting show?" He rubbed his hands together in anticipation. I couldn't believe his attitude.

"Don't you know about President Kennedy?"

"Oh, yes. But I decided not to interrupt the school day with this type of news. The students will find out about it soon enough when they go home."

"You can't expect us to sing on a day like this." Dick gave the principal a disbelieving glance.

"I do expect you to sing. The Beach Boys are in the gymnasium setting up their equipment now. They weren't too happy about performing either, but I reminded them that life does go on and we do have a signed contract."

I felt indignant. "We're really upset about this. How do you think the students are going to react when they go home and find out the President was assassinated and their principal decided to continue with the concert?"

"They will probably think we didn't know about the assassination at the time."

The principal gave us a smug look.

Dick's hands trembled. "Quite frankly, I'm too upset to sing. I can't just plant a happy smile on my face and go out and entertain people after such a shocking tragedy."

The principal observed the American flag hanging on the wall.

In his best authoritative voice he said, "Well, not everyone feels like you do about President Kennedy. Oh, I'm sorry he died, don't get me wrong. But he wasn't popular with everyone. In fact, some people might not be grieving at all. They might be glad to get rid of him."

Dick and I gawked at him.

"Anyway, let me put it this way," the principal declared. "You will either perform at the assembly today, or I will sue you for breach of contract." He sat back in his seat, his fingers linked behind his neck.

"Well," I said, surprised at the intensity behind my words. "I wonder what the readers of the Los Angeles Times will say when they find out that a principal in Orange County decided to force singers to perform in a high school assembly one hour after the President of the United States was assassinated. And the Los Angeles Times will find out, because I'm going to call them."

The principal glared at me. He slowly rose from his desk.

"You wouldn't do that."

"Just watch me."

He thought for a moment. "Well, if you're that upset about the assassination, I guess we'll have to reschedule the show."

He rummaged around on his desk for a calendar.

"How about a week from Friday?"

"Whatever, any day is fine," Dick said. "You'll have to check with the Beach Boys."

"Wait here! I'll be right back." The principal bolted from the room.

Dick and I sat, watching the industrial clock on the wall slowly tick the minutes. Bells rang and students hustled up and down hallways outside. To the students, it was just another high school day. To us, it was the day the world lost its heroic president. We sat in numbed disbelief. Finally the principal returned.

"Alright, the Beach Boys are available a week from Friday. So, if you'll just change the date on the contracts and initial them, I'll make you a photocopy and you'll be on your way."

We changed the contract, too upset to say anything else. Within minutes we were back on the freeway heading home.

* * * * *

For the next few days, I sat in Bill's apartment riveted to the television.

Time stopped. Nothing mattered but watching history unfold. What shock I felt to see the beautiful first lady, Jacqueline Kennedy, wearing a blood-splattered suit as she witnessed the swearing in of our new president, Lyndon Johnson. For better or worse, he now would guide our nation.

Several days after John Kennedy's funeral, Dick and I climbed into his maroon Cadillac to drive to a show in Sacramento. Bill decided to go with us, so we chose the more scenic route up the coast. Just past Pismo Beach we stopped at a motel for the night. As soon as Bill checked into his room, he invited Dick and me to join him as he flicked on the TV.

"They're transferring the assassin to a more secure jail," he said. "They're going to show the guy on TV."

We watched as several police officers brought out Lee Harvey Oswald. Suddenly, a man approached through the crowd, aimed a gun at Oswald and fired several shots. Oswald doubled over in pain. Our mouths dropped open. To see him shot before our eyes was almost as shocking as the Kennedy assassination. After the television coverage stopped, I turned to Bill and Dick.

"How can we perform in Sacramento?" I clutched my hands in my lap, my voice shrill. "I don't want to do anything."

Bill took a more practical view. "Well, you do have a contract and the show is scheduled. Even though great drama is going on nationally, people aren't as upset by the death of an assassin as they were by the president's death. It may be dramatic, but it isn't traumatic. Maybe it would help people heal to hear music and forget their troubles for awhile."

We proceeded to Sacramento, where Dick and I shared a bill with Bobby Vinton. His record "Roses Are Red" placed him on a national poll as the Most Promising Male Vocalist of 1962. We played to a packed house. Bill's instincts were right. People needed to hear healing music.

We walked out on stage, solemn but brave. As we sang "Turn Around" the audience became silent, as if hanging on each note, clutching each word. As we ended the song, no one moved. Several people in the front row had tears running down their faces. Finally the audience erupted into applause and we silently walked away, unable to sing a happy, up tempo number after that.

When we returned to Los Angeles, we drove to the high school in Orange County to make up the concert we'd missed on the day of the Presidential assassination. We only saw the principal at a distance.

It became apparent by the screaming and hysteria over the Beach Boys that their star had risen rapidly. That show was the last time we played with the Beach Boys as our house band!

CHAPTER EIGHTEEN

A Meditation Technique

As the country slowly started a recovery under the leadership of President Lyndon Johnson, I found my sorrow lessening. But in its place, a deep, empty space grew. Everything I'd believed had been suddenly shattered with the assassin's bullet; the beauty and grace of the times, the impression of the world as a safe place with well-intentioned people. All that vanished. I felt, in its place, distrust and confusion. Sometimes I wondered if I'd ever laugh again.

* * * * *

One cold afternoon I climbed into my car and drove along Sunset to the lake. The morning, gray and overcast, gave way to puffy clouds and filtered sunlight. By the time I turned my car into the lake grounds, I felt the winter sun warm my shivering arms.

Walking around the lake, deep in thought, I jumped when a hand touched my shoulder. Swinging around, I saw the face of the monk who had given me the pink crystal.

"Don't ever let down your guard." The monk spoke seriously. "It's important to always be aware of who is around you on all sides, especially behind you."

"But I feel safe here."

"I know, but still, you were daydreaming. It's a matter of being in the 'now' and 'fully present.'"

I smiled, suddenly overjoyed to see him again.

"Wait," he said. He walked to a pile of leaves on the ground and picked up a particularly beautiful one. "This is for you. You see, the leaf has left the tree in a glorious burst of color. But in leaving the tree, it also started its own death cycle. But what happened to the tree?"

Puzzled, I stared up at the tall, stately, magnificent tree.

I slowly answered, "It lives on. It loses leaves in the fall and grows new ones in the spring."

"Ah, is that a lesson for us?"

"I guess."

"Each one of us is born on earth for a purpose. We're here for a little while, and then we go behind the scenes again. It's a natural process, the way God created it."

"I suppose so. But death doesn't seem right sometimes. I just can't seem to get over the President's death. Why did he have to die? I feel so empty all the time."

"Remember, even the President had his destiny to fulfill. He lived the exact amount of time he was supposed to and accomplished much in his life. He went suddenly and without great pain. We mourn his loss but in doing so, honor his life."

The monk smiled at me. "Although it doesn't seem possible now, you will recover completely from this, for you have a long life ahead, with much to accomplish on your own."

He stared long and deeply into my eyes. Then he reached up and gently touched me between the eyebrows.

"I'd like to give you a meditation technique you can take with you. Any time you feel stress, anxiety or worry, just practice this and you'll feel calm immediately."

I sat straight and closed my eyes.

"Watch your breath," he instructed. "When you naturally inhale, you think 'peace in,' and when you exhale, think 'tension out.' Eventually your breath will slow down, your mind will slow and you'll feel peaceful and see with more clarity."

I practiced breathing in this manner for several minutes. When I opened my eyes, he smiled and said, "Go in peace."

By the time I drove back to my apartment, things felt different. I now knew everything would be alright.

The peace and tranquility of Lake Shrine.

CHAPTER NINETEEN

Competition and My New Car

The start of a new year brought optimism and new beginnings. Although "Turn Around" had reached number 27 on the national charts, it now headed down. We held great hopes for another hit record. What would 1964 bring for Dick and Dee Dee?

In a cheerful mood, Dick picked me up and we drove together to Bill's apartment. Dick knocked loudly on Bill's door. Bill, wearing a casual shirt and sweater, his dark hair perfectly groomed, welcomed us. I felt great joy seeing him again.

"Come in, come in," he said, all smiles. "I just got off the phone with a promoter in Tokyo. I'm packaging my first tour there. And guess who's starring in it?"

"Dick and Dee Dee," Dick answered, his eyes sparkling.

Bill looked startled and slightly guilty. "No, actually it's Paul and Paula. After all, they've got a top ten record at the moment."

Dick frowned.

"But of course I'm working on booking you and the Dovells there too."

"All the acts you manage," Dick replied.

"Right," Bill said. "Isn't that great? Over the holidays, Paula flew to L.A. from Texas and auditioned male singers to find a permanent replacement for Paul. She found the perfect person. So now everything's set for their first overseas tour."

"Great, I'm glad everything's set," Dick muttered. He stood up, suddenly and abruptly. "We've got to go." He grabbed my arm.

I looked at him, confused. An angry expression covered Dick's face.

The phone rang, loud and insistent. Bill picked it up, cupping his hand over the mouthpiece. "I'll only be a moment." Then he noticed us heading toward the door. "Why are you leaving? You just got here."

"We have to meet the Wilders," Dick replied. "I just remembered. We have an appointment with them."

Bill appeared momentarily distracted, but the caller must have said something clever, because Bill's face relaxed and he burst out laughing. Dick opened the door.

"Bye," I said.

Bill glanced at me, waved, and then focused his full attention back on the telephone.

* * * * *

Outside, Dick exploded.

"You know what's happening, don't you?" He didn't wait for my response. "He's putting all of his energy into building his management company for acts with hit records on the charts. He could care less about us."

"Dick, that's not true." I automatically defended Bill. "You know Bill always has our career in mind. He's done so much for us already."

Dick studied his bitten-to-the-quick fingernails. "Figure it out. If you had two male and female duos who would you promote, the duo with the hit record or the duo without one?"

"You think he's doing more for Paul and Paula than us?"

"Duh! I know he's doing more for them! Look who's going to Japan. He's doing more for all his acts than us. Just to keep us busy, he books us in stupid high schools. Then he spends the rest of his time promoting his other artists in places like Japan. We're busy running around doing local gigs, so we're out of his thoughts."

Dick studied me intently. "I thought you were going out with him. Did something happen?" That, of course, was none of his business.

"No, it's just that you and I are on the road so much, I don't see him that often."

"Well, you'd better find a way to change that or we're always going to be at the bottom of his roster of clients."

This line of reasoning annoyed me. I wasn't seeing Bill so he'd do more for the act.

"Or," I said sarcastically, "We could have another hit record. Maybe we should focus on that instead of my relationship with Bill."

Dick drove in unhappy silence and let me off outside the Barrington Plaza.

"I don't know why I picked you up today." His voice drifted from the open window. "You live so close to Bill you could have walked

* * * * *

Several days passed. Dick's words echoed in my head. Obviously, Bill found it easier to book acts with hit records on the charts. Was his focused attention on Paul and Paula a detriment to Dick and me? I trusted Bill but some concerns lingered in my mind.

Dick called the next evening.

"I finally reached the Wilders," he said. "Warner Brothers Records wants us to record an album before "Turn Around" drops off the top-forty charts completely. You won't believe this. They want us to do a folk album."

I smiled. Now he was talking about a type of music I totally related to. "I love folk music. You know that song "All My Trials?" Maybe we could sing that"

"There are all kinds of folk songs. We should do songs people are familiar with. And did you know most folk songs are over seventy-five years old? Their copyrights have run out. That means we can grab the song-writing credit."

I wondered if, in the grabbing, I'd be included as a song writer.

"Let's start gathering material," Dick continued. "Bring some folk songs over to my place on Sunday. I'll look for material too. It should be easy to pick a dozen folk tunes."

* * * * *

The next morning I'd just returned to my apartment from the swimming pool when I heard the phone ringing. I stumbled over Pepe trying to get to the phone.

"Hello!" I shouted.

"Where have you been?" Bill asked. "I've been calling constantly for the past hour and a half."

Surprised to hear his voice, I took a deep breath. "I was at the pool."

"What's wrong? I know you and Dick were upset when you left here the other day."

"Oh, Dick feels that you are giving more attention to Paul and Paula and your other acts than you are to Dick and Dee Dee. He thinks your focus has shifted."

"Oh, my God," Bill sighed into the receiver. "I think about you and Dick night and day. I'm always looking for new ways to further your career. You believe that, don't you?

"Look," Bill continued. "Paul and Paula had a major international hit. Right now, overseas, they're in much more demand than you and Dick. I can't help that. It's just the way it is. But I can develop contacts through booking Paul and Paula that will help Dick and Dee Dee in the future. Do you understand?"

"Yeah, that makes sense."

"Look, Dee Dee, when I go to Japan, I'm going to try to book you and Dick over there as well."

"You're going to Japan with Paul and Paula?" He hadn't even left and already I felt deserted.

"Sure, it will be a great career move, not only for Paul and Paula but for Dick and Dee Dee too." He paused and abruptly changed the subject. "In the meantime, let's get together. I know a great restaurant in Beverly Hills. Are you available tonight?"

Things felt out of control. I tried to control my scattered thoughts.

"I have plans to visit Sharon Sheeley."

"Oh, well, we'll pick another date. I'll call you next week."

Bill hung up. I felt confused and unhappy. Bill always knew the right thing to say and how to make every situation turn out in his favor. I had difficulty communicating verbally what I was feeling.

On a sudden impulse, I rushed out the door and took the elevator down to the parking garage. I climbed into my old Corvette and drove several short blocks to the Ford dealer in Santa Monica. Before the day was out, I'd leased a brand new Ford Thunderbird.

* * * * *

It had been a long time since I'd visited Sharon. I remembered her insisting we march into the president of Liberty's office and demand our release. Much water flowed under the bridge as a result of that scheme.

The drive to Hollywood took about forty-five minutes. As I finally pulled up in front of Sharon's house, I honked the horn. Sharon stuck her head out the door.

"For God's sake," she shouted. "The neighbors aren't deaf. Why are you honking?"

"I want to show you my new car!" I yelled. "Look, it's even got a retractable steering wheel."

Sharon squinted at the car, barely glancing at it. "Oh, yeah, it's great. Come inside. There's someone I want you to meet."

I parked against the curb, disappointed that Sharon wasn't more interested in my T-bird but still careful not to dirty the whitewall tires. I followed Sharon into her house.

"Go sit in the den," Sharon ordered. "I'll be right back with the tea."

I entered the small sitting room, sinking into a comfortable sofa. Sharon returned with the tea pot and three cups.

Following her was Jimmy O'Neill, one of the top disc jockeys in Los Angeles. I struggled to a standing position. Jimmy looked embarrassed.

"Please don't get up," he said.

"Do you know Jimmy?" Sharon asked.

"Sure. We met at KRLA ," I stammered. "Dick and I visited there promoting "Turn Around."

I walked toward the disc jockey and shook his hand. "Nice seeing you again."

Jimmy smiled and sat on one of the sofas. I studied his features. He had dark hair, parted on one side, a wonderful smile and a rich, resonant voice.

"What are you and Dick up to?" he asked.

"We're gathering material for our second album for Warner Brothers. It's going to be mainly folk songs."

"Yeah, I'm writing a song with Dick for the album," Sharon said. I glanced at her in surprise. Why was I the last to find out everything?

Sharon turned to Jimmy. "Can you do me a big favor, luv? Would you supervise the gardener? He's planting rose bushes out back, but hasn't a clue where to put them." Jimmy shrugged. "How do I know where they go?"

"Just use your best judgment. All four bushes need to be spaced evenly in the flower bed."

Jimmy reluctantly rose and wandered down the hall, headed toward the back of the house.

"We're getting married," Sharon whispered. "So far, you're the only one who knows. Jimmy took me to his mother's house for dinner last night, so I could meet her. I know she hates me. She served me meat loaf made from dog food!"

I started laughing. "It probably wasn't dog food. It just tasted that way."

"No, it was dog food alright." Sharon paused for dramatic effect. "I thought the meat loaf tasted strange and when I went into the kitchen for a glass of water, I saw six empty cans of Friskies dog food sitting on the counter. And she doesn't even have a dog."

Sharon took a sip of her tea. "Anyway, Jimmy and I are getting married. He's not a singer, like Eddy Cochran, but he is a good person. We get along well." I smiled, genuinely happy for her.

"He seems nice."

"He's going to be a huge TV star. I had this idea to create a television show patterned after the most popular musical TV show in London. Can you believe it? They actually have rock and roll artists on TV over there. Anyway, we've produced a pilot to sell to one of the networks. Jimmy's going to be the show's host."

Impressed, I asked, "What's the show like?"

Sharon's voice escalated and she waved her arms in the air. "It's a half hour of full-out musical performances, real high energy. We have dancers and back up singers for each act and a house band. Right now we're trying to decide what to call the show."

Sharon suddenly remembered something. "I've got to see what Jimmy's up to. I'm trying to get roses planted." She added, "Do you want to come outside and watch?"

"Actually, I've got to go. I've got a dog now and I left him alone in my apartment. He's still in his chewing phase. Anyway, say goodbye to Jimmy for me and congratulations."

Sharon gave me a hug and escorted me to the door. As I pulled away in my new Thunderbird I saw her heading around the side of the house and heard her yelling, "Jimmy! Jimmy! Where are on earth are you planting those roses?"

I drove back to West Lost Angeles, a smile on my face.

* * * * *

When I got home that evening Bill telephoned.

"How's Sharon?" he asked.

"Oh, she's developing a new television pilot and planning to marry KRLA disc jockey, Jimmy O'Neill."

Bill ignored the marriage news. "What's the concept of the show?"

"It's a format for rock and roll artists. She said something about musical performances, backed by singers and dancers. I don't know too much about it."

"Hmm, that's interesting." He paused. "Listen, I've got something to run by you. Do you think a hypnotist would make a good opening act for Paul and Paula?" I had absolutely no idea how to answer that question.

I finally stammered, "I don't know. I think kids mainly want to hear music."

"For Paul and Paula, I'm thinking way beyond rock and roll concerts. I'm thinking Vegas, world-class nightclubs."

"Well, just don't let the hypnotist hypnotize you."

Bill laughed. "That would never happen. I'd never turn control of my life over to anyone." Then he sighed.

"Actually, between you and Dick and Paul and Paula, I think I have more than enough acts to handle right now."

CHAPTER TWENTY

Will We Have Another Hit?

Bill booked us on a local television show, hosted by disc jockey Lloyd Thaxton. Bill met Dick and me in the studio dressing room. Dick's mood remained sullen on the drive over. Now he paced around, silent and unhappy.

"Is something wrong?" Bill asked him.

"No," Dick muttered, but he didn't sound convincing.

Bill said, "I think the producers of the show are planning to do something different with the taping, because they put a large studio monitor on the wall. They don't usually do that. Don't get distracted by whatever they show on the monitor. Just watch the cameras."

"Right," I said. "The one with the red light on it."

Bill and I laughed. Dick didn't.

When it was time to take our positions, a crew member led Dick and me to a small platform on the sound stage. We climbed up, standing side by side, silently waiting for our segment to start.

On one side of the room, Lloyd Thaxton interviewed a dancer. It was hard to see because the cameras and crew blocked my view, but I could watch the action clearly on the television monitor in front of us.

Suddenly we heard Lloyd say, "And now, here they are with another great hit record, 'Turn Around,' Dick and Dee Dee."

Applause morphed into the musical and spoken introduction of the song.

On the record, Dick spoke, "Life grows short, and man grows old, summers gone and the wind turns cold."

As we started to sing, I glanced at the monitor and saw the image of Dick and me. Turning back to the camera with the red light beaming at us, I tried to focus on the words and what we were communicating.

Slowly, the images on the monitor changed. Instead of seeing Dick and me singing, we started watching shots of children running across a field.

I heard Dick mutter and suddenly, without warning, he stepped down off the platform and walked away. I froze. Where was he going? What did he think would happen when the cameras returned to us and he'd vanished?

The second verse played and the children's pictures kept rolling across the screen. I've got to get Dick, I thought. He's got to get back up here.

I stepped down, my feet hitting hard on the wooden floor. Which direction had he gone? I headed toward the dressing rooms, starting to run once I reached the corridor. I saw an exit door to the parking lot. My intuition told me to head that way.

When I reached the asphalt outdoors, Dick and Bill stood arguing.

Dick yelled, "They have no right to book us on a TV show and never show us on camera."

Bill's hands trembled. He grabbed Dick by the arm and looked him directly in the eye. "You get back in there and finish that song immediately. If you don't, I'm resigning as your manager. This is totally unprofessional."

Dick pulled away, an angry look on his face. They both turned and saw me.

"Get inside immediately," Bill ordered. "Quick, before the song ends."

Dick and I hurried back down the corridor and into the studio. The song was nearly over. Images of children still filled the television screen. As soon as we climbed back on the platform, the cameras cut back to us as the song ended.

There was no interview. The cameras went to a commercial and Dick bolted for the dressing room. I slowly followed. Dick grabbed his garment bag from the clothes rack and headed for the exit.

"You can ride home with Bill," he shouted over his shoulder.

On the way home from the studio Bill said, "I don't know how much longer I can keep managing rock and roll acts. If it isn't one crisis, it's another."

I felt a wave of dread at the thought Bill might leave us. If he stopped managing our act, would I ever see him again? The romantic door had been closed for awhile and it appeared our relationship was simply professional. But I still felt great love for him. Only time would tell.

* * * * *

Dick and I picked six folk songs for the Turn Around album: "500 Miles," "The Riddle Song," "Freight Train," "Gypsy Rover," "Old Maid's Song," and "All My Trials." Dick made sure my name was included with his for song-writing credits. I felt warmth and gratitude toward him. We also chose a song Don Ralke had written called "Just Round the River Bend."

Dick placed two of his original songs on the disc, "The Gift," and "The World Is Waiting." He also included the song he had written with Sharon Sheeley entitled, "We Can't Help Crying for the World."

The final song chosen was "Don't Think Twice," written by Bob Dylan. Of course, no one messed with a Dylan song. Bob Dylan got the total song-writer credit.

Joe Smith, our contact at Warner Brothers, sent us to Studio Five, where a photographer took a series of photos of Dick and me. We took some shots in the studio and some outdoors at Griffith Park.

For the nature shots, Dick and I wore earth colors, a gold sleeveless dress for me and a paler gold knit shirt for Dick. He also wore an attractive forest green sport coat. We posed in front of tropical ferns and lush plants and trees. Warner Brothers chose an outdoor shot for the album cover. They felt it was more in keeping with the folk song image.

* * * * *

In late February, Warner Brothers released our follow-up single to Turn Around, the hauntingly beautiful "All My Trials" backed by the Bob Dylan song, "Don't Think Twice." The record company released the Turn Around album at the same time.

"All My Trials" climbed to the number 89 position on the Billboard charts. Everyone thought this indicated the start of a rapid climb to the top, but the single did a sudden reversal and fell off the charts within a month!

* * * * *

Bill, Dick and I sat in front of his television in early spring, 1964, watching the Ed Sullivan show. Tonight the Sullivan show would feature the first American appearance of the new singing sensation, the Beatles.

The British group held the top five positions on the U. S. record charts with their discs, "Can't Buy Me Love," "Twist and Shout," "She Loves You," "I Want To Hold Your Hand," and "Please Please Me."

Ed Sullivan introduced the Beatles and they appeared on stage wearing suits and ties, grinning and shaking their heads back and forth as they belted out the words to "I Want to Hold Your Hand."

"Wadda ya think?" Dick asked. He sounded unsure of himself.

"They're totally unique," Bill replied. "They're revolutionary."

"Oh, I don't know," Dick said. "They do have the advantage of playing their own instruments. They don't have to rely on random back up bands, like we do."

"They're cute," I said, staring at the TV. "I love their hair. And they've got such high energy." As the Beatles left the stage, Bill reached over and flicked off the TV.

"I want to talk to you about your choice of material, "he said. "It's fine to write your own songs, and you've written some wonderful ones, Dick. But I think it's time to record a sure hit, something so commercial it will blow everyone away the first time they hear it. Maybe it's time to leave the folk genre. Get back to rock and roll. Why don't you listen to some demos or albums of other singers. Try to find some song they haven't released yet."

Disappointed by the low sales of "All My Trials", but undaunted, Dick found an old Buddy Holly album. We listened to every cut carefully.

"I really like "Not Fade Away," I said. "I can hear our four voices on it."

"Yeah, that will work. Let's rehearse it."

We showed the song to Don Ralke, who worked up a simple rock arrangement for the musicians. With little fan fare, we recorded the song quickly, planning to place one of the songs from the Turn Around album, "The Gift," on the back side.

The week Warner Brothers Records scheduled "Not Fade Away" for release, I got a call from Joe Smith.

"I've got bad news," he said. "The Rolling Stones just released their new record.

It's a top pick in Billboard and Cashbox magazines. What terrible timing. They recorded "Not Fade Away."

Dick and I couldn't believe that we had chosen to record the same song as the Rolling Stones. Needless to say, the Rolling Stones' record rapidly climbed the charts while ours, now considered a cover record, drifted into rock and roll obscurity. Over the years, thirty-one singers released their versions of "Not Fade Away," including the Beatles in 1982.

Desperate for a follow-up hit, three months later Warner Brothers released another Dick and Dee Dee single, this one called, "You Were Mine" backed by "Remember When." Nothing seemed to work. When this record bombed out, I wondered if we'd ever have a hit single again.

CHAPTER TWENTY-ONE

New Song, New Manager, New Direction

"It's time for a complete musical change," Dick told me. I didn't remind him that Bill had been saying that for months.

"We have to get back to our roots, back to 'The Mountain's High.' I'm going to start listening to songs submitted from publishers."

While sifting through material, Dick discovered a song recorded by The Newbeats, a group from Louisiana. Their national hit, "Bread and Butter" currently sat at the number two position on the national charts, annoying Dick no end.

"They sound just like us," he complained. "They took our sound and now they have a national hit."

When he found "Thou Shalt Not Steal" on a Newbeats album he said, "This is it! This is our next hit single."

The Wilder Brothers agreed it was time for a change and we recorded the song in their studio, releasing the single in the fall. The song started a slow but steady climb up the national charts.

I called Sharon Sheeley. She told me she and Jimmy had married in a small ceremony with just family in attendance. "I'm going by Sharon O'Neill now," she informed me. I congratulated her. She also told me they named their new musical pilot Shindig.

* * * * *

Bill called a special meeting with Dick and me. When I entered his apartment, I saw the changes. The massive desk had vanished and the décor again resembled a living room.

"I wanted to tell you the news in person," he announced, waving his hands toward the furniture. "Please sit down."

Dick and I sat on the sofa.

"I've given this a lot of thought, and decided to leave the personal management business." I felt a strange feeling in my stomach.

"I'm going to work with Roz Ross as her assistant in a new company Dick Clark is forming in Los Angeles, Dick Clark Productions."

"What's going to happen to us?" Dick wailed.

"Well, different acts are making different decisions. For you and Dee Dee, I've contacted a management company in Los Angeles who is willing to take you on. You need to go meet them and see if it's a fit." Bill handed us a card.

"Call Shelly Berger and make an appointment. He's waiting to hear from you. Shelly works for Joe Scandori, who managers Don Rickles. The name of the management company is 'Scandore & Shayne.' I've already talked to Shelly about you two and I think you'll find him terrific to work with.

"It's been great managing acts for a year. I'm going to miss some of the crazy times. But, of course, I'll still be seeing you." He looked pointedly in my direction.

"Was it something we did?" Dick asked.

"No, it's a combination of things. All the acts have become more demanding. Frankly, it's like hanging out with a bunch of children. I want to work on creative television projects with adults."

He noticed our shocked and sad faces.

"Don't worry. I'm not going anywhere. You're more than welcome to call me for advice. It's just that I won't be managing your career any more. Trust me. This is the best move for everybody."

"You helped us a lot," Dick said quietly. "It's not going to be the same without you."

A sad look passed over Bill's face. I realized that he really did care deeply about his acts.

"No," he finally said. "It won't be the same, but you'll be in good hands."

When we left Bill's apartment, Dick did not appear happy.

"I know you don't really care about singing as a career," he said to me, "but I do. I'm going to be singing and writing songs for the rest of my life. And right now, Bill deserted us. That's a rotten thing to do."

I bristled at the criticism of Bill. "Dick, he had to do what was right for himself. He told us the acts were driving him crazy." I didn't mention Dick's storming off the Lloyd Thaxton television show several months earlier.

"Great!" Dick shouted. "We ask him to manage us and he calls us demanding. Well, screw that. I don't need him or you either, for that matter."

Dick pushed the pedal of the Cadillac to the floor and we shot down Wilshire. When he reached the Barrington Plaza, Dick let me out and then took off.

I tried calling Bill, but he didn't answer the phone. After several days of not hearing from Dick or Bill, the phone suddenly rang.

"Dee Dee?" she said. "Roz Ross. Bill has been practically living here ever since I arrived from New York. As he may have told you, we are developing a television project for Dick Clark Productions. Bill told me how creative you are. I wondered if you might come over and help us brainstorm."

I felt flattered Bill told Roz I was creative, but what was he doing "practically living" at her house? Were they involved romantically? Did she know he occasionally dated me? I decided there was only one way to find out.

I drove to Roz's rental house just off the Sunset Strip. Located several blocks above The Whisky (a hot new club), I parked against the curb in front of a small, secluded home. I knocked on the door and after several minutes Roz opened it.

"Dee Dee?" she said. "I'm Roz." She stood about five feet five inches tall. With short brown hair and darting brown eyes, I guessed her to be in her mid-thirties. She inhaled on a cigarette, blowing the smoke toward the ceiling. "Let's get to work."

Bill sat in the living room, slumped on the sofa. Left-over Chinese food containers and empty coffee cups littered the coffee table. Work, I would discover, consumed Roz. She loved nothing more than to focus on a project around the clock, stopping only to eat and grab a few hours' sleep.

This life style obviously appealed to Bill. He appeared animated and relaxed. He gave me a big smile. "There's some left

-over Chinese if you're hungry."

"Thanks, but I just had lunch."

Roz handed me a soft-drink bottle. "Basically we're working on a network pilot. It's like the concept of Shindig, which, incidentally, I hear is airing on ABC in the fall. However, our show will be taped on location. The working title is "Where the Action Is." We intend to go to various outdoor spots, like the mountains and the beach, and tape performers singing their hit records. What do you think of the idea?"

I smiled. "I think that's a great idea. There's room for more than one rock show on television. And I like the idea of going on location. It will give the show a different look each week."

Roz turned to Bill. "See, what did I tell you? I had a gut feeling that Dee Dee would be the right person to give us feedback."

They both smiled at me. Roz shoved a bowl of peanuts in my direction.

"I'm curious how you found out Shindig sold to ABC," I said. "Have they booked any of the shows yet?" I felt surprised that Sharon hadn't asked Dick and me to sing on the show. Then I realized we'd been in the studio a lot. We'd temporarily lost touch with Sharon.

"I don't know their schedule," Bill said. "You should ask Sharon Sheeley. She's largely responsible for creating the concept of Shindig. Anyway, here's the premise for Where the Action Is." He passed me a folder.

I worked with them the rest of that day and into the middle of the night. The three of us sat around the dining room table, drinking cup after cup of coffee. Finally, we broke to get some sleep.

"I've got to leave," I told Roz. "I left Pepe alone in the apartment all day and it really isn't fair to him."

"You've got to come back early tomorrow morning." Roz paced the floor. "Bring your dog with you. You will help us with this, won't you?" She stared at me anxiously.

"Okay." I hesitated. "How many days do you anticipate I'll be working here?"

"Oh, just a few more. Promise me. You'll return early tomorrow morning?" I nodded.

Bill remained with Roz. "I sleep in the guest bedroom," he said. "It saves all that driving time."

As far as I could tell, their relationship was only work related, but I worried nevertheless. I drove back to West Los Angeles, which didn't take long on the now deserted Sunset Boulevard.

* * * * *

Early the next morning, I woke feeling like I was coming down with the flu. Gathering up Pepe, I drove back to Roz's anyway. As the day progressed, after endless cups of coffee and numerous creative discussions, I felt lightheaded. I finally looked in a mirror and saw my face flushed with fever and my eyes bleary.

Roz took my temperature and discovered it was 103 degrees. She called the local deli and ordered hot chicken soup. Insisting I get into bed, she pointed toward her bed in the master bedroom! When I tried to protest, she insisted that she would sleep in the guest bedroom and Bill would sleep on the sofa in the living room. I felt too sick to argue.

For the next five days, I remained bed ridden. Roz kept reappearing, bringing me soup and crackers. I faintly heard their voices in the living room, discussing the pilot. Did they ever sleep?

When I was finally able to stand upright, I took Pepe and drove back to my apartment. I felt like I'd been gone for weeks. It took me several more days to fully recover.

* * * * *

A week later, Dick and I drove to Shelly Berger's home office on Kings Road in West Hollywood. We parked in front and knocked at the door of a craftsman style cottage. A short woman with dark hair opened it.

"Hi, I'm Ellie, Shelly's wife. Come on in. Shelly is in the den."

"Shelly and Ellie," Dick whispered to me. "Sounds like a dance team."

Shelly was sitting behind a desk in his study. He was a large man, with dark hair and compassionate brown eyes. After shaking our hands, he motioned for us to be seated.

"So, Bill tells me you're looking for management. Our company is owned by Joe Scandori," Shelly told us. "He personally manages Don Rickles. However, he is branching out and I have been hired to manage up and coming acts."

"Do you have any other acts signed?" Dick asked. "We don't want to get buried in a large talent pile, like we sometimes were with Bill."

"Right now, if you decide to sign with us, you're my only act. I want to give you one hundred percent of my time and energy." He passed us a dish of M & M's sitting on his desk. "What is your greatest challenge at the moment?"

I felt like saying, "Trying to figure out if Bill and Roz are having a personal relationship."

Dick spoke up. "We aren't getting the promotion we deserve. Something is radically wrong. Why would we have a hit folk song with "Turn Around," but not a hit album and follow-up single? Someone needs to check the type of promotion Warner Brothers Records is giving us.

"Also, the Wilders are taking a ridiculously high percentage of our recording income. We barely make anything. I think we should audit their books."

I felt like Dick poured a bucket of cold water over me. Was this what he really thought?

Shelly studied Dick intently, looking compassionate and deeply concerned. "First things, first," he said. "Those are all issues we can look into. In the meantime, we need to know what we can do to keep you working and in the public eye."

Ellie knocked at the door. "Would you like something to drink?" she asked. "I've got coffee...tea."

"Some tea would be fine," Shelly answered.

Ellie reappeared several minutes later and set the tea pot and cups down on Shelly's desk. Dick barely glanced in her direction. He appeared totally focused on Shelly.

I said, "Our friend, Sharon Sheeley, created a pilot for a television show. It's called Shindig. It will be the first show to feature rock and roll acts. The show airs on ABC in a few months."

"Who told you that?" Dick sounded angry.

"Roz Ross. I think Dick Clark Productions is creating a show to compete with Shindig." Dick looked annoyed that I had information he hadn't heard.

Shelly asked, "Do you two know Sharon Sheeley?"

"She's one of my best friends," Dick said. "We wrote a song together for the Turn Around album."

"That's great." Shelly stood up. "Here we are talking about promotion and you have the greatest opportunity in the world to appear on Shindig. Why don't you tell Sharon you want to be on the show? Think what national television would do for your career."

"Yeah," Dick said. "We need to sing "Thou Shalt Not Steal" on Shindig." He grabbed a handful of M & M's and popped them in his mouth. The smile on his face told me he'd decided our next career move.

CHAPTER TWENTY-TWO

Shindig

True to his word, Dick called Sharon immediately. She convinced the producer of "Shindig", a British gentleman named Jack Goode, to book us on one of the first few television shows.

Shindig aired weekly, starting September 16th 1964. It quickly topped national ratings and watching it became the cool thing to do on Friday nights. We were thrilled and honored to be on the show and pleased that the producers wanted us to debut "Thou Shalt Not Steal" on national television.

A week before our taping the show coordinators requested we come to a recording studio in Hollywood to sing and record "Thou Shalt Not Steal" with the house band, the Shindogs. They wanted to put our voices on a musical track for the show.

We sang "Thou Shalt Not Steal," virtually re-recording our song all over again. It sounded slightly different than the record, which was the point. The show producers wanted the TV audience to hear us singing live over prerecorded voices. I guess it removed a margin for error. In actuality, we would be singing live along with our own voice track.

On October 23, 1964, at 4 AM, I rose for a long drive from West Los Angeles to the ABC Studios in Hollywood at Prospect and Tallmadge. The roads appeared dark and deserted at that hour. I shivered with the cold and the excitement of this new venture.

When I arrived at the studio, after checking my name off a list, the gate man waved me through. I parked the car and, as dawn started to break, entered a side door to the sound set. Like a hive of anxious bees, the studio buzzed with activity.

"I'm here to tape Shindig," I said to a woman with a clipboard. "Dee Dee Sperling of Dick and Dee Dee."

"Please follow me." She led me to a small, nondescript dressing room. It contained a mirror, chair and clothes rack. It was small, but private. I loved everything about it.

"This is your dressing room for the week. Right now, however, you need to go sit in the studio audience with the rest of the cast for a briefing."

I found Dick wandering the halls and we walked to the theater, sinking into the plush theater seats. I looked around to see who else the Shindig producers had booked on the show. Leon Russell, the piano player who backed us at Pandora's Box a year before, sat in the front row. I also recognized a British rock group, Billie J. Kramer and the Dakotas, as well as Jackie Wilson and The Righteous Brothers. Sharon and her husband Jimmy were nowhere to be seen.

The cast assembled on the stage and the show's producer introduced us to the group of "regulars," singers or dancers performing weekly on the show. This category included the Blossoms, (three back-up singers featuring Darlene Love), the Shindogs, a small rock group, and ten to fifteen professional dancers.

For the next three days we rehearsed all day. I learned to walk to my mark, when to cross the stage, how to avoid crashing into dancers, and how to enter and exit quickly for the opening and closing numbers. I often found myself surrounded with huge cameras, a man riding on each one.

The director shouted, "We'll be switching cameras to get different angles, so you need to be vigilant. Remember, when you look into the lens, you are looking directly into the eyes of thousands of television viewers. It gives them the impression that you are singing to them personally."

The actual taping took place on a Friday evening before a live audience. That night I paced back and forth in the wings, watching numerous crew members bustle around, moving cameras and lights into place.

An aide took me to the makeup area, where a makeup artist sponged a tan base coat over my face, adding eyeliner to my upper lids and color to my cheeks. I looked in the mirror and frowned. My face looked artificial, plastic. The woman noticed my expression.

"Don't worry," she said. "You'll look beautiful and natural on camera."

I walked back to the wings and peered out at the audience. The seats contained mostly teens and people in their early twenties. I didn't recognize a single face. Where was Bill? I'd told him about the taping. Maybe he felt uncomfortable coming there, since he no longer managed Dick and me. Maybe he still remained sequestered in Roz's house, planning the pilot for Where the Action Is.

I also thought it unusual that Sharon wasn't there. And I had yet to see Jimmy, although I knew he was in his dressing room, waiting to go on.

Suddenly the lights dimmed. Jimmy O'Neill walked out in front of the cameras. I watched him on a studio monitor. He projected just the right blend of professionalism and clean-cut image.

Jimmy welcomed the audience to the show and announced the line up for that night. Each act received a warm round of applause, including Dick and me.

Then he introduced singer Jackie Wilson. Jackie ran out on stage, the music from the speakers playing the introduction to "Lonely Teardrops." I froze in place, mesmerized as his incredible voice soared to an amazing falsetto note at the end of the song. The audience clapped and shouted.

After Jackie exited, the Shindogs played a number, and then Jimmie introduced the Righteous Brothers. Bill Medley and Bobby Hatfield walked toward the cameras and audience, large smiles on their face. They launched into "Little Latin Loop de Loop." I loved their records and marveled at their soulful voices. They amazed me.

When Jimmy introduced us, Dick and I started moving, grooving to the introduction of "Thou Shalt Not Steal." As I sang I felt great joy and love for the audience. I smiled at Dick and he smiled back. This reminded me of our roots, what it felt like to sing in the beginning, to just have fun with the music.

All tensions of singing with Dick fell away and we reverted back to sharing the joy of music and letting the love flow through us to the audience. It was times like this that I remembered why I'd stuck with singing all these years.

We ended with a preplanned group finale in which all the acts sang together.

I stood next to Jackie Wilson and Bobby Hatfield of the Righteous Brothers. The spontaneous jam built to a climax. The audience roared its approval and when the director yelled, "Cut" and went to commercial, we had difficulty ending the song. We wanted it to go on forever.

* * * * *

In time, Dick and I became semi-regulars on Shindig, appearing on the show almost every other week. During the three years the show aired, we performed with some of the most famous groups and recording artists in the world.

Since Shindig producer Jack Goode hailed from England, he knew all the British acts with chart hits in the United Kingdom. As British artists rose in popularity in the United States, he booked them on Shindig. During its three-year run, Shindig became one of the most popular shows in America.

Interestingly enough, few American artists survived the British music invasion of 1964. The careers of hundreds of singers like Jan and Dean; the Crystals; Little Peggy March; Peter, Paul and Mary; Roy Orbison and even Elvis Presley floundered. Some Motown artists remained an exception, but almost all of the rest of the singers to climb the top-forty charts in the United States were British.

This illustrious group included the Beatles, who dominated the record charts for the entire year, Petula Clark, the Dave Clark Five, Cilla Black, the Honeycombs, Georgie Fame, Herman's Hermits, Gerry and the Pacemakers, Freddie and the Dreamers, the Kinks, Bill J. Kramer and the Dakotas, Manfred Mann, Peter and Gordon, Millie, the Moody Blues, the Searchers, and finally the Rolling Stones. Besides the Beatles and Rolling Stones, none of these acts had ever released records in America before. Most of them appeared on Shindig.

"Thou Shalt Not Steal" reached the number 13 position on the Billboard charts that first year. Our constant presence on Shindig helped expose our song to thousands of people.

I remember how excited I felt when we worked with British performers. I joined in the national fascination with anything British, including hair styles and clothes.

At the start of Shindig, in late 1964, British groups still wore suits and ties, as did the Americans. But British men wore their hair longer, making them appear trendy and youthful.

Both Dick and I changed our appearance, albeit gradually. Our hair lengthened, Dick's over his forehead and mine to my shoulders. By the time we'd performed on Shindig for a year, we looked more like British citizens than Americans.

Performing on 'Shindig.'

CHAPTER TWENTY-THREE

Recording Over Stones' Tracks in London

For a brief time, Dick dated Leslie Gore, pop singer of "It's My Party." He'd met her backstage at one of our shows. One day Leslie told Dick she'd been booked on a special rock and roll show to be filmed at the Santa Monica Civic Auditorium.

The show featured Jan and Dean, James Brown, Leslie Gore, and two of the first British groups to have chart records in America, Herman's Hermits and the Rolling Stones, singing their American hit record, "Time Is On My Side."

Dick began badgering Shelly to book us on the show. Shelly tried, but the show producer refused his request, protesting that he'd booked too many acts already. Still, Dick wouldn't give up. He tried to get Leslie to put in a good word for our stage performance. He tried calling the producer himself. Nothing worked. We were not booked on the Tami Show.

We were, however, invited to watch the show and were given a small concession: backstage passes. Dick and I appeared in the dressing room to say hello to Leslie Gore. We even dressed in stage clothes in case one of the acts didn't show up!

Standing backstage in the wings, we watched in awe as Jan and Dean skateboarded down a long ramp built out toward the audience. Leslie sang, "Its My Party," James Brown performed his fake "heart attack" routine on stage, and the Rolling Stones performed.

Afterward, we boarded buses to head for a live show at the Long Beach Arena, where Dick and I would open for the stars of the live show, the Rolling Stones. The bill also featured Ike and Tina Turner.

As we sat in the bus ready to leave, one of the cameramen from the Tami Show brought his camera on board and briefly filmed the singers sitting in bus seats. The camera scanned past me, catching me briefly on film.

Unfortunately, I smoked at that time, a nasty habit I managed to drop by my late twenties. Dick never did make it onto the Tami Show film, but I remained on film for posterity with a cigarette dangling from one hand.

* * * * *

That night, the Long Beach Arena filled with fans. As the show started, Mick Jagger watched from the wings as Dick and I performed. I carried a tambourine, which I usually played during some of our faster songs. Mick approached me backstage, just as the announcer called them on.

"Can I borrow your tambourine?" he asked.

I smiled and handed it over. I watched as Mick stood before the microphone, pounding out the rhythm on his hip. After the Stones left the stage, he handed the tambourine back to me. For several years after that, Mick often used a tambourine in his act.

The disc jockey announced Ike and Tina Turner. When Tina stepped onto the stage, the place went wild. As Tina danced and sang, Mick and several other Rolling Stones stared at her from the side of the stage, gaping in amazement.

During his performance on the Tami Show, Mick Jagger stood frozen in one place. But after he saw Tina, he began to dance all over the stage.

* * * * *

Determined to break open the British market, Dick made a bold and unusual move. He decided we should go to England for several weeks to promote ourselves there. Now that we had a hit record, all doors flew open. Joe Smith agreed that Warner Brothers Records would pay our expenses, so in October, we flew to London by ourselves.

Warner Brothers Records alerted the media of our arrival so we weren't surprised when a small group of photographers and reporters met our plane.

"Could you two hug each other and smile?" one man shouted, aiming his camera in our direction.

Thrilled by the attention, we eagerly complied with his requests. One man asked if we would assume a waltz pose so Dick could dip me over backwards, as if we were performing the tango. Laughing, we posed.

That photo appeared in the morning papers. However, they cropped it, only showing us from the waist up. It looked as if I lay on my back with Dick on top of me. Although we appeared fully clothed, the illusion suggested otherwise. Annoyed with the deception, I learned to be wary of requests from British photographers.

We checked into a beautiful hotel near Kensington Gardens. My lovely room looked small but featured a garden view. Dick stayed just down the hall. We spent our first day in a record store, buying albums of singers not yet popular in the United States. One of my favorites was a blues album by the Rolling Stones. It included "Time Is on My Side."

That evening, Dick and I decided to go clubbing with Michael Aldred, a young man we had met through Warner Brothers Records. Michael stood at medium height, with longish dark hair and large eyes. He was thin and wore dark clothes.

Michael took us to a private club in Kensington. When I saw Brian Jones of the Rolling Stones sitting at the table, my heart leapt into my throat. I tried to act blasé. "Dick, Dee Dee," Michael said to us, "This is Brian." He nodded at the other man at the table. "And this is the Stones' record producer, Andrew Oldham."

Michael pulled up a chair next to Brian and Andrew. Dick and I sat across from them. Before we even ordered drinks, Michael saw someone he knew at the bar.

"I've got to talk to someone," he said. "It's important. I'll be right back." He left the table abruptly.

I stared at Brian. His original dark blond Beatles-style hair cut had grown past his shoulders, in a pageboy style. He looked like someone from King Arthur's court. Shy and passive, he barely spoke.

When Andrew got up to use the rest room, Brian leaned over and quietly asked Dick. "Hey, mate, do you have any pills on you?"

Dick assumed Brian had a headache. "Yeah, I've got pain medicine," he said, pulling a bottle out of his pocket. Brian struck out his hand. Without even identifying what the pills were, he popped them in his mouth, washing them down with a swig of bourbon. The rest of the evening he just sat there saying nothing, a stoned look on his face.

When Andrew returned, Dick turned to him.

"Listen," Dick said. "Dee Dee and I need another hit record in America. I'm sure if we asked Warner Brothers Records, they'd be glad to pay for a session here in London. Would you be willing to produce it?"

Andrew looked startled. He glanced at Brian, sitting stoned in the corner and back at Dick.

"I don't know, mate. I'm awfully busy."

"It wouldn't take long. Just give us some songs and we can learn them in a day or two. I'll bet you have contacts at Decca where you record the Stones. They'll let you book a studio, especially if Warner Brother Records pays for it."

"Aw, I gotta think this one over. Can I call you at your hotel?" Andrew looked uncomfortable and glanced around for a way to escape. He finally jumped from his chair and dashed to the rest room. Dick turned to me.

"We've got to persuade Andrew to record us," he said. "I know the reason we aren't having consecutive hits is the Wilder Brothers and Don Ralke. They're outdated musically. We need a new, hip sound and Andrew is just the one to produce it." "But we have a contract with the Wilders."

Dick waved his hand. "Oh, don't worry about that. Those things can always be worked out. I'm sure Joe Smith would be thrilled to death if he heard Andrew Oldham was recording us."

I glanced at Brian Jones. He sat there mellow and smiling, saying nothing.

"How are you going to convince Andrew to take on this project?"

"I'm not going to let him out of my sight unless he agrees to a session date."

I wondered if Dick might be losing his mind.

When Andrew returned to the table, he quickly polished off his drink and stood up.

"Well, it was jolly good meeting you. I have to be leaving."

Dick leapt to his feet.

"I'll go with you." He turned toward me. "Dee Dee, Michael will see that you get back to the hotel safely. I'll talk to you in the morning."

The last I saw of Dick, he ran out of the club, chasing after Andrew Oldham.

Slightly concerned at being left alone in a strange city, I turned to Brian. He gave me a shy look. I observed his glazed eyes and slow reactions.

Michael Aldred noticed Dick and Andrew's sudden disappearance and returned to our table.

"Need a ride, luv? We can share a cab."

Brian trailed after us, following us into the taxi. The boys let me out first at my hotel.

"I'll call you soon," Michael promised.

* * * * *

The phone rang early the next morning. Dick sounded elated. "I did it. I worked things out. If all goes well, we'll be recording at Decca Records by the end of the week. Andrew is producing us."

I felt truly amazed. "How did you convince him?"

"I badgered him until he couldn't stand it anymore. He finally gave in."

I burst out laughing. "So what material are we doing?"

"Here's the thing. Andrew doesn't have time to bring in musicians and do an actual session. So he agreed to let us have several old Rolling Stones tracks they're not using. Mick Jagger and Keith Richards wrote the songs. He's going to drop Mick's lead vocals from the tracks so we can sing lead instead."

"But what if the songs are in the wrong keys?"

"We will make this work! I'm meeting Andrew later to get dubs of the master. We can practice to that. Meanwhile, call Joe Smith and tell him what we're doing. Ask him if Warner Brothers Records will pay for the session."

He wanted me to call Joe Smith and ask for money? After Dick hung up, I placed a call to Bill. After numerous rings, he finally answered.

"So, how's London? I've been reading in the paper that you're having great weather."

"Yeah, it's alright. Listen, I need to ask you something. Dick and I met Andrew Oldham last night in a club, you know, the Rolling Stones producer? Dick convinced him to produce a record for us. Now Dick wants me to call Joe Smith and ask if Warner Brothers Records will pay for it."

"Wait a minute. You have an exclusive production contract with the Wilder Brothers and Don Ralke."

"I know. That's what I told Dick. But he thinks this session will bring us the stardom we deserve. It is an incredible opportunity. I'm hoping something can be worked out. What do you think I should do?"

"You'd better tell Joe exactly what is going on. I'm sure he doesn't want to see a lawsuit between you and the Wilder Brothers. Since The Wilder Brothers lease your tapes to Warner Brothers Records, they might sue if the record company releases a disc they didn't produce. It sounds messy."

Bill took a deep breath and continued. "Call Joe, tell him the truth and see what he says. That's all you can do. Incidentally, I miss you. When are you coming home?"

"I miss you, too. Believe me, I wish you were here with us. Things are so chaotic. Well, we'll be home soon."

* * * * *

With trepidation, I placed the call to Warner Brothers Records in the United States. It took twenty minutes for the hotel to make the overseas connection. I could only guess what this phone call might cost. Finally, I heard Joe Smith's voice on the line.

"Hello, Dee Dee," Joe said. "How are things going in London?"

I tried to ignore the echo delay and launched into my reason for calling.

"Great. Listen, Dick asked me to call you to run something by you. Last night we met Andrew Oldham. You know the Rolling Stones producer? Dick convinced him to produce a recording session for us. Andrew doesn't have time to search for material and hire an arranger and musicians, so he wants us to sing on some old Rolling Stones tracks they're not using."

"That sounds rather unusual."

"It is. But Dick is convinced this session will result in a follow-up hit to 'Thou Shalt Not Steal.' So, the reason I called… he's hoping that Warner Brothers Records will pick up the tab for the session."

I heard silence on the line. Joe Smith finally spoke again. "Where is the session going to be?"

"I think it's going to be at Decca Recording Studios, where the Stones record.

It should be cheap because we're singing to tracks prerecorded by the Stones."

"What do the Wilders have to say about this?"

I took a gulp. "They don't know about it yet. We were hoping they might give us permission to use another producer just this one time. If the songs are a hit, it will only help all of us. After all, we're still under contract to them for several more years."

"Alright," Joe said. "Let me talk to the Wilders to see what they say. I'll get back to you."

About half an hour later, he called back.

"I worked it out. They weren't happy, but they agreed to let you record one session with Andrew. Why don't you have Andrew call me so we can work out the details?" I thanked him profusely and hung up, a smile on my face.

* * * * *

Dick arrived in my room carrying a portable record player and the Rolling Stones dubs, large records of vinyl. We wrote out the words to the songs on hotel stationery and started singing along with the music. Fortunately, they were in keys we could sing to.

The Rolling Stones played the instruments on the track and sang back-up vocals. Dick listened to Mick's lead vocal several times and then sang loudly over Mick's voice. I sang a harmony part. We practiced the songs for several hours, until we memorized them.

The next day Andrew called Dick and told him he'd talked to Joe Smith. Warner Brothers had offered to pay for the session. Andrew booked a studio at Decca Records and announced, "We're recording in two days."

* * * * *

The evening of the session, Dick and I arrived by cab at Decca Records. It rained that day and the city streets glistened. As we pulled up in front of the studio, we noticed another cab unloading Andrew Oldham, Brian Jones and Keith Richards. Andrew introduced us to Keith, who simply nodded, and we started into the building.

I had purchased a new pair of shoes that morning. They were black, pointy high heels. Walking through the glass doors of Decca Records, we crossed a large rubber mat containing hundreds of tiny holes. As I hurried to catch up with Dick, my right heel got caught in one of the holes. Unaware, I moved forward, but the heel held.

I lost my balance and fell hard onto my stomach, knocking the wind out of my lungs. Like a beached whale, I lay on the ground gasping for air.

Andrew, Dick, Brian and Keith Richards stood in a circle above me, staring down.

I felt my face flush as I struggled to breathe. "Ahhh. Ahhh."

Dick poked me with his foot. "For God's sake," he hissed. "Get up. This is embarrassing."

I responded with another gasp and managed to choke out, "I can't breathe!"

A security guard came running over. "Great steaming nit!" he shouted. "She's had the bloody wind knocked out of 'er. Just leave her be, mates. She'll be alright in a minute."

I lay there sprawled on the mat, trying to force air into my lungs. Everyone else froze. No one spoke. Finally, with a gasp, I felt air enter my lungs and after several more moments, made a half-hearted attempt to rise. The singers went into action, hauling me up by my arms, picking up the sheet music and the contents from my purse scattered all over the floor of the foyer.

"Are you alright?" Andrew asked.

I nodded. Dismissing the accident, our group paraded into one of the studios' control booths. Nobody said anything further about my dramatic entrance. I struggled to ignore the pain in my chest from the fall.

"I'm really fine now," I thought. If Bill were there, he'd have called the paramedics. Taking a deep breath, I decided to focus on the task at hand.

Andrew indicated Dick and I were to go into the large studio and stand before the single microphone. We put on earphones and listened while the musical track to "Some Things Just Stick in Your Mind," started to play. Andrew lowered Mick Jagger's voice until it faded away.

Over the tracks, Dick sang lead and I sang harmony. We could still hear the Rolling Stones faintly singing backup vocals in the background, "Bom, Bom, Bom."

We put our voices on four songs that evening. When Andrew handed Dick the master tapes, Dick thanked him profusely. We said goodbye to Keith and Brian. Dick carried the tape to the cab gingerly, as if it were made of glass.

"This is it," Dick said. "Our next hit record." I flopped back on the cab seat and closed my eyes, my body stiff and aching from the fall. While Dick chatted on I dreamed of soaking in a hot bath and climbing into bed.

* * * * *

The next day Brian Jones called and offered to take Dick to some of the trendy shops in Soho. Fully recovered, and not wanting to miss out on the fun, I went with them in the cab, but told them I wanted to take off to do some shopping on my own. I made plans to meet them several hours later.

At that time, London wore the proud title of "the world center of everything hip." Fashion, music, style…it all originated from there. The Beatles put England on the map as the center of the world's youth culture. I couldn't wait to visit London clothes stores.

The three of us exited the cab, and I headed across the street to check out a shoe sale. Cars and taxis raced through the rush-hour traffic. Double-decker buses honked as Dick and Brian stood on the street trying to determine which direction to go. A white school bus filled with adolescent girls pulled up at a stop sign.

"Oh, my God," a girl screamed out of the window. "It's Brian Jones of the Rolling Stones."

Brian glanced up at the bus. Suddenly, the bus windows shot down and the entire bus load of girls climbed out, dropping down onto the pavement like ripe oranges. To avoid hitting them, drivers honked, swore and slammed on their brakes.

Brian panicked and darted down an alley. Dick tore after him, followed by twenty girls screaming, "Brian, Brian, wait!" I stared dumbfounded, as they disappeared from sight.

The bus driver pulled over to the curb and opened the door of the now empty bus. I heard him mutter to himself. Ten minutes passed, with no sign of any of them. Finally, the girls filtered back, excited but also dejected. They'd lost Brian and Dick.

The girls climbed back on the bus and it finally took off. I waited awhile longer for Dick and Brian to reappear. When they didn't, I decided to get on with my shopping. Later in the day, I ran into Dick.

"You won't believe what happened," he said. "We ran for blocks. It was exciting, but also scary. I got the feeling if they caught us, they would have pulled out our hair."

"Anyway, we finally rounded a corner, found another alley and saw some empty trash cans. Brian threw open the lid of one of them, saw it was empty and jumped in. I did the same with the other can. We heard the stampede of girls charge by, but they never thought to look inside the trash. We stayed in there until we couldn't hear them anymore. Finally it got quiet and we climbed out. Brian started shuddering. He took a cab back to his flat." Dick grinned. "Shows you what can happen when you're a huge star."

* * * * *

My birthday happened to be the day before we were scheduled to return to Los Angeles. Dick decided to celebrate by throwing a huge party in a special suite of the hotel. I didn't realize he intended Warner Brothers Records to pick up the tab.

The afternoon of my birthday, Dick showed me the suite. Cream silk fabric covered the living room walls, sharing the space with hand-carved wood paneling. A baby grand piano stood in the corner. Fresh floral arrangements and antiques filled the suite.

The master bedroom, almost as large as my apartment in Los Angeles, featured a beautiful canopy bed. Dick told me that since it was my birthday, I should spend the night in the suite. I eagerly moved some of my things over. What a nice thing for Dick to do, I thought.

Michael Aldred helped Dick with the invitation list. He invited Brian Jones and many of his colleagues from the television shows, "Top of the Pops," and "Ready, Steady, Go." The hotel catered the affair.

That evening, waiters passed trays of starters. A bartender stood behind the mahogany bar in the corner. Several hundred people showed up. I missed Bill but felt better when a telegram arrived. Bill wished me a happy birthday and told me to hurry home.

Brian Jones sat quietly in the corner, observing the party scene. I joined him for a period of time, enjoying his silence and calmness. It was hard to stop looking at his blond page boy hair cut and perfect chiseled face.

"It's been great having you and Dick here this past week," he finally said.

"Maybe you'll be coming to the United States soon."

"Yeah, if the Stones play L.A. again, I'll give you a call."

By 3 AM Dick and I suggested everyone leave, but no one paid any attention.

I don't think half of them even knew who we were. Finally, in resignation, because people still partied in the living room and bedroom, I took my few possessions and returned to my regular room to get some sleep.

The following morning, Dick and I returned to inspect the hotel suite. A lone maid in uniform vacuumed the living room. But we observed, sticking out from behind the sofa, a pair of legs. Then we saw another person sleeping near the wall in the corner. People we didn't even know had spent the night in my hotel suite!

When we checked out, Dick told the cashier to charge the suite to Warner Brothers Records, along with our regular room charges. Unlike Liberty, Warner Brothers Records never questioned the extra expense.

Sad to leave a place where we'd met wonderful people and had such a great time, we boarded the jet headed back to LA . Dick hand carried the Rolling Stones session tape, holding it in his lap the entire trip.

We return from London with a new look.

"Some Things Just Stick in Your Mind"

CHAPTER TWENTY-FOUR

Murray the K's Brooklyn Paramount Shows

Disc jockey Murray the K booked Dick and me on his annual Brooklyn Paramount Theatre Christmas Show. One week after our return from London, Dick and I flew to New York City. Perhaps I should say, Dick, Pepe and I. When turned away from an overbooked boarding kennel, I made a last-minute decision to carry the dog to New York in a large straw bag. I felt there were no other options.

Snow covered the sidewalks as Dick and I wandered the streets, watching the ice skaters at Rockefeller Plaza and marveling at the holiday decorations in department store windows. Pepe stepped in snow for the first time and started shaking so violently, I thought his teeth might fall out. Realizing this California dog needed to be carried all the time, I left him in the hotel room while I headed out to exercise.

I found myself wandering through Central Park, staring into space, wondering what the future held. The silent, drifting snow flakes caused me to reflect on my life. I knew Dick and I wouldn't continue singing forever. But what real relationships had I built in my life? How would Bill and I find time to be together? Dick and I continually worked, traveled, always staying on the move. I started to think that, as great as singing was, there must be something more out there.

* * * * *

We rode a subway from Manhattan to Brooklyn. I finally staggered into the Brooklyn Paramount Theater, arms still sore from carrying Pepe, a hanging bag of stage clothes and a heavy cosmetic bag.

On stage, grinning maniacally stood Murray the K. He was middle-aged, medium height, thin, with dark hair and a large smile. I knew his reputation as king of the New York City airwaves, a disc jockey from 1958 to the present year, 1964 and beyond, on WINS radio, a 50,000-watt clear channel that broadcast for miles. I would also discover Murray's identity as a consummate showman. He billed himself as "Boss of the Swinging Soirée, Murray the K," and in the future, "The Fifth Beatle."

Murray produced rock and roll shows at the Brooklyn Paramount Theatre for about six years. I imagine he had secret aspirations to be a Broadway producer, as he told us we would all be doing an opening number together, which he wrote.

The entire cast ran on stage and burst into song.

"Another opening, another show,

We're back in Brooklyn and raring to go."

* * * * *

Since there were so many acts, it took hours to run through the cast rehearsal. Waiting our turn, we watched the Shangri-Las' rehearse. A girl's trio, in their late teens, they sang their new hit record, "Leader of the Pack," the story of a girl who falls in love with a guy from the "wrong side of town." He's finally killed in a motorcycle accident.

Murray arranged for a motorcycle driver to circle the stage behind the Shangri-La's on a Harley Davidson. As the motorcycle revved up and slowly drove in circles, the Shangri-Las started singing. Circling the stage, the motorcycle driver accidentally steered his bike into the back curtain. With a crash, he and the bike fell over. Several stage hands ran out. It took about ten minutes to untangle the man and push the bike upright.

Pepe, who slept in the straw bag during rehearsal, was jolted awake by the revving of the motorcycle and let out a growl. Oh, no. What if he disrupted the show and Murray kicked him out of the theater? I knelt down and felt for him in the bag, patting his head. "Good dog," I whispered. He finally went back to sleep.

I watched Dionne Warwick rehearse "Do You Know the Way to San Jose?" and "Message to Michael." As I stood in the wings observing her friendly manner and the ease with which she rehearsed the band, I envied her professionalism. She stood tall, with elegance, grace and charm. I sighed, feeling amateurish beside her.

Murray the K approached me, followed by a young woman with a huge black beehive hairdo that towered six inches above her head. She carried a clipboard.

"Dee Dee, you're assigned a dressing room on the fourth floor with Dionne," Murray said. I acknowledged his comment with a nonchalant nod. Perhaps I might learn something from Dionne. Being her roommate was definitely cool.

Then a stage manager called our names. After we rehearsed and walked off stage, we noticed the Shirelles watching us from the wings. One of the singers, Mickey, looked us up and down. "You know, you should exit the stage in a more professional manner. It looks sort of awkward the way you both half-ass bow and leave the stage."

I looked at Dick. He appeared shocked.

"Why don't you hold hands, bow together, then Dee Dee crosses in front of you with a twirl, ending up on the other side of you, holding your other hand. Then you could bow a second time and leave the stage. It might look more professional."

When we continued to stare at her, Mickey spun into motion.

"Like this," she said. She took Dick's hand, nodding that he should bow when she did. Then she swirled in front of him, releasing his right and taking his left. Again they bowed. She was right. It made a huge difference. Dick appeared uncomfortable. I didn't know if it was because Mickey was telling him what to do or because he felt awkward.

Dick and I practiced the bow several times, until Mickey applauded. "You've got it."

Dick and I used Mickey's bow every night we performed for the rest of our career together.

* * * * *

After the Shirelles, Jan and Dean, the Chiffons, Johnny Tillotson, the Kingsmen, the Thymes, the Ronettes, Smokey Robinson and the Miracles, the Dovells, Ben E. King, the Drifters rehearsed, Chuck Jackson, the starring act, closed the rehearsal with his soulful rendition of "Any Day Now."

Chuck had stage presence, raw emotion, and an amazing voice. I realized at that moment that this was the epitome of peak performance. I vowed to try to feel the lyrics of our songs on stage, to communicate the way Chuck did.

How spectacular to see performers on an official stage, with the proper lighting and orchestra behind them. It was so unlike our usual gigs, where we stood on a makeshift stage and tried to make it through the songs with an unknown four-piece band.

Johnny Tillotson, who performed with us on the Dick Clark Caravan of Stars Tour, arrived at the rehearsal with his attractive blond wife, Lou (short for Lucille), and reconnected with Dick and me. We all hugged each other.

"We're commuting from Manhattan to Brooklyn each day," Johnny said. "It's a long haul. Where are you guys staying?"

"In Manhattan," I answered.

"You know we're performing five shows a day, right?"

"Five shows? I thought we were doing two each night," Dick answered.

I felt shocked. That was way more than we'd anticipated.

"No, we start at ten in the morning and finish at ten at night. This commuting thing will be expensive if we take cabs. Why don't Lou and I meet you in Manhattan and we could take the subway together? As they say, there's strength in numbers." We agreed to take the subway back to Manhattan after the rehearsal ended that night, to try out his plan.

Pepe started whining, so I quickly climbed four flights of metal stairs to the dressing room. I found cold, drab cement walls and a single radiator for central heat. Across one wall stretched a large mirror. A counter faced it. There were no closets, but someone had placed clothes racks against the back wall. The room felt stifling. I tugged open the massive windows for fresh air, even though snow flurries flew in.

With a sigh, I hung my garment bag on the clothes rack and lifted my heavy makeup bag onto the counter. Pepe, now fully alert, jumped out of the straw bag and started sniffing the corners of the dressing room.

Moments later Dionne entered. She smiled when she saw Pepe. "I take it he's housebroken," she commented.

I laughed. "Fortunately, yes."

Dionne looked around the room at the drab, industrial green surroundings.

"Well, I've seen worse. Which side do you want?"

"I don't care. I have no preference."

"Alright, why don't you take the left side and I'll take the right."

I studied Dionne as she started unpacking her makeup bag, carefully placing cosmetics and a giant bottle of Jean Nate cologne on the counter. She looked more natural, less glamorous up close. I felt slightly nervous, but her friendly smile immediately put me at ease.

"I've got a dressmaker coming any minute," she said. "He creates the most beautiful floor-length gowns. Would you like to see a sample of what he does?" I nodded.

Within minutes a male dressmaker/costume designer entered, triumphantly carrying his latest creation for Dionne. It was a dramatic gown, with flared sleeves and a ruffled neckline.

"This is Dee Dee," she commented, waving in my direction. "She might like a gown, too." The man scurried over, opening a book with fashion sketches. I saw numerous pages of dazzling costumes.

"How long does it take to make one?" The man looked at his appointment book. "I can have a dress ready in three days."

There was a sudden knock at the door. The costume designer opened it. Murray the K stood outside, shadowed by his assistant.

"That's what I like, classy singers," he said, staring at Dionne's new gown hanging on the rack. "Just want to know, everyone feeling groovy?"

We smiled and nodded.

Murray stared at Pepe. "My God, for a moment I thought that was a rat. Make sure you keep him in the dressing room."

"I will," I said. With a thud, the door slammed shut behind him.

"What are the prices for your gowns?" I asked.

"Two-hundred-fifty dollars each. I think you'll agree it's a steal."

I gulped, but quickly rationalized that I'd be wearing the outfit often, if we performed in clubs. "That's fine."

The man pulled out a tape measure and took my measurements. I chose the sketch of a beautiful lavender fitted gown with long sleeves and ruffles at the wrist. I pictured myself slim and elegant, descending a long staircase, a vision in purple.

Pepe, who had been sleeping under the make up counter, suddenly roused himself and started pacing.

"I think he has to go out," Dionne commented.

"Right."

I picked up his leash and took Pepe down the metal stairs to the main level and out the stage entrance door, shivering in the cold while he did his business.

"You're not going to be able to go out that door by yourself after today," a stage hand said. "By this time tomorrow, there will be hundreds of screaming kids out there. Ya gotcha self a problem, lady."

I stared at him. He had a point. I hadn't thought about walking Pepe while we were at the Brooklyn Paramount Theatre.

"Joe's my name," the man said. "I'll walk him if you want. Of course, I need a little cash for my efforts." We agreed upon a price and that problem was taken care of.

However, I quickly discovered we were virtually trapped inside the theater. During their Christmas break most of the teens in Brooklyn either sat in the theater all day, watching the show over and over, or stood outside the stage door, waiting for singers to come out.

There was no way anyone could leave for dinner, so Joe provided take-out menus. I ordered Pepe the closest thing to dog food I could find, Salisbury steak with gravy and mashed potatoes. That evening, Dionne, Pepe and I ate our dinner in the dressing room off aluminum take-out trays. I found it ironic that we all ate the same meal.

I felt nervous as I dressed for the first show. Dionne wore a floor-length, form fitting gown. I wore a long silk skirt and sequined top. We both tottered around in three inch heels, although Dionne glided as she walked. I basically trotted. We managed to climb down four flights of stairs, holding up the bottoms of our skirts so they wouldn't collect dust.

Dick stood backstage, dressed in a shiny blue suit and tie. He looked nervous. "There you are," he said, pulling at my arm. "I was afraid you'd miss the opening." Dionne smiled at me and walked away.

We heard a loud drum roll and a voice boomed through the theater, "And now, the boss of the swinging soirée, Murray the K." Screams erupted from the audience.

The young people yelled and shouted, barely able to remain seated.

Dressed in an incredibly hip and expensive suit, wearing polished shoes and a huge smile, Murray ran on stage. In a moment of glory he shouted, "Ah Ba." The audience went ballistic.

"Ah Ba," they repeated. I heard another roar of approval.

Then he shouted what sounded like, "Bo Ma a Ma." The roar rolled over us. "That's what I like, a class audience. It's pretty groovy. And now, the cast of the show." I felt Dick push me from behind and, trailing after the other singers, we ran out onto the stage for the opening number, "Another opening, another show."

No one knew where to stand or how to move, but we made up for our awkwardness with enthusiasm. The crowd didn't care what we did. They yelled non-stop. I watched the rest of the show from the wings. Most of the acts did two or three numbers. Everyone looked glamorous and professional. And then it was our turn. Murray shouted, "And now here's an act all the way from Cal-lee-forn I-A, Dick and Dee Dee."

We ran toward the microphone set in the center of the stage. The color gels in the stage lights kept changing, flooding us with different mood-enhancing tones. For "Turn Around," blue and purple lights flooded over us. Respecting the mood of the song, the crowd lowered their screams to a decent level, but the moment it ended, the loud screaming commenced. It felt great to receive such love and support from an audience. I left the stage exhilarated.

Standing in the wings, I watched the rest of the show unfold much as it had during rehearsal, except this time, the motorcycle driver managed to keep his bike away from the curtains.

As Chuck Jackson sang his final note, the entire place erupted. Kids leapt from their seats, shouting and clapping. Murray shouted, "Come on out, everyone. Take a bow."

The entire cast walked on stage, smiling and bowing. The applause went on for five or ten minutes. Finally we wandered off stage. The lights came on in the theatre after the audience drifted out. A stagehand shouted, "Next show's in two hours!" I looked at my watch. We wouldn't be leaving the theater until after midnight.

Joe, the stagehand, beckoned us over. "Wanna see something cool?" he asked.

He put out his hand. "For just a buck each, I'll show you how to escape this joint."

Dick reached in his pocket. "Here," he said, handing the man two dollars. "It's worth it to see what you're up to."

We followed Joe through a maze of backstage cables and hallways, until we reached a wall with a large black curtain hanging over it. Joe pulled the curtain aside, revealing a hole in the wall large enough for a person to climb through. It looked like someone had taken a crow bar to the plaster.

Joe said, "This leads to the bar next door. Tony, the bartender, lets the performers enter the back of the bar through this hole. He's got several tables in there for you to sit. It's cool." I smiled at the ingenuity of former performers trapped in the Brooklyn Paramount Theatre. They'd knocked a hole in the wall and crawled through to freedom!

Lynn Easton of the Kingsmen, exploring the theater on his own, appeared in the dim light.

"Check this out," I said, pointing to the hole in the wall. "

Well, what are we waiting for?" Dick answered. "Let's go.

We ducked our heads and climbed through the hole, entering a storage closet. Facing a dusty closed door, we cautiously opened it. We walked into a private room with several tables crammed into the tiny space. A heavyset man, with a balding head, red face and strong biceps entered from the bar area. He wore a stained apron around his waist.

"Hey," he said. "Think of this place as youse guys' home away from home, you know whatta mean? So whad'll you have?"

"I'll have a Heineken," Lynn said.

"Bourbon and water." Dick's drink order startled me. We never drank before shows. I didn't like the taste of beer, but it sounded like a harmless thing to order.

"I'll have a Heineken, too," I said.

"The fans will never know you're here," the bartender commented. We could hear voices from the crowd on the other side of the wall. "I'll be back with the orders."

After he left I turned to Lynn. "So, what are the words to "Louie, Louie?"

He grinned. "It's a song about a man sailing a ship alone across the sea, thinking of his girlfriend constantly. When he finally sees Jamaica, he realizes it won't be long before he takes her in his arms again. But you wouldn't believe what lyrics people imagine we are singing. We've heard it all." Lynn leaned back in his chair and put his head against the wall. "It's great to get away from all that chaos, especially the constant screaming, don't you think?"

I started to relax.

Dick said, "After all the scum holes we've played, this is a pretty upscale place. You know, with the orchestra and all."

Lynn smiled. "Yeah, well, we play our own instruments, so the orchestra doesn't do us any good. But it is an upscale gig, that's for sure."

The bartender brought our order, setting the frosty glasses and bottles on the table. "Just shout if ya need anything. Oh, yeah, sign this tab. We settle up at the end of the week."

We sat in comfort and relative peace for about twenty minutes. The cold Heinekens tasted great. Eventually, we looked at our watches and left, ducking back through the storage closet hole in the wall to the backstage area of the Brooklyn Paramount. We arrived just in time for the second show.

* * * * *

Later that evening, after all the final bows and farewells, we waited an hour in the dark theater until the fans left. Finally, Dick, Lou and Johnny Tillotson and I, with Pepe in the straw bag, left the deserted building to walk out into a frigid New York night. At this hour, few cabs roamed the streets. We hurried toward a subway entrance a block away.

Huddling together under a dim overhead light in the nearly deserted subway, I felt nervous. The black subway tunnels stretched endlessly toward the unknown. Strange, unidentifiable sounds emanated from them.

At a distance, we observed the only other person in the deserted area. An old woman, dressed in what appeared to be black rags, eyed us warily from the shadows.

She slowly approached us. "I'm going to throw you on the train tracks," she hissed.

The four of us bunched closer together, trying to ignore her. To our great relief, the subway finally roared into sight and we climbed aboard the neon-lit car.

Pepe never woke during the entire episode. He definitely failed as a watch dog.

* * * * *

The next morning I got up, staring around the hotel room. For a moment, I didn't know where I was. I studied the faded rug. The honking cars and continuous hum of a city that never sleeps resounded through the windows and walls. My room contained a bed and desk. There was no dresser. Pepe slept curled up in the corner on a blanket.

I looked at my travel alarm. Oh, yeah, we're in New York. There was still plenty of time before we traveled to Brooklyn for the first show. I thought of calling Bill but realized it was three hours earlier in Los Angeles and he'd probably still be sleeping, so instead I ordered a room service breakfast.

The phone rang, loud and shrill. "Dee Dee," Dick said. "I just got a call from Johnny. He wants us to meet him at the subway entrance at 9 am. Will you be ready then?"

"Yeah, sure, I've just got to get dressed. I'll meet you in the lobby at 8:45."

Dick and I walked to the subway entrance. I carried Pepe, my makeup bag, purse and stage outfit in a hanging bag. The makeup bag banged against my legs as we struggled up Fifth Avenue.

I glanced at the store windows. Tiny villages complete with elves and Santa competed with elaborately decorated Christmas trees. A Salvation Army representative stood on the street corner, dressed in a Santa hat, ringing a bell for donations. Feeling loving and generous, I dropped some bills into his bucket.

Johnny and Lou stood at the subway entrance. Without incident, we boarded the subway and rode to Brooklyn. As we approached the theater, even at this early hour, thirty teenagers crowded around the stage door. Johnny studied them at a distance. "Well, that's the only way into the theater," he said. "I suggest we walk rapidly and don't stop for autographs or we'll be there all day."

When the teens saw us they started screaming and running in our direction. We found ourselves surrounded. Pepe let out a growl. Suddenly the stage door opened and Joe, the stagehand, shouted, "Come on! Come on!"

We pushed our way through the small crowd and climbed the steps to the stage door. "Johnny!" the girls screamed. Lou rolled her eyes.

"It's always like this here," she said.

Johnny waved at the fans. "I'll see you at the show," he promised. He turned to Lou. "Just be grateful they do scream."

By the time I got to the dressing room, I found Dionne dressed and ready to go on stage. She gave me a big smile.

"It must be difficult lugging that bag across town," she said as I dropped the makeup bag on the floor. "Here, let me help you."

Dionne took my garment bag and hung it on the metal clothes rack. I placed the straw bag containing Pepe on the floor and smiled back. Dionne acted so considerate, kind and, considering her success, amazingly humble. I felt fortunate to be sharing a dressing room with her.

When I went to unzip the garment bag I noticed a lovely lounging robe of Dionne's hanging on the rack, and a pair of pink fuzzy slippers on the floor.

"Why didn't I think of that?" I said. "What a great lounging outfit. I only brought street clothes to wear between shows. Well, at least I'll look decent when I go through the hole in the wall."

"The what?"

Before I could explain, we heard a loud knocking on the door.

"Ten minutes to show time!" a voice yelled.

I raced into action, unzipping the hanging bag and pulling out another silk skirt and sequined top, similar to the ones I'd worn the previous day, but in different colors. After checking my hair and makeup in the mirror, I told Pepe, "Stay. I'll be right back. Be a good dog."

Dionne and I walked together down the flight of stairs to the backstage area. You wouldn't think teenagers would pack a theater at ten in the morning and stay all day, but there they were. I stood in the wings and watched the performers until Murray called Dick and I on stage.

After we performed, Joe walked up to me and handed me a take-out menu. "Hey," he said. "For ten bucks I'll go pick up lunch for you and Dionne."

"Let me think about it. I need to see what Dick wants to do."

"You don't have any choice. You're trapped in the theater all day. Take-out is the only way to eat. Just find me when you're ready."

Carrying the menu, I walked back to the dressing room. As I swung open the door I saw Pepe sitting in the center of the floor. He looked up at me, a guilty expression on his face. The remains of Dionne's fluffy pink slippers surrounded him, like dead chicken feathers. He'd shredded them.

"Bad dog!" I shouted. "Bad, bad, bad!" Pepe just stared at me.

I'd cleaned up the mess by the time Dionne entered half an hour later. It took all my nerve, but I finally mumbled, "Dionne, I have something to tell you." She smiled at me.

"Pepe chewed up your pink slippers. I'm so sorry. Of course, I'll be happy to replace them."

Dionne glanced at Pepe lying innocently on the floor, then back at me and sighed. "It's alright. You don't have to buy me another pair. But could I make one request? Please tie Pepe on your side of the dressing room so there are no future incidents."

"Oh, sure," I responded, quickly slipping Pepe's leash onto his collar and securing it to the leg of my chair. I felt bad about Dionne's loss and determined to buy her another pair of slippers, no matter how unnecessary she said it was. I also vowed to have Joe walk the dog more often during the day.

* * * * *

When I returned from the second show, I noticed Dionne had decorated the dressing room mirror with silver Christmas garlands. It was three days before Christmas. I felt a deep longing to connect with my family. We'd only been gone four days, but it seemed like two months.

At least ten people stood in line to use the pay phone back stage, but that afternoon I didn't care how long I waited. When it was my turn, I made a call to Santa Monica.

"Hi, Mom," I talked so loudly several stagehands standing nearby turned and stared. "How are you?"

"Oh, we're getting ready for Christmas. Your Dad's getting the tree tomorrow."

"I have a crazy thought, what if all of you fly to New York for Christmas?"

Mom paused. "Well, that might have been nice if we'd planned it a little sooner. Patty is in a play at church this coming weekend and we're so busy baking and wrapping presents."

"Oh," I said quietly. "I just thought I'd ask. Merry Christmas."

I hung up and quickly dialed Bill's number.

"I was wondering when you'd have time to call," Bill said. I heard Christmas music playing in the background. The recorded voice sang, "It's lovely weather for a sleigh ride together with you."

"So how are the shows going?" he asked.

"Fine, they're fine. So, what are your plans for Christmas?"

There was a long pause. I suddenly felt insecure and slightly sad.

"Well, I'm pretty busy right now. After the first of the year, Dick Clark Productions is producing the pilot to 'Where the Action Is.' Roz and I are working around the clock."

Bill quickly changed the subject. "So, what's happening at the Brooklyn Paramount?"

I felt defeated. There was no point in asking him to come to New York. He clearly wasn't interested. All the Christmas spirit and joy vanished from my voice.

I said, "Oh, we're working hard. Bringing Pepe here wasn't the smartest move. But I'll tell you all about it when we get back."

"Well, if you can't get through to me again, have a Merry Christmas."

"You, too."

I wanted to be alone, but didn't know where to go to achieve that. I hurried up the stairs, my heels clanking on the metal, and opened the dressing room door. Pepe glanced up at me, a forlorn look in his eyes. I picked him up and hugged him. Then the tears came. I wanted to be back in Los Angeles. The shows no longer mattered.

I realized for the first time how awkward it was to talk to Bill, to have an indepth conversation about important things, like my feelings for instance. Suddenly I felt angry. Why did all the men in my life take me for granted? Bill only called occasionally. Dick used me as a prop.

Standing by the microphone show after show, a big smile planted on my face, I felt like a puppet. Play the music and the puppet dances and sings. Why did everyone seem to have a real life but me? I needed someone. It was Christmas! I finally dried my eyes, washed the mascara off my face and walked downstairs for yet another show.

* * * * *

Dick and I spent Christmas day, 1964, performing five shows at the Brooklyn Paramount Theatre. The only change from every other day was that we ordered turkey for dinner instead of Salisbury steak.

Dick and I decided not to give each other Christmas presents. I did go to Bloomingdales before the early show one morning and purchased a beautiful pair of slippers, which I presented to Dionne after the first show Christmas morning. She laughed as she extracted them from the tissue paper.

"Thank you," she said. "They're really beautiful."

I smiled back. They weren't pink, but they were lovely. It was the least I could do.

Dick and me in New York for Murray the K's
Brooklyn Paramount Theatre Show.

CHAPTER TWENTY-FIVE

Band Attack

Shortly after we returned to Los Angeles, Shelly booked us on the January 13th episode of Shindig. What a great way to usher in the New Year, back at the ABC Studios, surrounded by the dancers, The Shindog Band, and back up singers. I felt warm and comfortable on the set, like I'd returned home.

That night Jimmy O'Neill introduced us by saying, "And here are two of the nicest people in the business, Dick and Dee Dee."

We sang "Thou Shalt Not Steal" and our new release "Be My Baby." Although we'd returned from England with master tapes to the Rolling Stones songs, Warner Brothers had already pressed up "Be My Baby" as a follow-up to "Thou Shalt Not Steal." Warner Brothers slated a May release date for our British recording.

Bill booked Dick and me as guest artists on the Dick Clark Productions pilot of "Where the Action Is." We traveled to Snow Summit Ski Resort in Big Bear, where Dick and I taped a song in the snow. We watched as Paul Revere and the Raiders, the Supremes, Jan and Dean, Bobby Freeman, Bobby Rydell, the Four Tops, Frankie Avalon and Jackie and Gayle all performed numbers.

After five days, we trekked back down the mountain to continue shooting the pilot at Leo Carrillo Beach, north of Malibu. Dick and I sang at the shoreline, as a group of dancers called the Action Kids gyrated around us. During our number, the tide rose, sending waves crashing into the backs of our legs. No one stopped the cameras. When the song ended, water soaked my pants from the knees down.

"This show's going to be a big hit," Bill said. "You wait and see. It's going to give Shindig some major competition."

I realized how much our relationship had changed. Work remained the polestar of Bill's life. There didn't appear to be time for anything else.

* * * * *

A short flight of stairs led up to a small club named the Trip, located in a two-story white stucco building built in the 1940s on Sunset Boulevard. It was one of LA's first folk-rock clubs. The Byrds drew overflow crowds there whenever they played. When Shelly announced he'd booked us at the Trip, I wondered how the folk-rock crowd would react to our show.

The club featured a long, narrow room with a stage, P.A. system and space for about two-hundred people to dance. By the time Dick and I arrived one balmy evening in late winter, the room was packed to capacity.

After driving there on his own, Dick looked unhappy. His hands quivered and his eyes appeared bloodshot. He took me firmly by the elbow and pulled me toward the dressing rooms.

"Come on," he said impatiently. "We've only got half an hour to go over our material. Because the crowd is already here, we have to rehearse in the dressing room during the band break."

"We've had worse problems," I said. "It will be alright."

We entered a worn dressing area and sat on folding chairs. Dick impatiently yanked our sheet music out of the folder, trying to organize it on an empty bench.

Someone knocked on the door and, without waiting to be invited, pushed the door open. Two young men entered. The one holding a guitar looked to be twenty or twenty-one. He wore wild striped bell bottomed pants and a flowered shirt. His long dark hair touched his shoulders. The other man, tall and lean, appeared older. They both sported mustaches.

Dick rose to his feet, his body trembling.

"Here," he said. "Here's the sheet music to 'The Mountain's High.' Let's go over that first."

"Not, hello, how are you? Just 'here's the music?'" The tall man stared at Dick.

"Hey, man," the guitar player said. "The Mountain's High. That's an 'oldie but goody.'"

The other guy laughed. Dick didn't.

"Yeah, well, it went gold," Dick said. "You can't knock success."

"Yeah, yeah, yeah, yeah hee, yeah, yeah, yeah hee," the guitar player sang, in imitation of Dick's opening line of "The Mountain's High.'"

Dick glared at him. "Are you making fun of the song?"

"No, man, I dig it. It's a real blast from the past."

With trembling hands, Dick angrily snatched the music from their hands and dug into the sheet music folder, shoving in the scores to "The Mountain's High" and pulling out "Thou Shalt Not Steal."

"Well, here's a more current one," Dick said. "Ever hear of 'Thou Shalt Not Steal?' It went to number seventeen in the nation a few months ago. Is that current enough for you?"

"Hey, man," the guitar player said. "You don't have to get bent out of shape. What's your problem?"

"My problem is we have to rehearse in a dressing room half an hour before the show with only two members of the band who don't give a shit about our act or how we sound."

There was a knock at the door. A cocktail waitress entered, holding a large tray. I noticed her tight costume, a tiny mini-skirt that revealed the lower portion of her butt when she swung around. She resembled a Playboy bunny.

The waitress addressed the guitar player. "Danny, the guys want to know what's taking so long."

Danny rolled his eyes. "Tell them to cool it. I'll be right there." He turned back to Dick. "Look, man, if you want us to back you at all, you'd better hand over the sheet music. I've got about another ten minutes before I have to start the next set."

"God," Dick muttered. "How did we ever get booked in this dive with the band from hell?"

He threw the sheet music at the musician. Both men exchanged looks. One of the guitar parts to "Turn Around" fell to the floor, but no one bent down to pick it up.

"Look, I'm trying to make this work," the guitar player said. He flopped onto one of the folding chairs and quietly started playing the chords to "Thou Shalt Not Steal." He finally reached out with his boot and dragged "Turn Around" across the floor, depositing a huge black shoe print across the top of the page. After he ran through that song, he stood up.

"Well, I gotta go," he said. "See you on stage."

He took copies of the sheet music for the other band members and left the room, followed by the other musician.

Dick's face turned pale. He glanced in my direction. "Thanks for supporting me," he said.

That was it. I couldn't take it anymore. I turned and ran for the ladies' room. My stomach felt tight. This situation was intolerable. I gripped the edge of the sink and stared at myself in the mirror. "It's going to be alright. Just take a deep breath," I told myself. By the time I'd applied lipstick, checked my eyes for smeared mascara, and ran a brush through my hair. It was time to go on stage.

I joined a scowling Dick in the corridor as we stood near an open door, watching the band finish their last number. A wild rock song blasted forth. The audience danced and spun on the floor, arms and bodies gyrating. As the music wound down, the crowd stood panting and excited as the band leader announced, without enthusiasm, "Here they are, Dick and Dee Dee." A wild shout rose from the crowd. They wanted to party.

Dick and I put on our happy faces and climbed on stage. The colored spotlights blinded me. I heard the lead guitar player launch into the introduction to "The Mountain's High" and listened as Dick started singing. Behind him I saw the band leader snicker. He whispered something to the bass player and they both started laughing.

The crowd cheered and someone yelled, "Thou Shalt Not Steal."

"Yeah, we'll get to that," Dick said. "But right now, we're going to slow things down and sing a ballad that, thanks to you, was a big hit for us, "Turn Around."

As the band started to play the opening chords and Dick began to whistle, I realized something was wrong, terribly wrong. When we began to sing, it sounded horrible. Flat and off pitch, it shocked my ears. The audience picked up on it too. With confused looks on their face, they looked at us in alarm. I couldn't figure it out.

Why did it sound so bad?

By the middle of the song, like someone coming out of a stupor, Dick started to perspire and looked at me, eyes wide with shocked realization. He reached behind me and pulled me away from the microphone. His face flashed a warning my direction, conveying that the flat pitch was somehow my fault.

My face turned red. No way was this my fault. When we finished the song, the crowd silently stared at us. Dick turned to the band and muttered, "Thou Shalt Not Steal." After a long shuffling of sheet music, they played the brief introduction. As we began to sing, I realized nothing had changed. We sounded as off-pitch as ever.

Dick sneered at me, his lips tight and arms shaking. I tried to smile at the audience, but I just wanted to find a corner somewhere and hide. We finally finished the number. Dick abruptly left the stage with me trailing after him. We heard scattered applause. As the band launched into a wild rock song, the crowd started dancing again.

As we reached the corridor, Dick shouted, "Can't you ever sing on key?"

I turned and ran out the back door, bumping into someone, almost knocking him down. Bill grabbed my arm. When I recognized him, I burst into tears.

"What's wrong?" he asked. I just put my hands over my face and sobbed. Bill quickly led me down the stairs to the parking lot. He unlocked his Corvair and we climbed into the front seat.

"I can't take it," I sobbed. "Nothing is worth this."

"Take a deep breath and tell me what happened."

"Dick was in a bad mood the moment he arrived and we only had a brief time to rehearse in the dressing room. Only two band members showed up. Anyway, Dick insulted them and the band leader got bent out of shape. I don't know what they did to get back at him, but we sounded awful on stage."

"It probably didn't sound as bad as you think."

"Trust me, it did. It wasn't like we were a little off, it was disastrous. The audience just stared at us, like 'What's going on?' It sounded so horrible. So Dick, of course, blamed me. He started pulling me back from the microphone by the back of my dress. He thinks it's my fault."

"Look, let's go in and talk to Dick. You've still got the second show to do."

"No, I don't want to see him. I can't do a second show. I just want to leave. I want to quit the act."

Bill started blinking nervously. "Look, you're just upset. You have to do the second show because you have a contract. You don't want to be sued. Come on. I'll go with you."

"No, I can't go in there right now. I need to sit here."

"Alright, let me go talk to Dick. I'll be right back. Promise me you won't go anywhere." I just stared at him. Bill looked blurry through my tears. "Promise me."

"Alright." I turned away and leaned my head against the car window.

About an hour passed. I watched a plane fly over Los Angeles, miles high in the sky. How I wished I sat on that plane. Several couples left the club, joking and laughing. They climbed into a car and roared off into the night.

As the time passed, I started to get concerned. Why didn't Bill come back? What was taking so long? I finally pulled down the visor and checked my face in the mirror. I noticed mascara smeared under my eyes. I lifted my finger to my mouth, wet it and rubbed at the black stains, eventually eliminating them.

My eyes looked red from crying, but I couldn't do anything about that. With a sigh, I opened the door of the car and climbed the stairs to the club.

The band was on a break. People stood by the walls, or sat at tables with drinks. I made my way down the hall to the dressing room and opened the door. Bill and Dick, seated on folding chairs, glanced up at me.

"Come in," Bill said. "We were just finishing our conversation. Here, sit down."

He stood so I could sit in his chair. I ignored it and chose a chair a distance away, by the wall. He continued standing.

"Although the band won't admit it, from what I've gathered from people in the audience I've talked to, the band tuned the bass and guitar slightly off pitch when you and Dick started singing 'Turn Around.' No wonder it sounded bad. They wanted the audience to think you sounded flat, but it was really their instruments.

"When I asked the guitar player about it, he denied it, but I told them I had a portable tape recorder and was going to record the second set. I don't think they'll try that trick again."

I felt a wave of exhaustion flood over me. My head started to pound. I pressed my fingers against the pain and leaned my head against the wall.

"You'll get through this," Bill said. "Just get up there and do another show. I guarantee it will sound fine. Then, you're outta here."

During the second set, the musicians played in tune, a vast improvement over the first show. Unfortunately, most of the people had already left. After we sang, without a word to Dick or Bill, I climbed into my car and somehow managed to drive home.

* * * * *

The next morning I drove down Sunset Boulevard and entered the Lake Shrine grounds. I didn't expect to see the monk who'd given me the crystal, but I just needed to connect with the peace I had felt there years ago.

As I slowly walked around the lake, the tension of the night before lifted. I felt myself breathing deeply. The sound of the waterfalls and the singing birds created a sense of relaxation.

I stood on the path, near a fence facing the lake and closed my eyes. I could feel the sun on my face. A few moments later, I watched a snapping turtle surface the water, his tiny green head bobbing up and down. To my surprise, the bald-headed monk appeared on the path and headed toward me.

"You may not remember me," I said. "You once gave me a pink crystal and also a meditation technique."

"I do remember. You were deciding whether you should continue singing or not."

"Well, I did what you suggested. I've been traveling on the road for three or four years now."

"And you've had great success?"

"I guess you could call it that. Yes, we've had a number of hit records."

"And did this bring you the fulfillment you expected?"

In the distance, I heard a wind chime. I turned my head in that direction.

"Excellent," the monk said. "Right now you are fully aware in the present moment. So, are you happy?"

"Not really. Not with touring. Well, actually, there are highs and lows."

"What are the highs?"

"Singing before an appreciative audience, performing on television, meeting great people."

"And the lows?"

"Feeling like a ship without a rudder. Like life just demands I go in one direction after another without any chance to think or plan about what I really want to do or what I hope to get out of life. I sometimes feel like one of those hamsters in a wheel, running around and around in a circle, thinking I'm getting somewhere, but getting nowhere."

The monk burst out laughing. "Even hamsters get tired of the wheel."

He looked at me intently.

"I know you're strong and have the strength and courage to face these challenges. This is only one small segment of your life. Your singing career won't last forever. Just allow the changes to come. Just watch and observe. That's all you have to do. Be fully present, watch and observe."

We stood together silently, staring at the lake. I turned away to watch a swan chase a duck across the water. When I turned back, the monk had vanished.

I slept long and hard that night and woke alert, ready to tackle the world.

* * * * *

The next afternoon, Bill invited me out to dinner. We went to an intimate restaurant in Beverly Glen. Midway up the curvy road leading toward the San Fernando Valley sat the Four Oaks Restaurant. Entering, I felt like I'd walked into someone's home. The maitre d' seated us in a secluded corner. When the waiter took our orders, Bill turned to me.

"You want escargot, right?"

I was sure he knew by then that I couldn't stand snails, and I stammered, "Not really."

He laughed. "I'm joking." He turned to the waiter. "Please bring us a large caesar salad to share. For the main course, I'll have a steak. She wants the fish."

I smiled. It felt good to be with him again. Bill's blue eyes sparkled in the candle light. "I want to thank you for all you did for us the other night," I said. "If you hadn't been there, the act would probably have broken up."

Bill smiled. "I think Dick felt bad when he found out the problem was the band's fault, not yours."

I felt a pain shoot through my forehead. "Could we just not talk about Dick and Dee Dee tonight?" Bill looked surprised. We sat in silence for several moments.

"So have you sold Where the Action Is to a network yet?" I asked.

From the next room I heard the sound of soothing classical music. A dog's bark echoed through the canyon. Before Bill could answer, the waiter arrived, carrying a huge bowl of shredded romaine lettuce.

With a flick of the wrist, he broke an egg over the greens, sprinkled in some seasoning and scattered anchovies over the top. Lifting two large spoons, he tossed the lettuce in the air, each flip spreading the egg and flavoring.

With a flourish, the waiter scooped the salad onto two plates and placed them before us.

"Bravo," Bill said. "Well done." The man smiled, and then left the room.

Bill jabbed a piece of romaine with his fork and placed it in his mouth.

"We're taking it to CBS. We shot it for them as an independent. They've got first right of refusal."

Bill's eyes scanned the room. "Waiter," he called. When the man approached the table Bill said, "We'd like champagne cocktails. Tonight we're celebrating."

I smiled. "Are we celebrating the completion of your pilot?"

"Among other things. We're also celebrating our being together."

Our being together? I couldn't think of any two people less "together." I wondered what he was up to.

The waiter arrived with two sparkling glasses of champagne. Bill took a small sip, rolled it around in his mouth and swallowed. "Excellent," he said. "Here's to us. May we become even closer throughout the coming year?"

I felt cautious but my eyes filled with tears. Why did he have this effect on me? He could be so sweet. Love flooded my heart.

"Cheers," I said, laughing as a tear escaped and ran down my cheek. Bill reached forward and gently wiped it away.

"So, how are the Shindig shows going for you and Dick? Oh, sorry, I'm not supposed to mention Dick and Dee Dee. Well, how are the shows going for you?" I laughed.

"It's okay to talk about the act. Dick and I taped the last thirty-minute episode on January 13th. We sang 'Thou Shalt Not Steal' and 'Be My Baby.' From now on ABC is expanding the show from a half hour to one hour each week. Our next booking is on March 24th. And guess what we're singing?"

"I don't know, something retro? 'The Mountain's High?'"

"No, the producers want semi-regulars, like Dick and me, to sing material we didn't record. It's like having a separate recording session just for the show. We're going to sing the Bobby Freedman hit, "Do You Wanna Dance?" Can you believe it? That was one of my favorite songs in high school."

Bill handed me a small napkin-covered dish of sourdough rolls. I took one and placed it on my bread and butter plate. He tore his roll open, scattering crumbs on the linen table cloth.

"You know," he said, pointing his butter knife at me, "you and Dick are so dynamic live, but I'm not sure your records always reflect that live talent. Maybe you should record some of the songs other people have made famous, not just to sing on Shindig but to release as singles."

"Well, we tried that with 'Not Fade Away.' Anyway, the Wilder Brothers think 'Be My Baby' is a good follow up to 'Thou Shalt Not Steal.' But I know what you mean. It's a great idea to re-record a proven hit record."

When we finished our main course, Bill ordered small hot fudge sundaes for dessert. When he paid the bill, he must have left a generous tip, because the waiter gave a big smile and said, "Thank you, sir. And have a wonderful evening."

CHAPTER TWENTY-SIX

Stealing my Poker Chips

We taped a third Shindig show on April 21st, this one with the Beach Boys, the Shangri-La's, the Ikettes, Ian Whitcomb, Wayne Fontana and the Mindbenders and Cilla Black.

At one of the first rehearsals the cast sat together in the theater, listening as the production manager gave instructions. When we broke for lunch, Carl Wilson approached Dick and me.

"Hey, how are you?" Carl asked. "How's Bill doing?"

I remembered Bill acted as their agent and concert promoter when he booked them as our band almost two years ago.

"He's doing great," I told him. "He's actually left personal management and is developing a pilot for Dick Clark Productions. He doesn't manage us anymore. So, is your Dad still managing you?"

I saw a sad look briefly cross Carl's face. Then he quickly said, "No, we have another manager now."

Although the group's popularity now reached epic proportions, they still wore their matching striped shirts and looked identical to when we last worked together. During the actual show taping of Shindig, they stood on stage and sang along to a prerecorded track "Fun, Fun, Fun." They also sang "Help Me Ronda" and, oddly enough, opened with "Do You Wanna Dance?"

Dick and I sang "Freight Train" and "Be My Baby" from our Turn Around album.

Several weeks after the show aired, our manager, Shelly Berger, received a call from the Beach Boys' talent agency offering Dick and me a four-day tour of Reno, Salt Lake City, and St. Louis, with the Beach Boys. Instead of traveling by bus, we would fly.

Before we left Los Angeles, we taped another Shindig show. We didn't sing any of our own records, but instead two old rock songs, "Rockin' Pneumonia" and "(The Bees Are for the Birds) the Birds Are for the Bees." Since "Thou Shalt Not Steal" started to drop off the national charts, and "Be My Baby" wasn't rising, we felt lucky to appear on national television.

* * * * *

A month later, Dick and I and the Beach Boys climbed onto a commercial jet departing from Los Angeles International Airport and arrived late in the day in Salt Lake City. Besides us, the show included Glen Campbell. The Beach Boys hired him to stand backstage and add guitar licks to their rhythm guitars.

When we arrived at the rehearsal hall, we found a group of musicians setting up their instruments on stage.

"This is the group you're going to work with," Glen explained to us. "I'm going to sit in with both you and the Beach Boys."

We were grateful that a musician of Glen's caliber would help us rehearse the band and play lead guitar. Obviously, at this stage of their career, the Beach Boys did not back other acts.

That evening, Dick and I opened the show. With Glen's crisp guitar riffs, the musicians sounded fantastic. We received strong applause and did a one-song ovation. But when the Beach Boys walked out on stage, pandemonium broke out. The crowd sang and danced and partied like they'd been transported to State Beach in Santa Monica the night of a wild grunion run.

"Surfing music is just a fad," Dick said, as we watched the Beach Boys backstage. "When it ends, so will the Beach Boys."

"I don't know," I answered. "They're sure huge now."

I watched the Beach Boys smile at each other. Even Dennis, with his long hair flopping over his forehead and intense expression, appeared to be having fun as he wildly pounded his drum set. I felt a moment of wistfulness, sorry that Dick and I didn't share that feeling of closeness.

The next day, we flew to Reno. Everyone wanted to go to the casinos and gamble. Dick and I walked to a blackjack table.

"Let's try this," he said. He pulled some money out and swooped up a pile of chips, which he stacked in front of himself. Within five minutes, he'd lost it all.

He said, "This sucks. I'm going to play the slot machines."

I felt lucky and traded fifty dollars for a pile of chips. But instead of losing, I started raking in plastic. I felt a rush of adrenalin surge through my body. I might make a fortune. It appeared I couldn't lose.

Dennis Wilson of the Beach Boys played blackjack at another table. He finally ran out of funds and noticed the large pile of chips in front of me.

"Let me borrow a few of these," he said, swooping up handfuls of my chips. "I'll give them back when I win."

His luck never changed and mine took a downturn. We left the casino with nothing left but a handful of change.

"I don't have any money with me," Dennis said. "But I'll pay you back after the show tonight."

* * * * *

After the Reno show Dennis gave Dick and me a ride back to the motel in his rental car. As Dick and I started to climb out, Dennis said, "Dee Dee, can I talk to you for a minute?"

Dick gave me a strange glance and left for his room. I settled back into the plush upholstery and pulled the car door shut on the passenger side.

"We don't get paid for several more days," Dennis said. "Can you wait until then?" I nodded. I really didn't know how many chips Dennis had taken or what their value was.

Dennis smiled at me, a sweet grin. "You know, I used to go to Pandora's Box when I was in high school. I saw you and Dick play there several times."

I looked at him in the semi-darkness. Dennis appeared wiry, tough. He somehow looked older than his brothers.

"I was always attracted to you," he continued. I drew a quick breath. Where did this suddenly come from?

"I've had a vasectomy, so I can't have any children." He smiled at me with an impish grin. "I can't get anyone pregnant. I just thought you might like to know that."

I didn't know what to say. I thought of Dennis as a kid. He was certainly several years younger than I was. Then I thought of Bill. Did Dennis know I was going out with him?

Just then Dick pounded on the side of the car window. I jumped, startled.

"Bill's on the phone," he announced. "He wants to talk to you."

Slightly embarrassed, I climbed out of the car and gave Dennis a glance and smile.

"Thanks for sharing your medical condition," I smiled. "It does sound unique."

I figured Dennis used this line to pick up girls and found it amusing that he'd tried it out on me. For all his success and maturity, Dennis was barely out of high school. What was he, about nineteen now? I'd turned twenty-two.

I walked back to my room, flipped on the light, and waved goodnight to Dick before shutting the door. Lifting the phone receiver, I said, "Hello?"

"What took you so long?" Bill asked. "This long distance call is costing a fortune. I've been waiting on the line for five minutes."

"Oh, I was just saying goodbye to one of the Beach Boys. You know, they're just the way they were before all their success. It's pretty amazing. The only difference is how much better they sound now."

"Well, give them my regards. Incidentally, I've been working with disc jockey Bob Eubanks. He's opening up several clubs in the Los Angeles area, one in the Valley and one in Long Beach. They're called 'The Cinnamon Cinders.' He wants to book you and Dick. I referred him to Shelly."

I said. "Bob is one of the top disc jockeys in L.A. I'm sure his clubs will succeed."

"I'm sure they will," Bill said. "Incidentally, I want you to meet my parents when you get back. I've told them about you and they want me to bring you over."

Joy flooded over me. "That's great. I'd love to meet them." Isn't that a good sign when the man you're dating wants you to meet his parents?

By the time I hung up the phone and peered out the window, I noticed an empty car. I presumed Dennis had gone to bed. Flattered by Dennis' infatuation, but happy Bill wanted me to meet his family, I feel asleep with a smile on my face.

* * * * *

The next night we played St. Louis. After the show we sat around in Dick's hotel room with the Beach Boys and Glen Campbell. There was a sudden knock at the door and Dennis Wilson's girlfriend entered. She had been warned by one of the Beach Boys that Dennis hoped to spend time with me and flew in immediately from Los Angeles to head off a potential romance.

I felt amused by the situation and smiled at Dennis's obvious surprise and slight discomfort at her arrival. They didn't remain in the room long before leaving. When the brief tour ended, Dennis and his girlfriend took a separate flight back to Los Angeles. He never did pay me back for the "borrowed" poker chips.

CHAPTER TWENTY-SEVEN

Pi and Jerry/Ike and Tina

The Sunday after Dick and I returned from the Beach Boys tour, Bill drove me to meet his mom and step dad. Pi and Jerry lived in a historic old apartment building in Hollywood. As we rode the elevator up to their floor, I felt shaky, insecure. I hoped they would like me because I knew this meeting meant a lot to Bill.

"I'm sure you'll get along my parents," Bill said. "They're pretty cool."

Pi opened the door. She was a short woman, about five-feet, three inches tall, and slightly overweight. Her hair was blond and short, stylishly curled around her face. She had blue eyes and a radiant smile.

She grabbed both my hands. "We are so happy to meet you. Bill has told us many wonderful things." I thought, "He has?"

Bill mentioned some things about Pi as well. She had been a screenwriter, working many years for the studios. Under a nom de plume she had written the screenplay for the motion picture "Gilda," starring Rita Hayworth.

I immediately relaxed as she gave me a hug.

Jerry, tall and handsome with a full head of silver hair, sat nestled in a large leather arm chair, dressed in a bathrobe and surrounded by newspapers. He made no effort to get up.

"Jerry, this is Dee Dee," Bill said. Jerry smiled at me and nodded. Pi twisted her wedding band nervously.

"Jerry just woke up," she said.

Although unshaven, Jerry appeared suave, with styled hair and a tan skin, definitely a writer or actor. I knew he and Bill's father had been song writing partners. They had worked together in New York, writing and publishing hundreds of songs. When Bill's father passed away, Jerry married Pi.

"Sit down. Sit down," Pi continued, pointing to a comfortable chair.

I sank into the plush cushions, relaxing for the first time. Vivid pink and pastel flowers sprang from vases, the floral theme carried forth in the sofa fabrics. Paintings and lovely furniture filled the apartment. Sunlight streamed through the window.

We talked for awhile about my career and travels. Pi filled Bill in on family news and then offered us some iced tea. Jerry finally stood.

"Well," he said. "It's been nice meeting you. I've got to take a shower and get dressed." We gave Pi and Jerry a hug as we walked out the door.

"They liked you, I could tell," Bill told me in the car. "You're the first girl I've brought home since Marsha and I split up." I thought, "and I hope I'm the last."

Bill turned the radio to a top-forty station and started singing along to one of the songs. I watched out the window as the buildings and shops on the Sunset Strip raced by. At that moment, life felt pretty good.

* * * * *

The following weekend, Dick and I drove to the Valley to perform at the Cinnamon Cinder Club. We pulled up in front and stared up at the marquee. It read "Dick and Dee Dee Live Tonight." It was the first time since the Midwest tour with Jan and Dean that we'd headlined a show. In smaller print, the marquee read "The Ike and Tina Turner Review."

We didn't realize the power television possessed in exposing us to the public. After we appeared on numerous Shindig shows, people started recognizing us on the street. Folks often said hello in the market or when I stopped for gas. It felt strange. Ordinary people acted like they knew me personally.

Dick and I walked into the club dressing room and were met by a smiling Bob Eubanks. Tall, with dark hair and a large smile, he shook our hands.

"Well, what do you think?" he asked, pointing around at the walls and ceiling. "Come on. I'll give you a tour."

We followed him through the club, admiring the small stage in the corner, the dance floor and walls.

"This is the first club to welcome teens eighteen and over. Because we don't serve alcohol, the kids don't have to be twenty-one to come in and hear some decent music." Bob was proud of his club and the new concept of lowering the admittance age.

Dick and I were standing in the backstage area when Ike and Tina Turner arrived. Tina's long hair flowed around her face. She stood thin and tall and wore a very short dress and high heels. Her husband, Ike, walked to a corner and started tuning his guitar. He didn't have much to say.

Accompanying Ike and Tina were the Ikettes, a group of three female backup singers. They chatted among themselves in excited, happy voices.

Tina gave me a radiant and genuine smile when we were introduced. I felt drawn to her warmth and liked her immediately.

When Bob Eubanks called them on stage, Ike walked on first, followed by Tina. Within minutes, they launched into their former hit record," A Fool in Love," and the place started rocking.

The sheer volume and intensity of the band and the wailing of the backup singers excited the crowd. But Tina's amazing voice and wild, sensuous dancing evoked shouts. Soon everyone was cheering. Dick and I stared at Tina in total awe.

After the intense forty-five minute set, Bob Eubanks called for a ten-minute break before Dick and I went on.

"How are we going to follow that?" Dick asked.

Actually, following Ike and Tina on stage worked to our advantage because the audience crowded around the stage was already warmed up. They gave us a standing ovation before we even sang a note. Dick and I poured our hearts into the performance. Dick sang the lead on "What'd I Say" with more soul and feeling than I thought he was capable of. We left the stage perspiring, hearts racing, consumed with joy.

Tina passed us in the dressing room on her way out the door.

"That was cool," she commented with a warm smile as she disappeared into the dark of the San Fernando Valley night.

CHAPTER TWENTY-EIGHT

Engagement by Default

One day Dick Clark's wife, Loretta, called my apartment. Although I'd met her briefly on the Dick Clark Caravan of Stars Tour, I didn't know her well. Still, she invited Bill and me to a party at the Clark residence in Encino the following Friday night.

"I don't know if Bill can make it, Loretta," I told her. "Bill is so busy with his pilot project, he rarely takes a break."

"How long have you been going out with Bill?" Loretta suddenly asked.

I thought for a moment. "Well, I've known him four-and-a-half years."

"But how long have you been going together?"

"Well, the last few months we've been seeing each other steadily."

"Do you want to marry him?"

Wow, what a loaded question! I stammered for an answer. "Yes, I guess I do."

"Well, that's never going to happen unless you go into action. You're stuck in a rut with this relationship. Take my advice. I've been a matchmaker for several couples. You have to take an active role in this."

"An active role? Like what?"

"Tell him you need more of a commitment for the relationship to continue, that you'd like to get engaged. If he doesn't respond to that, break up with him and immediately find someone else and spend as much time with that person as you can. Usually, that does the trick."

Was she serious? I felt awkward and uncomfortable. Somehow this plan felt incredibly manipulative. Bill and I loved each other but my singing career caused long separations. I generally felt comfortable with the way things were. Did I really want to analyze our love relationship in the harsh light of scrutiny? Did I want to shake things up?

"Ok, Loretta, I'll think about it." I hung up but didn't sleep well that night.

* * * * *

The next day we began taping a new Shindig show. I couldn't get the conversation with Loretta out of my mind. Even standing on the brightly lit stage, dancing to the music with the Shindig dancers, our little talk haunted me. Loretta opened a whole new door of possibilities. All my longtime insecurities suddenly awaited examination.

I sometimes felt Bill moving in another direction with his time and energy and wondered how much he wanted me with him. Was my relationship with Bill part of my future? What did Bill truly feel about us as a couple? We'd never discussed it.

There was only one way to find out. I called him at Roz's.

"Bill, Loretta Clark wants us to attend a party at their house this Friday."

"That sounds great. I'm going back to my apartment for the weekend anyway. Roz and I need a break from each other. Tell Loretta we'll be there."

When I telephoned Loretta, she insisted I talk to Bill about "commitment" after the party, when he sat trapped in the car on the way home. Just the thought of the conversation sent excruciating jitters through my body. How could I bring up the taboo subject of marriage, one that had never been even remotely approached in our years together?

Several nights later, Bill and I entered Dick Clark's house, and followed Loretta down some stairs to the lower level party room. Already the place resounded with people dancing and talking. Dick's juke box, parked in one corner, played a constant variety of old hits.

I saw Lou and Johnny Tillotson. I discovered they'd moved to Encino from New York City and were living just up the street from Dick Clark. I also recognized Bobby Vee and met his wife, Karen. Dick Clark warmly welcomed us and then took Bill aside to "talk shop." Loretta grabbed my arm.

"You're going to talk to him on the way home tonight, aren't you?"

I cleared my throat and tried to answer, but could only nod my head.

She said, "Good. It's now or never."

I dropped a plate of nachos on the floor and spent the next few minutes trying to scrape up the guacamole.

* * * * *

I wanted the party to go on all night, but when we were among the last few people remaining, we said goodbye and walked down the driveway and climbed into Bill's Corvair.

Faint stars sparkled in the clear evening sky. Happy and in a good mood, Bill chatted about the party. How could I bring up the subject of marriage? Finally we were halfway home and I knew, as Loretta had said, it was now or never.

I cleared my throat. "You know, I've been thinking about our relationship. We've been going out together for several years now and...."

"And?"

"And I was wondering just what your long-term commitment was."

Bill suddenly swerved into the next lane, almost sideswiping another vehicle.

When he gained control of the car, he gawked at me.

"Where did this come from all of a sudden? We were talking about the great time we had at the party and suddenly you ask what my commitment to you is? Isn't it apparent that I love you since I spend time with you?"

"I know you care for me, but I'm talking about a long-term relationship and a future, maybe marriage and children. I was just wondering what you felt about those things."

"Whoa, talk about serious subjects. Alright, since you brought it up. I've been through two disastrous marriages and, right now, I'm not looking to jump into a third one. I think we have time. Is that what you want to know?"

I took a deep breath. "It's just that I don't want to waste years in a relationship if it's not going anywhere. I want to know that we're trying to commit to each other as a couple."

Then I forced out the most difficult words I had ever spoken to Bill. "If you don't feel that way, maybe we should start seeing other people."

"So that's what this is all about," Bill said angrily. "You have someone else you want to go out with and you have a guilty conscience, so you're finding a way to break up with me. Well, go ahead, date someone else."

"That's totally incorrect." I said.

Bill's jaw set firmly and he refused to look at me again. We drove in silence for awhile. When I tried to explain myself further, he said, "I don't want to talk about it anymore," and turned on the radio. The Byrds song, "Turn, Turn, Turn," blasted forth. "To everything there is a season, and a time for every purpose unto heaven." Tonight, my timing had failed me miserably.

* * * * *

Bill let me out on the street outside the Barrington Plaza. His eyes looked hurt and sad. Without another word, he drove away. I entered my apartment totally depressed. What on earth had I done?

The next few weeks reverberated with emptiness. I barely spoke to Dick. I did what I had to for the Shindig rehearsals, but I felt like I was sleepwalking. I had invested so much time in my relationship with Bill over the years that I had no other close friends. Now I felt empty, alone, and drifting.

Shelly Berger heard I had broken up with Bill and told me that one of the William Morris agents wanted to take me out, but I told him it was too soon. I needed some alone time. What I was really looking for was someone who would not command any of my emotional energy. I found that person in David.

Brought from England by producer Jack Goode to co-produce Shindig, David was soft-spoken and introverted. I only thought of him as a friend, but enjoyed talking to him about his native country and getting to know him.

We went out a few times and the word got around the Shindig set that we were seeing each other. Several weeks went by. Suddenly when I least expected it, Bill called.

"I need to talk to you," he said. "It's important. Can I come over?"

It was nine o'clock at night. My heart jumped into my throat.

"Alright," I said.

Minutes later, Bill knocked on my door. Pepe raced in circles when he saw him. We both laughed at the dog's reaction.

"I think he missed you," I commented.

"And did you miss me?"

I nodded my head. Bill slowly put his arms around me.

He said, "I've realized a lot during the past few weeks. This separation showed me how much I love you. So I've got a question for you. Will you marry me?"

I was absolutely shocked and stunned. I certainly hadn't expected this. But it felt so right. Since I couldn't speak, I just nodded. Bill took my hand.

"I don't have a ring yet, but we can go to a jeweler in Beverly Hills and pick one out together."

"I don't need an engagement ring. Let's just wear wedding bands."

Bill grabbed the telephone and dialed a number.

"Dee Dee and I are engaged," he announced. "No, I'm not joking. We just made the decision. Alright, here she is."

Bill put his hand over the receiver and said, "It's my mom. She wants to talk to you."

"Hello?" I said tentatively.

"We are so happy for you. In fact, we're coming right over now to celebrate. It's not too late is it?"

I put my hand over the receiver and said to Bill, "They want to come over."

"Great," Bill said. "Let's have a celebration."

Pi and Jerry arrived half an hour later, carrying a bottle of champagne. We toasted our engagement, toasted each other, and toasted life in general. I felt welcomed into Bill's family, loved and honored. My heart went out to Pi and her welcoming attitude.

After they left, Bill and I set a marriage date for July 9th.

"There's only one slight problem," Bill finally said. "I'm still legally married to Marsha."

My mouth dropped open.

"You're not serious."

"But that's not an issue," he hastened to say. "I've already talked to an attorney. All I have to do is leave the country, which I can do by going over the border from Texas to Mexico. There I can get a divorce that is recognized by most of the fifty states.

Then we can get married."

"What state is the divorce not recognized in?"

Bill got quiet. "California," he finally answered. "If we wanted to get married here, we would have to wait a year. But there's no reason to do that. We can get married in almost any other state."

"Like where?" What a strange turn of events. Would our friends and family travel out of the state for our wedding?

"Well, Vegas isn't that far. If we get married there, when a year is up, our marriage will be automatically recognized in California."

I pushed the wedding concerns out of my mind and hugged Bill, happy that he had found a solution to the divorce dilemma.

* * * * *

I heard a different story when I drove alone to my parents' house the next night. All the lights were out and they were in bed. I knocked on their bedroom door anyway. They were still awake.

"Come in," Mom called.

I tentatively opened the door. "Were you sleeping?"

"No, we just got into bed," Mom replied.

"And what good news did you bring?" Dad asked.

"Bill and I are engaged."

There was dead silence in the room. I struggled to see their faces in the dark.

"Oh, that's nice. When are you planning to get married?" Mom finally asked.

"In July."

"That's less than three months away! Don't you think you're rushing things?" Mom said. "He's much older, isn't he? And he's been married before. I think you should give this some time."

I sighed in exasperation. "Mom, we don't want to give it more time. We want to be married as soon as possible."

"Why? Are you pregnant?" Dad asked.

I couldn't believe he said that. My feelings were totally hurt. "No," I answered. "We just love each other and want to get married right away."

"You can have the reception in our back yard, if you want to," Mom finally said.

I paused, and then bravely continued. "Actually, we have to get married out of the state because his divorce won't be recognized in California for a year."

Dad sat straight up in bed. "This is getting awfully complicated. Why don't you just wait the year and do everything legally? You never know. A lot can happen in a year. You might even change your mind about the marriage."

"Thanks for being so supportive," I said, sarcastically. "I'm going home now."

* * * * *

While Bill flew to Texas and crossed the border to Mexico to fulfill the residency requirements and file for the divorce, Dick and I continued to tape Shindig shows. I loved the schedule, rising at 4:00 a.m. and driving across Los Angeles in the dark, arriving on a set bustling with activity. The studio isolated me from the rest of the world. I forgot my problems and immersed myself in singing and dancing. I wanted the Shindig shows to go on forever.

Pi and Jerry acted deeply concerned about my parents' response to our wedding plans. They even offered to talk to Dad. I told them my parents just needed more time to adjust to the situation. As the days passed, I kept hoping Dad might relax his strict requirement that we wait a year to get married. I didn't really believe he intended to miss our wedding ceremony.

Bill and I talked nightly by telephone. Holed up in a hotel in Mexico, he counted the days until he could get the document he needed to provide a legal divorce.

We discussed where to marry and decided on Las Vegas. One thing I remained adamant about was that we not marry in one of the commercial wedding chapels, but rather in a church. Bill suggested we go there and interview ministers, so we could choose a place and confirm the date.

I called Dick to tell him the plans.

"Wow, that is news," Dick said. "So how's your marriage to Bill going to affect our act?"

"Nothing's going to change with Dick and Dee Dee."

Dick replied, "We'll see."

* * * * *

In May 1965, seven months after our trip to England, Warner Brothers finally released two songs from the Rolling Stones session, "Blue Turns to Gray" and "Some

Things Just Stick in Your Mind." The Shindig producers booked us on the show and chose "Some Things Just Stick in Your Mind" as the Shindig Pick of the Week. We would tape the show the second week in June.

When Bill returned to Los Angeles from Mexico, he made an appointment to talk to my Dad. Bill approached the meeting with great optimism. He felt sure he'd convince Dad of our love and why we wanted to get married right away. He hoped to receive Dad's blessing for the union and his commitment to attend our wedding ceremony. That did not happen.

Dad remained stubborn and fixed on, as he saw it, "the letter of the law." With his sharp legal mind, he felt that since the divorce would not be recognized by the State of California for a year, if we got married elsewhere and moved in together in California as husband and wife, we would not be legally married and therefore "living in sin."

Although I would not call Dad a religious man, he attended the local Presbyterian Church weekly and was a strong supporter of church activities. Whatever his personal beliefs, he kept them to himself and never, ever proselytized. But he held firm to his belief system.

Divorce held a stigma on both sides of my family. Over the past hundred years, there had only been one divorce in our family and that was never discussed. Dad and Bill butted heads over the marriage issue and were unable to ever resolve their relationship.

When Bill's attempt to convince Dad to attend the wedding failed, I appealed to Mom. I told her our plans to get married in a church in Las Vegas and asked if she and my sisters would attend, even if Dad wouldn't. She told me that, as part of a marriage partnership and in respect for Dad's decisions, she needed to honor Dad's choice. None of my family would be there. I felt devastated.

As a last-minute attempt, I approached my Aunt Doris, who told me she needed to back Mom's and Dad's wishes, and Aunt Vera and Uncle Ralph, who also said that they would not be attending. Although terribly sad, I felt in my heart that Bill and I were doing the right and legal thing and that, even if my family chose not to support us, it was our wedding and we were going forth with it.

During this time I became quite close to Pi and Jerry. They thought it was "such a shame" that my parents were so unrelenting about the wedding plans. To make up for it, they redoubled their efforts to give us emotional support and love.

* * * * *

Bill and I flew to Las Vegas and interviewed various ministers at several churches. When we told them the situation with my parents, two ministers declined to marry us, as they felt the wedding shouldn't take place without parental approval. We finally found a minister at a Methodist church who agreed to a church wedding and booked the date.

I didn't want a long princess bridal gown, but something more sophisticated. I found a dressmaker in Beverly Hills who created a white lace dress. It was beautiful and elegant, with a lace jacket. Although I'd just turned twenty five, most of the young women my age married out of high school or during college. I waited a long time in deference to the singing career. Now I planned the ceremony. With a month to go, wedding plans occupied my every waking moment.

CHAPTER TWENTY-NINE

"Some Things Just Stick In Your Mind"

Way down Sunset Boulevard, past the sparkle of Beverly Hills and the funkiness of the Sunset Strip, where ordinary Angelinos struggled to survive, sat ABC Studios. I drove through the gate at 6:00 a.m., after giving my name to the guard.

I swung my car to the far end of the lot and parked as close as possible to the studio door. Today, as usual, we sat in the audience seats while the show's producer talked about this week's taping.

I liked the opportunity to be an audience member. I felt comfortable out of the spotlight. I loved watching it shine on someone else. Dick joined me, a garment bag slung over his right shoulder. As he eased into the seat, he whispered, "Sorry I'm late. Did I miss anything?"

"No, just the usual welcome speech. But we're going to watch the space walk on the T.V. monitors. The director said we have time before the taping starts."

All eyes remained riveted on the television screens. We saw the astronauts float around their cabin on Gemini 4. One of them prepared to go outside. In a massive, bulky suit, he left the space craft and, as I held my breath, floated alone in outer space.

"What if the line connecting him to the ship breaks?" Dick said.

I didn't answer. For about twenty minutes the cast of Shindig watched in silence as James McDivitt float/walked at the end of a golden cable. My heart soared.

What freedom! What an amazing moment in history! However, I felt great relief when he finally climbed back aboard the space shuttle.

The cast and crew left their seats and headed for the sound stage. Cameras hummed and the cameramen took their places. Don and Phil Everly walked to the microphone. Don Everly's dark pompadour and Phil's blond hair stayed neatly in place as they strummed their guitars and sang, "Wake Up Little Suzie."

As they launched into the opening medley, Dick and I walked out and joined them. We sang two verses of an Everly Brothers song, "Should We Tell Him?"

I felt the warm stage lights and the joy of singing live with the Shindog band over the prerecorded tracks. Great joy filled my being and all the challenges of life faded away.

Then Dick and I sang a song with Gerry Marsden, of Gerry and the Pacemakers, "Mrs. Brown, You've got a Lovely Daughter." Gerry's blond hair flopped to the side of his head. He grinned at me.

As that segment of the rehearsal ended, the director announced from the sound booth. "Alright, let's take a break. Remember your places and we'll pick up after lunch."

Dick and I walked to the commissary and ordered sandwiches.

"There are never any stars eating here." Dick said. "This place is filled with secretaries and executives."

"Maybe the stars eat in their dressing rooms."

"Well, you'd think they'd come out once in awhile."

Dick glanced at his watch. "Oh, man, the time goes by quickly. We have to change for our next number. Don't forget, it's really important to look relaxed and happy on this one. It's the first time we're singing "Some Things Just Stick in Your Mind" on national television."

I nodded. At last, the national release of our song from the Rolling Stones tracks. I'd brought just the right outfit for the event, a dark green velvet skirt and matching jacket I'd bought the day the girls chased Dick and Bryan Jones down the alley in London.

Twenty minutes later, Dick and I ran to the microphone. We sang "Thou Shalt Not Steal" and "Some Things Just Stick in Your Mind."

As we sang our new song, I couldn't help but realize how different our voices sounded compared to the vocals on "Thou Shalt Not Steal." I barely heard the top voices. Somehow in the mix, Andrew Oldham buried the high sounds. The brightness was gone.

I shoved all my concerns to the back of my mind, and smiled as everyone complimented us on our new single. And then the rehearsal ended. After the final encore, we left for the day, fourteen hours after we arrived. We'd be back in the morning for the actual taping.

* * * * *

The Shindig segment with "Some Things Just Stick in Your Mind" aired on June 16, 1965. We received good reviews of our single release in Cashbox and Billboard magazines. But good reviews and television exposure weren't enough to push the song onto the national record charts.

Spurred on by Dick's desperation, our new manager, Shelly Berger, recommended that Dick and I find a publicist to help promote the record. He told us a former colleague and press agent for the Beatles, Derek Taylor, had recently opened offices on the Sunset Strip. Derek handled publicity for many of the folk rock groups, such as the Byrds.

* * * * *

A secretary escorted Dick and me into Derek's office one afternoon. He stood medium height, thin, with a narrow face and dark eyes.

"What can I do for you?" he asked.

"We need some extra publicity, especially with the new record we just released," Dick said. "And we were hoping you would take us on as clients."

Derek leaned back in his chair.

"I've just recently moved here from London to set up my own company and I'm mainly working with bands, like the Byrds. But I'm willing to work with you and Dee Dee. The goal of publicity is to keep your name in the press. Shelly told me about your tie-in with the Rolling Stones. Sounds like we have something to write about."

We discussed a fee with Derek. He rose from his desk and walked to the door, signaling his receptionist.

"Set up another appointment with Dick and Dee Dee as soon as the contracts are drawn up." We left, feeling quite satisfied with how the meeting had gone.

When I got home, my answering service informed me that seven people had sent RSVPs for the wedding. My head reeled with details. I needed to get white satin shoes to match my dress. And we needed to book a private room at one of the hotels in Vegas for the reception afterwards.

I tried to stay as busy as possible in the last few weeks before the wedding. Sometimes I'd stare at the telephone, thinking that any moment Mom or Dad would call and tell me that they were attending, along with my two sisters, Aunt Doris, Aunt Vera and Uncle Ralph, but the phone remained silent. I buried the pain deep within and kept on moving.

Dressed in London outfit, publicity by Derek Taylor.

CHAPTER THIRTY

Something Borrowed, Something Blue

On July 9th in Las Vegas, Nevada, in a beautiful, simple ceremony, Bill and I married. Approximately thirty friends flew or drove in from Los Angeles. Bill's mother, Pi, and Dick St. John sat in the front row. Jerry volunteered to walk me down the aisle, since no one from my family attended my wedding.

Before the ceremony, as Jerry and I stood in the foyer of the large church, facing the backs of people sitting in the pews, Jerry smiled at me.

"It's a shame your family didn't come," he said. "But I want you to know it's an honor to step in as your surrogate father."

Tears filled my eyes.

"Thank you, Jerry. After today, you will be an official father to me."

A middle-aged woman in a print dress started playing "The Wedding March" on the piano. Jerry and I slowly walked down the aisle, arm in arm. I realized someone had placed a bouquet of yellow roses at the end of each pew. How lovely the church looked. The walls basked in muted sunlight filtering in through a stained-glass window. I gripped my flowers tightly in my left hand.

Bill, standing at the front of the sanctuary with the minister, turned to face me. His eyes glowed with warmth and love. I kept my eyes focused on him. I love him so much, I thought. I know this is the right thing to do.

Jerry joined Pi in the front pew and I took my place, standing next to Bill.

The minister read the wedding vows. When he reached the part where he said, "If anyone here knows why these two people should not be married, speak now or forever hold your peace," I half expected Dad to burst through the door stating the reasons the marriage would not be recognized in the State of California. But only silence resounded throughout the church.

Then the minister said, "I now pronounce you man and wife. You may kiss the bride."

Bill gave me a gentle kiss on the lips. His eyes glowed light and love. I took his arm and my heart soared as we walked down the aisle to lively piano music. Everyone rose and followed us out.

Surrounded by friends and Bill's family, the day was as perfect as it could be without a single member from my side of the family in attendance. But I understood the circumstances and felt no anger or blame…just an inner sorrow mixed with the joy of the occasion.

Our wedding reception took place in a small private banquet room. Then Bill and I flew back to Los Angeles to briefly attend to a few things before flying up to Monterey for our honeymoon. We rented a small cabin in the Big Sur woods.

* * * * *

Our first married morning, I woke to the sound of birds and took a deep breath of the incredibly fresh air. While Bill took a shower, I quickly dressed and set a table on the outside deck. I placed fresh orange juice, muffins and coffee on several place mats, adding a small jar of deep purple wild iris for color. I called to Bill that breakfast was ready.

Bill walked out on the deck, dressed in a striped shirt and shorts. He waved his arms at the trees surrounding the cabin.

"This is great," he said. "Let's go for a hike later."

I smiled and gestured toward the table.

"Come have breakfast first."

As soon as we sat down, Bill grabbed the Los Angeles Times, which he had purchased at the lodge, and proceeded to read it throughout the entire breakfast. This was our first morning as a married couple. I'd expected we'd talk about the wedding and our future. Instead, I felt extremely isolated and lonely. Something felt wrong with the situation.

Stuffing such thoughts deep within me, I decided I'd be the perfect wife, always agreeable to whatever Bill wanted to do. Wasn't that how you made a marriage work?

* * * * *

After several days, we returned to Los Angeles and started the process of finding a place for us to live, since neither one of us wanted to move into each other's apartment.

We wound up renting a house on Miller Drive, off the Sunset Strip. The two-bedroom, two-bath home perched on a hillside. Fresh air and sunlight filled the house. The living room contained Bill's furniture, and my possessions wound up in the second bedroom, which we converted into an office. In one of the bathrooms, the owner had built a wooden throne over the toilet!

I returned to Shindig tapings and Bill started working at the new offices of Dick Clark Productions, located on Sunset Boulevard near the residential section of Beverly Hills.

One day a huge delivery truck pulled up in front of our house and the driver handed me a giant box. When Bill and I opened it we discovered a full set of Lennox china. Mom and Dad had sent it, the only concession they ever made to our wedding. They never discussed it again.

Gifts from the rest of the family started trickling in as well. Aunt Vera and Uncle Ralph gave us The Joy of Cooking, which I started using immediately.

Eventually enough time passed and Mom and Dad invited us over for dinner. Everyone acted relaxed and happy. From then on, Bill and I were always included in family events as if I had never left the nest.

Bill and I on our wedding day.

CHAPTER THIRTY-ONE

The Great Year

1965 became my all-time favorite year for music. As I rode in the car, I sang along to Bob Dylan's "Like a Rolling Stone," Sonny and Cher's "I Got You, Babe," and the Byrds', "Turn, Turn, Turn." Waves of happiness flooded over me. It felt so good to be alive.

Dick and I kept busy performing on Shindig. Bill and I spent most evenings together, living the life of a happily married couple. We ate dinner at home. On weekends, I helped Bill decorate his office at Dick Clark Productions on the Sunset Strip.

As I drove down the winding road from our house each morning on the way to Shindig rehearsals, I'd arrive at Sunset Boulevard and marvel at the changes. Young people crowded the streets, dressed in bell-bottoms and furry vests. A tangible joy permeated the air.

Only one cloud darkened the horizon. In spite of Derek Taylor's publicity, Dick and I could not seem to get another hit record. Our Rolling Stones song, "Some Things Just Stick in Your Mind," slowly faded into obscurity.

On Shindig, we watched another duo, Sonny and Cher, don animal skins and bell bottoms, singing of their eternal love for each other. Their transformation amazed us.

Several years previous, Dick and I had sung in a star-studded show at the Long

Beach Area. One of the acts was a male/female duo called Caesar and Cleo. At the end of their singing number, Cleo pulled a little string on her skirt and it fell off, revealing only a bikini bottom! Now they wore furry vests and called themselves by their real names, Sonny and Cher.

Due to our television exposure, Dick and I remained popular and recognizable. But rumblings of distant thunder haunted our dreams. Without a hit record, a recording artist can only sustain a career for so long.

* * * * *

Still, the Shindig producers booked us. On the August 18th taping, Dick and I sang "Thou Shalt Not Steal" and "Don't Think Twice. By late August, Dick and I decided to record a song we'd learned from someone on tour, "Vini, Vini." Someone told us the words were in Tahitian.

Whatever possessed us to record such a radically different song, I'll never know. It's just that we loved singing it. It felt good, like singing calypso or reggae. But at a time in our career, when we needed a major national hit, we definitely picked a hard sell.

Looking back, I think the only reason the Wilder Brothers allowed us to release the single was their joy that we weren't recording with Andrew Oldham again. We returned to their production company, if not more humble, at least a little wiser.

We sang "Vini, Vini" on the September 28th Shindig show. The show producers didn't know what to make of the song, so they put us in Hawaiian leis and dressed the dancers in luau costumes. Dick wore a straw hat that made him look more like a Southern hillbilly than a native islander.

* * * * *

"Shindig has been dropped from ABC," Bill told me one evening. "They're putting a new show in its place. Remember the old comic book character, Bat Man? That's what the new show's about." Stunned, my body froze.

"I can't believe it," I said. "Why would they can with such a great show? Everyone loves Shindig."

"Not everyone, apparently. Believe me. They wouldn't drop it if the ratings remained high. I think Action took some of the ratings away from Shindig."

Shelly telephoned the next day. The Shindig producers wanted Dick and me to perform on the last Shindig show to be taped January 8, 1966. We were to dress in Bat Man and Robin costumes to help promote ABC's new show. I would be Robin and Dick would dress as Bat Man.

I just shook my head in dismay. I felt life careening out of control again. We needed a new direction. And we definitely needed another hit record. I didn't know it at the time, but that was not to happen again.

* * * * *

When we arrived at the final Shindig taping, we saw how much things had disintegrated. Only half the regular cast remained. An air of gloom permeated the studio.

Dick and I emerged from our dressing rooms, each wearing the ridiculous costumes. Dick started laughing when he saw me dressed as a boy. With my long hair, I did make an unusual-looking Robin.

"You're a sight to behold," he chuckled.

I wondered if he could imagine what he looked like dressed as Bat Man.

When we reached the sound stage, someone handed Dick a partial face mask. He reluctantly put it on, the mask covering his forehead, eyes and nose. Only his mouth stuck out. Totally unrecognizable, Dick's mood changed immediately from hilarity to depression.

We noticed cables strung from the ceiling.

"You don't mind if we strap you to a cable, do you?" the producer asked Dick. "We're going to have you fly. You know, like Peter Pan or Superman."

Before Dick was able to protest, stagehands snapped the cable to a hook in Dick's costume and hoisted him into the air. He waved his arms awkwardly, as he flew over the heads of everyone, swinging from one side of the stage to the other. I started to laugh, a crazy, out of control sound. Everyone else looked grim.

We sang "Lightning Strikes" as Dick sailed around the stage. I stood on the ground staring up at him, mouthing the words. The show, a shell of its former self, aired and went immediately into the archives. The new Bat Man Show premiered the following week and became a huge success.

Warner Brothers Records decided to release another Dick and Dee Dee album, a compilation of songs. They chose, as a title, Songs We've Sung on Shindig.

The album did not climb the record charts, although Dick kept insisting that we just had to give it time.

CHAPTER THIRTY-TWO

First Home

After our year's lease on the Miller Drive home expired, Bill decided it was time for us to buy our first house. We drove around the San Fernando Valley looking at places in Encino and Sherman Oaks.

When Bill got too busy at Dick Clark Productions to house-hunt any more, I continued searching on my own. I found a wonderful realtor, an older, distinguished British gentleman, who escorted me to various homes in his antique Rolls Royce.

The minute I walked into the house on Nobel Avenue, I knew this was the place for us. The house sat on a low hill, the front door just steps from the street. The back yard stretched up a sharp incline, tiered on several levels before reaching a back fence.

On one side of the house stood two large trees, filled with blossoms and the promise of future fruit. The realtor said one was an apricot tree and the other a plum. The house had a small, private patio outside. A giant sycamore tree in the center kept it shady and comfortable.

Inside, the living and dining rooms featured hardwood floors. There was a wood-burning fireplace along one wall of the living room and a small den with another fireplace.

Down the hall were two bedrooms and two baths. The master bedroom looked out toward the fruit trees. The master bath walls were painted a soothing shade of pale blue, matching the beautiful floor-to-ceiling blue curtain covering the tub. Round, decorator lights surrounded the tall mirror over the sink, giving it the look of a stage dressing room. Two tall windows looked out toward the back hill.

Bill and I ran a little short on the necessary deposit money. I remembered that Mom told me I was supposed to receive a small inheritance when I turned twenty one. No one had mentioned it for years. But now I was almost twenty four. I drove over to Mom and Dad's house.

"We've found a house we'd like to buy," I asked my parents, "I was wondering if I could get the money set aside for me?"

Dad looked concerned. "Of course you can have the money. It isn't much, but it might help. But the real concern I have is making sure a knowledgeable person inspects your house before you buy it. Have you and Bill thought of that?"

I said. "Of course we will do that."

Dad didn't look convinced. "You can't trust just anyone. Why don't I get a friend of mine who inspects property for Carnation Company to come check out the house?"

I hesitated, not sure I wanted Dad or his friend suddenly involved in a decision that might determine whether or not we got the property. Dad picked up on my hesitation.

"You don't have to follow this man's advice," Dad said. "But it's a good idea to know exactly what you are getting into."

* * * * *

A week later Dad and his friend arrived at the house on Nobel. Bill and our realtor huddled nearby. The inspector made a thorough inspection of the property, climbing up on the roof and crawling under the house with a flashlight.

"The only potential problem I see is the slope of the hill behind the house. In the rains, you might get a mud slide."

Bill and I thanked him for taking the time to do the inspection. We were grateful he found a sound roof and good plumbing. As soon as escrow closed and we'd moved in, the first thing we did was plant orange and lemon trees on the tiered hill to stabilize the earth.

I started to see another side of Bill, his handyman skills. He bought a tool box and started making small repairs around the property. The repairs merged into actual construction. After weekends spent pounding nails, he built shelves in the den closet and in one of the bathrooms. One of the shelves was slightly crooked, but I did not want to dampen his enthusiasm, so I remained silent.

Without a hit record in over a year, the bookings for Dick and Dee Dee decreased dramatically. We mostly worked clubs in the Los Angeles area. We hired a permanent guitar player, Eddy Bertrand, to accompany us. Eddy rehearsed the bands and played lead guitar, so we felt assured our music would sound good. I felt a huge burden lifted from my shoulders.

* * * * *

Early one morning Dick telephoned. His voice sounded flat, without energy.

"George Wilder just called," he said. "He had a conversation with Joe Smith at Warner Brothers Records. Warner Brothers has decided to drop us as recording artists."

I felt my stomach tighten in disbelief. "Why?" I cried.

"Oh, they're doing a massive reorganization of their rock and roll department. They're letting a number of singers go."

"What are we going to do?" I asked.

"I don't know. I want to talk to Shelly and see what he thinks. Maybe it's time to leave the Wilders for good and try to find another record producer as well as a new label. I'll let you know what he says."

Shelly recommended shopping our act to see what interest there was with other labels. He told us he'd get back to us when he had any news.

* * * * *

I found myself with time on my hands. A strong desire surged through me. I wanted to sing and play music. I wanted to get back to song writing.

Bill and I rented an upright Kimball piano, which we placed against the wall in the den. I spent hours playing and singing, mostly from memory or old song books. But one day I started writing songs again.

* * * * *

Dick and I continued to perform in the evenings, mostly in small clubs in the Los Angeles area. Without a hit record, our fan base basically dwindled. We focused on giving the most dynamic shows we could, throwing ourselves into dancing and communicating with the audience.

Interesting new instruments cropped up on commercial songs, some mixing East Indian flavored sitars with electric guitars. I loved the sound. It felt expansive, unique.

Suddenly the Beatles wore Indian clothes and meditated with the Maharishi Maresh Yogi. The world took note, trailing along after them. And Dick didn't miss the trend.

"We've got to start wearing Indian outfits on stage," he told me.

I sighed. "Dick, we're just playing small clubs in the L.A. suburbs. Everyone there is dressed in normal clothes. Isn't that going to look a little weird?"

"We've got to stay on top of the trends, or we're going to die. Here's the name of a clothing store in Los Angeles that sells Indian saris and Punjabis. I want you to get some."

I reluctantly drove to the store and chose several loose-fitting Indian Punjabis. When I wore one on stage for the first time, I felt ridiculous. The audience stared at us, sizing up this radical image shift. But when the music started and we began to sing, all was forgiven and it really didn't matter what we wore, because the music transcended all.

CHAPTER THIRTY-THREE

We Bite the Hand That Fed Us

Dick informed me that our manager, Shelly Berger, felt we should leave the Wilder Brothers and find new record producers. Since our contract with the Wilder Brothers was expiring, Shelly saw no reason to renew it.

Shelly finally signed Dick and me to Dot Records. We were told we could choose any record producer we wanted. Dick called with a suggestion.

"I think we should record with Quincy Jones. He's got a great track record."

"So this is it? We're leaving the Wilders for good?" I asked Dick.

"Why should we remain with them? They took advantage of us when we were starting out by giving us such a tiny percentage of the singing royalties. Now we get a chance to sign directly to a label without having to share our royalties with anyone."

I remembered what my boyfriend, Mike, had said years ago, "Fifty percent of something is better than one-hundred percent of nothing."

"They did help create our hit records."

"Look, Shelly's worked out a great deal for us. Trust me. This will be the best thing we ever did."

It felt strange leaving the Wilder Brothers and Don Ralke, my surrogate family. But we had been with them for five years and the contract was up. We were about to launch into new territory with no road map in sight.

I wanted to say goodbye to the Wilders, to feel a sense of completion. I picked up the phone and called George.

"Hello?" George's familiar voice came on the line.

"Hello, George, It's Dee Dee."

There was a moment of silence.

"What can I do for you?" He sounded guarded and formal.

"Well, I just wanted to thank you for all the years we worked together."

"You're making a big mistake leaving us. We know how to get the Dick and Dee Dee sound. Any other producer you hire is just going to do his job and move on. He won't have any real loyalty to you and Dick. And he won't know how the Dick and Dee Dee sound is created. Look what happened with Andrew Oldham."

"Well, Dick and Shelly think it's going to work out. Anyway, I just wanted to say thank you for all you've done. Will you convey my message to Walt and Warner as well?"

"Alright," George said. "And remember, you can always call me if you run into trouble."

We both laughed awkwardly. "I'll remember that," I replied.

* * * * *

Dick and I drove to Quincy Jones' home. A woman escorted us into a large living room and told us to wait by a huge baby grand piano. Finally Quincy entered.

"Sit down," he said, waving to the comfortable looking sofa and chairs. "I understand you're on a new record label and want me to produce a session."

"I've brought some songs I've written to show you," Dick said. "Is it alright if I play your piano?"

Quincy nodded.

Dick walked to the piano and sat awkwardly on the piano bench.

"They're sort of in the rough stage," he said. "Here's the first one."

Dick played the song. After he finished the room filled with silence. Quincy wrote something on a pad of paper. "What else do you have?" he asked. Dick ran through four or five songs in succession.

"Well, what do you think?" Dick looked nervous.

"I like the second and fourth songs," Quincy replied. "They sound more commercial. But what I think is not important. It's what you like that counts."

He glanced at me. "Which ones did you like, Dee Dee?"

Dick turned and stared at me. They both waited for an answer.

"I guess I liked the second one the best."

The truth was, I didn't relate to any of the songs. They didn't touch me on a deep level like much of the material I heard on the radio.

I knew Quincy's background included all kinds of music. I hoped he would get more involved in a new musical direction for Dick and me. But he allowed Dick to take the lead.

"You and Dick make a tape of the two songs you like the best and I'll do the arrangements," he said. From the far corner of the house, a phone rang. "Now if you'll excuse me, I have to take an important phone call." Dick gathered up his music and we left.

CHAPTER THIRTY-FOUR

Baby Chris

In 1967, I discovered I was pregnant. Bill desperately wanted a child, but I felt conflicted, caught between the necessity of performing each night and inwardly wanting to "nest" and prepare for the baby. I suppressed the desire to stop playing clubs, knowing Bill and I were dependent on the money. Even though I longed for quiet and solitude, I ignored my feelings. Life went on as usual.

Dick and I were invited back for a week's engagement in a large club in Scottsdale, Arizona. The last time we were there, we stayed in a luxury hotel in the desert and enjoyed a week of swimming and sailing on the club owner's small boat.

This time, I became bloated, starting to retain excess water. My ankles swelled. It was harder and harder to hide my growing stomach. I looked eight months pregnant.

On stage, I still felt the joy of performing before a live audience. I think the nightly dancing kept me in excellent shape.

Back in Los Angeles, on Sunday, June 4, 1967, I went into labor. It was the exact projected due date. The baby waited until after I'd eaten breakfast to start his entrance into the world. We drove to the hospital and four hours later, Chris arrived.

I held out my arms and they handed me my baby, wrapped in a blanket. Chris opened his eyes and stared into my face. His greatest asset was a full head of shiny black hair. He was the most adorable baby I'd ever seen.

I felt a wave of joy and relief. Bills eyes spoke volumes of love.

All too soon, the nurses carried him to the nursery and wheeled me to a private room to recover. By the time both sets of grandparents arrived from their respective golf courses, I'd eaten lunch and changed into a striped robe I'd purchased in England. The grandparents beamed with joy, as this was the first grandchild on both sides of the family.

* * * * *

I stayed in the hospital for three days. Dick called several days after the birth.

"So, you had a boy," he said. "Bill called me. Is it cute?" Without waiting for my answer, he forged right ahead. "I wonder how your having a kid is going to affect the act."

I felt a wave of impatience.

"Dick, lots of people have children and careers. I'll obviously have to find a babysitter or juggle things when we perform, but it will all work out."

"I don't know. What if we have another hit record and have to go on the road for a long tour?"

"Let's just focus on getting another hit record. As far as the baby goes, I'll bring him on tour or figure something out. Anyway, you don't have to worry now."

"Well, anyway, congratulations."

* * * * *

When we took Chris home from the hospital, summer reigned in splendor. In our yard the apricot and plum trees hung heavy with sweet fruit.

The first few weeks passed in a blur of sleeplessness and exhaustion. I slept whenever the baby did, taking short naps around the clock. The radio became my redeemer. I listened to songs about peace and love.

"Are you going to San Francisco?

Be sure to wear some flowers in your hair."

The Beatles released their Sergeant Pepper album. In my tired state, I lay in the den on the duo bed and, half asleep, listened to it over and over. When I shut my eyes, I saw swirling colors dancing to the music. It was unlike anything I'd ever heard. I felt uplifted, joyful. This album, I thought, was the most incredible record ever made.

Bill's younger brother, Jay, visited us from San Francisco. Full of stories about the love-ins and the hippie scene in Haight-Ashbury, he told stories of young people dressed in colorful clothes, with bells and love beads, dancing in the streets, passing out flowers to strangers. It was The Summer of Love."

I thought, "What a great time for Chris to be born, the Summer of Love."

Slowly, I returned to performing club dates in L.A. with Dick. After a three-week break, it felt good to appear on stage again.

* * * * *

One night, in the dressing room, Dick studied me intently.

"You've got to lose weight," he said. "Don't you know the look is super skinny, like that British model, Twiggy? And, while you're at it, get some false eyelashes. Your eyes look washed out. If we don't stay current and hip, we'll never make it."

Reluctantly, I drove to a drug store the next day and purchased false eyelashes and glue. The eyelashes were so long they practically touched my eyebrows. When I tried sticking the eyelashes to my upper lids, I got glue in my eye. But through trial and error, I finally managed to get it right.

It felt strange staring out of eyelash-enhanced eyes. I imagined black, long legged spiders sitting on my lids. Eventually, I got used to them.

As far as the weight loss went, I quickly resumed my normal weight, but realized I'd never be "skinny." The anorexic look just wasn't in my genes.

* * * * *

By fall, college students held strikes and sit-ins on campuses across the U.S. There were hundreds of demonstrations in opposition to the war. I watched the news in horror, as live footage showed American soldiers dropping bombs on Vietnamese civilians. I felt I had to do something. I joined Another Mother for Peace, an organization founded by actress Joanne Woodward. I proudly slapped a sticker on my car bumper, "War is not healthy for children and other living things."

The Dick and Dee Dee single, produced by Quincy Jones, was not a hit. In desperation, Dick connected with producer Ray Ruff who agreed to produce a session for us.

I drove to Dick's house to listen to some new songs he'd written.

"I was up all night writing," Dick said. "Listen to this." He pounded out a song on the piano. To me, Dick's material sounded uninspired and dated.

"Do you want my comments?" I asked. "I'm not sure the material sounds like what I'm hearing on the radio."

Dick glared at me. "I don't think you qualify as a music critic. I haven't done so badly writing hits in the past. Just learn your harmonies and leave the music decisions to me."

Without saying another word, I tried my best to memorize my notes. But when I left his house that afternoon, I'd already forgotten my part.

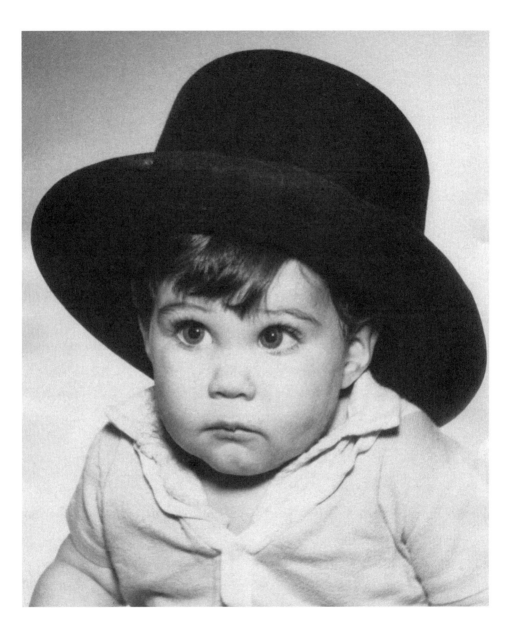

Baby Chris

CHAPTER THIRTY-FIVE

Assassinations and Snakes

In April, 1968, the television news brought reports and footage of another shocking event, the assassination of Dr. Martin Luther King. One minute he stood with friends and colleagues on a motel balcony and the next moment someone gunned him down. I felt sick, helpless.

I fell into a deep depression. As the days passed, I remained numb. Then in June, at the Ambassador Hotel while on the campaign trail for the presidency, an assassin shot Robert Kennedy. My world felt like it was falling apart.

* * * * *

Dick and I had met Robert Kennedy several months before, when we volunteered to perform at a rally in the Sacramento area to support Governor Pat Brown's re-election campaign.

When we arrived that day, several event organizers ushered us through the crowd to the outdoor podium, where we sang into an antiquated microphone, accompanied by our record "Thou Shalt Not Steal."

After the song ended, Dick shouted into the microphone.

"Don't forget. Re-elect Pat Brown." The crowd cheered.

As we were left the makeshift stage, we noticed a man surrounded by several security guards. As he approached, I recognized Robert Kennedy. We met in the middle of the outdoor asphalt playing field and the event coordinator introduced us. Kennedy took my hand and shook it firmly, staring into my eyes. His blue eyes radiated intensity and clarity. For me, the moment froze in time. Then he shook Dick's hand and headed for the small stage. We retreated to our car.

"We just met the future President of the United States," I remember thinking.

* * * * *

By October, the largest gathering ever, two-hundred fifty-thousand people protested the Viet Nam war at the Washington Memorial in Washington, D.C. My heart and soul resonated with the anti-war cause. Why was I singing "bubble gum" music on dingy stages when I could be protesting and making a difference? But the next morning we left for yet another club gig.

* * * * *

Shelly booked Dick and me in a night club on the outskirts of San Jose. Bill decided to accompany us and brought baby Chris along. We checked into a motel and Dick and I drove to the club for a rehearsal. A burly man in his forties greeted us at the door.

He stuck out his hand. "Joe Martinelle," he said. "You guys come in and meet the band." As we walked backstage, I noticed several covered cages against the wall.

"What are the cages for?" I asked.

Joe swung around in a panic. "Don't touch them. Don't touch them. They contain boa constrictors. One of the girls uses them in her act."

Boas? Her act? What kind of place were we in, a strip joint?

I felt better when the band, five guys on guitar, bass, drums, sax and keyboard, played our music perfectly. The rehearsal went well.

Before we left for the motel, Joe yelled, "You've got two shows tonight, eight and eleven. Don't be late. I've been promoting this show on the radio all week."

When I got back to my hotel room, I found Bill nervously pacing the floor with the baby in his arms.

"Chris has a temperature," Bill said. "I'm trying to get him to take extra fluids. Now that you're here, you need to watch him while I go get some medicine."

I took Chris and hugged him to me. Sitting on the bed, I rocked back and forth, telling him he was a good boy and how he would feel better soon. Bill returned with the medicine. Using the enclosed eyedropper, we gave Chris some of the bottled liquid. It made him groggy and he finally went to sleep.

I felt exhausted. Just as I lay on the bed to take a brief nap, the phone rang. It was my Dad.

"Hello, Mary?" he said. "You'll never guess where we are. I had business in Sacramento and we're heading down the coast for Los Angeles. We had the car radio on and heard about your show in San Jose tonight, so we pulled over and checked into a hotel. We're coming to the show. How do you get there anyway?"

I jolted awake. The last time my parents had come to one of our shows was at least five years ago, when we played a large arena in Los Angeles.

"Are you sure you want to do this? I mean, the club is in kind of a run down area and…"

"Of course we want to see you. Now just tell me how to find the place."

I gave him directions and hung up.

"I'm sorry I won't be able to go with you tonight," Bill said, "but I don't think we should leave Chris with a sitter, with this temperature and all."

"No, that's okay. I'll just go with Dick. We'll do two quick shows, and I'll be right back. The club is not that great a place anyway."

Bill ordered room service for us and put on his bath robe. I wanted nothing more than to take a hot bath, get into my own robe, eat a meal and climb into bed. Instead, I quickly ate and dressed in my stage outfit, what else but an Indian punjabi.

Dick knocked at the door and I waved goodbye to Bill.

"My parents called," I told Dick. "They're going to catch one of our shows tonight."

Dick looked startled. "Any particular reason?"

"No, they were just in the area."

"I haven't seen them in years. How are they doing?"

"Oh, the same as always, Dad's working and Mom's traveling with him."

When we got to the club and walked through the back stage area, I noticed the cage doors stood open. I bumped into a female dancer, dressed only in a bra and G string, with two large boas covering her neck and torso. I shuddered and stepped back.

"Don't be afraid," the girl said. "They're harmless. They can't bite. The only thing they could do is squeeze you to death."

I kept my distance and tried to smile. Just then, the band started to play and the girl dragged herself and the heavy boas out on stage and started an exotic dance.

I peered out at the audience seated at the semi-dark at tables and noticed my parents, front and center. They stared in fascination as the girl started dancing sensuously to the music, accompanied by the swaying snakes.

I saw burly men with tattoos and tough-looking women, some talking and shouting at the bar, paying no attention to the show on stage. This was definitely not our usual crowd.

Dick jolted me out of my reverie.

"We're on."

I sidestepped onto the stage, trying to avoid the exiting lady with the snakes. The crowd gave us polite applause. Dad yelled, "Yeah, Mary." I heard his voice echo over the clapping hands.

I tried to put myself in a happy mood. I tried to pretend I was young and in love, that we were the hit recording artists from Shindig, that the world remained a beautiful place, but tonight, for me, it just didn't work. I felt miserable, worried about Chris, nervous, embarrassed and depressed. Why tonight, of all nights, did Mom and Dad decide to come to one of our shows? And this club we were in. Was this what happens when you don't have a hit record for three years?

We made it through the show based on our professionalism alone. I hope people believed we were happy and carefree. Put on a smile. That's show biz. Never let them know clowns cry on the inside.

Mom and Dad walked backstage after the show, crowding against the snake cages.

"You were wonderful," Mom said. "You've certainly changed your act since we last saw you."

I couldn't believe she actually enjoyed it.

"Yeah, well, we've obviously added more songs."

"That was an interesting dance act," Dad said. "Do you think those snakes are dangerous?"

I shivered. "Only if they get loose and squeeze you."

We glanced at the snake cages.

"Well," Dad said. "We have to be going. Say hello to Bill."

"I will. Thanks for coming."

I had no intention of telling them that Bill and Chris remained at the motel, Chris with a temperature. Instead of taking care of him, I was singing in a club with strippers and snakes.

We sat at a deserted table in the back of the club between shows. I fell into a deep funk. I barely managed to stagger on stage for the second show, this time not caring if I bumped into the dancer laden with snakes.

After a lackluster show, accompanied by some turmoil at the bar which resulted in shouting and someone being ejected from the club, I sat on a bar stool in the semi-deserted club and waited for Dick to bring the car around to the entrance. I felt anesthetized, half asleep.

Through blurry eyes I watched a male singer take the microphone and start to sing a love ballad. The crowd chatted loudly, ignoring him. I felt sorry for him.

He tried a rock and roll song, which blasted out over the talking voices. As he neared the end, he took the microphone and started walking among the audience. He suddenly approached me and shouted, "Sing, sing!" He wanted me to join him on the chorus, to shake the crowd out of their lethargy.

I stared at him, startled. He leaned in closer. The spotlight lit us up, just the two of us. He hovered over me and I crouched defensively.

"Sing, sing!"

I couldn't deal with this any longer.

"Hey, I just finished two long sets," I told him, forgetting I was now speaking into a microphone. "My voice is strained and I'm exhausted. Sorry, I just can't help you."

For a moment, silence resounded. Even the bartender stopped clanking the glasses. Everyone looked in our direction. When the band started playing the song again, the singer jumped away from me as if on coiled springs, and he bounced back onto the stage, a grim look on his face. He started to sing a ballad.

When the spotlight left me, I felt terrible. That was the worst, most mean-spirited thing I'd ever done. I wanted to curl up and die.

I staggered to the exit and climbed into Dick's car, which he'd just parked at the entrance.

"I got paid in cash," Dick said when he arrived. "Do you want to count it out now?"

"Please, let's just go back to the motel. We can deal with it in the morning."

When I walked into the motel room, both Chris and Bill slept. I noticed Chris didn't look as flushed as before.

As I slid under the covers, I realized Dick and I were approaching the bottom of our career. I visualized the end of the roller coaster ride just around the next curve.

CHAPTER THIRTY-SIX

An Era Ends

When the revolutionary musical, Hair, opened at the Aquarius Theatre in Hollywood, Bill and I attended the opening performance.

As we sat in the audience with friends, we didn't know what to expect. But I suddenly noticed the cast members wandering the aisles, moving in slow motion. They looked like they walked on the moon. None of the audience members paid any attention.

Caught up in their frantic rush for seats and excitement about attending a world premier, they chattered excitedly, not realizing that an actual event was taking place simultaneously. The play began and no one noticed.

Finally I whispered to Bill, "Look at those people walking around in slow motion. Some of them are blowing bubbles."

The floating bubbles finally caught the audience's attention and they turned their gaze toward the stage. As the lights dimmed, the stage opened on a wild looking tribe of hippies. I stared, mesmerized.

As the music flowed, I listened to the most uplifting material I'd heard in recent years. How were Dick and I ever going to find a place among the revolutionary sounds taking place? What was to become of our "two verses, a bridge and closing verse" formula songs? This play forecast a leap into the musical future. I didn't want to be left behind.

When I got home, my head was spinning with the music we'd heard. I called Dick.

"Hi," I said. "Bill and I went to see Hair. It was so spectacular, Dick. The music lifted me out of my seat. A whole new era of sound is here."

"Okay, listen," Dick replied, paying no attention to what I said. "We're doing a session at Gold Star Recording Studios. Remember Stan Ross? He's going to be the engineer. We've produced many hits in that studio and we can do it again."

I sighed. "The Wilders always produced us at Gold Star. It's going to be strange being there without them."

"What's the matter with you? We don't need The Wilders. You'll be happy to know Don Ralke has agreed to drop by. Listen, I've written some new material. It's right in the ballpark of today's sound. You're going to love it. I've sent you a tape and I want you to memorize it. If we sing from the heart, we'll have another hit."

* * * * *

I listened to Dick's tape. The songs were pleasant enough, but nothing special. My mind was still in orbit with songs from Hair. What could I do to spice up the session, to make it unique and different?

I went to the piano and started working on my own material. Maybe I'd record a single someday. Maybe I'd have enough nerve to sing alone in public the way I sang in my den when no one was around.

* * * * *

The day of the Gold Star session, I gave Chris a hug and left him with a babysitter. I drove over Laurel Canyon to Gold Star Studios. As I walked down the familiar corridors, I marveled at all the hit records recorded in that building in the Sixties; Phil Spector's wall of sound, Sonny and Cher, the Righteous Brothers, Tina Turner, The Beach Boys, they'd all recorded there.

As I pushed open the heavy door to Studio A, I found Dick, Stan Ross and Don Ralke sitting behind the sound board.

"Hello, Dee Dee." Don welcomed me warmly.

"Hi, Don, Hi, Stan." I looked around in surprise. "Where are all the musicians?"

Dick said, "We recorded the music tracks earlier today. All you and I need to do is add our voices."

I looked at him, trying to grasp what he was telling me. Was I so far out of the loop that I wasn't even invited to sit in while the musicians recorded tracks for a Dick and Dee Dee session? What was going on?

Dick picked up on my unhappy expression. "Hey, you've got a busy life, right? Be glad you didn't have to waste half the day messing with musicians." I suddenly realized why this session was so important to the career of Dick and Dee Dee.

"Isn't this the last single we're required to provide Dot Records under our current contract?" I asked. "If we don't have a hit with one of these songs, they'll drop us from the label. I would have liked the opportunity to be involved with the music tracks."

Stan sat silently adjusting knobs and buttons. Don and Dick exchanged glances.

Dick said, "Yeah, that's right. We have to give Dot a final single. But right now, we're wasting time. Let's put the vocals down and see how they sound."

He stomped out of the sound booth. I followed him into the massive studio, now dark and cold. The ghosts of hundreds of talented musicians who played and recorded in this very spot floated around, their music silently humming in the atmosphere.

This was it, our last chance for us to record a possible hit. And the material Dick sent me to learn from the tape felt out of touch with what was making the record scene extraordinary. I felt a weight in my stomach.

Dick and I stood by each other and placed head sets on. The rubber ear pieces fit snugly on our ears.

"Let's do a sound check." Stan said into our heads.

The music began and Dick and I started to sing.

"Alright, that's fine."

I heard the squeaky sound of the tape rewinding. The introduction repeated and, again, Dick and I sang.

We completed the first song In several takes and quickly recorded a second one. But something felt wrong. The songs had no soul, no spark. My body started to tremble as I thought of all the hits we'd recorded in this studio. I remembered how excited we were listening back to some of the amazing sounds. What I was hearing now sounded dull and colorless.

I knew the final song, a ballad, had the best chance of becoming a hit record.

But it needed something more, something creative.

The song told the story of a young, innocent girl. I thought of the poetic beauty of the music from Hair. Summoning all my courage, I took a deep breath. Maybe if they heard my idea they might see the difference it made to the song. So, during the instrumental section, I started to speak, my voice wavering at first, but then loud and steady. I created poetry on the spot.

"She was a child then," I said. "drifting through the sands of time, picking an occasional daisy."

Dick stared at me like I'd gone insane. "What the hell are your doing?" he shouted. Stan hit the stop button and everything came to a halt. I saw Don Ralke peering at me through the glass.

"Are you crazy?" Dick yelled. "You ruined the song. Why did you talk?"

I babbled. "I just felt the song needed something creative and original."

Dick shot me a look of pure disgust. "You're not the lead singer. You just do background vocals. Now just sing so we can get this over with." He glanced at the sound booth. "Stan, can you erase that?"

After several seconds of numbing silence Stan replied, "Yeah, I can drop her speaking voice out."

"Too bad you can't drop her out of the singing as well," Dick muttered. I felt tears flood my eyes. My hands shook as I picked up the lyric sheet and tried to compose myself.

"Let's take it from the top," Don Ralke said into our ear sets.

This time, like a robot, I sang my part, mechanical and perfect. I hardly breathed during the instrumental. Everyone looked relieved when the song ended.

I had to get out of there before I burst our crying. I realized it was the end of the road for Dick and Dee Dee. This song was not going to be a hit but it didn't matter because I realized I could not longer sing with Dick St. John. The unique sound we'd once created as vocal artists no longer existed.

"I've got to go," I said.

Stan jumped up and took my hand. He looked into my eyes. "It was really great seeing you again after all these years.'

I felt like we were parting for the last time. Stan had witnessed many great Dick and Dee Dee sessions.

I managed to say, "It was good seeing you, too."

"Goodbye," Don said.

Unable to speak, I waved and headed for the door.

"I'll be right back," Dick told Don. "I'm just going to walk Dee Dee to her car."

When we got outside, Dick glared at me. "I don't know what the hell you were doing in there. Were you purposely trying to screw things up?"

"Dick, things are already screwed up." I turned and faced Dick, anger and rage finally surfacing. "I was trying to do something creative, original. Trying to break out of the box we've been trapped in these past few years."

"Well, I've got news for you. The box is already broken. Listen, before I came here today I made up my mind. I'm dissolving the act. Don Ralke is willing to record me as a single artist and it's time I focused on my own career. And I can do that now that you and I have completed our obligations to Dot Records."

I turned my back on him, climbed into my car and started the ignition.

"What do you have to say?" Dick shouted, his voice muffled against the window glass. I rolled down the window.

"When have you ever asked my opinion about anything? You just told me the act is over. But the truth of the matter is, Dick, it was over a long time ago. You're just now figuring it out." Dick stood and stared at me until I drove out of sight.

* * * * *

I felt angry, then incredibly sad. Tears streamed from my eyes. I could hardly see the freeway on ramp. I brushed the tears away, trying to ignore the huge void I felt in my heart. I'd been singing with Dick since 1961. Now the calendar read 1969, the end of an era as well as the end of a career.

I finally pulled up in front of my house and sat in the car staring into space, letting the tears subside. When I walked in the front door and looked at little Chris, he smiled up at me with wide blue eyes, overjoyed that I'd returned home. He put out his little arms and said, "Up, Mommy."

I gave him a big hug. We cuddled together on the sofa and I melted in a wave of love. I felt needed, appreciated, wanted. Here total joy existed and I hadn't begun to realize the depth of it.

At that moment I understood there was something far more important than my "Dick and Dee Dee" career. The drama of the day faded away like a shooting star.

Epilogue

I'm here at Lake Shrine listening to a distant waterfall. It's been forty years since I first sat on this bench near the water. I still remember the heat of that fall day, the vivid blue sky outside and that dark cloud inside my heart as I struggled with the decision of whether or not to continue singing. I was so young, scared and uncertain, yet I had my whole life ahead of me.

I'm holding the pink crystal the monk gave me many years ago And sitting here again, I can almost hear the monk saying "Close your eyes and let the peace of the crystal fill your being. Know that you are following the path you created for yourself and that everything will indeed work out for the highest good." And indeed it did. I survived and thrived on that long, adventurous road down the vinyl highway.

* * * * *

Bill and I divorced in 1975, but remained close friends, sharing our son Chris as he traveled back and forth from my home in Big Sur to Bill's residence in Los Angeles. Bill went on to become a successful network television producer. Two of the shows he created, "New Year's Rocking Eve" and "The American Music Awards" are still on the air today!

I cherish our years together. The dissolution of our marriage involved bad choices on both our parts, but we continued to remain supportive and positive toward each other.

Bill died of cancer in 1981, at age forty-four. Although we were divorced, I felt like I'd lost one of my best friends. Bill had been my agent, manager, lover, husband, father of my child and good friend. It took me a long time to move on after the loss.

Throughout the 1990's, Dick and I lived in the same town not more than a half-mile from each other! From time to time I'd run into him at the drugstore or the post office. Each time we met, it felt awkward. We both acted polite, but guarded and cautious—the way you act when you first meet someone and are on your best behavior. The last time I saw him, he asked about my family. He smiled when I mentioned Dad.

* * * * *

In December, 2003, while I was on vacation in Pebble Beach, a woman friend telephoned. She told me she'd read that Dick St. John died in the hospital ten days after a bizarre fall from the roof of his home. It didn't seem possible. I felt shocked and frozen.

Too many things were left unsaid. I honestly thought we'd someday sit together on a bench and reminisce about our singing career. Now I realize I can never show him this book, much less ever sing with him again.

Any minute now I expect the monk to appear, but that's not going to happen either, because he passed away in the early 1990's. When he knew his time was approaching, the monk gave away the few items he possessed. After he died, the other monks found in his room only one change of clothes and a harmonium (small keyboard). The monk truly exemplified the term, "non-attachment."

* * * * *

Yes, I survived the 'sixties' and it was a grand adventure—just as the monk predicted. Some people say that if you remember the 'Sixties', you weren't really there. Fortunately, I survived that era with my memory intact.

I loved singing with Dick as we traveled the vinyl highway, but little did I know what escapades awaited me in the 1970's when I headed "back to the land." Stay tuned for the next saga, "Love From Big Sur."

Billboard Magazine Discography

Dick and Dee Dee

<u>Year</u>	<u>Single</u>	<u>Chart</u>	<u>Highest Position</u>
1961	*The Mountain's High*	Pop Singles	No. 2
1962	*Tell Me*	Pop Singles	No. 22
1963	*Young and in Love*	Adult Contemp.	No. 6
1963	*Young and in Love*	Pop Singles	No. 17
1963	*Where Did All the Good Times Go?*	Pop Singles	No. 93
1964	*All My Trials*	Pop Singles	No. 89
1964	*Turn Around*	Pop Singles	No. 27
1965	*Be My Baby*	Pop Singles	No. 87
1965	*Thou Shalt Not Steal*	Pop Singles	No. 13

Dee Dee Phelps
Author of Vinyl Highway, singing as "Dick and Dee Dee"

Dee Dee began her career in journalism, songwriting and singing at age sixteen. Since that time she has been a newspaper columnist, top forty recording artist (singing as Dick and Dee Dee, one of the most popular recording duos of the Sixties), songwriter, performer, and author of the newly released narrative non fiction memoir, Vinyl Highway.

Dee Dee performed with such high profile artists as the Beach Boys, Rolling Stones, Dionne Warwick, Dick Clark, Tina Turner and many others. Her television performances include American Bandstand, Where The Action Is, Shindig, and the British television show, Ready, Steady, Go. Dee Dee sang in the motion picture Wild, Wild Winter and performed in the first precursor to videos, Scopitone. She toured the United States, Japan and Europe as Dick and Dee Dee (visit www.dickanddeedee.com to view vintage videos).

Some of Dee Dee's exploits are chronicled in other books. "Rock and Roll and Remember," by Dick Clark and "Liberty Records," by Michael "Doc Roc" Kelly. A UCLA writer's program student, she attended numerous memoir classes during the years spent writing Vinyl Highway. She also attended the Maui Writer's Retreat, 2003.

Vinyl Highway's initial success and requests from readers encouraged Dee Dee to begin work on the book's sequel, "Love from Big Sur," Back to the Land, a memoir of the Seventies.

Dee Dee currently lives with her husband, Kane, in the Los Angeles area. They have three adult children.

USA Price **$16.95**
Canadian Price **C$21.95**

ISBN: 978-1-934321-75-1